SABOTAGE

A Lou Gault Thriller

Dave McKeon

AHA Publishers

Editing/Publishing of *Sabotage* by AHA Publishers, an imprint of A Howard Activity, LLC

Cover Design by Bob Hurley, ImpressionsBookDesignServices.com

Cover Photo: Northwest Crown Fire by Steve Bunk / CC-BY-2.5

ISBN: 979-8-9912666-5-9 (paperback)

ISBN: 979-8-9902822-9-2 (eBook)

PRINTED IN THE UNITED STATES OF AMERICA

To Kevin, the best guy cousin I could have had
and
For Sandy, always

"Everyone needs beauty as well as bread,
Places to play in . . .
where nature may heal and cheer
and give strength to body and soul."

- *John Muir*

Chapter One

The only audible sound inside the parking garage came from the soles of Dominic Martino's fashionable Italian leather shoes hitting the concrete floor. As the echoes bounced off the inside walls of the cavernous cement building, his assassin waited in the shadows.

Martino was a gifted prosecutor, as well as a creature of habit. The killer had studied him for weeks and knew his routines. He also knew Martino would be the last to leave the office, and oblivious to his surroundings as he walked toward the parking garage.

As Martino approached his vehicle in the area reserved for the district attorney and staff, his mind was elsewhere.

Earlier in the month, a jury had handed him a hard-won victory. He smirked, thinking to himself, *why was I even concerned I might end up with a hung jury? I had a solid case . . . the jury listened . . . and justice prevailed...as it should.*

Days earlier, the assassin had scoped out the garage.

Choosing the location where he would take someone's life was never a random act. It was always a deliberate one which gave him the advantage over his prey. The element of surprise also seemed to sexually arouse him as he lay in wait for the kill.

The assassin's given name was Vincenzo, but after years of working the waterfront, his forearms had become grossly distorted. His massive forearms resembled those of the cartoon character Popeye the Sailorman. Those who worked beside him on the docks referred to him as "Popeye." Only a few select people knew of his avocation as an assassin-for-hire…and of his allegiance to Santino Varni.

As Martino approached a large puddle of oily water directly between him and his Mercedes Benz, he sighed. Clearly frustrated, he circumvented the water to avoid damaging the expensive soft leather shoes he wore. As he brushed up against a support stanchion, he thought it was a spider's web that had touched his face, until he felt a sudden tightening around his neck.

Within seconds his briefcase fell to the floor. Both hands instinctively reached for his throat. At the 10-second mark, his head began jerking wildly from side to side. He was desperately seeking to confront his attacker. But Popeye's massive forearms had already become an extension of the garrote, and Dominic Martino was being manipulated as if he was a marionette, on a string, made of papier- mâché.

Within 20 seconds, Martino was gasping for air. His fingers were frantically digging into the sides of his own throat in a futile attempt to release himself from the constraint that was cutting off his airway.

After 30 seconds his eyes were bulging. His mouth was open now, and his tongue was grotesquely extended.

At the 60 second mark, his brain was being denied lifegiving oxygen; he could feel the strength draining from his extremities.

After 90 seconds had passed, his lungs felt like they were on fire. He tried to scream…but the only noise he made was inside his head.

At the 120 second mark, the intensity of his struggle began to fade. Deprived of oxygen, Martino's body was shutting down.

When another 60 seconds had passed, Dominic Martino had lost consciousness and lay slouched against the chest of his killer.

The assassin looked at the Rolex stretched across his massive wrist. The elapsed time was reaching four minutes, the average length of time for someone to die once their airway was blocked. Yet, Popeye strained to maintain the tension on the garrote for a full six minutes, after which the chance of survival is nil. His victim would have succumbed to both an air choke and a blood choke. The blood choke was the more critical. Once the carotid arteries were unable to supply the brain with oxygen rich blood for a sustained period of six minutes, clinical death occurred.

In one smooth motion, the assassin released the garrote and slipped his arm underneath his victim's left armpit. Then he grabbed the right armpit for leverage and dragged the lifeless body of Dominic Martino into the darkness as if he were a rag doll. With his right hand, he slid open the panel door of an unmarked van. He had covered the cargo area with sheets of plastic. Then in one swift motion, Dominic Martino's body was unceremoniously dumped inside the van.

Just before closing the door, Popeye noticed the exquisite pair of Italian leather shoes on Martino's feet.

Stepping out of his own shoe, he tried on one of Martino's. The hand-made loafer fit Popeye's foot like a slipper. As he kicked off his other shoe, he removed Martino's second shoe and whispered *"Grazie."*

As he closed the door, he blew a kiss at the body sprawled in the back of the van. Whether the shoe would remain a *trophy*...or a curse...only time would tell.

Chapter Two

The fishing resort known as *Havre de Poisson* lay just under five hundred miles to the northeast of Boston. The sportsmen who journeyed this far into the Canadian wilderness were serious outdoor enthusiasts. They willingly accepted the morning chill and heavy dew that often clung to the open boats in exchange for a chance to haul in a trophy fish.

It mattered not that stars were still visible when they left the dock in the early morning. These people came to fish and early morning was when the sought-after monsters rose from the depths and began to feed. Most of the men had been on the water for well over an hour.

The early morning mist on the lake was a sure sign the temperature of the air was dropping faster than the lake water. Yet summer wasn't ready to give way to autumn, not now anyway. The forest's canopy was still dark green and the wavering sound of the loons calling to their mates still announced the coming of day.

Once the last boat left the dock, Lou Gault, proprietor of the resort, closed the door to the boathouse and retraced his steps back to his cottage.

It had been well over ten years since Gault fought in the Afghan war. Shortly after he returned to New Brunswick, his paternal grandfather, Grey Elk, had gifted the resort, and forty-five square miles surrounding the huge glacial lake, to Gault. The land was all that remained of the once vast ancestral lands of an eastern band of Abenaki.

Gault led a peaceful life now, far from the carnage of war. Yet, the warrior spirit that defined him in battle still remained deep within him.

As Lou passed through the screen door to the porch that spanned the front of his cottage, he turned and looked out across the horizon. His eyes searching for anything that looked different, anything that seemed out of place, anything that might be a threat to the environment.

By anyone's standards, Gault was a large powerfully built man. His wiry build was all muscle. His broad shoulders and rugged six-foot-two frame filled the entire doorway. He wore his hair short and his face was clean shaven, two habits he acquired while serving in Canada's elite JTF2 commando unit.

To many, Gault was the epitome of the quintessential outdoorsman. When it came to living in the out-of-doors and relying upon one's instincts, Gault was unquestionably the master of his fate. He was more than at home in the wilderness. From an early age he had learned to draw on his natural instincts and the resourcefulness inherent in his mixed French and Abenaki bloodlines.

. . .

GAULT'S RESORT was situated on the shores of an obscure lake in north central New Brunswick. Like many of the surrounding lakes, they were identified with a number, not a name. His lake was number 980. It was a moderate size lake, six miles long, and slightly over a mile across at its widest point. It was a cold-water lake, with considerable depth. The fish population was primarily rainbow and lake trout. The trout fed on the smelt that spawned in the streams flowing into the lake, and grew to enormous size.

Over the years, Havre de Poisson's reputation had spread across Canada and south into the States. To the truly avid fisherman, the allure of landing a trophy fish *never* went away. To the serious hunter, the *potential* of bringing down a record size buck worthy of being listed in 'Boone and Crockett' is like *The Call of the Wild*. People came to Havre de Poisson for one reason, to get into the record books.

The number of record-breaking trophies that have come from Havre de Poisson is a record unto itself. Combine that achievement with the pristine environment, the first-class accommodations, and the exquisite menus served by Chef Angelo, and it's no wonder so many sportsmen irreverently refer to Lou Gault's lodge as, 'Mecca.'

Although the essence of Havre de Poisson itself has stayed the same over the years, life at the resort has not. The year-round residents now numbered nine, three of whom were under the age of eight. The number of cottages available and the size of the dining room in the lodge had doubled. Cellular and internet service had become a reliable amenity. Every year now, by early April there's a waiting list.

. . .

SHORTLY AFTER LOU entered the porch, Kate, his wife of eight years, called out from the kitchen.

"Lou, are all the boats out?"

A slight smile appeared on Lou's face as he savored the lilting tone of his wife's Irish brogue. "They are. Everyone was eager to get an early start this morning, Kate."

Moving to the doorway leading out to the porch. she asked, "Do you have anything special going on this morning?"

"Not really. Well, there's a couple of things I need to do. Luigi Secondo is flying up."

"And what time is that?"

"Around ten. Why?"

"Could you watch the kids for me? I'd like to get my run in?"

"Yeah, sure. Are you doing five miles, or just three?"

Without saying another word, Kate stepped out onto the porch, lifted her five foot, six frame up on her tip toes and planted a passionate kiss on her husband's lips.

When she finally broke away from him, Lou brushed her long chestnut brown hair aside and placed his hands on her shoulders saying, "Kate, I can't believe how much it turns me on just to be your man."

"Well, you just hold on to that thought, because that's all we have time for until tonight. As soon as I'm back and showered, I'm on the phone for the rest of the day pulling next year's budget together for the Major Crime Unit."

"Are the twins up yet?"

"Up, fed, dressed, and watching 'Odd Squad' on PBS."

"And after that?"

"When the show's over, they have their chores."

With that, Kate put her hair up in a pony tail and was out the door.

As Lou watched the love of his life jog down the path, he thought to himself, *just about as fine a figure any woman could have, beautiful on the inside, smart as a whip, a wonderful mother, the best partner a man could have, and still as friggin' horny as ever.*

KATE HAD BEEN a *city mouse* before she met Lou, but she adapted quickly to life in the Canadian wilderness. She enjoyed the serenity of the forest and used the solitude it provided during her frequent runs to clear her thoughts and prepare for whatever was ahead.

When Kate returned from her run and began stretching out, she said, "Lou, I was thinking of Luigi Secondo during my run. today How many times has he been up here this year?"

"Ha…I've no idea. Luigi comes and goes as he pleases." After a pause he said, "Maybe every fourth week he's up for a few days."

"That man must have more money than he knows what to do with!"

"What makes you say that?"

"Well, for the last three years he's taken a cottage for the entire season, and he's hardly ever here. Now, that's a waste of money."

"It's probably cheaper and less hassle than buying a place."

"He always comes up alone. Never once has he brought anyone up with him."

"There's no harm in that."

"Well, if ever there was a man chasing the will-o'-the-wisp, he's the one."

"It's his life, Kate."

"Does he ever even take out a boat? Does he ever wet a line, or fish? No, he doesn't."

"He takes a boat out once in a while. Hey, he comes up here to get away and hang around with his pal Angelo."

"Well, of course, they're pals! Luigi brings Angelo all kinds of things from Italy. What the man needs to do is find himself a good wife and be happy."

Lou smiled, thinking, *Kate a man can be single and be happy.*

Using a more serious tone, Kate asked, "Lou, what is it that Luigi does for a living?"

"No idea."

"Stop! I don't believe this. In all the time he's been coming up here, and all the time you two have talked, you're telling me you've never talked about how the man makes a living?"

"Nope."

"Well, I find *that* hard to believe."

"Kate, I don't talk about things like that with the fellas who come up here. Hell, they come up here to get away from all of that."

Kate paused for a moment. "Well, you're always chatting with this one and the other one, what *do* you talk about?"

Lou shrugged his shoulders, before saying, "Well, we talk about fishing, we talk about hunting…tackle…bait…the lake…the weather…the guides…Chef Angelo…ya know, guy stuff."

"And you're not the least bit interested in knowing what Luigi Secondo does for a living?"

"No, I am not."

"Well, it may not make a wee bit of difference to you what the man does, but it does to me. And, I'll tell you right now, if there's one thing this Irish colleen you married is *going* to do, it's find out what the man does for a living."

Lou looked at his wife and smiled. *No kidding,* he thought, *that's why the Mounties wanted you to head up New Brunswick's Major Crime Investigative Unit.*

Eight years earlier, INTERPOL had loaned the services of a young Lieutenant Kathryn O'Grady to Canada, to help the Mounties bring down an international smuggling ring. Her investigative skills proved to be so effective, the Mounties ended up making her an offer she couldn't refuse. Shortly after, she transferred from Ireland's Directorate of Military Intelligence to the Royal Canadian Mounted Police.

"Kate, *relax.* It doesn't matter what he does back home."

Even though they were married, like many husbands, Lou had yet to realize, use of the word *relax*, quite often had the opposite effect.

"Well, I'll wager a goodly amount that Angelo knows."

"Kate, don't go sticking your nose where it doesn't belong."

THERE WAS a knock on their screen door. Unbeknownst to Lou, the quiet, peaceful life he strove to live had just begun to unravel.

Chapter Three

When Santino Varni's executive secretary entered his office, she had a passport in hand. "Mr. Varni, I have you traveling today as 'Luigi Secondo.' Your driver is ready whenever you are."

Looking up, he asked, "Does he have everything?" Santino had been sitting behind his desk, musing over the small article in the Boston Globe regarding the recent disappearance of an assistant district attorney.

"He does sir. I had your luggage, and the specialty items you requested, sent down a while ago."

Varni smiled. *Of course you did Nina, you take care of everything,* he thought.

"I have you flying out of Hanscom Field today, sir. Logan is stacked up."

Without saying a word, Varni turned and looked across the harbor toward Boston's major airport. After a moment he said, "Let *Matteo* know I need to speak with him."

For the past decade, Santino Varni had ruled over the

powerful local longshoremen's union with an iron fist. His unprecedented rise to power had coincided, not surprisingly, with a series of unfortunate accidents. Those accidents had claimed the lives of three other senior union officials, who many thought, were also in line for the top job. But Santino had been "the last man standing," so to speak.

WITHIN A MATTER OF MINUTES, Matteo Abruzzi, his trusted *consigliere* and childhood friend, sat on the opposite side of his desk.

"You're going to handle this *risk* we talked about?" Santino stared at him.

Without saying a word, Matteo stood up, walked over by the floor-to-ceiling windows in Santino's plush office, placed his hands in his pockets and stared out at Boston harbor. After collecting his thoughts, he turned, "Ya...don't worry."

"When's it happening?"

"Soon."

"What the hell does *soon* mean?"

Matteo sighed. *Santino you have so little patience*, he thought, then shifted his gaze away from his friend and again stared out across the harbor. "He's gonna go away in a couple of days. I wantcha outta town before he gets whacked, *capiche*?"

"Why?"

Turning sharply to his friend, Matteo said, "Whaddya friggin' mean, asking me *why*? We *talked* about this!" *This hit's gonna be all over the friggin' papers*, Matteo thought. Softening his tone, he said, "Look, Santino, I got this, okay? Let me do my friggin' job."

Santino leaned back in his chair. After running both hands

through his hair and locking fingers behind the back of his head, he said, "I want Jack Crevalle *dead*. He's a risk."

"It's gonna happen, Santino."

"I thought he was one of us," Varni said with some bitterness.

"Yeah, well, he pissed on his own grave, that's what he did." Matteo paused a moment. "He played us for the fool, and now he's gonna pay the price."

"How's it gonna happen?"

Turning back toward the window, Matteo said, "You don't wanna know."

Santino only half-listened to his friend. Instead, he muttered to himself, "Jack, I protected you. I *trusted* you. I even made you a freaking *steward*. And this is what you do?" Then he sat up straight again. "Matteo, when I ask you a question, I expect you to answer me."

Matteo turned away from the window and looked at his friend. "No, you gotta stay above this."

When Santino continued staring at him, Matteo rubbed his left hand across the back of his neck before adding, "It'll happen over in Charlestown. It's gonna look like the Irish made the hit."

Santino gestured with his hand, signaling that he wanted to hear more.

"Antonio's kid has a story going in the paper today. He's gonna infer how Crevalle's attorney is looking for a plea deal in exchange for him testifying *against* the Bunker Hill gang. The hit will look like somebody decided to silence him." Turning back toward the window, he took a deep breath before continuing, "The precinct captain on duty the night it happens will be one of ours."

Santino subconsciously slipped into Italian, *"Come ci sei riuscito?"*

Shaking his head, Matteo turned away from the window. "You don't need to know *how* I arraigned that."

Then Santino asked, "So, who replaces Crevalle as union steward?"

"I told D'Angelo we'd back him."

"All right." Santino nodded in agreement. "I need to catch a plane."

Turning sharply back toward the window, Matteo said, "Hey, so, you like this place you go to, huh?"

"It's out in the sticks. But, yeah, I like the place."

Matteo smiled as he turned to look at this friend. "I got Antonio's kid running a piece about you in tomorrow's paper."

"About what?"

"How you escape the pressures of work by communing with nature, catching fish, and all that bullshit."

Santino smiled and stood up. *"Tutto bene."*

"Yeah, *tutto bene*, everything's gonna be fine. Now just go. But do as I ask. Stay away for a week this time."

"Yeah, yeah . . . *ho capito*, I get it, I'm going, okay? *Ciao.*"

Matteo walked back to his own office while thinking, *If Santino Varni has an Achilles heel, it's this friggin' obsession he has with risks, and always having to be in control.*

WHEN THE LIMO arrived at Hanscom Field, the driver popped the trunk, got out and opened the rear passenger door. Although there were no overt physical changes, the man who emerged from the limo had already begun to take on a new persona. Like a chameleon altering its appearance to blend with its environment, Varni had begun to mentally shift into his alter ego, his alter persona, Luigi Secondo.

"This is an international flight, sir, you'll need to present your passport before boarding."

"I have it."

"Fine. I'll follow you over with your luggage."

When Santino Varni reached the foot of the Gulfstream G550's stairs, he presented his passport to the pilot.

After verifying the passport photo matched the face of his lone passenger, the pilot handed it back. "Welcome aboard, Mr. Secondo, we'll be on our way to Grand Falls, New Brunswick, as soon as we have your luggage stowed."

Chapter Four

After a knock on the screen door of Lou and Kate's cottage at Havre de Poisson, a familiar voice called out, "Kate, are you home?"

"I am, Koby, come in."

"I hope I'm not interrupting anything," Koby said as she stepped onto the porch.

"No, we were just talking. What's up?"

"I'm taking little Gigi over to Alessandra's. She's going to watch her while I staff the clinic at the village today. They're going to make cookies, then, go on a picnic. I thought the twins might want in."

"Nice! I'm sure they will. Let 'Nonie' know I'll be sending them over.

Upon hearing the voice of his cousin Jake's wife, Lou walked over to the doorway. "Hey, Koby."

"Hi, Lou."

"Before you head out, bring your boat over to the docks. I

wanna make sure that gas guzzler your husband bought has enough in the tank to make it down to Moose Cove and back."

"I will."

Koby Callahan had captured the heart of Lou's cousin, Jake, years ago. The two met on the isle of Guernsey, off the coast of France when Jake and Lou were in hot pursuit of the kidnappers of Lou's own wife, Kate. Koby, a globetrotting marine biologist, just happened to be in-between assignments at the time and was staying with friends who lived on the Channel Islands. In addition to being an internationally known, and well-respected marine biologist, Koby was also a registered nurse.

It was Jake, Koby, and their little daughter, Gigi, along with Chef Angelo, his wife, Alessandra, Lou, Kate, and their young twins who were permanent residents at the famed fishing resort and called it "home."

Now Koby balanced her time between raising their daughter, married life, staffing a drop-in clinic at the Abenaki village, and serving on a provincial board overseeing wetland habitats across the northern half of New Brunswick.

Jake still flew the mail plane on weekdays, with one difference. At the end of each day, the de Haviland Otter he flew to deliver mail, was now moored at Havre de Poisson. On Thursday evenings, he still flew over to Kedgwick to teach martial arts at the dojo he'd operated for years. Other than Thursday evenings, he enjoyed camp life at the resort, and occasionally helping Lou.

As Lou walked over to the boathouse, he noticed one of his

boats returning to the dock. Neither man looked especially happy.

"Any luck, fellas?"

"Nah, not even a single strike, Lou."

"How were you fishing?"

"We had two colors of lead-core line out."

"That's only twenty yards of line. That's not enough line. You gotta go down deeper this time of year. Are you going back out?"

"Yeah. We came in to refill the thermos with coffee."

"Try putting out four and a half colors on one line and five on the other. Whichever one gets a strike will tell ya what depth they're at. You're using about a seventeen-foot leader, right?"

"Yeah, just about."

"Good. Keep the speed around three on the trolling indicator. That should put the hook right above where the rainbows are. You're sewing the smelt on, right?"

"Yeah."

"If you're still not getting any strikes, back down on the throttle a bit."

JUST THEN, Koby came gliding around the point in a classic 26-foot mahogany barrel back Chris Craft runabout. Not long after Jake and Koby had married, they had hiked up to the headwaters of the stream, retrieved a few handfuls of gold nuggets panned from their land that he and Lou had hidden there, and acquired the classic. The only difference between Lou's runabout and Jake's were the serial numbers. Both vintage boats were Chris Crafts. They shared the same unique design, which was popular until fiberglass hulls changed that industry.

As Koby edged up to the dock, she threw the bumpers out and tossed the bow line to Lou.

"What's that little needle on the gauge pointing at Koby?"

Koby looked, then raised her eyebrows and tilted her head slightly. It's saying it's pretty thirsty!"

Once Lou topped off the tank and secured the cap, he gave Koby a thumbs up. With that, Koby cleared the bilge, pressed the start button and once again, the powerful inboard came to life. The throaty rumble the classics were known for momentarily drowned out every other sound. After the runabout had backed away from the dock, Koby eased the throttle forward, and as the craft moved ahead, the sleek bow came out of the water with ease. When the runabout reached the middle of the lake, it turned and headed west.

MEANWHILE, Lou began his daily chores. Every morning, he walked the shoreline, searching for even the slightest sign of litter or change in the aquatic plant life that grew in the pristine waters of the lake.

LIKE HIS GRANDFATHER BEFORE HIM, Lou willingly accepted the role of caretaker for what the Abenaki referred to as *N'Dakinna* (meaning "our homeland"). There was nothing ceremonial about the role. It was all about protecting the land and fostering the traditional ways of his people. Like his forefathers, Lou understood the ecological importance of the waterways. Water had always been essential to his people.

The lakes, the ponds, the streams were all critical to the plants. Even the wildlife in the valley depended upon the purity of the water.

In so many ways, *water* had always defined the Abenaki way of life . . . as it defined the life Lou led today.

Chapter Five

About the time Koby left the dock, a Gulfstream G550 began its approach to Grand Falls, New Brunswick. The lone passenger looked down at the vast impenetrable forest that stretched for miles on end. Within moments, his thoughts drifted back to the first time he had made this journey.

I never would have chosen this place, but it's really perfect. A smirk appeared on his face. *Funny how things turn out.*

Then, as if a switch had been thrown inside his head, it was Matteo Abruzzi's voice from long ago, that he was hearing. *Santino, we need to work on your image. It is no good for you to be around when things happen. When I tell you to go away, you need to go someplace respectable.* He smiled as he remembered the confrontation he'd had with his friend.

"*Who are you to tell me where I go?*" he had said back then.

"*Santino, per favore, listen to me, I will find a place for you to go!*"

When Matteo had first mentioned a remote fly-in sportsman's fishing lodge in the wilds of New Brunswick, Santino had laughed at the idea.

Now, as he looked out the window, the smirk on his face changed into a smile. *Matteo was right, I needed someplace squeaky clean.* With that, his thoughts were interrupted by the pilot's announcement: "Secure your seat belt and prepare for landing."

SECRECY AND DECEPTION defined Varni's world. Stealth, retribution, and unpredictability, those were the primary reasons Varni had been able to survive and remain in power all these years. There was *never* room for mistakes, or risks of any sort, or even the slightest hint of vulnerability in the brutal world Varni controlled. Everything that happened was deliberate, everything was done for a reason. There were never any *unintended* consequences.

And nothing was ever done in a manner that could point back to Varni. He was a cautious man, conscious to never leave a trail. Whenever Varni crossed into Canada, he traveled under the alias of "Luigi Secondo." Above all, Santino Varni abhorred taking unnecessary risks, which was the reason he was still alive. Santino Varni had enemies who watched his every move. Traveling under his *own* name was one risk he would never take.

The public image epitomizing Santino Varni as an avid sportsman, was strictly a ruse, a total sham, one that Matteo had carefully crafted for Varni. The frequent trips he made to Canada had absolutely nothing to do with any appreciation for the outdoors. It was his alibi. Plain and simple, it's where he hid out when he needed to distance himself from whatever mayhem he had orchestrated in his corrupt, brutal world. Then, to totally bury any connection, he was known by the name of Luigi Segundo at the wilderness camp.

ONCE VARNI LANDED in Canada and exited the plane, his behavior was entirely different, yet predictably consistent. He was an ordinary man. He carried his own luggage and there were no airs about him. After he cleared Canadian Customs, as Luigi Secondo, he predictably walked over to the Smyth Air counter and booked a charter flight to Havre de Poisson.

As he walked toward the terminal, a man loaded down with mail sacks bumped him from behind. "Oops, sorry, my bad! Hey buddy, hold the door open for me, will ya?"

Varni immediately stiffened. He hadn't quite finished making the mental transition into his alter ego and he took umbrage with being bumped . . . touched in any way. But as soon as he turned to see who was behind him, he heard a friendly voice. "Hey Luigi, it's you! I didn't expect to bump into you here. You just coming up?"

Upon hearing the name "Luigi," Varni morphed back into the unassuming persona of his alter ego. A warm smile appeared on his face, "Jake, I didn't recognize your voice! Yes, I just arrived."

"You heading over to the lodge?"

"I am."

"I gotta fly right by there on this next run. I can save ya a couple of bucks if ya don't mind sitting on a few mail bags."

Luigi momentarily squinted his eyes and tilted his head, as if he was pondering the offer. Then, the smile returned to his face. "Let's do it! I've never flown in a mail plane before!"

"Okay, wait here. I'll be right out. I just gotta exchange these bags."

When Jake returned, he gave Luigi a slap on the shoulder, "Okay, my friend we're all set, let's go."

"You're sure this is legal?"

"Absolutely."

"That's odd, I thought postal regulations would've prohibited you from taking on hitchhikers."

Laughing, Jake picked up his step, saying, "Don't worry about it. There's a lot of *grey* area in those regs."

Jake had parked the de Haviland he used to deliver mail a short distance from the terminal. When they reached the plane, Jake climbed in, turned around and motioned for Luigi to pass up his luggage. It wasn't until Luigi lifted his bag that he noticed a shiny, new Canadian 'airmail' stamp now adorning his shoulder.

When Luigi began picking at the stamp, Jake said, "Let that be! That's what makes you *legal* to be in the plane," and gave his trademark roguish smile.

As Jake taxied toward the runway, he turned to Luigi. Raising his voice, so he could be heard over the noise of the prop, he said, "Luigi! If you're hungry, there's a sandwich in the cooler with your name on it. I've got an extra bottle of Grey Poupon in there, too, if you want more flavor!"

"I'm good, thanks."

"Suit yourself."

The two men met the first year Luigi had rented a cottage at Havre de Poisson for the entire season. They instantly became friends and had often enjoyed a cigar with Chef Angelo at night under the stars.

• • •

AFTER KOBY LEFT THE DOCK, Lou had walked quite a distance along the shoreline. When he heard a float plane coming up the valley, he looked at his watch. *Hmmm, that should be Luigi, but it sure as hell sounds like Jake's mail plane.*

As Lou headed back toward the dock, the conversation he'd had earlier with his wife came to mind. *Kate's right, Luigi's been coming up here long enough; I should know a little more about what he does for a living.*

Lou had walked a good distance away from where the plane would be coming in. Now, he quickened his pace to return when he looked up and saw the pilot make a tight turn into the wind. By the time he reached the resort, the passenger had already deplaned, and the float plane was taxiing out to the center of the lake. Over to his left, Lou saw Luigi Secondo and Chef Angelo walking together toward the lodge.

Why have I never asked Luigi how he's able to get away and come up here so often? But what the hell, Angelo's happy every time his friend comes up, maybe I shouldn't worry about it at all.

BEING NEITHER A FISHERMAN NOR A HUNTER, Luigi rarely took out a boat when he was at Havre de Poisson. Early on, the Abenaki guides began referring to him as, "the one who comes, but does not fish."

The only reason Varni, known only as Luigi Secondo to everyone at the resort, even considered returning a second time was because of the exquisite Italian cuisine Chef Angelo prepared day-after-day. Over time, the friendship between the two men flourished. Whenever Luigi was in camp, the two of them took their noon meal together. They would talk for hours on end, covering everything under the sun, always speaking in Italian.

It was not unusual for a sportsman to come to Havre de Poisson to fish in the spring, then again in the fall to hunt. However, Luigi Secondo was, and remained, the only person to ever inquire about taking a cottage for the *entire* 23-week season.

When Lou Gault and Luigi shook hands on a seasonal agreement, it included two unique clauses which catered to Luigi's idiosyncrasies. Instead of receiving a box lunch, Luigi would take his lunch in the lodge with Angelo. Secondly, instead of weekly housekeeping, Luigi would receive daily service.

Luigi visited the resort often enough that he was on a first name basis with the year-round residents. However, it wasn't until the year he took a cottage for the *entire* season that he truly assimilated into the camp culture and added a unique element to it. Along with Chef Angelo, he built a regulation bocce court near the lodge. Weather permitting, the two of them took on "all comers" in a best-out-of-three bocce match. During dinner, whenever Angelo emerged from the kitchen to sing an Italian song, he would motion for his friend saying, "Luigi, come! We'll do this one together!" The melding of their rich tenor voices always ended with applause and shouts of *bravo*.

In every aspect, the life Luigi Secondo lived while at Havre de Poisson was the polar opposite of who he was in Boston. What began as merely his alibi, had slowly become the alternate universe in which he lived.

Over the years, the friendship between Angelo and Luigi evolved to the point that Angelo looked forward to hearing, "Hey *paisan*! What's for lunch today?" In return for the special dishes Angelo always prepared for his friend, Luigi kept *his* friend supplied with a variety of Italian delicacies.

Most days, once the two men finished lunch, they'd spend an hour or two walking the forest trails together. Luigi favored the path that looped down past the old logging road, as it was the easier trail. On inclement days, the two men hung around the lodge talking and feasting on whatever "small plates" Angelo had decided to prepare for lunch.

Although Luigi came and went with little notice, he was seen as a semi-resident of the resort. When he was in camp, he'd sit in with Angelo and Alessandra when they tutored the three Gault children in Italian. Once the lesson was over, the children eagerly gathered around Luigi, as if he were a beloved uncle, and listen to him tell story after story in Italian. His young audience sat mesmerized, as he drew them into his stories using different voices, inflections, and grand hand gestures that embellished his tales. When the last story was told, the youngsters would jump up, give their beloved storyteller a hug, and trot off to their cottage most often for sleep.

The conversations that Angelo and Luigi enjoyed knew no boundaries. Angelo would often open his heart to his friend. It was no secret that Luigi was Sicilian. Yet, Angelo would jokingly say, "You know my friend, you are not really Italian, you're an Arab." Yet, the furthest thing from Angelo's mind was that his friend was *anything* other than the gentle, God-fearing man he appeared to be.

Chef Angelo and his wife Alessandra had come over from Italy, themselves, fifteen years earlier. They had intended to work for only a season but they never left. Alessandra was her husband's capable sous chef. She also ran herd over the housekeeping staff.

Despite Kate's desire to know more about Luigi, she, too, accepted him as part of the resort's inner circle. Yet, there was one resident who continued to watch Luigi closely.

Chapter Six

For the past few days, the weather in central New Brunswick had been ideal, a little crisp for this time of year, but sunny.

Five hundred miles southwest was an entirely different story. A cold front had moved in, settling over the warmer water of Boston's harbor, blanketing the docks in a thick fog. Throughout the day and into the night, the waterfront had taken on a somewhat ghostly grey appearance.

Adding to the visual murkiness which engulfed the docks, the sounds within the harbor were different. The dampness seemed to mute both sight and sound. Intermittent warnings from fog horns seemed more distant. The rhythmic clanging of bells attached to buoys was softer; lapping of water against stanchions seemed strangely more melodic. Even the irritating noise from winches were soft, and sirens that periodically broke the silence at the piers, seemed muffled.

In some inexplicable way, the familiar sounds of the harbor had been transformed into a poorly orchestrated opus, garishly akin to a score from The Phantom of the Opera, only hauntingly off key.

But Jack Crevalle was oblivious to all the sounds of the harbor. As usual, he sat hunched over a small desk in a dilapidated weathered shack along the waterfront. The structure had never been much of anything; it was hot in the summer and cold in the winter. It was where the union stewards sat when they made out their duty rosters. So, it didn't matter to Crevalle that it was foggy. Boston's weather never prevented men from working as they loaded and unloaded cargo on huge ships tied up at Boston Harbor.

The only thing powerful enough to bring the docks to a standstill was a nod from Santino Varni, president of the Longshoremen's Union. Periodically Varni flexed his muscle; other than that, it was business as usual.

At this particular hour, the longshoremen on second shift had taken over the docks. Jack Crevalle was halfway through making out the third shift crew assignments when he heard a knock.

"Hey, Jack . . . you in there?"

Without taking eyes off his laptop, Crevalle called out, "Yeah, I'm here."

"Hey, a few of us are going over to that new club . . . the one over in Charlestown. They got some hot babes there . . . wanna go?"

At first, Crevalle didn't recognize the deep booming voice coming from just beyond the open doorway. Swiveling around in his chair, he put the voice and face together. "Hey, Popeye . . . how you doing?"

"I'm okay. Hey, put that shit away and come with us."

"I can't, I gotta finish up."

"Okay, so, finish up! I'll wait . . . we'll go together."

"Ahhhhh, I don't know. I should go home and change. I'm grungy, in work clothes."

"Nah, you're fine. What's the matter . . . you think you're going to a friggin' funeral?"

"No . . . no, but look at *you*. You look nice, look at the fancy shoes you got on."

Smiling, Popeye lifted his right foot while pulling up a pant leg to show off the cordovan hand-made Italian leather shoes he had on. "You like? I got 'em off some stiff."

"Popeye, come on! I'm gonna be the only one not dressed up, I'm gonna feel like a fish outta water."

"Ahhhhh, frig that, Jack! Ain't nobody gonna *give* a shit."

Jack thought for a moment. "All right; gimme five minutes to finish up."

"Okay, I'll be in the car."

It was closer to ten minutes before Jack Crevalle slid into the front passenger seat next to Popeye. "I thought you said a few of the guys were going?"

"They didn't wanna wait. Said they'd save us a seat. You wanna beer? I got a cooler in the back seat."

"Nah, I'm good."

As Popeye pulled out of the parking lot, Jack's eyes took in the plush interior and the insignia on the dash and thought: *This car is just like the one Matteo drives. And I'm drive a friggin' Toyota. How the hell does this guy get to drive around in an S-Class Mercedes?*

Popeye continued with the small talk, keeping it friendly, but he was never one for idle talk. As they drove toward Charlestown, Jack kept thinking.

Popeye's a strange one, I never thought the bastard liked me.

Why the hell is he going out of his way to include me tonight? Ha, he must be looking for some OT to pay for the friggin' chariot he's driving.

When they came to a stoplight, Popeye glanced at the Rolex stretched across his massive wrist. It was close to time the captain assigned to night watch in Charlestown would be coming on duty.

When Crevalle noticed Popeye looking at his watch, he broke the momentary silence, "I ain't been to a strip joint in ages. Do these dames go all the way, or do they just tease?"

"Hey, who the hell *cares* . . . it's a friggin' night out, right?"

"Jimmy's daughter did that shit for a while."

Popeye glanced over at Crevalle after this comment and shrugged a shoulder. "Ya, but she did it out in the open. She wasn't two timing nobody behind their back, like *you*, ya piece of shit," Popeye muttered it so low that Jack never caught it.

"I ain't been to Charlestown in ages," Crevalle lied.

"Yeah, me neither," Popeye also lied. "I'm gonna bang a right turn here onto Water Street; they got everything blocked up ahead."

"I always go up Warren. It bypasses all the crap at Harvard Square."

Popeye smirked. "I thought you said you ain't been over here in ages?"

Crevalle hesitated, realizing his mistake. "Ya, well, I meant . . . hey, all I *meant* was when I *used* to come over here, that's the way I went. That's *all* I was sayin'."

When Popeye suddenly took a sharp left into an alleyway, Crevalle sat up straight. "Hey, where the hell are ya *going*? I thought this place is on Warren Street."

"Paulie said the place ain't got no parking right now. Said

he's been using the lot behind *these* buildings. So, big deal, we gotta walk a little."

"Ahhhhh, Paulie's a friggin cheap bastard just like his old man. The place we're going has valet parking. All ya gotta do it pull up in front."

Popeye smiled to himself.

THE ALLEYWAY WAS DARK, lined with dumpsters, empty barrels, boxes, assorted junk; you name it, it was there. Walls were peppered with graffiti and the further you went in, the more the walls felt like they were closing in on you.

Popeye took his time navigating the Mercedes deeper into the poorly lit maze before finally pulling over. Turning to Crevalle he motioned with his head as he said, "Okay, Jack, let's go."

"You parking *here*?"

"Yeah."

Shaking his head Crevalle said, "Okay, which way?"

"Straight ahead, I'll be right behind you."

As soon as Jack Crevalle walked beyond the sedan's elongated hood, Matteo stepped out from the shadows. Jack saw him, Santino Varni's consigliere,

"*Whoa, Matteo* . . . what the frig? Holy *shit,* man, you scared the ever-loving crap outta me!"

At just about the same time Jack realized something might be amiss, a thin wire passed over his face and a garrote tightened around his neck.

The more Crevalle resisted, the further back Popeye leaned as he applied full force to the garrote. Crevalle was considerably shorter than Popeye and at a point during the struggle, Crevalle's feet left the ground. Matteo watched the macabre dance in front of him. Crevalle was jerking around like a drunken marionette on a string controlled by a masterful puppeteer.

Ten seconds passed, twenty seconds, thirty seconds, sixty seconds; Crevalle's brain was being denied the necessary life giving oxygen it screamed for. Popeye could sense the fight draining from his latest victim.

At the ninety-second mark, Crevalle had lost consciousness, and lay slouched against the chest of his killer. The assassin maintained tension on the garrote until a full six minutes had passed.

Once again, an unsuspecting victim had fallen prey to the strength of Popeye's huge forearms, and his talent with the garrote.

Chapter Seven

In many ways, Santino Varni and his contrasting alter ego, "Luigi Secondo," could aptly be described as a modern-day Jekyll and Hyde.

Although he'd never been officially diagnosed, Varni suffered from a rare mental health condition since an early age known as *dissociative identity disorder (DID)*. Previously, the affliction had been referred to as *split personality disorder*.

People with DID had two or more separate identities. Each personality controlled its own behavior completely independent from the individual's "other" personalities. Each identity had its own personal history, its own traits, its own likes and dislikes. The "core" identity was the person's usual personality. Common medical terminology for the non-core personalities was simply *alter* identities.

Santino Varni's *core* persona was a ruthless, self-serving mobster. Varni lived a life of crime, greed, and willfully imposing misery upon others. Varni gave no quarter and expected none in return. He controlled those around him through fear. Santino Varni had the power to virtually take whatever he wanted in life, whenever he wanted it, and by whatever means he chose. To him winning was everything, whether through bribes, intimidation, or acts of unspeakable violence; his world was pure black and white.

In stark contrast, the man known as "Luigi Secondo," who frequented Havre de Poisson, was an alter personality of the public figure known as Santino Varni. The personality of Luigi was a kind, gentle soul. He was an interesting conversationalist, scholarly, yet never officious or patronizing. He got along well with the other sportsmen, and they enjoyed his company. The fresh clean air, as well as the sights and sounds of the unspoiled wilderness seemed to invigorate him. More than once, Chef Angelo had commented to his friend, "Luigi, when you come up here, you're tense. But, by the second day, you're a different man, even your posture is more relaxed."

The only response Chef Angelo ever received from Luigi was, "*Eh*, what can I say, huh?"

The stress-free environment of camp life, and natural camaraderie that existed among the sportsmen, made it easy for Varni's 'alter' persona, Luigi Secondo, to flourish whenever he was in camp.

For someone who grew up in the city, Secondo's needs were minor. He came across as being quite comfortable with the low-profile, off-the-grid lifestyle existing at Havre de Poisson. He seemed to relish the trusting relationships he had established with the Gault youngsters, and appreciated the unassuming friendships he enjoyed with the older, year-round residents at the resort.

By the time Varni's alter persona, Luigi Secondo, arrived in camp, the mental and physical transformation had already occurred. Incredibly, for the duration of his stay, he'd have no difficulty *sustaining* the alter image throughout the day. The gentle Luigi Secondo was the only personality everyone knew.

However, after dark when he was alone, the drama he endured was an entirely different story. At night, the voice of the more powerful "core" personality, Santino Varni, would come to Luigi. That's when Luigi Secondo struggled to stay in his *altered* state of mind and remain the 'alter' persona.

Luigi was fully aware that the *only* reason he, himself, existed was because his creator, the core persona Santino, *allowed* him to exist. The conundrum he struggled with was that his own values were at complete odds from those of his creator, Varni. But he knew Santino would come into his thoughts at night, and he always tried to be prepared . . . to stay in control.

Not one night was any different from another. Whenever Luigi stayed at the resort. He would lie in his bed, in the dark, waiting for the inevitable conversation the two diametrically opposed personalities would have in his head. The pressure from Varni never changed, nor did Luigi's resistance. It was truly a battle of wills, akin to a game of chess played between two grand masters, neither willing to concede to the other.

Now, Santino Varni was extremely risk adverse. He had only survived in his violent world because he eliminated risks *before* they became real threats. To Varni, any environment that he didn't have absolute control over . . . was a risk.

Varni's patience had worn thin. One night, not long after

Luigi had slipped into bed, the voice of Santino Varni entered his *alter* persona's subconsciousness.

Luigi . . . did you pose the question today?

Luigi tossed his head back and forth, in a futile attempt to clear his thoughts and rid himself of the invisible bond that held the *alter* persona to the *core* persona.

But Santino had never been a patient man. When Luigi didn't respond, the voice entered Luigi's mind again, stronger.

Did you pose the question today?

Luigi knew he had no choice but ultimately to submit. He knew the question would be repeated ad nauseam, until he responded.

No. No, I didn't. It is too soon, another day.

Then Santino cut through Luigi's deflection, like a surgeon with a scalpel.

You know I don't like taking risks, Luigi, you know that.

Luigi sighed before thinking: *Santino, there are no risks here. We are safe. These are good people.*

Luigi, you and I know both know that is not true, don't we.

It is true! Please . . .!

No, it's not. If anything were to happen, I would be unable to protect either of us here. We are in danger and you know I don't take risks.

The muscles in Luigi's face tightened and he winced, as if in pain. Finally, he responded in his mind: *The opportunity to ask the question has not presented itself.*

You tell me that every night, Luigi. Why is that?

I'm waiting. I'm waiting for the right time, that's all; that's all it is, Santino.

There was a pause; then the voice invading Luigi's head took on a darker tone. *I don't understand why you won't do this one thing for me. Perhaps I need to have someone else do it; someone more . . . persuasive, ask the question.*

Luigi struggled to clear his mind so his thoughts wouldn't betray him. But it was impossible. Varni knew.

Luigi, you are here in this place only because I allow it. What do you think will happen if you don't ask the question?

Realizing his back was against the wall, and weary of this nightly battle of wits, Luigi gave in. *Okay, okay, I will ask the question tomorrow.*

Long after the voice of Santino left Luigi, he lay awake, soaked in sweat, resigned to the fact he could no longer placate his nemesis with delays and promises. Before the next night, when the two personas would speak again, he expected to have an answer . . . to the question.

Chapter Eight

It was well after dawn the following morning when Luigi Secondo showed up at the dock with a boxed lunch in hand. The surprise in Lou's voice was obvious since the man had rarely set foot on the water. "Hey Luigi, good morning. You taking a boat out?"

"Morning Lou. Yeah, I woke up thinking I'd like to get out on the lake today."

"Want me to fix you up with a guide?"

"No, no, I'll be fine, Lou."

"Yeah?"

"Yeah, I . . . I just wanna spend a little time out on the lake, that's all.

"Okay. I'll get you some fresh bait and rig up a line for you."

"I don't even think I'll do any fishing."

"No?"

" Nah, I think I'll just spend a little time with my thoughts."

"Well, if you change your mind, come on back in."

Close to three hours passed before Luigi returned to the dock. Then, after having motored up the full length of the opposite shore and back, Luigi walked the trails. He walked the full length of the old logging road out to route 385 and even took a picture of the mile marker 221 sign out on the highway.

When he returned to the main resort area, Luigi wandered over to the brook that flowed past the old sawmill. As he approached the brook, an intermittent glitter of light caught his attention. At first, he thought it was merely the reflection of the sun's rays dancing off the water as it splashed over a shallow section of the stream bed. When he reached the embankment, he raised his left arm, and shielded his eyes from the sun with his hand. Then he realized the glitter was a combination of the sun's rays on the water and on a small bright yellow stone. Yielding to his curiosity, Luigi bent down, rolled up his sleeve and fished the stone out. As he looked down at the pebble in his palm, he thought: *Probably fool's gold, but I'll have it checked out.* With that, he placed the stone in his pocket and walked back to his cottage.

Before dinner that evening, Luigi joined his friend, Angelo, for an *aperitif.* "Tell me my friend, how much longer do you plan on working here?"

"Ha! This is my *home,* this is my life; *forever* I guess, my family is here."

"No. Your family is in Italy."

"Well, yes, *that* family is in Italy . . . but *this*, my friend, *this* is my family now."

"Would you leave if Lou sold the place?"

Shaking his head, Angelo said, "That won't happen Luigi."

"Which? You wouldn't leave, or Lou wouldn't sell?"

"Both."

Luigi took a sip of his drink before continuing, "Why not?"

"Well, because Havre de Poisson is not for sale."

Smirking at his friend's simplistic view of things, Luigi said, "Angelo, everything is for sale, *everything* has a price."

Holding up his index finger, Angelo said, "That may be true for many things, but not for *every*thing."

"You don't think Lou would sell if the right offer came along."

"No, this is his home. He grew up here, this is where he chooses to raise his family."

Luigi nodded and smiled, but thought, *Well, we'll see about that my friend. Everything has a price . . . and everyone can be bought.*

Angelo changed the subject. "So, how would you like *coniglio* tomorrow for lunch, huh? I'll cook it Sicilian style."

"Of course."

"Good, we'll have it tomorrow. You and I."

Luigi placed his glass on the counter. "Actually, I've had a change in plans. I'm going to leave right after dinner tonight."

"Oh, I'm sad to see you go so soon. But I'm sure the rabbit will be pleased to know it will live to see another day. So, when will I see you again?"

"I'm not sure . . . but soon."

. . .

THE MAJORITY of guests had finished their evening meal and already retired to their cottages when the sound of a float plane coming up the valley reached Lou's ears. Surprised that a plane was coming in so late, he headed down to the docks to turn on the huge flood lights for its landing.

When the Smyth Air charter taxied up to the dock, Lou was waiting and secured the leading edge of the pontoon to the dock with a tie down strap.

"Thanks for throwing on the lights, Lou, it would have been one *helluva* challenge navigating in with just the one headlight."

"I wasn't expecting a plane tonight, what's up?"

"We got a call this afternoon for a pickup."

Lou tilted his head to the side and waited for the pilot to continue.

"A Mr. Secondo needs a ride over to Grand Falls."

Lou frowned. *That's odd, Luigi didn't say anything about leaving tonight . . . but, like Kate says, he comes and goes like the wind.*

As Lou bent down to secure a second tie down strap, the unmistakable howl of a wolf penetrated the stillness of the night. Shortly after, he heard the mournful response from a second wolf.

The first wolf was quite a distance down the valley, but the second wolf wasn't far away. After having left the valley for over a decade, the wolves had returned. Their presence forced the exodus of pesky coyotes who had filled in as the apex predator once the wolves had left.

As soon as Lou finished securing the second tie down

strap, he heard footsteps on the dock. Turning, he recognized the silhouette of the man walking toward him.

"Hey, Luigi, is everything okay?"

"Everything's fine, Lou. I just need to get back."

"Well, hop in and I'll pass your luggage up."

"Sure, but I need to ask you something first."

"Fire away."

Luigi looked down and to the right before saying, "Lou, how much do you want for this place?"

"What did you say?"

"I asked how much you wanted for this place. What's your price?"

Laughing, Lou said, "I don't have a price."

"Come on Lou, *everybody* has a price."

Lou ignored Luigi's question and handed the single piece of luggage up to the pilot.

"How's two and half million sound?"

When Lou didn't answer, Luigi pressed again. "Seriously, Lou, what's your price? What would work for you? I'd keep you on to manage the place. You'd pull down a hefty salary. You'd be in control; everybody will still see this as your place. Angelo would stay on; Jake could continue to live here. Think about it, *nothing* would really change."

"You're chasing a wild goose, Luigi. Havre de Poisson is not for sale, at *any* price. So, when are we going to see you again?"

Luigi ignored Lou's question. "*Come on*, be honest! I'm talking *cash*, how much? You'll still get to run the place. You'll be your own boss, live here for free. You'll enjoy a nice salary without the headaches that go along with being the owner. Nothing else changes. Sound like a deal?"

"Seriously, Luigi, when are you coming up again?"

"Lou, name your price. Give it to me in Canadian dollars and I'll pay you that in U.S. dollars. How's *that*? You even make an extra, what, twenty-five percent on the exchange rate?"

Lou paused and looked Luigi straight in the eye. "Luigi, Havre de Poisson is *not* for sale, period." The intonation in Lou's voice made Luigi stop. Lou was serious.

"Okay, *okay*, I guess you haven't given much thought to this yet. Give it some serious thought, Lou. I'll be back up." With that Luigi climbed into the float plane.

Once Luigi was aboard, Lou released the tie down straps, pushed the pontoon nearest him away from the dock with his foot, and stood back.

As the plane headed out to the middle of the lake, Lou shook his head, as if to expunge the conversation he'd just had with Luigi from his mind. He waited until the plane lifted into the evening sky before turning off the landing lights.

Then just as Lou reached the top stair of the deck that ran across the front of the lodge, he heard the plane circling back. *Well,* he thought, *if you're gonna have engine trouble it's best to have it someplace where you can land safely.*

Lou returned to the landing, switched the landing lights back on and stood waiting at the dock. When the plane came in, Lou again grabbed a line and secured the plane to the dock, thinking Luigi and the pilot would be staying overnight. Instead, the pilot kept the engine running and Luigi stepped out of the plane.

"Lou, listen, maybe I caught you a little flat-footed, and I'm sorry about that. Look, you know I *like* you, and I want you to know that I intend to do the *right thing* by you. You don't have a price in mind right now, so here's what I'm going to do. Before I get back, I'll have a reputable real estate professional work up a *fair* offer. All that will change is you won't have any cash flow headaches, or carry the financial burden. Everything else will remain the same. Whaddya say, Lou . . . *deal*?"

Lou stood there dumbfounded.

"Okay, Lou, I know this is sudden. But don't pass it up; don't let this slip through your fingers. You'll still get to live the life you want. The only difference is you'll be set for life. We'll talk next time I'm back up."

Lou smiled, shook his head, and looked Luigi straight in the eye, his gaze steely-tough. "Luigi, Havre de Poisson is *not for sale;* it *never* will be for sale. Period . . . end of story. I'm sorry, but that's just the way it is. That said, you're welcome to come up *as a guest,* just like everybody else, but that's all, that's it."

Lou's words seemed to bounce off Luigi like a ball at a carnival stall.

"Lou, like I said, I don't need an answer right now. Sleep on it. Think about the advantages for you. *Seriously,* think on it."

Chapter Nine

When Lou returned to his cottage, Kate was there. He shared the gist of his conversation with Luigi Secondo.

"Seriously, Lou?" Kate asked. "He *honestly* thinks he can buy you out?"

"Who knows?"

"Is it even possible?"

"Of course *not*. The land belongs to the Abenaki people; I'm merely this generation's guardian."

Kate crossed her arms. "Lou, what do we really know about him?"

"Not a *helluva* lot. He must be well-heeled to be offering me two and half million in U. S. dollars. Cash, no less."

"He must be doing something *right* to be throwing that much money around. What's he do for a living?"

"I've no idea."

"You don't know?"

"No . . . and I don't care."

"Well, I *do*! I think I'd like to know who this guest of ours really is."

"Kate, don't go wasting your time; this will all blow over."

"You said he told you to 'think on it.'"

"Well, maybe those weren't his *exact* words, but it was something like that."

"Lou, that means he's still looking to make a deal."

"No, he got the message, loud and clear."

Kate looked at her husband, tousled his hair and said, "Sweetheart, sometimes you can be just a little *too* naive."

"No, he heard me."

Kate let out a sigh. "And sometimes you can even be blind."

Lou sat down and shrugged his shoulders. "Hey, if he brings it up again, I'll just tell him the same thing. Now, let's put it aside."

Kate looked at her husband and shook her head. *As smart as you are, Lou Gault, you can be too trusting at times.*

When Lou saw the expression on Kate's face he said, "What?"

"Like I said, I'm going to find out who this man really is who's coming up here as often as he does and doesn't do anything but sit and think."

"Okay, sleuth, do that. Right now, it's getting late and I'm over at the village tomorrow for a tribal council meeting."

"Oh, before I forget, Koby said to remind you she'll be traveling with you tomorrow."

"*You* wanna tag along? You haven't been to a council meeting for a while."

Kate almost responded with, *Oh, joy!* but opted for, "No, I'll pass this time."

"Suit yourself."

"I'm on a conference call tomorrow with the major crime unit. The baby boomers are beginning to retire *en masse*, and the Mounties aren't able to do any recruiting until budgets are final. So, they've asked us to come up with a few interim staffing solutions."

Kate could tell by the look on her husband's face that whatever it was he was thinking about, it had nothing to do with the Royal Canadian Mounted Police with whom she was involved.

As she placed her hand on Lou's forearm she said, "I think you're ready for bed, hon."

"I am."

Kate stood up, kissed her husband, and said, "Good, because this Irish colleen you've been neglecting these past two nights is ready for some good old-fashioned lovemaking."

ELSEWHERE, the pilot behind the controls of a private charter flight from Grand Falls, New Brunswick, received word they'd been cleared to land at Logan airport. The *alter* persona of Luigi Secondo had faded into the background hours ago and the *core* persona of Santino Varni was back in total control. As the lone passenger looked down at the lights below, thoughts of how he might persuade Lou Gault that it was time to sell his business entered his mind.

OVER THE YEARS, Santino Varni had become accustomed to having his way. The words "no deal" didn't exist in his vocabulary, neither did the word, "sorry."

Years earlier, when he had decided to live in a home overlooking the ocean, he didn't contact a real estate agent, he merely told his chauffeur to drive north along the coast. When Santino saw a cliff home he desired, he simply said, "Pull over."

Back then, Santino stepped out of the limo and walked boldly past two "No Trespassing" signs on the property. As he walked passed the house, he inspected the siding and the windows. He noticed the view in the back overlooking the ocean was breathtaking.

When a female's voice asked, "May I help you?" He turned and smiled.

"Yes, I'd like to purchase your property."

"I'm sorry . . . it's not for sale."

"What's your asking price?"

"You do realize this is private property and that you're trespassing."

"You didn't answer my question."

At that moment, the sliding door to the rear patio opened, and a man emerged. The women turned to him saying, "Honey, this man thinks our home is for sale."

"Sir, this is private property. It's not for sale. I'm going to ask you to please leave."

"What's your asking price?"

"I just asked you to *leave*."

"You didn't answer my question."

"All right, enough of this," he said. "I'm going inside and calling the police."

Later, when the couple's daughter couldn't reach her parents for two days, nor had they returned her calls, she drove over to their home. She found her parents sitting in their car, inside the garage, hands cuffed to the steering wheel. The car wasn't running, but the ignition key was turned on. There was a lingering hint of exhaust inside the garage.

The coroner's report listed both deaths as apparent suicides due to asphyxiation from carbon monoxide.

Months later, an agent representing Santino Varni acquired the estate at public auction. Several potential buyers had also expressed interest in the prime location and were present at the auction. However, after Matteo Abruzzi briefly spoke with them, those who did remain declined to bid. In the end, the only bid for the property was from Santino Varni.

Chapter Ten

The following morning, as Lou raced toward Moose Cove, his thoughts were definitely not on his mahogany runabout. The conversation he'd had the night before with Luigi weighed heavily on his mind.

Whenever the tribal council meetings coincided with the days Jake's wife, Koby, staffed the clinic, the two would travel down the lake together. Usually, they passed the time with small talk. Today was different; while Koby was traveling with him, there was no conversation. Instead, Lou stood with one knee on the seat, his head extending above the windshield. Even after making love to his wife, he'd had a restless night, and the rush of crisp air in his face helped him stay awake and focused.

As they approached Moose Cove, Lou backed off the throttle allowing the hull to drift silently over the shallows between the barrier islands that sheltered the cove. Koby broke the silence when she whispered, "Lou, look; directly ahead, the loons are in the cove."

At the sound of Koby's voice, Lou jettisoned the conversation with Luigi from his thoughts, and mentally returned to the present.

"I see them."

"There's four of them."

"That pair has nested in this cove for well over ten years."

"I see *two* pair."

"No, there's only one *mating* pair. The other two are this year's hatchlings. They'll abandon the younger ones when they fly south."

"I can't blame them for nesting here year after year. This cove is the most picturesque place on the lake; it's so beautiful in here."

"You'll get no argument from me or Kate on that."

As they drifted under the feathery limbs of the ancient white pines that stretched out over the water, the sandy bottom dropped off sharply.

"Lou, did you and Jake come here often when you were growing up?"

"On and off, we did. Most of the time we hung out in the village with our friends."

"You didn't swim here?"

"Sometimes, but more often than not, we swam at the first feeder pond."

"The water is so clear in here, it's difficult to gauge the depth."

"It's about eighty feet in the center," Lou said. The two had made this run numerous times, and each knew their role. Still, he changed the topic and directed, "I'm coming about; prepare to toss the bumpers over the side."

As Lou secured the runabout to the cleats on the dock, Koby walked over to the mini-garage at the tree line and backed out the ATV parked there, then waited for Lou to join her.

As they traveled through the forest, Lou talked over the noise of the ATV. "Do you need me to bring anything before the council today related to the clinic?"

"No, we're good. Aside from a few poison ivy cases, there's not much going on right now, Lou. But you can let everyone know the annual flu vaccine will be arriving by the end of the month."

Since moving to the resort, Koby had literally worn two professional hats: On Monday and Thursday, she staffed the clinic at the village of Grey Elk. On the third week of the month, she flew to Grand Falls for an all-day meeting as a marine biologist. Her credentials had earned her a seat on New Brunswick's Wetland Habitat Management Board. The rest of the time, she was a mom, a wife, and an integral part of the inner circle of the year-round residents at Havre de Poisson.

JUST BEFORE THEY entered the village, Koby turned to Lou saying, "Lou, I'm curious, what is it that Luigi Secondo does for a living?"

Lou smiled to himself. *Now I wonder who she's been talking to?* Then he responded to her question. "I really have no clue . . . all I know is that he comes up from Massachusetts."

"He's really become a fixture at the resort, hasn't he? The kids love him. He has my five year old going around the cottage talking in Italian."

"Yeah, the twins too!"

"I'm glad Gigi is growing up with her cousins. The three of them will be as close as you and Jake."

"Family means a lot to us, Koby. Jake and I were robbed of that when we were young."

"No, you weren't," she protested. "Jake said your grandfather, Grey Elk, stepped in and raise the two of you like his own sons."

"True, but we missed out on a few things by not having a mother."

The sense of family that existed among the year-round residents of Havre de Poisson was strong. Every holiday was a special event. It mattered not whether it was Christmas, New Year's, Boxer Day, someone's birthday, Kate's Saint Patrick's Day celebration, Feast of the Assumption, which Angelo always revered, National Grey Poupon Mustard Day, which Jake observed, or National Indigenous People's Day. Everyone always came together and celebrated.

When they reached the village, Lou brought the ATV to a stop in front of the council lodge.

Tall Tree, husband to Lou's only girl cousin, Laughing Gull, was standing in front of the council lodge. "*Raven Claw*, welcome! It is good to see you, my friend."

Lou was known as Raven Claw among the Abenaki residing in the village of Grey Elk.

"My eyes are glad to see you too, my friend." Then, looking down at Tall Tree's feet, he said, "How is it that your moccasins are wet?"

Tall Tree nodded. "My son and I just returned from fishing at the feeder ponds. The rocks are slippery."

"Really?"

"There is more algae in the upper ponds than ever before . . . but the fish don't seem to mind."

Lou paused for a moment, thinking about what Tall Tree had just said. "I don't recall algae being a problem up there."

As Koby donned her backpack, she said, "That isn't anything new Lou. We're getting reports of algae blooms showing up all over the province."

"Really?"

"We're seeing three different types of algae, actually. We're working with a couple of labs to determine the cause." Then she turned and started to walk away. "I'll meet you here as soon as my shift is over, Lou."

For the last half dozen years, Lou had presided over the tribal council. His presence and guidance recreated the much-needed leadership and structure that existed when his grandfather, Grey Elk, had been alive.

Foremost on the council's agenda, this day, was the long overdue discussion on forest management. It had been well over a decade since the mature trees in the ancient forest had been harvested. Since then, the growth along the fire breaks and emergency access roads had reached a point that, in the event of a fire, they no longer would meet the needs of their intended purpose.

A last-minute addition to the agenda was an impromptu discussion on the algae that seemed to be increasing in the small ponds at the western end of the valley. The ponds were an integral part of the watershed and eventually emptied into the huge glacial lake. The Abenaki have always revered water and saw it as the lifeblood of their environment. The pristine water in Lake 980 was a key to that environment, as were the fish that beckoned the sportsmen to Havre de Poisson.

Council meetings traditionally ran overtime, as everyone

present had a voice. Unlike the previous council in past years, decisions were now being made, regardless of the challenges that came before the council.

This day, before the council meeting ended, an agreement was reached to solicit bids from several forest management firms to thin out sections of the forest and clear the fire lanes. Additionally, consensus among those present was that steps should be taken to eradicate the algae in the ponds before it spread into the main lake.

It was after 5 p.m. when Lou joined Koby at the ATV. As they drove back to Moose Cove, Lou shared news that the council had discussed looking into the algae situation.

"Lou, don't do anything until I hike over to those ponds. I'll collect a few samples and send them off to the labs for analysis."

Lou thought about Koby's request for a few moments. Finally, he nodded. "Okay, I'll have one of the Abenaki guides go with you."

"Oh, that won't be necessary. I'll just follow the streams."

"Many have gotten lost going there."

"Seriously?"

Lou nodded. "Very few choose to go there alone."

"Why?"

"Well, for one thing, it's where Azeban, the trickster, dwells."

"Azeban. Ha! He's that mischievous little spirit that's a raccoon, right?"

"Well . . . yes and no. He's not *really* a raccoon, he only takes on the shape of one when he chooses to reveal himself."

"I've listened to Jake tell Gigi stories about the tricks that little fellow likes to play."

"There are many stories of how that *trickster* has deceived my people. He seems to favor the area around the ponds."

"Well, I'm fairly confident I'll be able to hike in and out without a problem."

"Tall Tree will go with you."

"I think I'll be able to make it on my own, Lou," she insisted. "But thanks for the offer."

Chapter Eleven

Santino Varni surprised his executive secretary, Nina Cataldo, when he arrived at his office.

"Oh, Mister Varni, sir! I wasn't expecting you today. Matteo said you'd be away until tomorrow. Did everything go well?"

Varni looked at Nina for a few seconds, taking in everything about her. She was as strikingly beautiful as she was efficient. Long ago, he had decided she was off-limits to him because he needed her in other ways. Finally, he said, "The trip was fine."

"I'm glad, sir. I'll be right in with your folder."

"Let Matteo know I wish to see him, then give Frederico Passiatore a call. Ask him to stop over."

"Do you mean Mr. Passiatore, the jeweler?"

"Yes."

As Santino passed Nina's desk, she thought: *That's odd, he doesn't wear jewelry. I wonder why he wants to see the jeweler.*

Nina, who's full given name was Antonina, knew *exactly*

the kind of man she worked for. But she also saw a human side of him that very few ever did. She understood the complexities of the man, the influence he had, the power he wielded, his personal idiosyncrasies, and his demons. She had earned his trust because she was loyal, discreet, and wise enough to never ask inappropriate questions. She was well-compensated, and when needed (which wasn't often) she wore the rank of boss on her sleeve. Additionally, whenever it was expected that he attend social events with a guest, she accompanied him.

THE FIRST THING Santino did when he settled down behind his desk was scroll through the contact list on his cell phone. Just as he pressed the call button, Matteo walked into his inner office, coffee in hand. Santino waved his hand, pointed to a chair, and brought his cell phone up to his ear.

The voice on the other end said, "Lombardi Realty, *Nardo* speaking."

"Nardo, *como stai* my friend."

"Santino, is this you?"

"Yes."

"Ah, *molto bene!* What can I do for you, my don?"

"I'd like to acquire a lake."

"You wanna buy a *lake*? A whole lake?"

"And the land around it."

"Where?"

"In New Brunswick."

Nardo paused a moment. "As in Canada?"

"Precisely."

"Is there a specific lake you have in mind, or are we talking about any lake?"

"The lake I want to own is Lake 980. There's a sportsmen's lodge on it called Havre de Poisson. I'd like you to work up a fair offer for me."

"Understood. Give me a few days and I'll be back in touch."

"Grazie, Nardo."

When Santino ended the call, he sat back in his chair; his body language telegraphed he was deep in thought.

Matteo waited a few moments before saying, "Here's your folder. I thought I'd save Nina a few steps."

At the mention of Nina's name, Santino snapped back to reality. "Matteo, does she have anyone special in her life?"

"Who?"

"Nina."

"Of course not."

Santino tilted his head in surprise. "She doesn't?"

"Come on, man, no one's gonna go near her."

"Why? She's a beautiful woman."

Matteo shrugged his shoulders. "She's untouchable."

"What the *hell* does that mean?"

"Everybody thinks she's *your* woman. No one is gonna screw around with her."

Santino just shook his head. "That's crazy."

"Hey, perception is reality, man. They see pictures in the paper of you two at all the fancy shindigs you go to. What the hell are they *supposed* to think, that she's just window-dressing?"

Santino sat back in his chair, shaking his head in a dismissive gesture. *This is crazy.*

Matteo shifted the conversation. "I thought you were gonna stay away until tomorrow."

"I don't like being off the grid. Besides, I wanna put someone outta business."

"Who?"

As Santino tapped the tips of his fingers together, he said, "The guy who runs the place I just came from."

Matteo's forehead furrowed. He paused, trying to process what he'd just heard. "You wanna take a guy out of business who lives in the friggin' *woods*?"

"Yeah."

"You're shitting me, right?"

"No. My going there is *becoming* a risk."

"What risk? There's no friggin' risk with you going out to the boonies."

Santino ignored the question, swiveled in his chair, and stared out across Boston Harbor. Finally, he said, "He has a choice, either he sells to me, or I eliminate the risk by putting him out of business."

"What's the risk? Tell me what the friggin' risk is."

Santino closed his eyes and reflected on the conflict that was within him. *It's me,* he thought, *I'm the risk. It's this damn alter ego I have. I can't trust him, that's the risk I'm dealing with.*

When Santino didn't answer, Matteo pushed, saying, "What's the risk? There *is* no friggin' risk, and you know it."

Varni pursed his lips. *The only way I stay on top is by eliminating risks.* Finally, he took a deep breath and shook his head, as if to clear his thoughts. "*We* need to be in control when I'm there."

"You're friggin' crazy. You *are* in control. You can come and go there as you please. Nobody even knows who the frig you *are*."

When Santino didn't respond, Matteo waited before saying, "You're really serious about this."

"I am."

"*Shit*, man, we got a lot bigger bones to crush than this."

Varni again dismissed his friend's comment. "No,, he's going to sell, or I put him out of business."

"This is totally crazy. Where you gonna get the money?"

"From the pension fund."

"You can't *do* that, man. The Fed's will be all over you."

"It'll be a loan."

"A loan? *Bullshit!* Come on man, you can't keep dipping into the fund!"

"Hey, who's in charge here, huh? *I'm* in charge, not *you!*"

Matteo took a breath before saying, "Then make him a friggin' offer."

Santino smiled. "I tried to."

"And?"

Santino responded by shaking his head. "He wouldn't give me a price."

"So, come up with a price."

Santino hesitated. "He's not motivated yet."

"So, all you gotta do is motivate him."

When Santino didn't say anything further, Matteo gestured for him to continue.

Santino looked directly at his friend and pointed his finger. "That's what I want *you* to do."

"What?"

"Motivate him."

Matteo shook his head, stood up and walked over to the floor-to-ceiling windows. "How the hell am I gonna do that? I don't have any friggin' influence up there."

"So, get some."

"Yeah, right. Like *that's* gonna happen."

"Maybe it's time you fly up there with me. You know . . . do a little *fishing around* on your own."

Chapter Twelve

N ot long after, Lou and Koby left for the village of Grey Elk, Kate walked over to the lodge to have a cup of tea with Alessandra. Over time, a friendship between the two had evolved into a close, pseudo-mother-and-daughter caring relationship.

As they sat down, the first thing out of Kate's mouth was a question. "Alessandra, what do you know about Luigi Secondo?"

"Luigi? He's quiet, but he's a nice man."

"What else?"

"Well, he and Angelo get along well. He's certainly kind to the children, and he seems to enjoy helping us tutor them in Italian."

"That's not exactly what I meant. What do you *really* know about him."

Alessandra thought for a moment. "Well, when you put it *that* way, not all that much. I know he's Sicilian. He seems to like it here. I think he must be single. But why do you ask?"

"I'm just curious." After a pause, Kate asked, "What does he do for a living?"

Alessandra inhaled deeply. "Oh, *that* I don't know, maybe Angelo does." Raising her voice, Alessandra called out, "Angelo, do you have a minute?"

It wasn't long before Angelo came out of the kitchen, wiping his hands on a cloth. "Wassup, my dear?"

"What does Luigi do for a living?"

"Luigi Secondo?"

"Yes."

"He's in charge of something, but I don't know what."

Kate tilted her head to one side in a questioning fashion. "Wait! The two of you are always together. *How he makes a living* has never come up in conversation?"

"No, it never has."

Kate was skeptical. "Come on, really?"

Angelo merely shrugged his shoulders in response.

Kate shook her head. *Men.*

"Is that it? I gotta get back into my kitchen."

Kate smiled. "Yeah, that was all, Angelo, thanks."

LATER, when Kate returned to her cottage, she had a little time before her conference call with the major crime unit task force began. She intended to search for the name of Luigi Secondo.

Years earlier, Lou had acknowledged his wife was far more competent in technology than he was. From that point forward, anything and everything related to technology at the resort had been under her bailiwick.

As soon as Kate's computer powered up, she clicked on the file marked *guest registration.* Every visitor was required to fill out and submit a registration form along with their reservation request. After selecting current year information, she scrolled down until she reached the name "Luigi Secondo." When she clicked on the name, instead of seeing the fields filled in with the usual data, an asterisk appeared along with the words: *See prior year.*

When Kate clicked on the previous year, it was the same, *See prior year.* When she clicked on two years prior, it was the same, *See prior year.*

What is this guy, a ghost? she wondered.

It wasn't until she had gone back four years that the data fields for Luigi Secondo began to appear. As she scrolled through the fields, much of the information requested had been left blank. The electronic signature on the document wasn't even Luigi's, it was someone named "Antonina Cataldo."

The design of the online guest registration form had never involved Kate, nor had she ever accessed it before. And just as she stared at the name "Antonina Cataldo," Kate's cell phone gave her a five-minute warning that her conference call with the unit called Major Crimes was approaching. Given that she was the host, her thoughts shifted towards preparing for her upcoming meeting.

MEANWHILE, on the seventh floor of the Longshoremen's Building, Nina Cataldo walked into Santino Varni's office. "Mr. Varni, Mr. Passiatore, the jeweler, is here to see you."

"Show him in, Nina, then bring us each a cup of espresso."

"Certainly."

As Nina turned and walked away Santino watched her. *Am I really the reason she has no lover in her life?*

FREDERICO PASSIATORE HAD A POMPOUS PERSONALITY. He was a knowledgeable jeweler, but he overplayed the part of being prosperous and debonair. That, in addition to the pretentious attire he always wore earned him the nickname *"the peacock."* He sported a pencil thin mustache; his nails were always professionally manicured, and he wore a toupee. He had inherited his jewelry business from his father who had been a successful jeweler in Sicily long before emigrating to America.

As Frederico Passiatore entered Santino Varni's inner office, he paused . . . and genuflected.

"Frederico! Welcome my friend. Come, sit."

"How may I be of service to you, Santino?"

"Tell me, how's my godchild? How's your family?"

After making the sign of the cross, Frederico responded "She's good; my wife is good, everyone is good. My daughter, she's big now, you wouldn't recognize her. She's already in the third grade. These little ones, they grow up right before your very eyes, Santino."

Varni smiled, but the christening of Frederico's child was nothing more than a distant memory.

"I read her the story about you that was in the paper," Passiatore offered. "The one about how you like to go fishing. Now she wants *me* to take *her* fishing! I said: 'Sure.' What else could I say, huh? But what do I know about fishing, huh? *Nadda!* Nothing. Maybe she goes fishing with *you* some time, huh?"

Santino dismissed Frederico's suggestion. "How's business? Are you doing okay?"

"What can I say? My business is nothing this time of year. If it wasn't for people getting married, and holidays, I'd have no business."

Santino was about to tell Passiatore why he had summoned him, when Nina walked in with two cups of freshly brewed espresso. When Passiatore saw the ornate demitasse cups he said, "Ah, *Murano* glass."

Nina, nodded and, uncharacteristically, spoke. "Why, Mr. Passiatore, you have a very fine eye."

Santino waited for Nina to leave the room before continuing. "Frederico, you're a busy man, so, I won't take up much of your time."

"How can I be of service to you, Santino."

Varni reached into the top draw of his desk, took out the yellow stone he had retrieved from the stream near the sawmill, and placed it on the edge of his desk. "What do you make of this?"

When Frederico Passiatore picked up the nugget and felt the weight, he took out his jeweler's loupe in his vest pocket. The magnifying glass would only tell him so much. "Do you mind if I scratch this to see what's underneath?"

Santino shrugged his shoulders. "Go ahead."

After scratching the specimen with a penknife, Frederico carefully placed it back on Varni's desk. "Santino, I should do an acid test to be certain, but I believe this is a solid gold nugget. How did you come by it?"

Varni ignored the question and only responded, "What's it worth?"

"Gold is close to two thousand dollars an ounce; this feels like it's a little over an ounce. It's in a raw state and would need to be alloyed down for jewelry. But it would be my pleasure to do that for you, but only if you'd like."

Frederico's words fell on deaf ears. Varni was lost in thought. *Two thousand dollars an ounce; there must be others in that streambed.*

When Varni didn't respond, Frederico nervously asked, "Santino, if you wish to sell it, I'll give you an honest price."

Santino Varni had never doubted that Passiatore would recognize the stone. The man had been a jeweler all his life. Passiatore was the fence Santino Varni used, and protected. Varni's past endorsements had made Frederico an extremely wealthy man. Now his thoughts shifted.

Frederico, my friend, I think soon you will have the opportunity to repay all the debt you owe me.

Suspecting there might be more nuggets where this one came from, Frederico offered, "I can move things like this . . . discretely, of course, in small quantities. Let me know if I can be of service to you."

Finally, Varni responded. "I was just curious what it was."

"Understood."

With that, Santino Varni stood up, signaling the meeting was over.

As Frederico started to leave, Santino said, "Wait." When the jeweler turned around, Santino tossed him the stone. "Let me know what the results are after you do the acid test. Then give this to my godchild."

"Thank you, my don."

Chapter Thirteen

The physical, active lifestyle that Lou led kept him in excellent shape. On the other hand, Kate's lifestyle was far more sedentary. She wasn't compulsive about exercising; however, she did follow a regular routine. During the week she alternated between the Mounties' functional strength and conditioning program and jogging. On the days Kate jogged the forest trails, Koby Callahan "laced up" and ran the five-mile trek with her. The only exception was when Koby was in Grand Falls attending the New Brunswick Provincial Wetland Habitat board meetings.

On this day, Kate knew Koby would be in Grand Falls, so she set out alone. When she reached the point where the path circled around the marsh bordering the beaver pond, she stopped and placed her hands on her hips. Looking straight ahead, a thought ran through her mind. *It's not even thirty yards across and it's dotted with hummocks. I've hesitated to suggest this to Koby, but today I think I'll go straight across.*

With that, she took off, nimbly jumping from one grassy

hummock to the next, as if she was playing hopscotch. Shortly after she started out, she heard a splash, but it didn't deter her from continuing.

More than a few times, she found herself quickening her step to maintain her balance after landing on a wobbly hummock, but she managed to stay upright until she made it to the far side without getting wet.

As soon as she reached the shore, she looked back. *Well, that was different.* Then abruptly, she took off running again, glad to be distancing herself from the mugginess that always engulfed the marsh during the summer.

Kate traveled through the forest silently with all the grace and endurance of a true athlete. She had grown up in the city; yet, the sounds, smells, and ways of the forest had all become familiar to her since moving to Havre de Poisson.

After traveling just over two miles along the forest trail, she rounded a bend and abruptly pulled up. Directly ahead, in the middle of the path, was a huge grey wolf. The wolf's ears twitched forward as soon as Kate came into view. The remains of the rabbit the predator had been eating at its feet.

The wolf seemed to be alone. Kate's right hand instinctively went for the bear repellent she carried, only to find the belt loop holding the container, was empty.

Humph, she thought. *Well, now I know what that splash was back at the marsh.*

Kate stood motionless, staring directly into the beast's yellow eyes now clearly focused on her. Even from a distance, she could see blood from the wolf's kill mingled with saliva, dripping from the hair surrounding its mouth.

The wolves had reestablished themselves in the valley around the same time the twins were born. Once they had returned, the less dominant coyotes had fled. Like coyotes, wolves roamed in packs and hunted as a pack. But this full-grown male, with a shoulder height well over thirty inches, was alone. Encountering a lone wolf in the wild was only *slightly* less dangerous than facing an entire pack.

The beast appeared to have completely forgotten the half-eaten rabbit at its feet. Licking his lips, the animal moved slowly toward Kate, his tail twitching back and forth ever so slightly. Kate locked eyes with the wolf and remained motionless. She was aware of its every move as the wolf narrowed the distance between them.

When the beast lowered his hindquarters, signaling he was about to spring, Kate recognized the behavior. She stepped backwards and prepared for its next move.

In less than the blink of an eye, the beast was upon her! His large front paws covered her shoulders, pressing against her neck. The smell of fresh blood on his breath was nauseating. The wolf was full grown, and she struggled to remain upright. But the added weight on her shoulders caused her to step backwards two or three times before she'd had enough.

"Hector, get down!"

As she ran her hands across the nape of the wolf's neck, she said, "I know! I know! You're happy to see me, but I really don't need the blood from your half-eaten breakfast all over my face. So, get down." Her voice was playful. But when the wolf didn't respond, she barked, "Heel!"

Upon hearing the command, the wolf dropped to all fours and quietly sat back on his haunches.

"Good boy! You ran off on me this morning, didn't you. I *wondered* where you'd gone. I thought about carrying food for you, but I know you like to hunt." Scratching the top of the wolf's head, she asked, "You *do* like to hunt, don't you boy?"

The wolf's ears twitched at the sound of the word *hunt*, and his senses were instantly on full alert. *Hunt* was another command the wolf understood, but he had also been taught to remain motionless until he heard the word *release*.

Knowing the wolf would now remain with her, she said, "Come on, Hector, you and I will travel together." With that, Kate set off at a more leisurely pace. Like the apex predator he was, Hector sauntered along beside her, without a care in the world, leaving his half-eaten rabbit behind for others in the forest to eat.

Three years earlier, while jogging in the woods, Kate had come upon the days-old wolf pup. He had been standing next to a dead she-wolf who had borne him; the pup was hungry and whimpering. Tracks on the trail told the story of the mother valiantly trying to protect her pups from a cougar. Obviously, the she-wolf had gone off by herself to have her litter. Then alone, and weak from having just given birth, she was no match for the talons of a large cat. There had ever been a question in Kate's mind other than bringing the pup home and raising him.

In the beginning, Lou and Chef Angelo were against harboring a wolf at Havre de Poisson. But Kate persevered, and finally, everyone agreed to allow Kate and the wolf pup a brief zero-tolerance trial period. Initially, Kate used a baby bottle to feed the pup, but he quickly made it known he wanted solid food. Over time, the adults saw how readily the young wolf responded to Kate's commands, and their concerns eased somewhat. But it was still questionable as to who had adopted whom.

Since wolf packs tend to be matriarchal, the alpha female is the one who rules the pack. The role of the alpha male is to lead the hunts and breed with his mate. Hector instinctively accepted Kate as the dominant alpha female of his pack. The niche he carved out for himself was that of the enforcer, a beta wolf, the one responsible for protecting the pack. Had the wolf viewed either of the twins, their cousin Gigi, or any other full-time resident at the resort as a lowly omega wolf, there would have been trouble.

Omega wolves are misfits in the pack. Omegas are not seen as a peer in the pack. They have no social standing and are repeatedly tormented, until they are ultimately driven from the pack, or killed.

Kate had agreed early on that if there was even the slightest indication of Hector treating anyone as an omega, the wolf would be destroyed.

Lou took the wolf pup's training seriously; he spent hours patiently working with the pup, teaching him basic commands. Most importantly, he taught the wolf how to co-exist with humans. And Hector had proven time and time again that he was trustworthy. Eventually, he was allowed to roam about freely.

That having been said, from the time Hector was a pup, Lou cautioned every visitor upon arrival that although the wolf *seemed* domesticated, he was still an unpredictable wild animal; and as such, he was extremely protective of his pack members – the family.

Chapter Fourteen

Nardo Lombardi made his bones brokering controversial real estate deals. The more entanglements a deal had, the more complicated the deal was, the more he enjoyed it. He knew the ins-and-outs of the Boston market like the back of his hand. He also knew which palms needed to be greased upon occasion. But the main reason Nardo was on top of his game was because he did his homework.

Once he had time to familiarize himself with the market in New Brunswick, he picked up the phone and reached out to Santino Varni.

"Santino Varni's office. How may I help you?"

"Nina, hi, this is Nardo Lombardi. I'd like to schedule a meeting with Santino."

"May I ask the subject of the meeting?"

"It's a follow-up to a conversation he and I had recently. He wanted me to do a little research for him."

"I see. Please hold." As Varni's executive admin glanced

at his calendar, she asked Nardo: "How much time do you need?"

"No more than a half hour."

"In person, or over the phone?"

"In person, if possible."

"Are you available at 1:15pm today?"

"I can be."

"Fine. I'll let Mr. Varni know." Nina had always been very professional.

At exactly 1:10 p.m. Nardo entered Santino Varni's outer office, Nina looked up, and smiled. "Are you Mr. Lombardi?"

"I am."

"Have a seat please. I'll see if Mr. Varni is ready for you."

The commercial real estate market in rural central New Brunswick was virtually non-existent. Yet, Nardo Lombardi had done his homework, and he was very optimistic when he arrived at Varni's office that afternoon. He had barely seated himself when Nina reappeared.

"Mr. Varni will see you now."

With a smile on his face, and not much more than a few ideas, Nardo Lombardi walked into Santino Varni's inner office.

"Nardo, my friend, come in, have a seat. You know Matteo, yes?"

Nardo nodded at Matteo, then sat in an ornate club chair directly in front of Santino's desk.

"Santino, I have some information to discuss with you. It's not everything you asked for, but it's a start."

Santino dismissed the caveat with a wave of his hand and waited for the realtor to begin.

"I've researched the property in New Brunswick that you have expressed interest in. There's not a whole lot to go on; the area is largely undeveloped."

Santino shrugged his shoulders, again indicating his indifference.

"Here's what I was able to find out: Title on the property surrounding the lake transferred to the current owner, about a dozen years ago; someone named Lou Gault."

Santino nodded that he understood.

"That transfer occurred through probate. It was a single tract of land encompassing roughly fifteen square miles. I was unable to obtain any provincial records regarding the assessed value, or real estate taxes on the property. However, I was able to verify that Lou Gault *is* the name of the proprietor who operates the resort that is situated on the lake."

Again, Santino nodded.

"About eight years ago, title to two separate, similar-sized tracts of land, which abut the first property, transferred to Gault. That also happened through probate. Shortly after those title transfers occurred, a document contesting the legality of a court ordered sale by eminent domain was added to the file. I haven't read the legal argument, however, it must have held up, because there has been no subsequent title transfers. I did find an earlier transfer approved by the provincial government back in 1921. There is a minor reference to a treaty going back to 1796, which I haven't investigated. But we'll need to find out if the land is considered tribal lands. Tribal lands are sometimes handled differently, but that won't necessarily preclude it from being sold."

Nardo sensed he may have given a data dump and

paused to see if there were any questions. Santino gestured with his hand for the realtor to continue.

"Regarding a valuation, I was able to find a few commercial real estate transactions involving other lake front properties in New Brunswick. However, based on the brochure I saw for the lodge on Lake 980, and the property descriptions of what has recently been sold, they may not be a valid comparison."

Santino frowned. "Why not? Were the others also lake front resorts?"

"They all had lake frontage. However, the other properties were on lakes that were minuscule, and were bank foreclosures, therefore, sold at auction."

Santino nodded again. "So, how do we come up with a reasonable offer for the location I asked you to look at?"

"We'll need to be creative. But I'll come up with a range. A couple of wood lots sold in the general area a few years back; we can start with that. I'll do a more complete search on undeveloped waterfront property in relatively remote areas. I'll also talk to some contacts I have on how to value a body of water. The other thing we'll want to know is the physical condition of the buildings. Will the current owner allow an onsite, due diligence inspection?"

Santino smirked. "I rather doubt that."

"Is the owner motivated to sell?"

"Not yet."

"Well, it's *critical* that we understand what condition the buildings are in, and inspect the infrastructure. How many buildings are we talking about?"

Santino looked at the ceiling and appeared to be mentally counting the number of cottages. Finally, he said, "I'll be going up there again; I'll get back to you on the number of buildings."

"Would it be possible to take pictures while you're there?"

Santino shrugged his shoulders. "Sure."

"Good. We'll use photos if we're not able to do any onsite due diligence."

Santino nodded.

"I'll need a few close ups of the roofs. Get the inside and outside of the buildings, the kitchen, the docks, boats, whatever. Plumbing is always an issue, so take pictures of that."

Santino turned in his chair and looked directly at Matteo. "You got that?"

"Yeah, I got it."

With that, Varni stood up; the meeting was over. As Nardo got up to leave, he looked at Santino. "It'll only take me a couple of days to work up the numbers for the land once I have the photos. When do you think you'll be going back up there?"

Santino glanced at Matteo, then he turned to Nardo. "Soon, very soon."

Chapter Fifteen

When Kate and Hector jogged back into camp, her twins emerged from nowhere and were instantly all over their playmate, scratching him behind the ears and gently rubbing his back as all four of them walked toward their cottage.

The wolf had grown up with the twins; early on he had learned to tolerate their playful affection. There was no question that he considered them fellow beta members of *his* pack.

As the foursome approached the screened porch surrounding their cottage, Kate abruptly stopped, turned around. "Hector, lie down! You two, inside; it's time for lunch." Her voice indicated there would be no discussion.

From the very beginning, Hector had been obedient to the one who raised him; now he meandered over to the area he claimed as his own under the porch and settled down.

. . .

THE ARRIVAL of winter in the North country often came early. Lou was anxious to address the forest management concerns of the tribal council. It wasn't long after bids came in for planned services that a reputable contractor was engaged.

Within a matter of days, crews were roaming the ancestral lands of the Abenaki, selecting and marking trees in the ancient forest that would be harvested. Other teams were evaluating the condition of fire breaks and where additional emergency access lanes needed to be cut into the immense forest.

Shortly thereafter, sounds of chain saws and the crashing of tall timber could be heard off in the distance.

MEANWHILE, back in Boston, Santino Varni looked across his massive desk at his friend Matteo. "Let's talk about how we're going to *motivate* this seller."

"I don't even understand why we are talking about this," Matteo protested. "Let it go. We got enough to do. The union elections are coming up. Why are you being *crazy*? You don't need to buy this place. Everything's perfect just the way it is."

"There are risks."

"Then I'll find you someplace else to go."

"No."

"I'll find you another hideaway."

"I said, *no!*"

Matteo bristled slightly at the sharp retort. He dropped his eyes, took a deep breath, and waited. Santino drummed his fingers on the arms of his chair before speaking. "Matteo, what are your thoughts about how we can help Mr. Gault come to the realization, it's time to sell?"

Matteo stared at the rug a few moments. Then he recited

the recipe he thought his boss wanted to hear. "He's gonna get a message that his business is up for sale, and that it's in his best interest to cooperate."

Santino sat back in his chair, subtly shaking his head. "No, this time, we need a different approach."

"Why? He's no different from any of the others."

"Actually, he is."

Matteo smirked. "He'll crumble; they're all the same."

"Not this one."

"You watch."

Santino completely dismissed Matteo's comment. "This time, it needs to be done with *finesse*. It needs to be so subtle that he never suspects I'm the one behind anything."

"Why?"

"Because he's different. And I have my reasons." Matteo gestured with his hands, as if to say, *tell me.*

"I want him to see *me* as his *last* hope, his *savior*, the one who throws him a lifeline," Varni said.

"Santino, you're making this a helluva lot more involved than it needs to be." But when Santino didn't respond, Matteo continued. "Okay, so, you wanna go in a different direction. Then let's talk about it. What does he value? What's important to him?"

Santino swiveled in his chair and stared out at Boston's waterfront. "There are at least a half dozen things he treasures: his family, his friends, his reputation, the land, the eco system. Those last two seem to be intertwined. He prides himself on being independent, and he cherishes the quiet life he lives."

"All of which are easy to exploit," Matteo added. "How about we snatch his wife, hold her for ransom? He'll have to come to you for money."

Santino laughed. "Somebody already *tried* that. It didn't work out too well for them. Actually, I think they were dames."

"Then, maybe he gets a message about how *now* would be a good time to sell, before somebody close to him has an *unfortunate* accident."

Without warning, the voice of Luigi Secondo drowned out all the other thoughts within Santino's head.

No, Luigi yelled.

The absolute authoritative tone in Luigi's voice startled Santino. Luigi had never come to him like this before. Luigi had never existed in Boston. Yet, it was Luigi's voice he'd heard.

Who are you to come to me, Santino thought. *I created you!* Santino closed his eyes, thinking, *Luigi, be careful, or I will snuff you out as if you were the flame of a candle.*

Matteo stared at his boss, surprised at the look on his face. He waited for a response. Finally, he broke the long silence. "You wanna go with that?"

The sound of Matteo's voice brought Santino out of his trance. He opened his eyes. "No. Knowing Gault, and the stories I've heard about him, that would be like kicking a hornet's nest."

"He's up there all *alone!* He's out in the friggin' boonies! Maybe he gets roughed up a little, spends a few days in the hospital with a broken wing or something."

"Matteo, I sense that any attempt to physically threaten Gault will have quite the opposite effect."

Matteo shook his head in frustration. "I don't get it. Why do you wanna run this friggin' place?"

"I don't want to *run* it. All I want to do is *control* it; to eliminate the risk I feel. He'll still run it for me."

"You don't think he'll walk away, if he sells?"

"No, he *loves* the place. All that needs to happen is for him to see the difference between *owning* the place versus *running* it as two entirely separate things."

Matteo ran his hand through his thick hair and down across the back of his neck. Then, he let out a sigh. "Santino, you keep tying my hands behind my back. So, just tell me *how* you want me to do this."

"It needs to be surgical."

"What the frig does *that* mean?"

"I want the place left intact. No one gets hurt."

Matteo sunk back in his chair and smiled. "Surgical, huh? Ha! How 'bout we eliminate the friggin' fish? Who's gonna bother to go there after that, huh? Would that be friggin' *surgical* enough?"

Santino smiled. The thought had never occurred to him. "How do you propose to do that?"

Matteo walked over to the tall windows overlooking Boston harbor. "How the frig should I know. We poison the damn water! Maybe we burn him out!"

"I said *surgical.*"

"Okay, we go after his money. We force him into debt; get him in so deep he can't get out."

"How?"

"Maybe some friggin' fisherman gets hurt and sues him for everything he's got. Maybe the place burns down, and he's got no insurance, and he comes to you hoping you're some friggin' angel investor?"

"He's not that stupid, he'd have an umbrella policy covering something like that."

"So, maybe something happens to his policy. Maybe his friggin' policy lapses. Maybe his insurance agent gets a letter telling him to cancel the policy, that he's changed agents. I'm just thinking out loud here."

"That could be a piece of it." Varni's voice was smooth. He was thinking.

Matteo turned and walked back to the chair in front of Santino's desk. "The only way people get in there is by plane, right?"

"There's a logging road, but basically, yeah, everyone comes in on float planes."

"So, we take the float planes away."

Santino leaned back in his chair and looked at Matteo. "You think you can persuade the float planes to stop flying there?

"Maybe there's a rash of mechanical problems, and they all get grounded."

"Don't be stupid. You'd need an army to pull something like that off."

Matteo winced at the putdown; his years of devotion didn't deserve talk like that. Still, he boldly retorted, "Santino, maybe *you* have the better eyes on this. What do *you* see?"

"What do I see? I see him coming to me and asking me if the offer is still on the table, *that's* what I see."

Matteo wasn't over the putdown and he waited before saying, "Maybe there's a series of interruptions: His drinking water goes bad. Maybe we cut off his food supply, maybe his supply of gasoline goes bad. He's in the woods, right? Maybe his generators fail. Maybe his reputation goes down the crapper. Maybe a couple of his guests die from food poisoning. Suddenly word spreads that the place is a freakin' disaster. He's being sabotaged from within, and he can't figure out how the hell it's all happening, or how to stop it."

"Ha! Sabotage, I *like* that approach."

"Yeah?"

"Yes, but it needs to be subtle. Whatever you do, it can never be traced back to me."

Matteo paused for a moment. "Santino, I don't get it. Why are you dancing around with this guy? What's so friggin' special about this place? It's in the friggin' *woods*."

When Santino didn't respond, Matteo said, "Why don't you just buy some land on a friggin' lake and create your own friggin' retreat? Screw him! We don't need to drive the son-of-a-bitch out of business."

"That's *Plan B*."

"What is?"

"I go into competition with him. I drive him to the brink of going out of business. *Then* I take over."

"Why can't that be Plan A?"

"Because it's *not* . . . for the moment, anyway."

Matteo stared at the ceiling. "I can't believe I'm even having this friggin' conversation with you Santino."

"Well, believe it."

"You said you wanted to take him out of business surgically, right?"

"Yes."

"And you want *me* to run this, right?"

"Yes."

Matteo paused before saying, "All right, but this ain't gonna happen overnight."

"Thank you."

"You're welcome."

"Matteo, I want you to come with me the next time I go up."

"No way."

"You need to have a lay of the land."

"*Shit!* I knew I shoulda sent you to Las Vegas in the beginning, like you wanted . . . at least there's broads there."

"So, bring somebody up with you. There's three bedrooms in the cottage."

Matteo took a long look at Santino, a man with whom he had traveled many a dark road; a man he was bound to serve. "Maybe I will," he said.

Yes, maybe he would.

Chapter Sixteen

The following morning, Santino Varni arrived at his office and stopped at the desk of his executive admin. "Nina, when you have a moment, I'd like you to come in with my calendar."

"I'm free now, sir."

With that, he made a motion with his right arm indicating: *Ladies first.*

Like Santino Varni, Antonina Cataldo had grown up poor on the streets in Boston's North End. She had been two years ahead of Santino in school, but even when they were both in grade school, he had known of the beautiful girl everyone said had a "face like the goddess Venus."

Years later, when Antonina's husband had disfigured her during a drunken rage, her father came to Santino seeking retribution. Santino agreed the husband needed to be taught a lesson.

Her husband was a large, powerfully built man. When Popeye went to . . . *counsel* . . . him, Antonina's husband took umbrage and stupidly resisted. At the funeral that followed, Santino let Antonina's father know that he took full responsibility. As he embraced her father, he said, "Antonina will never be a financial burden to you."

Over the years, Antonina had undergone numerous facial reconstruction procedures. Through the grace of God, a few carefully selected plastic surgeons, and the deep pockets of Santino Varni, her facial features, and self-esteem, had been restored.

SANTINO FOLLOWED Nina into his office. The contour of her hourglass figure, her walk, her poise, her exquisite attire, the slingback shoes, and the provocative scent she always wore were not lost on him.

When Nina headed toward one of the chairs directly opposite the dark ornate desk at the far end of the room, Santino said, "No, we'll use the sitting area."

Nina turned, smiled, and walked toward the plush club chairs which had been arranged in a circle. As soon as Santino took a seat, Nina sat down, crossed her legs at the knee, placed Santino's calendar on her lap, and looked up expectantly.

"I will be traveling as 'Luigi Secondo,' again."

"Understood. When will that be, sir?"

"That all depends."

Nina paused, waiting. When Santino didn't respond, she asked, "Depends on what, sir?"

"I'd like you to join me this time, Nina."

Nina's thoughts began to race, but she managed to nod her head. *I didn't see this coming. Why is he asking me to travel with him? He's never asked me to go away with him before. It's not like he needs an escort at a black-tie event.*

"You'll need a passport. You have one, right?"

Nina could feel her face blush. "No, I . . . I do not."

"Call Representative Conti's office. He'll expedite the process for us. Tell him I would consider it a *personal* favor if we had it in a few days."

"Yes, sir."

"I would like to travel as soon as you have your passport."

Nina nodded, again. "Understood. I'll start looking at flights and hotel arrangements now. Where will we be traveling?

"Havre de Poisson."

"The resort?"

"Yes."

"Will we be there the entire time?"

"Yes."

Nina hesitated. "Okay."

Santino saw concern in her eyes. "Let's talk about this trip. From the time we leave this building, until we return, you are only to address me as 'Luigi.' Is that understood?"

"Of course."

"The full-time residents treat me like family. They will wonder who you are." Santino paused before continuing. "I'm going to introduce you as my fiancée, my lover. While we are there, you must remember that you *don't* work for me, we met through a mutual acquaintance, that's all they need to know. *Capiche?*"

Nina nodded her head; her face felt flushed. *I'm your fiancée?* Her thoughts raced. *What does that mean?*

"Naturally, they will be curious, and will want to know all

about you. You must be impeccable with what you say, *never* divulging who I am; tell them *nothing* about me, and as little about yourself as possible."

Nina nodded again. *If we're engaged, does that mean we hold hands? Is he going to kiss me? How is this going to work?*

Santino sensed Nina's uneasiness. "What's running through your thoughts?"

Nina modestly tugged at the hemline of her dress. "If you tell them we are engaged, that we are lovers, they will expect us to be affectionate toward one another."

"Will that make you uncomfortable?"

"No, I . . . I, I just need to know what your wishes are." What she wasn't sharing were her deepest desires. *Santino, why are you are so blind? I want to be with you in every possible way. Why do you think I am so devoted to you?* She had kept her true feelings hidden for so long; she had never wanted him to think she was repaying his kindness with anything physical.

Santino broke the silence. "Good. Matteo will be joining us. Check with him; he may or may not have someone traveling with us. We'll stay at the cottage I have up there."

Nina hesitated for a moment. "How long will we be gone, sir?"

"A few days, three, four, maybe five. Have someone cover for you while we're away."

Santino noticed a faraway look in Antonina's eyes. "Is something wrong?"

After a moment she said, "No, no sir, I . . . I . . ."

"What?"

Laughing, Nina said, "I don't have anything to *wear*! I've never been in the woods before."

Santino reached for his wallet and took out a credit card. "Here, go knock yourself out."

When Nina hesitated, Santino looked her straight in the eye. "Take it. Just keep in mind this place is in the *sticks*, they all dress like they stepped out of an L.L. Bean catalog."

Nina's emotions were raging. She wasn't a traveler. The farthest she had ventured from Boston's north end was an occasional girl's weekend trip to Cape Cod.

"Are we good?"

Nina took in a deep breath before nodding her head. "Yes, we're good." With that, a very flustered Antonina Cataldo stood. "Will that be all?"

As if Nina's question had been a scripted cue, Santino Varni stood up.

"No, there's one more thing."

Varni came close to her and leaned forward; putting a hand behind her head, he drew her close, tilted his head and gently kissed Nina on her lips. Her first instinct was to pull back because she had suppressed herself for so long. Then she returned his kiss, with just a hint of the passion she'd held within herself for him.

As Nina turned and walked toward the door leading to her work area, Santino's eyes never left her. "Why have I ignored this beauty who's been sitting directly under my nose?" he whispered to no one.

At Havre de Poisson, it seemed every fisherman in camp had arrived *en masse* at the docks, stowed their gear, and already set out for a day's fishing. Once they'd all launched, Lou headed back to his cottage.

True to form, the first thing Lou did when reentering his screen porch was turn and face the lake. Then he carefully scanned the landscape, searching for anything that seemed different, or out or place.

When Kate heard the screen door open and close, she stepped out onto the porch, turned her husband around to face her, raised up on her tiptoes, and planted a passionate kiss on her husband's lips. Next, she began lightly caressing the inside of his thigh. Once she sensed her husband was sufficiently aroused, she broke away and turned in a pirouette. "Are you the slightest bit horny?"

"Well, after *that* greeting, who wouldn't be?"

"Good, because the kids are already on their way to the village, and this Irish colleen, you married, is in the mood for an early morning delight."

As he watched the love of his life head toward their bedroom, he thought, *How the hell did I ever get this lucky?*

By the time Lou reached the bedroom, Kate had already disrobed and was standing next to the bed running her hands through her chestnut brown hair. She smiled as she pulled back the covers, slipped into bed and propped her head up on her pillow; now she waited for the man she loved to undress.

"Ya' know what, Kate?"

"What, hon?"

"Like I said the other day, I can't believe how much it turns me on just to be your man."

After slightly arching her back, Kate let out a heavy sigh. Then, with a provocative voice, laced with dulcet tones of her lilting Irish brogue, she said, "Well, my man, come hither; let this fair maiden show you just how true that is."

Chapter Seventeen

I t was close to noon when Angelo took off his apron and headed up the grassy knoll behind the lodge to collect a few eggs. He'd left the onions near the edge of the stove, to continue caramelizing over a low heat. The pecorino cheese had been freshly ground; leftover baked ham had been expertly sliced, julienne style. The fennel bulb was shredded and red bell peppers had been diced to just the right consistent size. Fresh peas had been rinsed and parsley sat on the cutting board, waiting to be rough chopped. All that remained was whisking eggs before the dish he was preparing could be assembled and placed on the stove top.

Today the lunchtime culinary delight would be a traditional Italian frittata, made from a few odds and ends needing to be used up. Having limited access to a supply chain was a downside of living far off the grid in such a remote location as Havre de Poisson. Chef Angelo had always been masterful at planning and repurposing everything in store; very few supplies coming into Angelo's kitchen ever went to waste. No lunch he prepared for year-round residents of Havre de Poisson was ever made to order.

As Angelo headed to the hen house, his thoughts were on the number of eggs he needed to collect.

Then, a noise caught his attention. Coming around the building, his worst fear came into view. Hector was aggressively pacing by the large cage housing the fowl, snarling like the wild beast he was. Birds inside the pen were agitated. They were squawking, scurrying about, and fluttering into the air. It was pure chaos as the birds kept running into each other, desperately attempting to find shelter somewhere inside the limited enclosure.

Angelo had *never* been a fan of having a wild beast like this wolf in camp. He had reluctantly tolerated the carnivore's presence in exchange for a commitment from Kate. She had assured him that at the slightest sign of aggression, the wolf would be euthanized, humanely . . . or, otherwise. The drama unfolding before his eyes was all the proof he needed. That day had finally come.

Hector, he thought, *damn you! Get away from my birds!*

Angelo quickened his step, shouting as he waved the flimsy wire basket in his hand back and forth over his head, hoping to distract and deter the wolf.

"Get away! Go, *damn* you! You *devil*! Get away from my birds! *Go!*"

Yet, instead of fleeing, the wolf became even more aggressive and seemed to be attacking the enclosure itself. Suddenly, he jumped up on the side of the cage, as if trying to reach the top.

Angelo saw frothy saliva around the edge of the wolf's

mouth, and froze; a telltale sign of rabies. His thoughts were racing. *That damn wolf is trying to scale the fence; he's mad with rabies and after my birds!*

"Lou!" Angelo yelled. His eyes searched the ground for a sturdy stick, a long-handled shovel, a rake, *anything* to defend himself from the beast, if it turned on him.

Then, in a fleeting second, Angelo's eyes saw a young fisher cat scamper across the netting covering the top of the enclosure.

Hector was following every erratic move the fisher made and never took his eyes off the cat. When the intruder finally leaped from the top rail of the coop toward a neighboring tree, Hector was waiting underneath.

The two animals went airborne simultaneously. Hector's timing was impeccable; he intercepted the intruder in midair. With the fisher's head held firmly between his powerful jaws, Hector came down, violently shaking his head back and forth. The fisher may have been in a stranglehold, but he wasn't immobilized, and instinctively began to fight back.

The cat flailed wildly with his front and back legs, desperately trying to reach his attacker. The front legs of a fisher cat aren't exceptionally long; but its claws could easily sever an artery in the wolf's neck. Then, as if the wolf decided the contest was over, there was a popping sound as the wolf's powerful jaws came together. The fisher's body stiffened and went limp; its head crushed; its spine severed at the neck.

Angelo stood motionless, stunned, trying to comprehend what had just played out before him.

With the threat to the hen house eliminated, Hector released the fisher cat from his mouth and sat back on his haunches. The wolf's tongue hung from the side of its mouth, as he panted. The body of the defeated fisher cat lay at his feet. Hector sat there . . . looking directly at Angelo.

What happened next caused Angelo to blink several times. *Was that my imagination?* Angelo thought, *Or did that damn wolf just cock his head and wink at me?*

For a second, Angelo and the wolf remained motionless; their eyes locked on each another. It wasn't until Angelo heard Lou's voice that the trance between them was broken.

"Angelo, what's up? I heard you call."

"I think I'm gonna give that damn big wolf of yours a hug."

"Hector?"

"Yeah," Angelo said, nodding his head.

"Why?"

"When I came around the building, I thought he was after my birds, but he wasn't. It turns out he was *protecting* them. I'll tell ya' though, Lou, if I'd had a shotgun instead of a basket, he'd be the one laying on the ground right now."

"Where is he?"

Angelo motioned with his head, "He's over there, smug as hell."

"Over where?"

Angelo turned around, but the wolf was gone. "He was just there, sitting beyond the coop, just a second ago."

Lou glanced over, but only saw the motionless body of a fisher cat at the far end of the enclosure.

"I had that wolf pegged all wrong, Lou."

"Well, we all tend to see what we choose to see; and believe what we want to believe at times."

Angelo ignored Lou's comment, and was now lost in

thought. *These birds won't be laying any eggs for a while after this scare. I'm gonna need Jake to fly some in.* Then he let out a sigh. "At least the cage held up."

"Take another look, Angelo, we've got a rip in that top screen. Maybe it's time we put the same gauge wire up there that's on the sides."

"Lou, I didn't even see that! How the hell did *you* see that?"

"Eyes like the raven, man, eyes like the raven," Lou replied, referring to the name the Abenaki elders had given him.

Angelo nodded his head. "I'll ask Jake to bring some of that wire in, along with some eggs. I'm gonna need to buy eggs for a while."

"That wire's *way* too heavy to bring in on a float plane. Wire like that's gotta come up the logging road. I've got a fuel delivery coming in next week; I'll have them bring it in."

WALKING BACK TO THE KITCHEN, Angelo's mind flashed back to an incident over a decade old. It happened right after he and Alessandra had first come to Havre de Poisson. A pack of wolves had defeated the fragile coop he had constructed, and he had lost every bird. That winter they dined mostly on fish and venison. The following spring, he and Lou rebuilt the coop, this time with a studier structure.

Years later, well after the wolves had left the valley, a pack of coyotes attempted a nighttime raid. That time the structure had held. And the coyotes were dispatched by a group of well-armed Mounties, who just happened to be in camp at the time.

Now, as Angelo climbed the back stairs leading into the

kitchen, he stopped on the landing and glanced over at his vegetable garden. Alessandra and both of Lou's young twins were in the garden, cultivating rows. A little further away, near the tree line, was the wolf sitting on his haunches, watching over his pack.

Chapter Eighteen

Kate fired up her laptop. She had been surprised that Angelo, the one person who spent the most time with Luigi Secondo, knew so very little about him. Undaunted, she was determined to find out who this frequent visitor was, one way or another.

When she keyed in the words *Luigi Secondo* and *Boston*, multiple hits came up. Seeing some matches went as far back as the 19th century she refined her search by adding "21st century." When she hit the enter key, images of individuals named Luigi appeared. But no photo came even close to resembling the man she was seeking. There were a few hits without photos, but she discounted them due to their ages.

Hmmm, she thought, *maybe he doesn't live in Boston. I'll widen my search by using the word 'Massachusetts.'* Additional images appeared, but again, none matched the Luigi Secondo she knew. Widening her search even further, she keyed in *"New England."* But, even then, none of the matches resembled the Luigi Secondo who visited Havre de Poisson.

Kate sat back in her chair. *What is this? Am I chasing a ghost? Why isn't he showing up online?* Then Kate added the words *"business owner"* to her search criteria. A new screen came up, loaded with hits. Quite a few looked promising, and Kate clicked through them. One after the other, however, she dismissed them.

Maybe he doesn't go by 'Luigi' professionally. She modified her search to the surname *'Secondo.'* Again, a lot of matches came up, but nothing was linked to the man she was interested in finding.

But Kate was undaunted. *Well, my friend, you may not be showing up in social media, but you obviously have a lot of money, so let's see if I can find you somewhere else.*

With that, Kate logged into her RCMP account and gained access to the Canada Border Service Agency's database. In no time at all she pulled up the most recent crossing record for Luigi Secondo. The record contained the date, place of entry, and passport number.

Now I'll find out who the hell you are and what you do, she thought.

Armed with a passport number, Kate sent off an official request to the U. S. Department of State, from her RCMP email account, requesting a copy of the passport information on file for Luigi Secondo.

ABOUT THE SAME TIME, in a small trattoria in Boston's north end about five hundred miles to the southwest, Santino Varni's consigliore was just finishing his lunch. As he pushed his plate aside, he looked across the table at his companion.

"Espresso?"

"Yeah."

Matteo sat back, placed his napkin on the table and motioned for the waiter.

"Yes sir?"

"Two espressos."

"Of course."

It was approaching 2 p.m. The lunch crowd had emptied out and returned to work. Except for a couple sitting next to a window, they were alone. Matteo looked over at them. The woman was staring at her wine glass. Her index finger slowly caressed the rim. The man was leaning across the table saying something to her. She smiled.

Lovers, he thought. *He's giving her a line of bullshit, hoping to get in her pants, and she's loving the attention. She'll probably let him.*

The tables were far enough apart that neither could overhear the other's conversation. Yet, when Matteo turned to the man sitting across from him, he spoke softly. "I have a proposition for you."

The man across from him nodded and continued eating.

"You'll need a passport."

The man shrugged his shoulders, inferring indifference.

"This is not a one-and-done."

Matteo waited to see if he could detect a change in the other man's expression, but he didn't.

"Are you interested?"

"Say more."

"Santino wishes to buy a business."

The man across the table stopped his fork in mid-air and smirked. "Ha, so you want me to make someone an offer, eh?"

Matteo inhaled before responding. "No, it's more

complicated than that. The owner is not ready to sell. Santino wants to use a light hand. He wishes to be seen as the owner's *savior*, not motivator."

"What, is he getting soft?"

"No. He wants the owner to stay on and run the business for him."

"So, no muscle?"

"Correct."

"Then, why do you need *me*?"

"I need help to work on his . . . psyche."

"Whaddya think, I'm a friggin' shrink?"

"Naaah. But you're discreet, and you follow through. You're gonna help me get in his friggin' head, that's all."

"So, we *dick around* with him for a while. After that, what? Do I make him an offer?"

Matteo smiled, "No. We're gonna overwhelm the son-of-a-bitch with so much *shit* he's gonna want out. We'll hit him with one punch after another. We're gonna make him think owning a business is a living hell."

"Then what?"

"He gives up and comes to Santino for help."

"When's all this gonna happen?"

"It's been green lighted."

"And I need a passport for this?"

"Yeah."

"So, where the hell is it?"

Just as Matteo was about to respond, he saw the waiter approaching. "Wait." Matteo held up a finger to silence his companion.

"Gentlemen, your espresso I also bring your check. But I assure you, there is no rush. You take your time, *capiche?*"

Matteo nodded. As soon as the waiter was beyond earshot, he continued. "It's in Canada."

"Yeah, well, Canada's a big friggin' place. *Where* in Canada?"

"Where Santino goes."

"You mean where he goes to fish?"

"Yeah."

Matteo waited for a response. When there wasn't one, he continued. "He needs a little help motivating the owner to sell, that's all."

The man sitting across from Matteo pursed his lips and nodded.

"Are you in?"

"Yeah, I'm in."

Matteo raised his espresso cup saying, "To our success."

Raising his own cup, Popeye added, "Yeah, in the freakin' woods."

"Relax. This'll be a walk in the park. We just gotta get up there and get a lay of the land. After that we'll figure out how we motivate this guy."

"You sure you don't want me to just go up and beat the crap out of him?"

"Santino doesn't want that."

"So, we gotta go pussyfootin' around in the freakin' woods. When's *that* gonna happen?"

"Next week."

"For how long?"

"Three, maybe four days."

Popeye looked down at the stylish Italian leather loafers he had on. "We gonna be in the friggin' woods all the time?"

"Some of the time."

"Then I gotta bring a couple pair of shoes."

. . .

WHEN FREDERICO PASSIATORE performed the simple acid test on the nugget Santino Varni had gifted his daughter, the results floored him.

Passiatore dealt in retail jewelry. Occasionally, he'd agree to buy back or take gold jewelry in exchange for something, but he'd never dealt in unrefined gold. That said, he was familiar enough with gold that he could tell from the color whether a ring was 10-carat, 18-carat, 20-carat, or higher.

In their natural form, nuggets ranged from 83 percent purity to as much as 92 percent. The stone Varni had given him was an unusually deep rich orange-yellow color. Even at first glance, Passiatore knew the purity of the nugget would be on the higher end. But when the nugget came in at 98.0 percent, twice, he performed the test a third time. The result was the same.

The highest purity nuggets were generally found in the southern hemisphere, in places like Australia and Southeast Asia, not in eastern Canada.

So, when Passiatore called Santino to give him the results, he said, "Santino, the gold you gave my daughter has an unusually high purity."

"And?"

"Most nuggets found in the northern hemisphere are valued around a thousand dollars an ounce. This one would be closer to *three*." He was excited.

Santino simply said, "Interesting." However, his thoughts were very different. *If there's one in that stream, there's more.*

"Santino, this is too valuable, I cannot accept this gift from you."

Although Santino had the phone to his ear, he wasn't

listening. His thoughts were on the hidden treasure that would soon be his for the taking.

"Santino, I'm going to return this to you."

"No, keep it. It's a gift to my godchild."

Chapter Nineteen

Traffic was unusually light the morning a limo picked up two passengers at the Longshoremen's Building and headed over to Boston's Logan Airport. By the time Matteo showed up, the man who had earlier passed through TSA as "Luigi Secondo" had been sitting in the Charter Terminal lounge for twenty minutes.

As Matteo walked over to his friend, his eyes scanned everyone sitting at the gate area. "Hey, Santino, where's Nina, I thought she was coming with us?" The woman sitting directly next to Santino, dressed in upscale outdoorsy attire, lifted her eyes from the paperback she was reading, and smiled.

"Hey, Nina! *Damn*, I didn't even recognize you!"

Nina smiled. "It's the outfit," she deadpanned. Matteo matched Nina's quick wit.

"Yeah, like *you're* gonna blend."

Santino cleared his throat, "Where's Popeye?"

"He's coming. TSA pulled him aside." But when over five

minutes passed and Popeye still hadn't joined them, Matteo stood up. "I'm gonna go find out what's going on."

Just then Matteo saw Popeye enter the lounge. "Okay, he's here." With that, Santino stood up, which his fellow travelers understood to be the signal that it was time to leave.

Once they were all seated in the Gulfstream G550, the pilot came on the intercom. "Folks, the tower is letting us jump in ahead of these big Delta jets, so we're now third in line for takeoff. The weather looks good all the way up to Grand Falls, New Brunswick. It should be clear sailing."

When the pilot clicked off, Nina reached for a box she had brought onboard. As soon as she broke the seal, the aroma of freshly baked Italian breakfast pastries called *cornettos* filled the cabin. Similar to a *croissant*, these were only slightly sweeter and filled with custard, jam, or Nutella.

As the box of pastries made the rounds, Nina poured out four coffees from a thermos she had arranged to have onboard. As she passed them out, she said, "Luigi tells me there is a cappuccino machine where we're going. But this morning, we're settling for caffe Americano."

Popeye raised his cup. *"Alla vita!"* His companions all followed suit, saying, "To life!" in unison.

After taking a sip of coffee, Luigi turned to Matteo, "Have you decided if you are coming to the cottage?"

Matteo nodded his head. "We're not. When we reach Grand Falls, we'll rent a car. I'm gonna drive around for a couple of days, just to get a feel for it."

"So, when will I see you?"

"In Boston."

"I said *when*, not where."

"We'll fly back late on the third day."

Luigi nodded, and pursed his lips, a signal that he

approved of what Matteo planned to do. "If you change your mind, there's an extra room at the cottage. It has two beds in it; that'll be yours."

From the beginning, Nina had been the one who made arrangements to rent the cottage. She knew the cottage had three bedrooms. She reflected on what he'd just said. *Hmmm, I guess the plan is that I have my own room,* she thought.

JAKE COMPLETED his routine morning preflight inspection and walked over to the kitchen. "Hey Angelo, how many eggs did you say you wanted me to bring back?"

"Eight dozen, my friend."

"That's all?"

"For now."

"White or brown?"

"What do I care, eh? An egg is an egg!"

"So, whatcha got going for supper tonight? The message board is blank."

"Tonight, I make us a special dish."

Jake looked over at the sous chef table and saw the long line of salmon filets neatly dressed out. He had flown them in the previous day. "Are we having what I think we're having?"

"Tonight, I make *filet of salmon, alla Jacques!*"

"Aah, my absolute favorite! You're sure you have enough Grey Poupon for that?"

Dismissing Jake's comment, Angelo said, "Luigi will be here for dinner tonight. This time he brings his lady friend."

"How do you know?"

"What? You think we don't talk when he's away? He calls me."

"Okay. I gotta go. Oh, and so you know, there's already a couple of hungry fishermen sitting out there in the dining room."

Angelo blew Jake a kiss, saying, "*Ciao!*"

AROUND MID-DAY, the wheels of the Gulfstream from Boston touched down in Grand Falls. The flight had been smooth. For most of the journey, Nina had her nose planted in a romance novel.

As the pilot taxied over to the terminal, Nina reached into her carry-on bag. This time she took out two small, unmarked rectangular boxes. As she handed one to Matteo, and one to Popeye, she said, "Here, you'll need these; they're fully charged."

Nina noticed the quizzical look on Popeye's face. "Popeye, do you have a question?"

"Yeah, what's this?"

"It's a burner."

"I got a burner."

Nina held out her hand. "May I see it, please?" Popeye took out his cell phone and handed it to Nina, who looked at it, and handed it back.

"That's a regular cell phone."

"So?"

"That phone works off of terrestrial towers. There aren't many towers up here. Take this, you need a phone that works off satellites."

Popeye nodded, saying, "Thanks."

Once the four travelers passed through Canadian customs, they split, and went their separate ways. Matteo and

Popeye headed toward the Avis counter while Luigi and Nina walked toward the Smyth Air Service counter.

Well aware that Santino Varni used an alias when he was in Canada, Nina was completely *un*aware of the full transformation that occurred once his feet literally touched Canadian soil. Even the most minute aspects of his "core" persona of Santino Varni disappeared. In every aspect, she had literally never met the man now walking by her side. Santino Varni had once again morphed completely into the alternate persona of Luigi Secondo.

When Luigi began talking with the agent behind the Smyth Air counter, Nina was taken aback. Amazed at the soft, yet masculine tone of his voice, the sudden change that had come over Varni astonished her. She subconsciously tilted her head, trying to take it all in. Even Luigi Secondo's posture was different from Santino Varni's. Santino's posture was rigid. He often appeared tense, like a cat ready to pounce. Luigi's posture was more relaxed; there was a certain grace about him.

As she watched him, she stepped back and stared at the man standing next to her. *He doesn't even sound like himself! I've never seen him this patient with anybody about anything. If I didn't know that he avoided drugs, I'd swear he was on something.*

When Luigi finished the transaction at the counter, he thanked the young woman behind the counter and turned to Nina. "We're all set, dear; they have a plane for us, and we should be able to board now. Do you need to use the ladies' room before we head out?"

Nina looked around to make sure no one was close enough to overhear her. "This is an *act*, right? You're modeling how we're going to play it while we're at this place, right?"

Luigi looked at her. She could clearly see the surprise and uncertainty in his eyes. "I don't understand what you're saying, Nina, dear. Is everything okay?"

Nina blinked a few times. "No. No, there's no problem. I'm . . . I'm fine. Everything's fine."

"That's my gal. Wait here, I'm going to get a luggage cart. No sense in either of us carrying these things when we can throw them on a cart."

Before Luigi walked away, he kissed Nina on the cheek. "Be right back!" Nina stared after him.

My god, he's good at this. I'm glad I know he's just pulling my leg.

Two hours later, when the unmistakable sound of a single engine float plane reached Lou's ears, he looked up at the sun. *Yup,* he thought, *just about the time I figured we'd see Luigi.*

When Angelo had given Lou a heads up to expect Luigi about mid-day, Alessandra had gone over to Luigi's cottage, aired it out, and freshened things up a bit. As the plane taxied in, Lou was standing at the end of the dock.

After securing the plane's pontoons to the dock, Lou opened the door to the cockpit and waved to the pilot.

"Afternoon, Lou, I've got a couple of guests for ya,"

A couple? Lou thought. *Angelo said Luigi was coming up.*

Luigi poked his head out of the cockpit like he had been shot out of a cannon. The first thing he did was place a hand on Lou's shoulder. "Lou, I hope I wasn't out of line when I was leaving here last time. I don't know what came over me. Please forgive me for pressing you about selling this place. I *know* how much it means to you."

"Hey, that's all forgotten," Lou said, slightly relieved, remembering it well.

"Good. That said, if you ever need any financial assistance, I want you to call me. Okay? Are we okay?"

Lou smiled. "Of course, we're okay. That kinda stuff doesn't bother me."

"Good, I was worried I might have weakened our friendship."

"Not a chance." Then Lou noticed movement in the passenger area of the plane. "Did you bring someone up with you?"

"I did, Lou. I want you to meet someone who's very special to me." Sticking his head back inside the plane he said, "Nina, do you need a hand getting out?"

"I think I could use a hand," a warm voice said from inside. As Nina Cataldo emerged from the de Haviland Otter, both Luigi and Lou held out their hands.

"Lou, I want you to meet my fiancée, Nina . . . Nina Cataldo! Nina, this is Lou Gault."

Instantly impressed with the firm hold she took of his outstretched hand, Lou thought her warm smile seemed to take over the very essence of Nina's face.

"Very nice to meet you, Nina."

"And you. I've heard so much about you," she said as Lou continued to hold her hand.

"Step onto the pontoon first, then the dock," he instructed. Nina seemed to perform a dance as she maneuvered from the pontoon onto the dock.

"Whew, I didn't expect the plane to be rocking in one direction and the dock in another," she laughed.

"That's why I held onto your hand. We've been able to

tame a few things up here, but synchronizing the pontoons to the docks isn't one of 'em, yet," he said.

As Nina looked around, Lou checked her out. *Hmm, personable and quite the 'looker.' Luigi, my friend, I think you did just fine.*

Nina turned to Luigi. "Is that big building where the kitchen is?"

"It is."

"I'm looking forward to meeting Angelo," she said.

"Well, once we drop our luggage off at the cottage, we'll do just that."

"Luigi, let me help you with that luggage," Lou offered.

"Lou, you've got enough to do keeping this place running. If I need to make a second trip, it's no bother."

Listening to the conversation between the two men, Nina turned her face away so she wouldn't reveal her disbelief at the person Santino Varni had become.

Chapter Twenty

When Luigi and Nina reached the front door to his cottage, he set down the luggage, opened the screen door, stepped aside, and motioned with his arm, saying, "Ladies first!"

Nina still wasn't quite sure what to make of this totally different behavior from Varni, but nodded and went along with "Luigi Secondo's' invitation.

As she entered the cottage, Luigi said, "Nina, the room directly ahead is the one I usually sleep in. Matteo and Popeye can have the room with twin beds, if they show up. I'd like you to take the room on the left, adjourning mine.

Deep inside herself, Nina wanted to say, *Why don't we just share a room?* But all she said was, "Fine."

"Once we unpack, we'll head over to the lodge and I'll introduce you to my friend, Angelo."

When Nina entered the bedroom, she expected to see the exposed rafters. What surprised her though, was how thoroughly clean the room, indeed, the entire cottage was.

Then, out of the corner of her eye, she saw movement. Turning, she realized the door connecting her room with Luigi's was slightly ajar.

Interesting, she thought. *Who would have thought a cabin in the middle of nowhere would have adjourning rooms.*

It wasn't long before Luigi had unpacked and was ready to head over to the lodge where the guests ate in the dining hall and where Chef Angelo created his culinary masterpieces.

Luigi knocked lightly on the adjourning door and entered Nina's room. "Dinner won't be for a while yet, but Angelo will be in the kitchen." Taking Nina by the hand, he said, "Come with me."

About halfway down the path, Nina stopped, turned her head toward the lake and took a deep breath, filling her lungs with fresh air. "What *is* that wonderful outdoorsy fragrance? It smells like Christmas."

"It's the balsams."

"The what?"

"The pine trees, they emit an oily substance from the pores in their needles. That's what you smell."

"How do you know that?"

"Well, when you come up here enough times, you get to know the sights, sounds, and smells of the place."

As they stepped onto the deck of the lodge, Nina paused again. To the west, the horizon was ablaze with various shades of amber and brilliant fiery reds, framed by purple clouds. "Are the sunsets always like this?"

"Pretty much. In the early spring, the sun is positioned a little differently. It goes down a little more to the right. At sunset, the reflection on the water is magnificent. It's almost as if the water is on fire."

Nina gazed at the brilliant display of color for a few moments before Luigi took her hand again. "Let's go in; I want you to meet Angelo. Oh, a word of caution, don't *ever* refer to him as a 'cook.' It's *chef* Angelo."

As soon as Nina entered the lodge, she was impressed with the large openness of the dining room, and that white linen cloths draped the tables.

This is definitely not as rustic as I anticipated, she thought.

"Come, this way, Angelo will be in here."

As they entered the kitchen, Luigi spotted the chef. "Hey, Angelo, *Ciao!*"

His friend turned around. "Hey, Luigi!" Angelo immediately stopped what he was doing and wiped his hands on a towel.

"Angelo, I want you to meet my fiancée, Nina." His face was beaming.

Looking directly at Nina, Angelo said, "*Que Bella Donna*! Your boyfriend, Luigi, he told me you were coming, but he said nothing about your beauty. I forgive him for keeping you a secret," With that, Angelo took Nina's hand and kissed it. "I am pleased to meet you. Come, I have a table for you."

Angelo led them to a table set for two by a window with full view of the lake. The tent card on the table read: *Reserved*.

"Luigi, do you trust me to pair the wine for you tonight?"

"Of course, my friend."

"Good." Turning to Nina, he asked: "And you, *signorina*, which would you prefer right now, an espresso or prosecco?"

Instinctively, Nina looked at Luigi. When he didn't hint at a preference, she said, "We'll save the prosecco for dinner."

"Understood. I will only be a moment." Then Angelo

raised his arm in a graceful motion and shouted, *"Uno minuto!"*

WHEN ANGELO RETURNED with the espresso, he also had four small plates on the tray. "Luigi, I bring you a little something special. Just a taste to snack on."

"Grazie."

"Prego!"

Nina stared at the appetizers Angelo set before them. *I really didn't know what to expect, but it certainly wasn't this.*

Angelo placed his hand on Luigi's shoulder. "Now, my friend, I need to go back to work. *Mangia!*"

As Nina's eyes scanned the delights before her, she dismissed the assorted cheeses and reached for a sautéed mushroom bruschetta. After tasting the combination of fresh thyme, marsala, pecorino cheese and savory creamy mushrooms hitting her palate, she rolled her eyes.

"Oh, Luigi, this bruschetta is *beyond* delicious. I've never tasted anything even *close* to this before."

"Would you like the recipe?" Nina nodded as she took another bite.

"For you, my dear, I'll ask."

Nina kept looking at him. *What is happening? There is nobody here to impress with his act. Either he is planning to stay in character, or something else is going on with him.*

EVERY EVENING during Lou's twenty-three-week season, Alessandra and Kate would pitch in and take on the task of serving and clearing the tables in the lodge.

Earlier, when Lou had mentioned that Luigi's fiancée had

flown up with him, the news traveled rather quickly among the year-round female residents. That evening, Alessandra was the first to arrive at the lodge. Before she even went into the kitchen, she walked straight over to the table were Luigi and Nina sat.

"Nina, welcome! I am Alessandra, Angelo's wife. I need to get ready for the rush now, but I wanted first to say, 'hello.' You and I, we'll catch up later, yes?"

A broad smile spread across Nina's face as she nodded in agreement.

Moments later, when Kate arrived, the same scene played out. "Nina, please stay behind after dinner. We're all anxious to get to know the woman Luigi is marrying. Again, welcome."

LATER, after all the meals had been plated and brought out to the guests, Angelo emerged from the kitchen. He motioned to his friend Luigi, and mouthed the words, "Luigi, come, join me."

Luigi smiled, placed his napkin on the table, excused himself to Nina and stood up, then walked over to his friend. Nina sat back in her chair, wondering what was happening.

As soon as Luigi joined his friend, they turned their backs to the diners and whispered to one another. After a brief discussion, Angelo pressed the button on a fob he held in his hand and music flooded the room. Then in unison, the two men faced their audience and began singing the iconic Italian song, "Quando, Quando, Quando".

Their rich voices blended perfectly. Over the years, these two tenors had frequently entertained lodge guests with

Italian songs, often singing as a duet, one singing melody, the other harmonizing.

Tonight, even before they finished singing "Quando," the guests had begun applauding. When they finished, and without reluctance, the men gave in to shouts of "Encore!" After a rousing rendition of "Volare," the two impromptu entertainers bowed to well-deserved applause, shook hands, and parted ways.

As Luigi returned to their table, Nina couldn't help but notice both Kate and Alessandra's eyes following him. When he sat down, she smiled and touched his forearm. Leaning close, she whispered into his ear. "Well done."

"Thank you, my dear. By the way, how's the fish?"

"It's delicious. What is it?"

"Filet of salmon alla Jacques."

"That sounds French. Is it?"

"It's not. When Angelo created the dish, he named it after Lou's cousin, Jake. Jake has this rather strange affinity for Grey Poupon. You know, the mustard."

"I thought I tasted that." As Nina took another bite, she said, "I think I'd like this recipe, too."

Chapter Twenty-One

Luigi held Nina's hand as they left the lodge after dining and walked back to their cottage. The night air was unusually warm, and the moon was almost full. Luigi playfully squeezed her hand more than once as they walked along the moonlit path.

I wonder if he meant anything by singing that song, 'Quando, Quando, Quando,' she thought. *Besides its beauty, I saw him look at me several times. Was he hinting at something?* The whole scene both confused and excited her as her mind raced with anticipation of his intentions.

When they reached their cottage, Luigi held both her hands and looked into her eyes. But his words disappointed her. "It's late; let's go to bed."

Nina nodded, and said, "Okay, but let me use the bathroom first."

After finishing her nightly routine, she called out: "Next." Then, tiptoed into her own room, changed into a revealing nightgown, and turned off the small table lamp. Then she waited.

The door separating their bedrooms was slightly ajar; the light in Luigi's room silhouetted the outline of her own door. When she finally heard him leave the bathroom, she pulled the covers up a bit, just to be coy. But the light in Luigi's room went out.

Nina took a breath. *Now, he will come to me.*

But when no one came through the doorway separating their rooms, Nina's thoughts began to wonder. *He must be expecting me to come to him. He didn't say 'goodnight,' so he must be waiting for me. He's deliberately left the door open, so that must be it. He's playing a game.* Nina let out a sigh. *Why does this have to be so damn confusing?*

As she continued to think, she heard voices coming from Luigi's room. Surprised, Nina tilted her head to the side. *Is there someone else in the cottage?*

The words were spoken in hushed tones, but it definitely sounded like two people having a conversation.

Try as she might, she was unable to clearly hear what was being said. Finally, curiosity got the best of her; she slipped out of bed and tiptoed over to the door to listen.

"There is no risk here."

That's Luigi's voice, Nina thought. *Who is he talking to?* Then she heard the sound of the authoritative second voice, and froze. *Santino!*

"No, the danger is *real*. But, not for long," Varni's voice protested.

Nina caught her breath as her right hand covered her mouth. *Santino,* she thought. *Oh, my, he has forgotten which role he is playing.*

Nina opened the door a little further, just enough to get a

better look inside Luigi's room. The light from the moon streaming through the window was enough to see Luigi lying in bed, alone.

He's dreaming, she thought, *he's talking in his sleep; there's no one else here with him.*

Nina remained by the door listening as the two voices argued. At times the conversation was intense; at other times the words were garbled. She watched in amazement as each time Luigi's body suddenly jerked, he seemed to be struggling with some invisible bond as if trying to free himself. Clearly, whatever nightmare he was having, was agitating him.

"No, Santino, this is *wrong*!" she heard Luigi's voice say. Finally, Luigi turned on his side. "No! Go away! Leave me!"

Nina waited a few minutes before venturing into Santino/Luigi's room. Her eyes were now acclimated to the dark and she focused on his face. Looking down at the man she wanted to love for so long, she placed her hand lightly on his forehead. Then she leaned down and kissed him on the cheek.

"Go to sleep and rest, my love," she whispered. He stirred slightly. *Did he hear me?* she wondered, as she watched his form. When he didn't move again, she tiptoed back to her own room, and its lonely bed.

Early the following morning, when Koby woke from a deep sleep, she sat straight up in bed, startling her husband, Jake.

"Koby, are you okay?"

After letting out a deep breath, Koby said, "Yes."

Jake rolled over to face his wife, "Then, what's the matter?"

"I need to go to the feeder ponds."

Jake thought a second, then he rolled over quietly saying, "Thank you for sharing."

Koby looked at her husband. "I'm sorry Jake. It's just that I woke up realizing I'd asked Lou not to do anything about the algae in the ponds until I sent a sample off to the labs. That was days ago."

"And?"

"And now I'm holding everything up. I haven't done it yet."

"Go back to sleep; he's a big boy. He'll get over it."

"I *can't*. You know how protective the Abenaki are about their waterways. The people in the village were anxious to eradicate the algae a while ago until I put the brakes on."

Knowing sleep time was over, Jake sat up, placed both feet on the floor and ran his left hand across the back of his neck. "What time is it?"

"Almost a quarter to five."

"Tell me, again, why you need to go there."

"We're dealing with three forms of algae across central New Brunswick. Each requires a different management approach. We need to know which species are in those ponds."

"You going there today?"

"Yes, I need to. I've put it off long enough."

"Have one of the guides go with you."

"I can find my own way."

"Koby, *no* one goes there alone."

Koby rolled her eyes. "Why? Because Azeban lives there?"

"Basically, that's the reason."

"Look, Jake, I think the stories you read to Gigi about Azeban are really cute. They're entertaining, but he's not real! There's no such thing as a spirit that's capable of turning itself into a raccoon. It's mythology."

"My people don't think so."

"Jake, I'm a big girl. I think I can handle this. Okay?"

Chapter Twenty-Two

Whenever Kate had an afternoon free from conference calls, she liked to stretch her legs and take an afternoon tea with Alessandra. If Koby was in camp, the three of them would gather and enjoy each other's company.

Kate and Nina Cataldo had spoken briefly after dinner last night when Nina and Luigi had arrived. But it was a lengthy travel day for Nina and she excused herself rather quickly.

But now, as Kate made her way over to the lodge, she noticed Nina sitting in an Adirondack chair and reading on the porch of what everyone referred to as "Luigi's cottage."

Kate smiled. *Luigi is probably out walking with Angelo. Let's see how much I can find out about Luigi Secondo over a cup of tea.* As Kate walked over, Nina was absorbed in the book she was reading and never heard her approach.

"Is it a good read?"

Startled, Nina looked up quickly. "Oh, it's so peaceful here, I didn't even hear you."

"It must be a good read, then."

Letting out a sigh, Nina replied, "Yes and no. It's just another 'bubblegum for the brain' romance novel. I do like this author, though, at least her books aren't the usual 'cookie-cutter' drivel."

"I'm heading over to have a cup of tea with Alessandra. Would you like to join us?" Kate looked at her with anticipation. When Nina hesitated, Kate said, "Or you can have a cappuccino. Chef Angelo *insisted* on having a high-end espresso machine."

"Oh, I don't know," Nina said. "Mister . . . I mean, *Luigi* said something about going for a boat ride this afternoon. I wouldn't want him to find me gone."

Kate tapped her Apple watch, "Well, you've got time. Luigi and Angelo won't be back from their walk for a while yet." Smiling, she pressed harder. "Come on, I'm overdue for a little girl-talk."

With that, Nina dog-eared the page she was on, closed the book and stood up. "Okay, I'm in. This city-girl can only take so much peace and quiet."

"It does take a little getting used to," Kate said. "Although, it's not uncommon for wives or significant others to be here in camp. Some women truly enjoy fishing; others just come to relax and chill out with their man. Even though you're the only woman here right now."

As they walked toward the lodge, Kate began thinking. *Hmm, she started to refer to Luigi as 'Mister,' then corrected herself. That was odd.*

"Kate, I'm trying to place your accent. Are you Canadian?" Nina asked.

"No, I'm an Irish colleen. Born and raised in the Emerald Isle, the land of the shamrock. But *this* is my home now. What about you? Are you a 'proper Bostonian'?"

"Hardly. My last name is Cataldo. I was born in Italy, but my parents came over when I was very young."

"Lou and I had a wonderful time in Italy a few years ago; it's so beautiful. Do you go back often to visit Italy?"

"No." Her comment sounded sad. Then without skipping a beat, Nina said, "So, what brought *you* over here?"

Well, Nina, that was skillful how you shifted the focus back to me, Kate thought. They were almost at the lodge, but to keep the conversation going, Kate answered the question. "Like so many things in life, it was work-related."

"I see."

As Kate opened the screen door leading into the dining room, she asked, "Nina, would you prefer, a cappuccino or tea?"

"Oh, a cappuccino would be great."

In a louder voice, Kate called out, "Alessandra, would you make a cup of cappuccino, please?"

A voice from the kitchen called back, "You're not having tea today?"

"I *am*, but we have company; Nina is here."

"Oh, okay!"

Kate decided to share more personal information, hoping Nina would open up a bit. "So, getting back to what I was saying, it was through work that I came here which is actually how I met Lou. It's funny, when you're trying to meet your *Mister Right*, you never do. Then, when you're *not* looking, the universe just seems to connect you somehow with who you're supposed to be with!"

Nina smiled and nodded in agreement but offered nothing.

Kate paused. *Okay, Nina, that was your cue to say something. Wonder why you're not saying anything.* Determined to keep the conversation going, Kate added, "I can't even begin to tell you how much we all enjoy having Luigi here."

Nina decided to interject a little irony. "I'm not too surprised. He's a totally different man here than back home."

"Really? How so?"

Nina saw where Kate's question was leading and changed direction. "You and Lou have two children, is that correct?"

Kate smiled to herself. *Sweetie, you need to be Irish to get away with answering a question with a question.* Then she replied, "Yes we have twins, a boy and a girl."

"Oh, I thought I saw a third youngster, a girl."

"Lou's cousin and his family also live here. That would be their daughter."

"Oh."

"Lou and I were married a little over a year when the twins came along. They're going on seven now, but I think my daughter is beginning to show signs of being a teenager, already."

When Nina didn't say anything, Kate continued. "If you don't mind me asking, how long have you and Luigi known each other?"

"We both grew up in Boston's north end. It's like a little Italy there, everybody knows everybody else."

Ha, another non-answer, Kate thought. *She's good! I'll need to phrase my questions better.*

When Nina didn't elaborate further, Kate said, "The Irish are like that, too. When I'm over in Ireland, it's one big happy family. I've totally lost track of how many third, fourth, and fifth cousins I have now."

With that, Alessandra emerged from the kitchen, carrying a tray loaded with tea, a cappuccino, and biscotti. "Nina! *Como stai?*"

Instinctively Nina responded in Italian. *"Sto bene. Grazie."*

"Prego!" Then realizing Kate's understanding of Italian was minimal, Alessandra quickly added, "It's nice that you've joined us."

When Nina reached for the cup of cappuccino, Kate noted with surprise there wasn't a ring on Nina's left hand. *That's odd,* Kate thought, *she's not wearing an engagement ring. Knowing Luigi, he must have given her a diamond. She probably just took it off.*

After everyone had taken a sip of their beverage, Kate reached over and lightly touched Alessandra on the knee. "Oh, I meant to ask you earlier, what are we having for dinner tonight? I saw the entree was blank on the message board."

Alessandra rolled her eyes. "My husband . . . he's like a young child. He's making *Coniglio alla Molisana.*

Kate tilted her head. "I don't believe I've ever had that."

"It's boned rabbit and sausage, on a skewer. Angelo dresses it up a little; he pairs it with a mushroom marsala reduction sauce. We made it often in the old country. You'll enjoy it. For *sides,* he's doing a Tuscan rice dish and broccoli *'a crudo".*

"It sounds delicious, but why the change?"

Alessandra shrugged her shoulders. "Luigi's here! So, you know everything is going to be about Luigi."

Nina smiled saying, "Mister . . . ah, Luigi *does* enjoy rabbit.

And what's not to like about broccoli sauteed with wine and garlic."

Kate glanced at Nina and smiled. *She did it again.* She shifted in her seat to have a better view of Nina's face. "Nina, does Luigi have a *favorite* dish? What's the one thing he likes you to cook for him on special occasions?"

Nina totally dodged the question. "His work hours are erratic. He, ah, we . . . we tend to eat out a lot. We're blessed, though, there are so many *ristoranti* in the north end, and they're all within walking distance. Naturally, we have a few favorites, but it's often difficult to choose which one to go to."

Kate had a follow-up question, but then, Alessandra pointed at the plate of biscotti. "*Mangia*, please, enjoy."

"I will have one, thank you," Nina reached for a biscotti. "They look delicious. My mother always added cranberries to her biscotti during the holidays. Have you ever done that?"

"Oh yes. They grow wild here."

My, my, Kate thought, *she's really good at changing the subject. But I'm going to take this conversation in the direction I want it to go.* She took a sip of her tea and looked directly at Nina.

"Luigi is up here quite often; is he retired?"

"No, no, he's not retired." As soon as the words came out of her mouth, Kate could see Nina knew she had made a mistake. It was like she could see Nina's stomach tighten.

Kate had 'teed' up the opportunity she was looking for, and wasn't going to let it pass. "Oh, so what does Luigi do for a living that he's able to take so much time off?"

Nina froze. Kate knew she had backed her into a checkmate position. Nina cleared her throat and lifted her cup of cappuccino as if she was going to take a sip before responding. But it was a ploy. Instead of taking a sip, she fumbled the cup and the entire contents spilled down the front of her clothes.

"Oh, darn! Oh, I *can't* believe I just did that!"

Alessandra quickly offered a couple of napkins. "Ah, *tutto bene*, everything is fine."

Feigning embarrassment, Antonina stood up. "Oh, I'm such a klutz. I need to go soak this blouse or it will be ruined. Coffee is *so* difficult to get out once it sets in."

Alessandra got up quickly. "Wait, you need some baking soda; I have some in the kitchen." Speaking over her shoulder, she kept talking. "Make a paste and work it into the stain; let it sit for a half hour before you rinse. Maybe you do this twice, three times, perhaps. *Capiche?*"

"Yes, yes, I understand. Thank you, Alessandra." With that Nina followed her into the kitchen. "I'm so sorry."

"What? What are you sorry for? Did you do this on purpose? No. It was an accident."

"I'm just embarrassed."

As Nina came back out from the kitchen, Kate had analyzed the entire incident. *What a very clever move, Nina, but why so evasive? What are you hiding?*

As Nina walked out the door, Kate watched her. *Not once, but twice, you started to refer to Luigi as 'Mister.' Why would you do that if you two are engaged? Maybe the real question is whether that's true: Are you really engaged to him? Nina, you're definitely hiding something. Whatever it is, it makes you nervous, and I'm going to find out what that is.*

Chapter Twenty-Three

When Kate returned to her cottage, she fired up her laptop. Next, she pulled up the resort's guest registration file and scrolled down the list of names until she reached the last name of 'Cataldo.' As she maneuvered the mouse and clicked on the link, her mind was in complete search mode. *Okay, let's see what information we have on you, Nina Cataldo.*

As soon as the page changed, Kate sat back in surprise. *Whoa, what's with all the blank fields?* The only information Nina had filled out about herself were, name, phone, and occupation. Kate stared at the record. *Okay, so your full name is Antonina. I'm glad you thought it was important to let us know you are an executive administrator. I thank you for that.*

Kate let out a breath and shook her head as she sat back in her chair. *Lou, if you're asking for all this information, and you really want it, the fields need to be designated as 'required' from now on.* Sighing, Kate picked up a yellow sticky pad, made a note to herself to have their webmaster make the program change, and exited the file.

Next, Kate opened a *people finder* search app and initiated a query on "Cataldo + Boston." When seventeen pages of names resulted, Kate backspaced and refined her search to the name "Antonina Cataldo." *Who knew 'Cataldo' was such a popular name in Boston?*

In seconds, Kate was scrolling down a much shorter list of "Antonina Cataldo" names. No sooner had Kate clicked on the first listing then she backspaced and modified her search further to exclude obituaries.

Of the newly refined list, only a few matches had pictures, and none resembled the Nina Cataldo currently removing coffee stains from her blouse at Havre de Poisson. Finally, Kate came across the profile of one Antonina 'Nina' Cataldo who was a valedictorian graduate of Boston's *Katharine Gibbs School*. It caught her attention. There was no photo attached, but the graduation date was consistent with a timeframe Kate suspected Nina might have been in school.

Hmm, Katharine Gibbs, I'm not familiar with that school, but it sounds like it's private. So, let's click on the link and see what Gibbs is all about.

"Oops," Kate whispered, "Katharine Gibbs closed all locations in 2011." She backspaced a few times and scrolled down her screen a little further. "Ah, here we go, Katharine Gibbs *Alumni*. Let's take a look here."

After a quick scan of the home page, Kate whispered, "This looks like a member-only site. Maybe the contact tab will light up if I position the cursor over it." A second later, she found success. "Yes, it does, and it has a phone number."

After jotting the number down, Kate moved her curser around the screen to see if there were any other hotlinks. As soon as the curser hovered over *School History*, it lit up like a Christmas tree and Kate double clicked.

From reading the brief synopsis, it was obvious that Katharine Gibbs was a professional secretarial school. Kate sat back. *So, Nina, you went to secretarial school. But wait, that's not what you go by today, Now, it's either administrative assistant or executive administrator.* Kate glanced away from her computer. *I wonder if I can find a Nina, or Antonina Cataldo listed in* any *professional organizations for admins?*

Three organizations popped up: American Society of Administrative Professionals (ASAP), International Association of Administrative Professionals (IAAP), and Executive Assistants Organization (EAO). Kate knew she'd be denied access into the sites, so, she took a different approach and called each organization on the phone. After identifying herself, temporary passwords were sent to Kate's official RCMP email account.

Antonina Cataldo's name showed up twice in the organizations. One listing had her aligned with a Boston Chapter, the other with a New England Chapter. The Boston chapter had the words *Past President* after Nina's name. Kate keyed the word *officers* into the search box at the top of the page. Suddenly Kate's screen was filled with group photos.

In a picture taken seven years earlier, the name *Antonina 'Nina' Cataldo* appeared among the names under a photo. Kate moved her cursor and enlarged the photo. Her hairdo was different, but the facial features were a match.

Kate clicked back to the membership listing. The employer listed for Nina was International Longshore and Warehouse Union.

Okay, Kate thought, *you started to call him 'Mister' twice, so let's see if the name Luigi Secondo appears on the International Longshore and Warehouse Union site.*

Kate googled the ILWU and clicked on *Boston*. When she clicked on the tab titled "Officers" a list of names came up, without headshots. The name of Luigi Secondo was not among them.

MEANWHILE, Nina Cataldo was down at the water's edge sitting in the bow of an open boat. As Luigi backed the boat away from the dock, he asked, "Is that the same outfit you had on earlier?"

"No, I've changed." She was surprised he had noticed.

"Well, where would you like me to take you Nina?"

"You're asking *me*?" She was even more surprised.

"Yes."

Nina glanced up at the sky; it was a perfect day, clear except for a few wispy cirrus clouds high in the lower reaches of the stratosphere. Nor was there a ripple on the lake. Turning her attention to Luigi in the stern, she smiled. "You're the boss, sir."

Damn, she thought, *I did it again.* "Let me rephrase that," she said quickly. "Anywhere you'd like to go would be fine with me."

Luigi held his finger up to his lips and looked around. They were alone. Finally, he whispered, "Nina, call me 'Luigi.'"

Nina blushed and lowered her eyes. "I know; I'm sorry. It won't happen again."

"Did you have an opportunity to take any photographs?"

"A few. I've walked around the resort. I've also drawn a map and included all the buildings. I was able to get a look inside the kitchen which is actually quite impressive; the equipment is all high-end. Vulcan stoves and grilles, Artic Air refrigeration units; everything looks fairly new."

"Good."

As the boat headed out toward the middle of the lake, Luigi said, "Angelo once told me that the most beautiful spot on the lake is a cove west of here. He called it 'Moose Bay,' or something like that."

Nina reached inside the pocket in her slacks and pulled out a small map of the area. Spreading the paper open, she scanned it before pointing to a spot. "I see a place called Moose Cove."

"That must be it. We'll head down there."

Chapter Twenty-Four

A small hamlet known as "Five Fingers" lay thirty miles north of Moose Cove, the way the crow flies. There, Matteo and Popeye were nursing a couple of drafts at a local watering hole. They'd had a long day traveling around the countryside and were bone tired.

"Matteo, this is friggin' nuts, man. There ain't no friggin' way we're gonna find anybody up here to help us. This is real backwater country, man."

Matteo took a long sip and sat back. "I'm not so sure. Let's just sit here and scope out the local gentry."

Popeye shook his head. "Matteo," he whispered, "I'm telling ya', there ain't nobody that's gonna talk to us; we're strangers."

Matteo's eyes never left the long row of locals sitting at the bar. "Just wait. I think if we stay long enough, somebody who just doesn't fit right, is gonna walk through that door."

"And?"

"And that's the one we're gonna hit on."

"Yeah, well you do whatever you wanna do. I'm gonna go see what the hell they got for a menu around here."

As Popeye stood up, Matteo called out, "Hey!"

"What?"

"Grab a pitcher of beer on your way back."

"Yeah."

Matteo stretched out his legs and watched people sitting at the bar. He knew the kind of person he was looking for. If he saw the right personality, he had the skills to gently separate them from the herd and recruit them. Once anyone became his minion, he knew exactly how to steer them into doing his bidding. So far, however, from what he could tell, not one person sitting at the bar was a candidate. Not one of them looked successful at anything beyond just getting by. Not one fit the profile he was looking for.

When Popeye came back from the bar with another pitcher and a single page laminated menu, he set them on the table. "You really think you're gonna find some backwoods piece of shit in here to control?"

Matteo nodded his head. "Yeah."

"Well, *shit*, I'll pay money to see that."

Matteo just smiled and refilled his mug with beer. What he needed was someone who knew the area, lived on the edge, wasn't afraid to take risks . . . provided the reward was worth it . . . and maybe had a burr up their butt about something. Most likely his perfect candidate would be someone who was shunned, had a chip on their shoulder, or was just plain angry.

Popeye busied himself checking out the menu. It read:

Hamburger

Cheeseburger

Double Cheeseburger

Hot Dog
Chili Dog
Chips

Popeye tossed the menu in front of Matteo. "Hey, check this out. They got quite the friggin' menu."

Just then, the door opened and Popeye instinctively looked up. As soon as he saw the slovenly dressed young man, he nudged Matteo with his elbow. Their eyes followed the newcomer as he walked the full length of the bar and took the stool furthest away from everyone. What captured Matteo's attention more than anything, was the reaction of the men sitting at the bar as the newcomer walked past. Even in the dim light, he could see the subtle elbowing and heads turning as if they all knew something about him.

Popeye whispered, *"Misfit."*

Matteo nodded and raised his mug of beer like a salute.

As gregarious as the bartender seemed to be with other patrons, he took his sweet time before heading down to the newcomer, and barely said a word to the young man sitting all alone at the far end of the bar. Matteo and Popeye watched the scene play out. Occasionally, someone said something, heads would turn toward the newcomer, and a few laughs were heard.

After a while, Popeye leaned over to Matteo. "It appears the new guy ain't the most popular fella in the room."

Matteo nodded. "I was thinking the same thing."

"You want me to go over and talk to him?"

"No."

"You want me to do *any*thing?"

"Just watch my back."

With that, Matteo stood up, left his beer mug on the table and walked over to the bar. He deliberately went to the far end and sat one stool away from the newcomer. The top of the bar was sticky, the edges dotted with cigarette burns. He stayed silent for a moment before saying anything.

"Can I buy you a drink, friend?"

"I ain't yor friend."

Matteo lightly slapped his hand down on the bar. "Well, I'm new here, and I hate to drink alone. If you don't *mind* . . . and if you'd *let* me . . . I'd like to buy you a drink."

"You can, if you got a mind to it . . . but that don't make us *friends*."

Matteo raised his hand and caught the bartender's attention. "I'll have another draft . . . and give *him* another of whatever he's drinking."

The bartender nodded his head, and turned away. A number of others at the bar also turned away. But other than that, nothing much else happened.

"My name's Matteo, what's yours?"

After a long pause, the young man kept his eyes down, but answered. "Oswald."

"Pleased to meet you, Oswald. You live around here?" The young man responded with a slight nod.

"You live in the Abenaki village?"

"*No.* I ain't no Abenaki."

"Oh."

"I'm a Turnbridge."

"Sounds like you don't care much for the Abenaki."

"They nearly kilt my cousin! Shot him full of arrows; that's what they done."

"Is he all right?"

"He's alive." Oswald played with his shot glass. "He's in jail now and he ain't never coming out. All 'cuz of *them*."

Matteo zeroed in on Oswald's weakness and bias. "Well, I

can certainly understand why you're not a huge fan of the Abenaki. He let a few moments of silence pass. "So, Oswald, do you work around here?"

"Ha! Ain't nobody looking to hire a Turnbridge."

"No? Why is that?"

Oswald Turnbridge turned the half-filled shot glass around a few times with his fingers before he lifted the glass and slugged down the rest of the whiskey. "Cuz, there ain't nobody round here that takes kindly to us."

This is way too freaking easy, Matteo thought. Then, after taking a sip of his beer, he played his card. "Well, *I'm* looking to hire someone."

Matteo waited a few minutes. When Oswald Turnbridge didn't say anything, he repeated himself. "I need someone I can trust to do a little work for me."

"Doing what?"

"Oh, just a few odd things, nothing hard. You familiar with the woods around here?"

Oswald snorted, "Ha, been traipsing around these damn woods since the day I was born."

"You're sounding more and more like the kind of fella I might be looking for, Oswald, even if you are a Turnbridge. Hell, maybe even *because* you are." Matteo watched the newcomer's face, but it showed no emotion.

When Oswald didn't respond, Matteo said, "You interested?"

"What's I gotta do?"

"Nothing you couldn't handle." Again, Oswald just sat there without any comment, or reaction. Matteo waited a few more minutes before asking, "What kind of work have you been looking for?"

"Shit, I ain't even been giving that a whole lot of thought."

"Are you interested in a job where you could make your own hours, work independently, and make a lot of money . . . *under* the table?"

Oswald smiled. His lips pulled back, exposing yellow, twisted teeth. "Who the hell wouldn't?"

"Well, then, I just might be able to use someone like you."

"Yeah?"

"Yeah." With that Matteo slid off the bar stool. "Come with me. I wanna introduce you to my associate. He's sitting over there."

"Yor *what*?"

"My friend."

THE NEXT MORNING, still in Five Fingers, Matteo and Popeye sat in a small café reading a local edition of The Brunswick News. They still had a slight buzz after the long talk they'd had with Oswald Turnbridge the night before.

"Matteo, what's the plan for today?"

"I'm not sure yet. I'm still trying to wrap my head around the pieces to this puzzle."

"Well, ya' got this knucklehead we squeezed last night. Whaddya thinking? Ya don't need a friggin' army up here."

Matteo sipped his coffee. "Turnbridge is one piece of the puzzle, but I need a few more pieces to make this work."

When the waitress came over to take their breakfast order, Matteo asked a question. "Would you happen to know a young fella named Oswald Turnbridge?"

"Nope, not familiar with that one," she said.

Matteo smiled. "I was thinking of hiring him. This being a small town and all, I thought you might know him."

Before the waitress said anything, she looked around to

see if anyone was listening. "Mister, I know the Turnbridges, and unless you're looking for trouble, folks around here would tell you to stay well clear of them inbreds."

"What kind of trouble?"

Without a pause, the waitress replied, "You name it, they *done* it. 'Course ya gotta feel sorry for the young'uns they brung into this world. Hell, ain't none of them got a snowball's chance in hell of breaking that mold and making something of themself."

"Is that a fact?"

"Yessir, right hand up to God. Now, what's it gonna be for breakfast: eggs, or flapjacks? We got ham, bacon, hash, sausage, and home fries, too, if you want any."

"Where would I find him?"

Thinking the conversation had moved to ordering food, the waitress paused before saying, "Who you talking about? You still asking, 'bout that Turnbridge kid?"

"Yes, I am."

"That I don't rightly know. Ain't nobody I know that pays attention to what their kind do, or don't do. Now, what can I get you to *eat*, honey?"

Matteo smiled, "I'll have the breakfast special and another pot of coffee."

"And you?" she looked at Popeye.

"You got bagels?" he asked after studying the single page menu.

"We got English muffins, white or wheat toast; take yor pick, that's all we got."

"Gimme three eggs, salsa, ham, and wheat toast."

"Ain't got no salsa. Ketchup is on the table. How you want them eggs?"

"Looking up at me." Popeye said and handed her the menu. She took it and walked into the kitchen.

"Friggin' woods!" Popeye said and let out a breath.

"Are you finished with that other section of the paper?" Matteo asked.

"Yeah. Check out the article on page four."

"Which one?"

"The one about some damn friggin' fish from Europe that's got 'em all upset up here."

Matteo read the article several times, before he put the paper down and smiled. "I think we've just found another piece of the puzzle."

"Yeah?"

Matteo nodded. "Yeah, but first we gotta go find this Turnbridge kid."

"You got something in mind?"

"Yeah, he's gonna go catch us some fish."

Chapter Twenty-Five

Jake couldn't sleep after Koby had bolted upright in bed and awakened him. He dressed and left the cottage earlier than usual, figuring he'd get an early start delivering the mail. But before he even undid the protective covers on the de Havilland single-engine plane, he walked over to see his cousin.

"Lou?" he called out.

"I'm in the boat house, Cuz, what's up?"

"Koby's got it in her head to go down to Moose Cove, then hike over to the feeder ponds all by her lonesome, today."

"Is that so?"

"Yeah."

"Well, don't worry, I'll handle it."

"Thanks, Cuz. I gotta go."

"Hey."

Jake paused, "What?"

"What time is Koby heading out?"

"Oh, it won't be a while yet."

"Okay, that gives me enough time. That fog is pretty ugly this morning. Why don't you join me for a coffee and wait until it lifts?"

"Nah, this is nothing; it's just coming off the lake. I'll be fine once I get above it."

"Okay. Just be careful taxiing out. There's twenty-three boats out there somewhere."

LATER THAT MORNING, Koby dropped their five-year-old daughter, Gigi, off with Kate and headed over to the private boathouse Jake had built near their cottage.

The first thing she did, after removing the canvas boat cover, was to check the fuel gauge. *Three quarters full, more than enough,* she thought. With that, she hit a toggle switch to blow out the bilge, started the engine, released the ropes, and pulled the bumpers onboard.

As she backed the 26-foot mahogany launch out of the boathouse, the damp fog surround her. She shifted the throttle into neutral and looked around. *Mmm, it's thicker out here on the water. I could wait, but, nah, this'll burn off.* She turned the running lights on and slowly moved the throttle into forward gear.

Like Lou, Koby Callahan faced whatever life challenges came her way head on and with confidence that she would figure it out. She was familiar with the lake and traveled down to Moose Cove solo, usually twice a week to staff the clinic. Additionally, after years of being on the world's oceans, she was no *rookie* when it came to adapting to foggy maritime conditions.

This morning, when she reached the center of the lake, she

pulled back on the throttle and stood up. *See? Fog's not as bad out here,* she thought as she pushed the throttle forward. *With a little luck, the sun will come out and this will all lift.*

For most of the ride down to Moose Cove, her thoughts were focused on the three types of algae New Brunswick was dealing with. It wasn't until she backed off the throttle and glided over the shallows entering the cove that she realized how disorientating the fog was.

Hmmm, it's even heavier in here, she thought, as she tied up at the dock. *Had I known it was going to be this foggy here, I would have said 'yes' to someone leading me to the streams where the ponds come in.* Just then, she heard a deep baritone voice.

"Ready to go?"

Koby looked around just as Lou emerged out of the fog.

"Lou! What are you doing here?"

"I came down earlier. Jake asked me to be your guide today." The heavy fog had obscured the other boat already sitting at the dock.

Koby smiled. *Guess it's not such a bad thing when husbands don't always listen to their wives.* "Actually, I'm really glad to see you!"

Once Koby finished adjusting the boat bumpers so the runabout wouldn't rub up against the dock, she stood up, donned her backpack, turned toward Lou, and said, "Lead the way!"

Lou nodded and without saying a word, turned and walked off the dock into the mist.

Visibility in the cove was limited to some fifteen feet in any direction. The air was heavy and moist. The ground was wet, even the usual sounds of the forest were muted by the dampness and fog.

Koby was in good physical shape since she regularly

jogged with Kate along the trails around Havre de Poisson. Yet she found her breathing a little more labored than usual as she kept pace with the long strides Lou was taking.

It's going to be slippery because of the fog, she thought, *and there's no need for us to hurry. So, how do I say 'slow down' without Lou thinking I'm a wuss?*

As they left the shoreline and entered the forest, Koby was certain the pace would slow down, but it didn't. Smiling to herself, she had an idea. *Maybe if I engage him in conversation, he'll slow down.*

"Will this trail take us to the feeder ponds?"

"Yes."

Well, I did ask a simple 'yes' or 'no' question, Koby reasoned at his brief answer, then smiled. Shifting to an open-ended approach, she asked, "Lou, how far is it to the first pond?"

"Not far."

"How big are these ponds?"

"Not big."

"Are they in a chain? Does one feed into another?"

"You'll see."

Koby nearly laughed out loud when she realized he wasn't going to respond as she expected. Adjusting the shoulder straps of her backpack, she thought:, *Lou, you would have never made the debate team.*

The path from Moose Cove to the feeder ponds was not much more than a game trail. After hiking through the underbrush for close to a half hour, they came to a clearing directly below a waterfall. The water was cascading directly down from a ledge fifteen feet above. The volume wasn't heavy, but the thin, opaque sheet of water coming off the rock was steady and stretched close to ten feet across.

"This is truly majestic; I didn't expect this. It must be breath taking when the sun is out," Koby marveled.

"In the time of my great grandfather's father, this is where our village was."

"Right here at this waterfall?"

"Just above."

"It's so beautiful here. Is there a name for this waterfall?"

"It is known as Azeban's Cave. Come, let's go."

"Wait, wait! Why is it called Azeban's Cave? It's a waterfall."

"Because this is where he lives."

"Who?"

"Azeban."

"Where?"

"Behind the falls there's a cave. You can't see it from here, because of the water, which is why the trickster chose this place to be his home."

As Lou spoke, she scanned the small pool at the base of the waterfall for signs of algae.

"Lou, does this water come from the feeder ponds?"

"Yes."

As she looked up at the towering rock on either side of the waterfall, she wondered: *Okay. So, do we scale this ledge, or do we go around it?*

"Follow me, there's a trail to the side." When Koby hesitated, Lou said, "Come on, let's go, Azeban doesn't need to know we are here."

Oh, my god, Koby thought, *does Lou really believe all this stuff about Azeban is real?*

Chapter Twenty-Six

The article Matteo read appeared on the front page of the Brunswick Daily News, below the fold. It was written by K. A. Zimmer, the reporter who covered monthly meetings of the New Brunswick Wetland Habitat Management Board. The article read as follows:

The recent meeting of the Wetland Habitat Board proved to be livelier than usual. Everything was quiet until the board began discussing the recent capture of several fish known as Tench in the Kedqwick River. This fish is not native to the Americas and is considered to be an invasive threat. The Latin name for this fish is "Tinca, tinca." It is common throughout Europe and parts of Asia. Experts believe they were unintentionally introduced into the Saint Lawrence when ships arriving from Europe released their bilge water into the harbors.

The danger the Tench represent to any body of water in the western hemisphere is devastating. It competes against native fish species for space and resources, usually winning. It uproots large masses of aquatic vegetation, which alters the habitat for native species, and negatively impacts the water quality.

Tench eggs have a mortality rate of only seventy percent, whereas the eggs of indigenous sport fish native to the western hemisphere, like the trout, suffer a ninety-eight percent mortality rate. Additionally, one female Tench lays hundreds of thousands of eggs, whereas fish like our native trout will lay no more than a few thousand. The Tench can also tolerate extreme changes in temperatures and water quality . . . they are truly survivors.

Koby Callahan, a board member, and certified marine biologist, spoke at the meeting urging the board to address this issue with vigor. According to Callahan, once the Tench invades a body of water, if not eradicated, it will cause the existing ecosystem to collapse.

First to go will be the bottom of the pyramid, the small snails and bivalves. She went on to say that once those are lost, algae blooms will become commonplace even if they have never occurred before,. Next will be a decline in the population of smelt, and other small fry which larger fish feed upon. She concluded by saying once the population of the food fish declines, the larger fish, like trout and bass will collapse, leaving only the Tench.

Al Becker, the newest member of the board commented that, in his opinion, there were bigger fish the board needed to fry (no pun intended) and adding this to the pot would simply water down existing resources. After a lengthy discourse, Becker made a motion to table further discussion on the Tench.

Longtime board member Mark Gilbert took umbrage with Becker's position and urged the board to take action now.

After a heated exchange, Chairman, Jack Davis, asked Callahan if she had any knowledge on how soon this might be an issue for central New Brunswick. Callahan said that now is the time to act. She stated that depending on the size of any specific body of water, a complete collapse could be measured between months or a matter of a few years.

After the meeting, this reporter asked Chairman Davis if he had any further comment regarding the Tench. Davis stated: "It's out in the open now. We'll have to deal with it."

Stay tuned folks, this one's got all the makings of being a humdinger.

Reported by K. A. Zimmer

The Canadian Wildlife Services organization understood the threat the species officially known as *E. Tench* represented to the environment. What they weren't aware of, was how extensive the Tench population in Canadian waters had become.

Not only had the species established a solid foothold in the brackish estuaries near Quebec City, it was thriving. Huge sections of aquatic plant life, once prevalent in the marshes had been uprooted. As the lower rungs on the food chain began to disappear, the shallow water in the marshes became murkier and the oxygen levels declined.

The Tench's presence will often go undetected because of its muddled green coloring and tendency to remain in seclusion during the day.

A light-colored Tench is a rarity. The odds of a mutated fish reaching maturity are low, due to predators. Yet, a light greenish-gold specimen had managed to avoid detection and reach adulthood.

Like the other females, she had lived a solitary life, existing in the shadows. The very act of keeping to herself had allowed her to beat the percentages. She had survived because of discipline, caution and her instinctive survival skills.

Shortly, like the other females, she would leave the shadows. Her biological clock would force her to embark upon a solo journey to deposit her eggs.

She was healthy, her reflexes were sharp and she was in perfect physical condition. She had almost reached the headwaters of a river flowing into the Saint Lawrence the previous year. This time, if she could elude detection, she would travel even further before completing her mission.

It was twilight when she moved out. She had deliberately waited until dusk. It was the time of day that light played tricks with the shadows, which gave her an advantage.

She was cautious. She would travel by night, concealing herself during the day. Although she was totally in her environment, she moved with caution. The year before she had narrowly evaded death.

AFTER THE BATTLE of wills Luigi Secondo had gone through the previous night with his core persona, Santino Varni, and lost, he hadn't slept well. He awoke exhausted the next morning, to the point of actually giving thought to skipping his daily walk with Angelo and giving in to a nap. However, when he laid down and closed his eyes, Santino's demands filled his thoughts, again. Never before had Santino's voice invaded Luigi's thoughts during the day. But, today, from the moment Luigi had opened his bloodshot eyes, there was a new normal. Santino was now sending him a barrage of subliminal messages, at will.

The messaging wasn't nonstop, but it was akin to a

broken record. The message never changed: *Pick Angelo's brain, he's the Achilles heel; pick Angelo's brain, he's the Achilles heel. Do it, do it now!*

At first Luigi was able to merely shake his head and the message would go away. If someone was talking to him, Santino's message was nothing more than a distant background noise in Luigi's mind. However, as the morning wore on, it became more difficult for Luigi to dismiss the subliminal messages coming from his core persona.

That morning, when Nina and Luigi walked up to the lodge for breakfast, Angelo's first response when he saw his friend was, "You look tired."

"I didn't sleep well."

"So, take a nap. We'll walk tomorrow."

"No, we'll walk today."

"Nina, are you planning on joining us?"

"No, I'll pass; but thank you for asking, Angelo."

At that time of morning, every other guest was out on the lake, so Angelo pulled a chair up to the table and joined his friend. More than twice during breakfast, Santino's voice was so loud in Luigi's head that it actually drowned out what Angelo had said. Each time that happened, Luigi tapped him on the forearm, and said: "Say that again."

When Nina noticed both men had finished their meal, she stood up. "You two go for your walk. I'll clear the table."

Luigi stood and kissed Nina lightly on the cheek; then the two men headed out. As they walked toward the path that led to a wooden gate by the old logging road, Luigi said, "Last night, you said you wanted to tell me about a letter you received from Italy, yes?"

"Things are not good there. My cousin, he writes that the olive trees are all dying."

"Do they know why?"

Angelo let out a breath. "It's an epidemic. He says the land looks like Chernobyl after they had the reactor incident. The hills look like an endless sea of dead grey tree trunks. He says they are taking frantic measures to control the spread, but it is no use. It is a shame. I know those trees. It's where the oil I use comes from. They've been in my family for generations."

As Angelo continued talking, the voice of Santino Varni began to pulsate inside Luigi's skull like a bullhorn: *Pick Angelo's brain, he's the Achilles heel. Do it now, do it now!*

Angelo was completely unaware of the verbal harassment and test of wills that was going on inside Luigi's head as he continued talking. "My cousin, he is being forced to cut his trees down. He says there will be nothing left to harvest this year. Some of his trees are centuries old. They say it's a bacteria. How do you fight something you cannot see, eh?"

Again, Santino's voice brutally invaded Luigi's thoughts becoming louder, more insistent: *Do it! Do it! Do it now!* Santino seemed to have a stranglehold on Luigi's consciousness and refused to let go. Finally, Luigi had had enough of Santino's badgering. He came to an abrupt stop on the path and forcefully shouted out the word: *"No!"*

Angelo also stopped and looked at his friend. "What? What does *'no'* mean? I am telling you a story about the old country. It *is* happening there."

When Luigi didn't answer, Angelo could see a far-away look in his friend's eyes and rephrased his question. *"Luigi, s'matter for you?"*

When Luigi still didn't respond, Angelo grabbed him by both shoulders and shook him. "Hey, *paisan!* What's s'matter for you? You okay?" The physical shaking was enough to refocus Luigi's thoughts on the here-and-now.

Somewhat embarrassed, Luigi said, "I'm sorry, my friend, I was daydreaming and for some reason . . . it felt real."

"Are you okay? Do you need to rest?"

"No, no, I'm okay. I'm just, I'm just tired."

"Then there is nothing wrong?"

"No, I'm fine. I'm, I'm just overtired."

"You scared me," Angelo said. "But if you say you're fine, then it's okay." Just then, a doe and two yearlings burst across the path not more than twenty feet ahead of them. Angelo pointed toward the deer. "Did you see that? That my friend, that is why I choose to live here."

Angelo's comment gave Luigi the opening he needed to begin doing Santino's bidding.

"Angelo, how long have you and Alessandra actually been here?"

"That, I am not sure, maybe a dozen years. But what is time? What does time mean? Time means so little to me."

"You like it here?"

"Of course! Why else would I stay, eh?"

"So, what do you think is the one thing that makes Havre de Poisson stand out among all the other fishing lodges?"

"Ha, that I do not know."

Luigi let the questioning go, for the moment, and the two men walked a good distance while engaging in small talk. But Luigi knew he would try to pick Angelo's brain, again.

"Angelo, I've heard fishermen refer to Lou's place as *Mecca*. Why is that? What's the one thing, the key thing, that you believe makes people think this is such a special place?"

"Ha, that I don't know. I guess they just like to come here. I've never given it much thought."

"Me neither," Luigi lied. "But let's you and I *give* it some thought." Luigi paused for theatrical effect, then said, "I have my own ideas, but in your opinion, if there was *one* thing, and I'm talking just *one* thing, that elevated Lou's place above *all* the others, what would you say it was?"

Angelo didn't answer and the two men traveled in silence for a while. Finally, Angelo responded. "If you put it *that* way, I would have to say it's his reputation."

Following a fake laugh, Luigi said, "And here I expected to hear you say it was your culinary expertise."

"No, food makes no difference to the ones who come here. They come to catch the trophy fish, the monsters that lay in wait in the depths of the lake. The fish . . . and this beautiful setting . . . *that* is what draws them here. Look, look around you. Look at how beautiful everything is." Angelo waved both arms around them.

"Yes, Lou does walk his talk when it comes to caring about the environment."

"It is the way of the Abenaki people."

The two walked only a short distance before Luigi broke the silence again. "Earlier, when you said, 'reputation,' did you mean Lou's *personal* reputation or the *resort's* reputation?"

"How can you separate them?" Angelo asked. "You can't! One is the reflection of the other. He has no choice, it is *Alnobaiwi.*"

"What's *that* mean? I've never heard that word before."

"It's a word the Abenaki use. It's in their language. It translates to '*in the Abenaki way.*' He is part of those who have chosen to preserve the life ways of his people, the traditions that have been handed down to them by prior generations."

Not yet satisfied, Luigi waited a few moments before

trying a different approach. "It must take a lot of work to run a place like this. What do you think is the most difficult thing Lou has to wrestle with during the season?"

Angelo didn't hesitate one-second to answer this question. "Ha, keeping everyone happy, so they keep come back again."

"I can see how that would be a challenge," Luigi said. "How *does* he manage that?"

"By keeping everything running smoothly."

"When you say, 'everything,' what do you mean?"

"You know, the boats, the outboard motors, the condition of the cottages, enough guides for the season, getting the right food in on time, whatever."

"I never thought about all that," Luigi lied.

"He makes it *look* easy, that's all. But I have never known anyone work harder at making it look easy." Angelo said.

"He is carrying a lot of risk. Everybody wants to sue people today for the littlest thing. I hope Lou has adequate insurance coverage."

"Ah, don't you worry about Lou, he's a smart businessman."

"He's got insurance?"

"Of course.

"I would have thought it would be difficult to get insurance for a place like this, so far off the beaten track."

"Not really. Except for the big cities, most of Canada is off the beaten track."

"So, who does Lou use for a carrier?"

"For years he was with Maritime Commercial. But a few years back, when we enlarged the kitchen and he started building more cottages, they balked. So, he took his business over to Brunswick Mutual Casualty." Guileless, Angelo did not realize he had spilled important information. But Luigi did.

As they continued their walk, Luigi mulled over the key aspects he had drawn out of Angelo: *Trophy fishing, stellar reputation, unspoiled pristine environment, specific insurance information.* Then the voice of Santino invaded his thoughts, again. *And, now, we will turn each one into his biggest nightmare.*

Chapter Twenty-Seven

Koby's intention was to make a beeline hike to the ponds, collect a few samples, send the algae off to a lab and when the results came back, advise the tribal leaders how best to treat the ponds.

In and out, one and done, straight forward; all I want to do is 'check the box,' she thought.

When they reached a plateau directly above the falls, Koby felt a breeze on her face; movement off to the left caught her eye. When she glanced left, the fog swirled, exposing for a split second what appeared to be the outline of small buildings. Startled, she blinked, but the image had faded into the mist.

She called out. "Lou, where exactly was the village you said used to be around here?"

"Right where we're standing. Come, the ponds are this way."

She blinked her eyes again. *Wow, is it my eyes, or the power of suggestion playing tricks on me?*

Koby was used to hiking trails, but she was tired from the pace they'd kept on the way to the ponds. Just as Lou turned and set out again, disappearing into the fog, a second gust of wind came across the plateau. Like before, the breeze was refreshing, and she turned toward it. Again, the mist seemed to part and for a second time, the image she had just seen reappeared. She leaned forward and squinted into the mist. *Am I getting a glimpse of something that no longer exists?*

Whatever the image was, it vanished just as quickly as it had the first time. *No,* she thought, *between the fog and the power of suggestion, my imagination is totally playing tricks on me. Now, which way did Lou go?* She turned around. *Damn fog.* Looking down, she saw the path at her feet. *He must have gone in this direction,* she thought.

As she took a step forward, a fairly large raccoon emerged from the mist not more than ten feet in front of her. She expected the raccoon to scamper off. Instead, he stood up on his hind legs, looked directly at her, and momentarily bared his teeth, as if he was grinning. Then he dropped to all fours and disappeared into the mist.

Koby closed her eyes, shook her head, and smiled. *Nope, I'm not going there; you're not real!*

Then Lou emerged from the fog, motioning her to follow him. "Come on, the ponds are just up ahead."

THE FOG SHROUDING the resort had dispersed shortly after Koby left and Luigi and Angelo set out on their walk. Nina again wandered around camp, discreetly taking pictures, with her cell phone, of every structure and facility at the sportsman's resort from different angles. Twice, when she noticed Alessandra staring at her, she waved and placed the phone up to her ear, as if she was on a call.

In addition to taking pictures, Luigi had also asked Nina to nonchalantly meander over to the stream that powered the sawmill and look for anything in the water that might look like a gold nugget.

The morning ground fog had disappeared, but it was still overcast, and the grass felt wet on her open-toed shoes. As she approached the stream, she hesitated when she saw Hector trotting along on the opposite bank. Remembering Lou had cautioned them upon arrival that a wolf roamed the camp, she stopped. "Although he might appear domesticated," Lou had told them, "give him a wide berth."

Hector had now become a creature of habit, whether instinctively, or because he lived among humans. His daily routine was pretty consistent. In the morning and late afternoon, he'd set out to find something to eat. He clearly saw his role within 'the pack' as that of the *protector*. As such, three times a day he made a complete circle of the resort's outer perimeter. When he wasn't hunting, or *out on patrol*, as Lou referred to it, he just relaxed in his lair, under Lou's porch.

The wolf had been aware of Nina's presence long before she had seen him. When he reached a point on the bank directly opposite Nina, he sat back on his haunches and looked at her with his yellow eyes. The stance he took almost mirrored a sentinel. When Nina kept walking toward the stream, the wolf leaped across the water in a single bound, then sat back on his haunches, next to an "off limits" sign. Nina immediately understood the wolf's message, did an about-face, and returned to Luigi's cottage.

· · ·

THAT SAME DAY, Matteo and Popeye checked out of the motel they stayed at in Five Fingers, and drove around the lake to Kedqwick. This was the day they'd check out the logging road that Lou referred to as, "the back door" into Havre de Poisson.

The old logging road leading to the resort was on the south side of the lake, off Route 385, near mile marker 221.

They'd practically driven the full length of the northern side of the lake and were coming up the south side when Matteo, turned to Popeye. "What was the number on that mile marker we just passed?"

"It was somewhere in the one seventies. We got a-ways to go; we gotta go through some village called 'Knick-Knack,' or something."

"Nictau."

"Yeah, whatever."

"When we get there, keep your eyes open for a place to eat."

"I thought you said you wanted to see this friggin' logging road and then fly back to Boston?"

"I did."

Popeye shook his head. "Then why the hell are we stopping to eat? We can eat at the friggin' airport."

"We're coming up on another mile marker," Matteo said.

"Yeah, so, how about slowing down, so I can get a look at it."

Matteo ignored Popeye's comment. "We'll get something to go."

As they passed the marker, Popeye said, "This one's number 173, we got just under fifty to go."

"Keep your eyes open for a takeout place."

Popeye stared out the passenger side window mumbling,

"Whoop-dee-friggin'-do, we're gonna have a friggin' picnic in the friggin' woods."

Matteo heard the comment and responded. "We'll eat in the freaking car, okay? I just wanna go up that logging road, look around and then we'll head over to the airport."

Matteo and Popeye had been together on this trip longer than they'd ever been in each other's company before. They'd been getting along, but they each had their individual quirks and were used to running their own show. They respected each other, but, they were beginning to get on each other's nerves.

"I ain't running around in the friggin' woods."

"All we're gonna do is look *around* a little; that's *all* we're gonna do."

"Yeah, well I ain't playing no friggin' Davy Crockett walking around in the friggin' woods."

"What's s'matter?"

"Ahh, you coulda said something before we left. I ain't got the right shoes on for this *shit.*"

Matteo took his eyes off the road and glanced over at the fancy Italian leather shoes Popeye had on.

"Hey, it ain't muddy; it'll be fine!"

Chapter Twenty-Eight

As Koby continued on her trek to the feeder ponds, the once level trail had become a steady uphill climb. Eventually, the damp fog dissipated, and her field of vision returned to normal. As soon as they crested a barren rock ledge, the first of the feeder ponds came into view.

That's interesting, she thought, *when I heard the word 'pond,' I expected they'd be small. This is a good-sized body of water, maybe four, even close to five acres.*

Lou stood silently at the edge of the pond, eyes scanning the shoreline.

"Are the other ponds like this one?"

"No, they're not as large."

Koby could tell by the rocky shoreline that the pond had most likely been created when the glaciers covering most of North America had receded in the Holocene period.

"Lou, how deep is this one?"

"In the middle? Maybe ninety feet."

"Do the upper ponds feed into this one?"

"Yes."

Koby wiggled out of her backpack, took out a few plastic vials, labeled them as "Pond 1," and knelt down at the water's edge. As she reached into the water, there was a swirl not more than a few feet from her hand.

"Lou, what variety of fish are in the ponds?"

"Trout, rainbow smelt, that's all."

"Do many people come here to fish?"

"We come here at night."

"At night . . . why at night?"

"This is where we fish . . . like our ancestors."

It wasn't until Koby walked around to the far side of the pond that she saw the birchbark canoes. Torches ladened with soot and traditional long fishing spears the Abenaki had used for generations were laying inside them. She kept silent.

The water in the first pond was relatively clear to the eye, but rocks along the water's edge had a growth of algae. The water in the second pond appeared cloudy. The third pond was totally covered in what appeared to be green scum.

Once Koby had collected samples from all three ponds, she donned her backpack, took a deep breath, and looked at Lou. "Okay, let's head back."

"It'll be easier going back."

"No kidding, it's all downhill."

"No, we'll take the road back."

"Wait! What? There's a *road* that comes up here?"

"Yes, it's one of the new fire access roads. It's much easier for my people to come here at night now."

Koby looked at Lou in total disbelief. "Then *why* didn't we take the road up here?"

"It comes from the village, not Moose Cove."

"Lou, I don't need to go to the village, I need to get back to Moose Cove."

Lou had a funny smile on his face. "When we return to the village, we'll borrow an ATV. Come this way. The road is right here. Watch the poison ivy."

Not even thirty yards east of the ponds, just before the tree line, was a twenty-foot-wide fire lane. As Koby watched Lou disappear into the brush, she wondered: *Was I set up?*

It was close to mid afternoon when Matteo and Popeye turned onto the old logging road that served as a back door for Havre de Poisson. There were a few spots where Matteo had to let up on the gas, but for the most part, the SUV rode high enough, that it navigated the dips and rocks with ease.

Popeye looked out the side window. "So, we're gonna follow this to the end, then what?"

"We'll take a look around, get something to eat, and head over to the airport."

When they reached the wooden gate, Matteo threw the SUV into park, and got out. "Okay, let's see what's on the other side of this gate. It looks pretty dry; we'll stay on the road. Let's go."

Popeye looked at the condition of the road. *It does look dry, I guess I won't mess up my shoes.* With that he grabbed his coffee and stepped out.

The two walked beyond the gate until the path turned left toward the lodge area. When Matteo saw the roofs of buildings through the trees, he whispered, "Stay here, I'm gonna take a walk and see if I can get a better look."

"Go ahead, 'cause I ain't traipsing around in the friggin' woods."

After a few minutes, Matteo returned. "Okay I got an idea what this place looks like, let's go." Popeye suddenly leaned to the right to get a look behind Matteo who said, "Is someone behind me?"

"Just a big friggin' dog."

"*Screw* the dog. Let's go."

With that, Matteo began walking back down the road, but Popeye didn't move. Like Hector, Popeye was a creature of habit. He sensed the threat, reached into his pocket and took out his garrote. When the animal didn't move, Popeye said, "Come here, boy. Come on, you wanna come to Poppa?"

Hector sat back on his haunches; yellow eyes locked on Popeye. Popeye's eyes locked on his target. The two killers stared at one another; neither moved. Their primal killer instincts were in control.

From a distance Matteo yelled, "Hey, Popeye! Let's go man, we gotta stop off in Five Fingers before we head over to the airport."

Slowly Popeye began to back away. When he sensed the animal wouldn't charge, he turned and headed down the road. When he caught up with Matteo, he asked, "Did you get a whiff of smoke in the air?"

"Yeah."

"Be a shame if this place burned down, wouldn't it?"

Matteo had a smirk on his face. "Yeah, wouldn't it."

Popeye turned to take one last look back. The lone sentinel with yellow eyes was still watching.

THAT SAME AFTERNOON, when Lou returned from Moose Cove, he hung around the dock putting a few things away. He thrived on being organized. His grandfather had drilled into him that everything had a place, and everything needed to be *in* its place. Although he'd never said it, he agreed with Grey Elk's philosophy; being organized and being on top of things was worth the aggravation.

Just as he finished rearranging his gear inside the boathouse, he heard a craft coming in at full throttle.

"Lou! Lou! Are you in there?"

Lou stepped out of the boathouse, waved, and walked over to where the boat was coming in. The men seemed anxious about something.

"Lou, there's a fire out there somewhere. Take a look to the west! You can really smell it out on the water." Lou turned to see a thick plume of white smoke rising up a few miles off in the distance.

"Not to worry, fellas, we're doing a controlled burn today. The Forest Service gave us the greenlight." He saw the men's faces relax a little.

"We thought the whole place might be going up. It'd be a damn shame if what those wildfires did in California happened here."

"Nah, there's plenty of tanker trucks standing by, and the weather people said the conditions would be acceptable for a coordinated burn today."

"Okay, we were just concerned."

"Thanks, fellas. Now, tell me, what kind of luck did you have today?"

"We got a few hits around noon, nothing since then."

"How were you fishing?"

"We were trolling. We had three colors of lead core out."

"Are you interested in hauling in a lunker, with some light tackle?"

"Yeah."

"Well, hold on a minute and I'll give you a couple of light tackle rods."

The sportsman, who was midship, wrapped a line around a cleat to prevent the boat from drifting away from the dock. Within less than half a minute Lou emerged from the boat house. "Here ya' go, guys. Now, head west and go down the lake until you come to a huge pine tree that's leaning out over the water. You'll see it on the right, maybe a good half mile down."

"I know the tree you're talking about."

"Okay, good. There's an underwater ledge that juts out about twenty feet from shore. The big ones wait down below for the fingerlings to come off that ledge. They'll come right up from the depths any time of day to feed. Throw the hook so you're about forty feet offshore, then cast onto that ledge and slowly reel the smelt toward you. Hell, if it ain't beneath you, you can even hook the smelt under the dorsal fin and use a damn bobber."

"We'll give that area a try."

"I've got some cork bobbers, if you wanna try that."

"Thanks, but there ain't a fisherman alive that doesn't have a bobber hidden somewhere in the bottom of the tackle box."

"Okay, go get 'em."

Chapter Twenty-Nine

Ten years ago, Lou had an altercation with a different member of the Turnbridge clan. One of their family had repeatedly trespassed onto Abenaki land and killed a number of deer, just for their antlers.

It took a while for Lou and his cousin, Jake, to determine who the poacher was. It also took them and a number of warriors from the village of Grey Elk to capture him and bring him to justice.

A young, impressionable Oswald Turnbridge had been present that day long ago, and had witnessed his older cousin, Arthur Turnbridge, stumble onto their porch, soaked in blood, and riddled with arrows. Shortly afterward, the Canadian Mounties had converged, in force, upon the Turnbridge compound. A trail of his blood led the Mounties straight to Arthur where his female cousins were caring for him. He had been taken into custody and subsequently charged, and convicted, of murder.

That harrowing day back then was the last time twelve-year-old Oswald ever saw his cousin. Testimony given at the trial of Arthur Turnbridge resulted in the Canadian Centre for Child Protection stepping in and placing every Turnbridge youngster under the age of fourteen into a foster home. Since that day, Oswald had hated the Abenaki and blamed Lou Gault for separating him from his parents.

So, to say Oswald Turnbridge wasn't a fan of the Abenaki, was an understatement.

The Turnbridges were among the earliest Europeans to settle in the area. Since colonial times, they'd kept to themselves and had somehow found a way to live off the land. Unfortunately, as a result of generation after generation of mating with close blood-relatives, their individual genetic diversity was low. The abnormalities and harmful recessive traits that now existed among the Turnbridge clan were numerous. With few exceptions, the Turnbridge children, who occasionally attended school, were relegated to remedial programs.

Whether it was a quirk, or divine intervention, Oswald was an exception, he was born with fewer recessive traits than most of the Turnbridge children in his generation. Although he'd never be the sharpest knife in *any* draw, he did have an IQ significantly higher than most other Turnbridges. In fact, Oswald was actually the first of the Turnbridge children, who had been placed in foster homes, to graduate from high school. When he turned eighteen, and was free to leave, he returned to live with his birth family, at the Turnbridge compound.

It was because Oswald had spent so many years in a foster home that he was comfortable venturing out from his family's compound and walking the streets of Five Fingers.

That said, he had no outside friends and was shunned whenever he frequented the local watering hole in town.

Like many Turnbridges, Oswald had a large physique and powerful arms from working on the farm. The locals had always mocked him whenever he came into the bar, but after one fool had picked a fight with him, and had his jaw broken, the others knew well enough to leave him alone.

AFTER TALKING WITH OSWALD, Matteo knew the Turnbridge Clan lived somewhere off Route 17, south of the community known as Five Fingers. Exactly where, he wasn't sure, but he'd find out.

There wasn't much in Five Fingers except the watering hole, a small diner, and a scattering of houses.

"Matteo, how're we gonna find out where this puke lives?" Popeye asked.

"We're gonna ask around."

"Ask! Ask *who?* What the hell are ya' gonna do, knock on doors?"

"There's a diner up ahead, remember? Someone *there* will know."

"Five Fingers ain't a real town," Popeye shot back.

Just as they were approaching the diner, a pickup coming from the opposite direction, pulled into the parking lot. Matteo pulled in right beside him.

"Popeye, roll down the window." As soon as the driver in the pickup got out, Matteo called to him, "Hey, fella!"

"What?"

"Can ya' tell me how to get to the Turnbridge place?"

"What the hell do you wanna go *there* for?"

"You know where they live?"

"Yeah, but I'd stay the hell away from there, if I was you."

"Where do they live?" he repeated

"You know that place is a *shithole*, right?"

Popeye had heard enough; he was frustrated they couldn't get a straight answer. But when he unbuckled his seatbelt, Matteo put a hand on his thigh, signaling for him to stop.

After letting out a deep sigh, Popeye said, "Look, can ya' just help us out here. All we're askin' is where they live."

The local pointed in the direction he had come from. "Go down about two miles. There's a dirt road on the right. It's the only one you'll come to. Turn there, and you'll find them . . . or smell 'em first."

"Thanks, much obliged."

As Popeye rolled up the window, Matteo backed out of the parking lot. The first dirt road they came to was overgrown with grassy weeds and certainly didn't look like it'd had much wear.

"You sure this is the right friggin' place?" Popeye asked, as Matteo turned onto the road.

"We'll find out."

It was late afternoon. The sun was low in the sky, and trees along the sides of the road blocked out most of the sunlight.

After traveling close to half a mile, they came around a bend and saw someone walking up the road.

Popeye squinted. "Maybe this is him." Matteo shrugged his shoulders, came to a stop, and waited. As the figure came closer, Popeye thought, *This ain't him, this guy's too old.*

Matteo opened the driver's side window. "Hi there. Could you tell me where I might find Oswald Turnbridge?"

"You the law?"

"I am not." Matteo laughed low.

"If you ain't the law, then why you here?"

"I've come to talk with Oswald Turnbridge."

"Whatcha wanna talk to him 'bout"

Who's this guy, the friggin' gatekeeper? Popeye thought.

"Oswald and I met the other day, I told him I might have some work for him, that's all." The old man stooped down and peered inside the SUV at Popeye.

"Is *he* the law?"

Matteo shook his head. "No, he is not."

"Well, if you wanna talk with him, you best git yerself down to the barn. Last I seen of him, he was busy sloppin' hogs."

"I'll do that."

THE BARN WAS a good quarter mile further down the road. When they pulled into the yard, Matteo hit the horn once before turning off the SUV.

"All right Popeye, let's go see if we can find our boy." As soon as they opened the doors to the SUV, the stench from the pigsty hit their senses like a Mack truck.

Popeye emerged from the vehicle bent over with dry heaves and could barely whisper, "What the *frig*! This place stinks! Holy *shit*, how the hell can anybody stand this?"

Matteo placed a handkerchief over his mouth and nose, but it barely made a difference. Not long after, Oswald and two others emerged from the barn, pitchforks in hand. They came to see who the intruders were.

Matteo recognized Oswald immediately. "Oswald! It's Matteo. I'd like to talk with you about some work."

One of the men standing beside Oswald said, "We ain't hiring nobody today mister, so *git.*"

"He ain't talking to you," Oswald dismissed the other Turnbridge. "He's talking to *me.* So, *you* git!" The other Turnbridge looked sullen.

"Oswald is there someplace we could go talk in private?"

"Here's good a place as any. They'll leave us be."

"All right, let's do it inside my vehicle."

Popeye was back in the SUV in a flash, thankful to have the vehicle's door between himself and the stench. Oswald opened the rear door on the right side and got in. When Matteo got in, he turned sideways in the front seat and faced the rear.

"Oswald, I have a job I'd like you to handle for us."

"I'm listening."

"You can read and write, yes?"

"I ain't no fool . . . 'course I can."

Matteo handed him the article about the European Tench that had appeared in the newspaper. "Take a few minutes and read this."

Oswald took his time reading the article, then looked up. "So?"

"I got something I'd like you do with these fish."

Chapter Thirty

When the Smyth Air Charter taxied down the lake and lifted off for Grand Falls, the man sitting beside Nina Cataldo was Luigi Secondo. By the time their connecting Delta flight touched down in Boston, the man sitting next to Nina had morphed back into Santino Varni.

The shift from one persona to the other had been gradual, but even as the man slept, Nina sensed the changes taking place in the seat beside her.

The marked difference between the two identities was constantly running through her mind; sleep had eluded her for the entire flight. Finally accepting his split personality, she wondered which persona was more attractive, which man she most wanted to be with.

When the plane arrived at the gate, they exited, walked into the terminal, and Nina settled into her normal world again. As they went through customs, she watched the person she knew so well present a passport with the name

"Santino Varni" on it.

He's himself, again, Nina thought. *How does this happen?*

BACK IN CENTRAL NEW BRUNSWICK, it was business as usual as the week came to an end. But for the next two weeks, the lodge would shut down for the annual midsummer break. The anticipation among the year-round residents of Havre de Poisson had risen to a peak.

By late July, the lake's water temperature traditionally rose to the point that forced the fish to go deeper and fishing was slow. The vacancy rate during the final week of July and first week of August had always been high. Well over a decade earlier, Lou had decided to take a mid-season break during those weeks and shut down the camp.

Now that Jake had a family, and Havre de Poisson was once again his home, he also took those weeks as vacation.

There was a time when Lou had considered staying open and welcoming families during those two weeks. But once Kate pointed out the vast differences in that business model, and how hard the change-over effort would be, he "kicked that can to the curb."

As the guests from the previous week boarded planes and headed out, a small group sat on a grassy knoll watching the exodus. Jake, his daughter, Gigi; Lou's twins, Ayleen and Tyrone, and Hector waited patiently until each plane taxied out to the center of the lake. Then, Ayleen would whisper, "Now, Uncle Jake?"

Jake would reply, "On the count of three." When he reached three, he and his "charges" would wave and softly sing the chorus of *Happy Trails to You.*

Like his cousin, Jake had been orphaned at the age of

four; he and Lou were raised by their paternal grandfather, Grey Elk. Growing up together, the cousins were inseparable. Both became masterful trackers, wise in the ways of the forest and of the Abenaki. In their late teens, the Royal Canadian Mounted Police recruited them as auxiliary members, to assist in search and rescue missions. Then they both joined Canada's Joint Task Force Two commando unit. Now veterans, they shared the same values. Yet their personalities were quite opposite: Lou grew up to be the more stoic and serious of the two; Jake evolved into a fun-loving, free spirit.

When the last plane took off, the small group headed over to Rocky Point, an outcrop just west of the resort, and picnicked on burgers, dogs, and watermelon.

After twelve weeks of non-stop full occupancy, the residents at Havre de Poisson were taking a breather. For the next two weeks, life at the resort would be easy living. It would be all about family and the kids. Lou's cousin, Laughing Gull, and others, would come from the village with their own youngsters most days.

DURING THE MIDDLE WEEKEND, a flotilla of boats arrived from the village of Grey Elk filled with friends and family who were anxious to celebrate *Alnobaiwi,* the Abenaki way of life.

The celebration began by placing dried tobacco on drum skins, as an offering. Then Mother Earth was awakened by a few gentle beats on the drums. Once homage had been paid to her, it was non-stop games, laughter, food, and fellowship.

The celebration stretched well into the night, long after darkness had taken over the sky. When the dancing finally ended, and stories that needed to be told were told around the fire, those who had come made their way to the empty cottages for a restful sleep over.

For those two weeks, life at Havre de Poisson was peaceful; it was the way life should be.

On the same weekend the villagers traveled to Havre de Poisson to celebrate the Abenaki way of life, Oswald Turnbridge and his cousin traveled in a different direction. For the same few days, they camped on the banks of a tributary leading into the Upsalquitch River on the northern New Brunswick border, netting a strange fish, ones they were being paid to catch, but not release.

The following Monday, on the seventh floor of the Longshoremen's building, Matteo sat across the mahogany desk from Santino, patiently waiting for him to get off the phone with Nardo Lombardi.

Once Nardo had received the photo images Nina had forwarded to his phone, it was only a matter of hours before he was ready to sit down with Santino. But it was Varni who wasn't ready yet.

"Nardo, I can't see you today, perhaps tomorrow. Stay on the line, Nina will pick up; she'll set it up. Talk to her."

"I will. Thank you, Santino." Then with the push of a button, Varni hung up his desk phone.

"It sounds like Nardo is anxious to see you."

Santino nodded. "So, Matteo, what do you have to tell me?"

"I have a couple pieces of the puzzle in play."

Santino gestured for Matteo to continue.

"I've found a way to marginalize the friggin' fish in his lake. It won't happen overnight, but I have someone working on it as we speak. In the meantime, we can spread a few rumors about his lake which will begin to weaken his reputation."

"Do we know this person?"

"*I* do; you don't."

"Can we trust him?"

"We'll see."

"Keep an eye on him. What else?"

"Popeye and I visited that logging road. He's going back up soon. He'll make sure things don't run as smooth as usual."

"What else?"

"I was thinking of putting him in *your* cottage."

Santino shrugged his shoulders. "What else?"

"That's it for now."

"Are you aware they're doing controlled burns in the forest?"

Matteo smiled, "No."

"You didn't smell the smoke?"

"I did, but I figured it was coming from wood stoves."

"It would be a shame if a fire threatened the village across the lake and none of his guides, or housekeepers, showed up."

"Now, that *would* be unfortunate."

"Yes. Here's something else for you to play with: He's insured through Brunswick Mutual Casualty."

Chapter Thirty-One

The controlled burns taking place in the forest had been underway throughout Lou's two-week shutdown. Not only had the potential threat to the village been reduced, but wildlife would benefit from the tender new growth that would occur in the coming spring.

It wasn't long after Koby submitted her collected water samples to the labs when results came back. The Abenaki were dealing with two forms of algae in the feeder ponds: green and red.

The smallest pond had a well-established colony of green algae common in stagnant or slow-moving water which usually appeared during early to mid-summer months. Although this type of algae might look unsightly, it was actually important to the environment.

A different form of algae known as string algae, red in color, was found in each of the other two ponds. The two lower ponds weren't quite as lentic, or still, as the smaller, upper pond, therefore, the red string algae colonies weren't as well established as the green algae. Even so, if left untreated, the red algae presented a risk to the aquatic ecosystem.

The water samples Koby had taken at Moose Cove came back completely devoid of any algae.

After meeting with the tribal council, she reported on how to safely eliminate the current bloom: first by treating it, then by finding, and eliminating the cause.

"Algae, like most plants, produces oxygen. However, when the bloom is as extensive as it is in these ponds," she said, "it has the potential of actually using up oxygen in the water and creating toxins. It's the toxins that are harmful to both humans and the environment."

Next, she planned on discovering the source. She made a second trip to the ponds, this time via the new fire lanes. As she had suspected, the culprit was agricultural run-off. And the farm most likely contaminating the stream beds that eventually flowed into the ponds were fields belonging to . . . the Turnbridge clan.

When Lou learned the source was the Turnbridge fields, he laughed. "There isn't a snowball's chance in hell of us influencing the Turnbridge clan to change their agricultural practices."

From the beginning, Lou had chosen to mitigate the situation independently. He designed a series of leaching beds and retention ponds along the perimeter of the Abenaki lands to cleanse the run-off water well before it entered the first pond. A deal was worked out and the income from the additional trees harvested, covered the cost.

. . .

Unlike most of the Turnbridges, Oswald Turnbridge had eventually earned the right to "make the walk" and receive a high school diploma. His academic success was largely due to the liberal philosophy of "no child left behind" that prevailed at the time. After hours of intense individual tutoring, he squeaked through the standardized testing required for graduation on his second attempt.

But Oswald's prowess was not in the classroom. Whatever success would come to him in life, would be in areas far beyond the world of letters. The lone exception to his anemic academic record was his stellar performance in gym class.

Even as a teenager, he had a powerful build; both the football and wrestling coaches desperately wanted him on their teams, but his grades repeatedly disqualified him from participating in any school sport.

Like many Turnbridges who had come before him, the things he seemed to enjoy most in life were in the out-doors. He was a natural when it came to hunting, fishing, and living off the land. He had courage and never shirked at doing his chores. And he was loyal. If he gave his word, he usually kept it, even though he was prone to distractions upon occasion.

Well North of Lou's resort, the two Turnbridge cousins spent the better part of a week fishing on a fairly large tributary leading into the Upsalquitch River.

The recent uproar over the presence of European Tench in New Brunswick waters came about when news of a few being caught in the Upsalquitch watershed had spread.

Since then, Oswald had scouted the area and selected a campsite on one of its tributaries. He wasn't sure how long it would take him to catch a sufficient number of this Tench fish, but however long it took, his next need was to keep the fish alive. He recalled reading how Scottish people used cages in the lochs to farm Atlantic Salmon and decided to build a cage of his own.

The first thing Oswald did was to pitch a two-person dome tent directly across from a gravel bar that had a deep pool on one side and a fast-running current on the other. Then, he sunk a 4 x 4-foot mesh cage into the deep pool in hopes of keeping alive anything they caught.

Oswald stood on the gravel bar, with a long-handled net. His reflexes were sharp, not many fish got by him.

When a light greenish-gold colored fish darted away from his net, he wasn't sure exactly what it was. But, once he did net it, the distinctive shape of the fins identified it as a Tench and he tossed it into the cage. In short order, the world the fish was in became small. She was trapped, her ability to travel forward came to an end.

On the third day, his cousin asked, "How many of these dang fish you wanna catch, Oswald? You ain't gonna try catch to 'em *all* are ya?"

"Hell, no."

"I don't know why anybody wants these fish in the first place. They ain't no damn good to eat. They's bony and they's got a muddy taste to 'em."

"Well, maybe we just ain't figured out how ya cook 'em. You ever thought 'bout that? No, 'course you ain't. You complain 'bout everything, you know that?"

As Oswald walked across the gravelly sandbar to count how many fish were in the cage, his cousin mumbled, "Ain't so."

He pulled the cage out of the water and counted the fish.

"I guess we got enough," he said. "We get any more and we ain't gonna have room enough to transport 'em."

The odd colored fish stood out among the slew of muted green fish Oswald had in the wire holding cage.

"Hey, Oswald, you got a different colored one in there."

"I knows."

"What kind is it? It ain't like them others."

Oswald knew if he didn't answer his cousin, he'd never let up. "It's a Tench."

"They kinda look like bass, Oswald, but they ain't bass, is they?"

"They ain't bass."

"You gonna keep that different color one, or let it go?"

"It's a Tench. I'm keeping it."

"Can we go home now?"

"Yeah, but I need a hand bringing these fish over to the pickup. We gotta get 'em in the coolers first."

Oswald had thought about releasing the odd colored fish, but when he lifted the heavy cage out of the water and began emptying the contents into the coolers, the greenish-gold fish slid out with the others.

TWO DAYS after Santino had returned to Boston, Nardo Lombardi sat in Santino's office, anxious to go over the real estate proposal he'd pulled together. Nardo was pleased with his own efforts, yet, as he watched Santino review the prepared proposal, he fidgeted in his seat.

Santino looked at him. "You're comfortable with this?" Nardo cleared his throat before answering.

"Yes, Yes, I am."

When Santino didn't say anything further, Nardo said,

"I'd start off by extending an offer at the low end of the range I've indicated." Santino nodded and continued leafing through Nardo's proposal.

"This is good. It's thorough. It's what I expected," Santino finally said.

Nardo inhaled deeply, relaxed a little, and nodded. Then, unexpectedly, Santino shot him a question. "What's this reference to 'first nations' land?

"Well, the whole area seems to be designated as ancestral Abenaki land."

"Is that a problem?"

"It shouldn't be. I couldn't find any historical significance of that adding intrinsic value."

Santino sat back in his chair. "What about sentiment?"

"That doesn't change the actual commercial value of a property. All sentiment can do is drive a seller's *perceived* value of their property up beyond any true realistic market price. Sellers always want to get as much as they can."

When Santino didn't say anything, Nardo offered, "It's the *buyer*, not the seller, who determines true market price. It's what a buyer is willing to pay."

Santino mused over the proposal on his desk a few minutes longer. Finally, he looked up. "Let's go ahead with the plan B we talked about."

Nardo was expecting further questions on the purchase proposal. "What?"

"I want you to look around for a likely location. It needs to be prime and near this one. The lake needs to have trout and be large enough for float planes to land on it."

Nardo was dumbfounded. "Santino, I can find you real estate in the wilderness, but I'm no contractor."

Santino stood up, signaling the meeting was over. "I know that. Come back to me when you have something to discuss."

Nardo debated the pros and cons of attempting to further discuss the proposal he had pulled together for Santino about buying Lou out. When he saw a completely insincere smile on Santino's face, he thought better of it, and respectfully took his leave.

Chapter Thirty-Two

The start of what Lou referred to as his "second season" always began with the usual commotion. Float planes were lined up, jockeying for position at the docks. Guides were busy going back and forth transporting luggage from the docks to the cottages. Guests no sooner stepped foot inside their cottages than they were back on the docks anxious to get out on the water and wet a line. Through it all, Lou had the patience of Job.

No matter how chaotic things became, no matter how many questions people asked, Lou had a smile on his face, and made time for everyone. His posture and demeanor conveyed a sense of total calm. He went out of his way to greet every guest, making them feel welcome at the sportsmen's paradise so many referred to as *Mecca*.

As Lou walked up and down the docks, mingling among his guests, he was peppered with questions.

"Lou, there was a lot of smoke in the air at the far end of the valley. Are you aware of it?"

"Very much so. We're doing controlled burns this year."

Another said, "Lou, you've had a couple of real hot weeks. How far down are the fish?"

"The lakers should be at about eighty-five feet; the rainbows are hanging at sixty, no more than sixty-five."

"Any special time you want us off the water?"

"Nope, that's up to you. Just remember, Angelo closes the kitchen at 7 p.m."

JUST AS LOU turned around to walk back up to the lodge, a first-time guest approached him. "Lou, I'm gonna need to borrow some gear. Half of my stuff didn't make the connecting flight."

"Don't worry. I'll fix you up with whatever you need."

"Thanks. I brought my kid up with me. He's got a few food allergies and he's lactose intolerant. I hope the kitchen can work around that?"

"Did you mention that when you sent in your reservation?"

"Absolutely."

"Then you're all set. Angelo is aware." Lou was unflappable.

Still, no matter if a guest had a question or not, no one left the dock without hearing one essential safety message: Namely that Hector, while appearing to be fully domesticated, was *not*.

"He's a wild animal and needs to be given a wide berth," Lou said to each and every one of them.

Another first timer arriving was "Vincenzo Pierro." Nina Cataldo had called ahead letting them know that Vincenzo would be coming up and taking Luigi's cottage for the week.

When Lou approached Vincenzo, he couldn't help but notice the huge forearms on the man.

Lou stuck out a hand in welcome. "Hi, I'm Lou Gault. Welcome to Havre de Poisson."

Popeye grabbed Lou's hand and pumped it. "Yeah, thanks. I'm Vincenzo, Vincenzo Pierro. I'm glad to meet you; heard a lot about you."

Lou was no slouch when it came to strong handshakes, but when he felt the enormous strength in Popeye's callused hand, he was taken slightly aback. *Whatever this guy does for a living, it sure in hell isn't done sitting at a desk.*

"You're a friend of Luigi's, right?"

Popeye was completely aware that Santino Varni went by a different name at the camp and responded. "Yeah, yeah . . . well, sort of. Yeah, that's right."

"Well, any friend of Luigi's is always welcome here," Lou smiled. "Did you come up to do a little fishing?"

"Nah, I just came up for a little R&R."

"Well, make yourself at home and let me know if there's anything I can do to make your stay more enjoyable."

By the time Popeye arrived at the lodge for dinner, everyone else had been seated. The only table available was a table for two at the far end of the room. As soon as he pulled the chair out, Alessandra rushed over.

"Please, please, don't sit down yet. Let me join this table with another so you won't be dining alone." Popeye waved his hand dismissing her concerns.

"I'm fine."

"No, no please, let me do this."

But Popeye continued pulling the chair out, sat down, and placed the cloth napkin on his lap. "I'm fine," he said again.

"I'll arrange the tables differently tomorrow," Alessandra said apologetically. "This won't happen again."

Popeye waved his hand in a manner to convey he wasn't upset. But the situation only served to make Alessandra take extra measures in meeting the needs of her one "lone diner."

Later, when Popeye got up to leave, he stuffed a few packages of sugar in his pocket.

THE FOLLOWING MORNING, not just one boat, but *two* of them barely made it twenty feet from the dock when their engines died. No matter how many times the bulb on the gas line was squeezed or the electric start button was pushed, the boats were dead in the water.

It wasn't long before Lou heard distress calls: "Hey Lou, we need a hand here."

The guys in the second boat had already reached for the oars; one of them hollered, "Yeah, us, too!"

Lou ended up throwing a line to each of them and manually hauling them back to the dock before sending them off in different boats.

When his guests left the dock for their second time, Lou stood thinking, *At least the engine on Luigi's boat is finally getting some hours on it; the kids can go a day without their boat, too.*

Then, as Lou turned his back to the water, he heard someone shout: *"Woo-hoo!!"* The fellas in the second boat had no sooner left the dock and put a line out when they had a fish on. Satisfied his guests would now be fine, he turned to look at the failed engines.

All right, Lou thought, *let's see what's up with these kickers.*

The outboards were only 25 hp engines and Lou easily lifted them off the transom. After bringing each into the boathouse, he set them up on stands with the shaft of one immerged in a bucket of water.

As he removed the cowling, he thought, *This is odd, I haven't had a single issue with these Honda kickers, yet all of a sudden two of 'em decide to act up on the same day.*

As soon as Lou took the fuel pump apart and saw the filter he said, "Well, no wonder you wouldn't start, you little sucker, your filter's plugged up."

After cleaning the filter, Lou connected it to the fuel line and the engine started on the first try. It ran for about thirty seconds before it shut down again.

"Well, let's take another look at this; maybe something else is going on."

Lou checked for air in the lines, worked the air intake valve, everything looked fine. Finally, he pulled the fuel pump filter, it was clogged again.

"Must be something in the tank."

Sure enough, when Lou pointed a halogen light inside the gas tank, he saw a white granular residue on the bottom. "I'll be damned. Well, guess I'll need to pour this gas through a mesh strainer, clean out this can and start all over again."

It took more than a few rinses to eliminate whatever it was in the gas tank. The first thing he did after pulling the cowling off the second engine was to check the filter on the fuel pump. It too was clogged. As he unscrewed the cap on the second gas tank he thought, *Well, let's take a look-see at this one. Yup, same thing.*

• • •

THAT EVENING when Lou went over to pick up the twins at Jake's cottage, his cousin was sitting on the front porch. "How'd it go today, Cuz?"

"Got off to a rough start, but everything else went fine."

"What happened?"

"Ah, a couple of fuel filters clogged up, that's all. I had to throw a line to two boats and haul 'em back to the dock. First time that's ever happened."

"Whaddya think it was?"

"I don't know. Something got into the tanks, but I got 'em working again."

"So, how long were those guests sitting around?"

"Not long, I put one in Luigi's boat and the others went out in the boat the twins use."

"Lucky you had a couple of spare boats."

The tanks in both boats had something in them that got sucked up into the filters. I checked all the other boats when they came in, but they were clean. Really glad I figured it out. I'd hate to have somebody get stranded out on the lake."

Chapter Thirty-Three

The following morning, when Angelo walked into the kitchen, the first thing he noticed was a spiderweb crack in the huge plate glass window.

When Lou stopped at the lodge for a cup of coffee before heading down to the dock, Angelo motioned him into the kitchen and pointed toward the window.

"What?"

"Look at the window."

When Lou saw the crack in the glass, he walked into Angelo's kitchen to get a closer look. "Well, the bird that slammed into that window broke its neck. That's really thick glass. I'll give Brunswick Mutual a call to find out who they're using for glass repairs these days. Someone will have to come out and measure. In the meantime, I'll get a ladder and put some duct tape on it, just to be safe.

Lou exited the lodge through the back door just off the kitchen, so he could get a look at the window from the outside. He expected to see a dead bird laying on the ground.

When he didn't, he was surprised. *Something must've carried off whatever flew into that window, 'cause it sure in hell didn't get up and fly away on its own.*

As Lou stepped back to get a better look at the damage, he nearly twisted his ankle on a rock somewhat larger than a tennis ball lying on the ground. The area behind the lodge was basically a thick bed of pine needles. Lou looked at the rock, then up at the broken window, then back at the rock. He did this a couple of times, before dismissing it. *Naaah, that's just coincidental; it had to be a bird.*

A SHORT TIME LATER, when guests started streaming out of the lodge, anxious to be out on the lake fishing, box lunches in hand, Lou was down at the dock, waiting. Each boat had been set up with fresh bait and he'd wiped the dew off every seat cushion.

Within minutes, the morning stillness was shattered as twenty-three outboard motors all seemed to fire up at once. For a moment, the sound was almost akin to the start of the Indianapolis 500 Speedway as the boats all began moving out.

What happened next, caused Lou to wonder if he was re-living the movie "Groundhog Day" where events kept repeating themselves. The same two boats that had engine problems just yesterday morning were, again, sitting dead in the water not more than twenty feet from the dock.

"Hey, Lou, ya gotta give us a different boat!" one guy yelled out.

"Hold on, I'll get you a couple of new ones, fellas. I'm not sure what's going on with those two; they've been working fine all season. But that's *my* issue not yours."

. . .

ONCE THE FOUR anglers had changed boats and left the dock for a second time, Lou pulled both engines into the boathouse. Again, the issue was clogged fuel pump filters, once again there was a granular residue inside the gas cans.

It took about a half hour to unclog the filters, remount the outboards and clear out both gas cans. Next, Lou grabbed a roll of duct tape and an extension ladder and headed over to the backside of the lodge.

The lodge backed up to the woods. There wasn't anything behind it other than pine trees and a bed of pine needles. The reddish-brown needles had been accumulating back there for years, and covered the ground like a thick carpet.

As Lou braced the ladder up against the building, something in the corner of his eye grabbed his attention. A good-size area in the bed of needles had been disturbed, the rest of the bed was as smooth and as flat as a pancake. To someone without Lou's woodland tracking skills, the difference might have been written off as the work of a squirrel, but Hector had pretty much rid the area of the furry little rodents once he'd moved in.

Lou walked over and knelt down to examine the area. The disturbances were clearly not the work of a squirrel. Squirrels dug small round holes a little larger than the diameter of a silver dollar. The disturbances Lou saw were close to the size of his shoe. *Something a helluva lot bigger than a squirrel has been back here, messing around. No telling what it was looking for.* Lou stared at it a little longer, but, given the thickness of the bed, it was impossible to make sense of what that might have been.

. . .

THAT EVENING LOU again walked over to Angelo's cottage to have a cigar with the chef and Jake.

Lou lit a match and drew on his cigar. "Jake, remember how I told you about those two motors fouling up?"

"Yeah. How'd they work this morning?"

"Same damn thing happened."

Jake tapped the tip of his cigar on the edge of the ashtray. "Same two boats?"

"Yup."

"You probably didn't clean out the tanks well enough."

"*Bullshit*, those tanks were clean."

"Same two boats, you said?"

"Yeah."

"Which boats?"

"The first two."

"The ones right at the beginning of the dock?"

"Yeah, right next to the boat house."

Jake paused, thinking. "Did you buy the long shafts or short shafts on those kickers?"

"The long shafts, otherwise, I'd have to modify the transoms. Why?"

"It's kinda shallow where you dock those two. I was just wondering if the props might be kicking something up, but that wouldn't have anything to do with the fuel pump anyway."

"Nope, not one bit."

"Strange that it's only those two."

Lou took a puff on his cigar and turned to Angelo. "Chef, I duct taped the outside of that cracked window."

"I saw. What did the insurance company say?"

"I wasn't able to get through to them. I left a message. They'll call back."

"Did you find the bird that flew into it?"

"No, something got to it before I did."

"Probably Hector

"Hell no, he'd have to be damn hungry to eat something he didn't kill."

Jake changed the subject. "Hey Angelo, tell Lou what you said about Luigi's fiancée."

Angelo took a long draw on his cigar before saying anything. "All I said was she was a nice lady. I think it's good for him to settle down, take a wife."

"No, not *that*. You know what I'm talking about."

"Oh, *that*," Angelo laughed. "Ha, I think she must have wore him out the first night they were up here. He was so tired the next day we almost didn't take a walk."

Lou stayed quiet for a few minutes, tapping his cigar on the ashtray and thinking. "Angelo, what does Luigi do? Kate's on a mission to find out."

"*That*, I don't know." Angelo took a puff on his cigar. "It doesn't matter to *me* what a man does, as long as he's a good man. I like Luigi, he's a good man."

Lou snubbed out his cigar. "Well, tomorrow comes early for me. I'm gonna call it a night and hit the sack."

"Yeah, well, I'm right along with ya' Lou. They got me flying down to Fredericton tomorrow."

"Why the hell are you going all the way down there?"

"Ask Kate."

"Whaddya mean, 'ask Kate?'"

"She had me bring a package over to Grand Falls just before the shutdown. Now, she's got something else she's sending down to Mountie headquarters."

"I didn't think you flew down there anymore."

"I don't usually. The regular guy is on vacation. Kate's package is express delivery, the boss doesn't want it hanging around."

"Well, gentlemen, you're welcome to stay here as long as you like, but I'm gonna say, *buona notte!*" Angelo said, standing up.

"Yeah, us, too. Good night, Angelo."

As Lou and Jake headed across the clearing toward their cottages, they saw Hector roaming along the shoreline.

"Looks like someone pulled night patrol, eh, Lou?"

"Yeah, he makes the rounds a couple of times every night. I just keep praying no one runs into him on their way to the outhouses."

Chapter Thirty-Four

The following morning, Lou greeted the men staying in cottages one and two when they arrived at the docks near their boats.

"You fellas should be all set this morning."

"Let's hope so." His guest's tone of voice told Lou that he meant, *three strikes and you're out.*

Lou smiled. "Let 'em run a few minutes at the dock before you leave, just in case."

"Not a problem; we gotta get our gear squared away anyway," one said.

Both engines started right up and were purring like kittens until the bow line on boat two was untied. Then the engine conked out.

"Aww, come on! Not *again!*" Lou was beyond frustrated.

Moments later, the kicker in the other boat sputtered twice, coughed, and went down for the count. Lou winced when a man in the first boat muttered to his companion, "This is getting *way* too old for me."

Lou pursed his lips and let out a frustrated sigh. *I can't friggin' believe this.* "Damn, I can't figure this out," Lou said out loud. "I'm sorry, fellas. I'm gonna permanently move you guys into different boats. I've never had an issue like this before."

"Do these kickers have a lot of hours on them?"

"No, they've only had a few seasons; they're not that old. I'm not sure what's causing this, but it isn't the experience I want you fellas to have. So, I'm gonna adjust the rate you guys paid.

"We appreciate that, Lou," two of the men said at the same time.

"Well, I'm sorry about this."

"Aaaah, sometimes shit just happens, Lou."

"Yeah, well, I appreciate that, but not three days in a row, fellas. That's just plain wrong."

"Yeah, I heard the third time around was supposed to be a charm," another said. The man was joking, but Lou picked up a sarcastic tone in his voice.

NOT LONG AFTERWARDS, when everyone except Vincenzo Pierro was finally out on the water, Lou's cell phone rang. When he looked at the screen, the caller ID displayed Brunswick Mutual Casualty.

"Hello?"

A young, pleasant sounding female voice responded, "Mr. Gault?"

"This is he."

"We received your request for a call. What can we do for you, sir?"

"I wanted to know who you're referring policy holders to

for window replacements."

"Give me a moment, while I click over to a different screen." She was momentarily silent, then said: "Here we go. That would be, Noonan Glass."

"What's my deductible? I've got a crack in a big thermal plate glass picture window."

"I'll check."

A moment later, the young woman came back on line. "Mr. Gault, I'm not seeing an active policy for you."

"Look again. It's most likely under my business name. Check under Havre de Poisson."

After a slight pause the young lady came back again. "I'm sorry, sir, I'm not seeing *any* policies under that name, either. Oh, wait, here's one . . . but that policy was just cancelled."

Lou furrowed his brow and held the phone out at arm's length, anger beginning to build. "Whaddya mean *cancelled*? I didn't cancel anything. I've been doing business with you folks for *years*."

"It appears that you did, sir. The note in the remark's column says: *Closed at customer's request.*"

"That's absurd; I *never* told you to cancel my policy!"

"I'm looking at the text message you sent to us two days ago instructing us to cancel your policy."

The warrior spirit deep within Lou suddenly stirred. He took a deep breath before carefully choosing his words: "Look, I don't know what's going on, but I *never* sent you, or anybody else, a text cancelling *anything*. You've got me crisscrossed somehow with somebody else. So, just do whatever you need to do to reactivate my policy."

"I'll let Mr. Hendrix know that you'd like your policy rewritten."

"Tell me, what's the phone number you have that the text was sent from? Do you have that on your record?"

"I'm not seeing it."

"Well, that text was sent to you by somebody else, 'cause *I* sure as hell didn't send it."

He heard the woman take in a deep breath. When she didn't say anything, he asked, "Is there a claim form online?"

"There is." The woman's voice had changed from pleasant to icy cold.

"Good, I'll submit the claim when I get an estimate from Noonan Glass."

"How long ago did the damage occur."

"It happened sometime during the night."

"Last night?"

"Yes."

"Sir, I'm afraid we won't be able to process that claim. You haven't had any coverage with us for the past forty-eight hours."

Lou smirked before saying, "Well, you can tell Bud Hendrix that if he's got any questions about the claim, he can call me."

"Is there anything *else* I can help you with?" The curt tone of the woman's voice left little doubt she was ready to end the call.

Lou cleared his throat. "No, I think I've had enough help for one day. Thank you." After he hung up, Lou thought, *This is crazy. First a couple of motors are giving me trouble, now I'm getting hassled by my own insurance company. What the hell's happening?*

Chapter Thirty-Five

After the Turnbridge cousins filled their plastic coolers with water and transferred the fish from the holding cage, they began lugging the containers over to their pickup.

"Oswald, we gotta dump some of this water out."

"Can't."

"No, we *gotta* 'cause it's sloshing, an' it's heavy!"

"Don't be stupid; we need the water to keep the fish alive."

"Oswald, don't you go calling me stupid."

"Then stop bellyaching."

"How far we gotta carry these fish once we get back?"

"Just to the water."

"I ain't never been on Abenaki land 'fore."

"I ain't, neither."

"Well, how far is it to the water?"

"I don't know. I just told ya', I ain't never been there!"

"I gotta set my end down. I ain't got no damn handle to grip."

"The handles broke off. Just stop ye'r bellyaching."

"I ain't bellyaching, I'm just *saying*."

It took several trips before the two cousins had all the plastic coolers sitting in the back of the only pickup truck the Turnbridge clan owned.

It was a long drive back to Five Fingers, and Oswald had his challenges. The coolers were old, the covers weren't tight, the springs on the truck were long gone, and the road was in bad shape. Because of that, Oswald couldn't travel over 25 mph. If he did, far too much water sloshed out of the coolers. The center of the road seemed to be smoothest so he hugged the center line.

It didn't take long before he had a caravan of vehicles following behind him. Just about every one that passed him either gave him the finger, or a toot on the horn *along* with the finger. The cousins traveled in silence until the land of the Abenaki came into view.

"Oswald, you know they been cutting and hauling logs outta here."

"I know that; I ain't stupid."

"I betcha they's a road that goes to the water, Oswald.

"If we find one, we'll take it."

"Well, you just passed one."

"I saw it."

"Then why didn't ya *take* it?"

"It was a *fire* lane, stupid."

"I dun told you not to call me that!"

"Then stop whining . . . you ain't no baby."

"You know what, Oswald?"

"What?"

"I ain't never doing nothin' wit you agin."

After that, they traveled in silence for a while before Oswald pointed to the roadside. "Here's a road coming up."

"I see it."

As they approached the turn off, Oswald slowed down. "Look! Look at all them tire tracks. Now, this here one's a road."

After turning off the highway, they traveled quite a distance before Oswald saw what looked like a break in the tree line to his left. "Stay here, I'm just gonna pull over and go see how far we are from the water." Oswald's cousin bristled at being told what to do, but he stayed put.

As it turned out, Oswald had turned onto the fire lane that ran parallel to the first feeder pond. He hadn't walked more than thirty feet from the truck when he circled back to the vehicle and let down the tailgate.

"The water's just a little ways away. Come on outta the truck. We ain't got all day."

"I'm coming."

When Oswald pulled the first cooler toward him, his first thought was that it was a lot lighter than before. When he lifted the cover, the fish were still wet, but that was about the size of it. Most of the water had either been jarred out or seeped out from a crack in the side. The fish weren't moving much, if at all.

"Come on, we gotta move! We gotta get these damn fish in the water, 'fore they all die."

"Well, some of 'em is dead now," his cousin pointed out. "Why we carrying dead fish?"

"They ain't *all* dead."

"*Some* of 'em is."

Oswald, sighed. "Okay, put the damn thing down so's we kin throw out the dead ones." Close to a dozen fish ended up in the brush.

When they finally reached the pond, they waded a few feet out and tipped the cooler upside down. The greenish-gold specimen Oswald had netted was among the first batch of fish that made it into the upper pond. Her body was enlarged from the eggs, but days would pass before she was ready to spawn.

As soon as the fish hit the water, most of them sensed they'd found freedom, and scooted off. A small number floated on the surface, their gills opening and closing periodically, they'd been without sufficient water far too long. Now, they were dying.

"Gather up the ones floatin.' We ain't leaving 'em in the water."

"Why not? Whatcha gonna do with these dead ones?"

Oswald glared at his cousin. "Just put 'em in the cooler."

"They ain't no good for *eating*. Whatcha want 'em for?"

"I don't *want* 'em. I just don't wanna *leave* 'em floatin,' that's all. Come on, help me pick 'em up."

"Where ya' gonna put 'em?"

"We'll just leave 'em in the bushes; something will come along and eat 'em."

When Lou returned to his cottage, Kate immediately looked up from her laptop. "Hon, what would you like for lunch today?"

"I don't care." The curt reply was totally unlike him.

When he closed the door to the bathroom, he overheard his wife say: "Well, aren't *we* in a good mood."

He emerged a minute later. "I'm sorry Kate, I'm just frustrated."

"About what?"

"Those same two engines wouldn't start again today; it's the third time in as many days."

"Did you put the men in other boats, like you did before?"

"Yeah."

"Well, then it's not such a big deal to be worrying yourself about now, is it?"

"That's not the only thing, Kate. Some bird hit the huge plate glass window in the kitchen and cracked it."

"So, call Brunswick Mutual."

"I did. They told me I cancelled our policy."

"Why would they say that?"

"Because they say I sent them a text canceling the policy."

"Did you?"

"Of course not!"

"Then it's just a mistake, they'll fix it."

"Well, they better, or Bud Hendrix is gonna get a piece of my mind."

"Lou, don't go getting yourself all riled up, somebody made a mistake."

Lou shook his head, "Everything's been running smoothly all season, not one hitch, then all of a sudden, boom! I have three issues to deal with."

Kate tilted her head. "*Three* issues?"

"Yeah, the two kickers, the broken glass, and now my insurance company is giving me a hassle."

"Well, everything happens in threes."

Lou looked at his wife. "What?"

"I said, 'Everything happens in threes.' It's an old saying."

"I've never heard that before. Is that another one of your silly Irish beliefs, like the banshee story?"

Kate had listened to enough. "Lou, go take a nice shower, you'll feel better." He was about to say something else when he rubbed his hand across the back of his neck and felt the tenseness in his muscles.

"I just might do that."

"Good. Take a fresh towel in with you, there's none on the rack, I'm doing a wash."

No sooner did Kate hear Lou begin to draw the water than his cell phone rang. At first, she thought about letting it just go to voicemail, but then she noticed who the caller was on the display.

"Hello?"

"Hi, this is Bud Hendrix, Brunswick Mutual. I was hoping to speak with Lou. Is he available?"

"Oh, hi Bud, this is Kate; he just stepped into the shower. Can I help you?"

"I don't know Kate, but let's try. Lou sent us a text a couple of days ago telling us to cancel his policies. Now, he says it wasn't him. Today, he told one of my staff members that he's going to submit a claim for a window, but technically, he's not covered."

"He mentioned that to me. Do you still have the original text cancelling the policy?"

"Ya, I'm looking right at it."

"Somewhere on that text is the number of the phone it came from. What's the number?"

"Ahhhhh, let me see. Okay, I see it."

"Read me the number."

When Bud read the number, Kate said, "That's not Lou's

phone number, Bud. That's not even a Canadian area code. I'm online now; let's see where that area code is located." Kate clicked over to Goggle and keyed in the area code. "That's the area code for Tulsa, Oklahoma."

"Where?"

"The area code for the phone that sent you that text is for Tulsa, Oklahoma. Lou's phone number has the 506 New Brunswick area code."

"Does he have another phone?"

"No, he only has the one. Bud, he didn't send that text to you."

Bud took a long pause. "Well, someone sent this text and signed it 'Lou Gault.'"

"Hold on, let me get into another account. Maybe I can find out who that number belongs to." Kate was already working behind the RMCP system's firewall when Bud called, and clicked on a phone tracking app. When she keyed in the number, nothing came back.

"Bud, the number's not showing up in the public listing. All it's telling me is that the carrier is Amazon. There's a tool behind the Mountie's firewall I can use to trace it through to the carrier, but it'll take a while."

Bud took a breath and paused before responding. "Well, tell Lou not to worry then, and to send that claim in. I'll let Brunswick Mutual know *we* made the error. I'll make sure the policies he had in place are reinstated."

"Thanks Bud. I'm sure he'll be glad to hear that."

"Oh, and tell him I need a diagram of those new fire access roads he's putting in over at the Abenaki village. Once I have those in hand, I should be able to work a slight discount on the village policies."

"I'll let him know that Bud."

When Lou came out of his shower, he called out. "Kate was that my phone I heard ringing earlier?"

"Yes, Bud Hendrix called."

"I hope the hell you gave him a piece of my mind?"

"We got it all straightened out, everything's fixed."

Lou thought about that for a moment. *Hmmm, I wonder if she knows anything about fixing outboard motors?*

Chapter Thirty-Six

Late that afternoon, Lou was coming out of the lodge just as Jake was coming up the steps juggling more than a few cases of eggs. "Hey, Lou, hold the door for me, will you?"

"Sure thing, Cuz."

As Jake entered the lodge he hollered back, "Hey, how'd you make out with those two motors this morning?"

"You really wanna know?"

Heading toward the kitchen, Jake shouted over his shoulder, "Yeah, but wait a second, I gotta put these eggs down. I'll be right out."

Lou rested both hands on the deck's railing and scanned the lake waiting for his cousin's return. *In spite of a few hassles, it's been a perfect day weather-wise,* he thought. Off to the West, the sky was aglow with crimson reds, fiery oranges, and brilliant yellows. *Well,* Lou mused, *looks like tomorrow will be another perfect day.*

Finally, Jake came out of the lodge and walked over to Lou. "Don't tell me you had problems, again."

"At least it happened while they were still sitting at the dock."

"Same two boats?"

"Yeah."

"Three days in a row, same two boats?"

"Yeah."

"All the other kickers are working fine?"

"Yeah."

"What's that tell ya?"

"Someone's messing with me."

"That's what *I'm* thinking."

"Who?"

"Doesn't matter, long as you catch 'em."

Lou snorted. "You're right."

"Exactly. So, tonight, we'll keep a set of eyes on the boats, and we'll catch the bastard."

"Jake, I am not pulling an all-nighter. I'll put a trail camera down there."

"Do that if you like, but I've got a better idea."

"What?"

"We'll use Hector. Hell, he makes the rounds every night anyway."

"He won't stay by the boats; he roams all over."

"Not if we *tie* him to the boathouse."

"Shit, we can't do that; he'll go nuts if someone he doesn't know comes around the boats late at night."

"Isn't that the point?"

"Jake, he's a *wolf*, not a *guard* dog!"

"So, you put him on a short leash. All he has to do is scare the shit out of the bastard that's doing this. Then, in the morning, all you have to do is check butts. The first one who's got a brown stain on their back side is your man."

Lou shook his head and laughed. "Jake, you are one crazy son-of-a-bitch."

"So, are you game for this?"

"Totally."

LATER THAT EVENING, after the guests had finished supper and dishes were cleared, Alessandra began the nightly task of setting up for breakfast. When she came to the table Vincenzo used, she noticed the sugar bowl was empty . . . again.

As she refilled the bowl, she thought, *Someone has a real sweet tooth.*

WHEN KATE LEARNED Hector was going to be tied up for the night, she wasn't pleased. She insisted that Lou at least put a blanket on the floor of the boat house, for Hector to sleep on. But Lou pushed back.

"Kate, he sleeps on the ground under the porch. He doesn't need a blanket."

"I don't care. You're interrupting his normal pattern and sleep cycle."

Lou knew it was fruitless to argue with Kate once she had her mind set. With everything else going on, the last thing he needed was for Kate to get her "Irish up."

ELSEWHERE, sitting in his cottage, Vincenzo, known to many as merely Popeye, sat patiently waiting for the year-round residents to settle in for the night. Earlier, well before he planned to head down to the docks, he had called the night editor of the Brunswick News. They had spoken at length and he had given him a convincing story about the unsatisfactory conditions existing at Havre de Poisson.

Then, once he sensed everyone had settled in for the night, he exited his cottage via a rear window. The first thing he did was sneak around to the coop where Angelo kept the hens. Rather than make a hole in the enclosure, he merely unhooked the front latch and propped open the door. The birds were an integral part of the resort's supply chain, providing not only eggs, but on occasion, a source of protein for meals. Their loss would add to the increasingly upsetting atmosphere. Vincenzo scattered feed on the ground near the gate, hoping to entice the birds to leave and wander into the woods, where they'd fall prey to the predators that roamed the forest.

Next, he slunk from shadow to shadow and entered the maintenance shed where Alessandra's washing machines were located. She depended upon the machines every weekend to achieve a quick change-over. Vincenzo sabotaged them by slicing into the belts just enough so they would fail the next time the machines were used. Then, he entered the back door of the lodge, and tripped the breaker for the walk-in freezer hoping everything inside would be defrosted by morning.

Finally, he went around to the lodge; standing on tables, he unscrewed every other light bulb in the dining room's ceiling fixtures halfway. He backed them off just enough so none of them would work in the morning. Before he left the lodge, he went into the kitchen and cracked open the door to the walk-in freezer.

When he left the lodge, he headed back to Luigi's cottage.

He wasn't done for the night, but needed to make a phone call.

First thing he did, after entering the cottage, was pour himself a double Scotch. Then, sitting down, he kicked off his fancy Italian leather shoes and made a phone call to Smyth Air to request a pickup the following evening at six p.m.

It was well after 2 a.m. when Vincenzo slipped his shoes back on and slowly opened the door to his cottage, intending to head down to the docks. His knife in one pocket, the burner phone Nina had given him and a few sugar packets in another.

Although high in the night sky, the waning moon was still bright. Even in this remote location Vincenzo was cautious and would stay in the shadows as much as possible. He waited on the cottage steps until his eyes became accustomed to the night. Then, he quietly made his way down toward the dock area, as he had the previous three nights.

Meanwhile, Hector was stretched out at "his post" in the boathouse, not in the best of moods. The wolf had always been a free spirit and wasn't at all keen about being tied up. He was accustomed to roaming the grounds at will; being restrained by a leash was foreign to him. Now, a wolf's hearing far exceeds that of its domestic cousin, the dog. Wolves are capable of hearing sounds at least six miles away in the forest, and as far as ten miles away across open ground.

When Hector heard the door to the cottage open in the distance, his head raised up, instantly he was alert to the sound he'd heard. The doorway to the boat house was open; Hector was laying just inside the threshold. The way the shadows played, he was nearly invisible to the human eye.

As Vincenzo approached, the tail of a large fish disturbed the surface of the water. The noise brought him to an abrupt halt and he froze to listen. Vincenzo wasn't the jittery type, but he had learned to err on the side of caution; it was a trait that kept him alive. Several moments passed before Vincenzo was comfortable enough to move forward again.

In addition to excellent hearing, wolves have superior night vision. Hector's keen eyesight had spotted Vincenzo's shadowy silhouette as soon as it left the cottage. Now, as the figure approached, the wolf squinted and locked eyes onto the human coming toward him, studying every movement.

As soon as Vincenzo put one foot on the dock, all hell broke loose. Hector lunged out of the boat house, snarling and snapping his jaws wildly. The only thing that protected Vincenzo from certain death was the short leash Lou had used on the wolf.

Vincenzo reacted fast, but not fast enough. The wolf had latched onto the tips of Vincenzo's right ring finger and pinky. Had the leash been a little longer and the wolf's jaws closed around Vincenzo's entire hand, the beast would have easily pulled him closer, and the battle would have ended quickly.

But now, Vincenzo instinctively pulled back in horror, wrenching his bloody hand free. But the wolf continued snarling and lunging forward, his jaws snapping wildly. On the last lunge, Hector grabbed hold of the intruder's jacket, barely missing any human body parts, and wouldn't let go.

Vincenzo's bravado had vanished. His mind raced wildly. For once, the mean-spirited killer had no control over the situation; his usual cruel character, cockiness, and nasty spirit gave way to complete fear. For the first time in his life, Popeye was scared . . . for his own life.

By now, Hector was in a frenzy, froth spewed from his mouth. He shook his head back and forth violently tearing the lower section of Vincenzo's jacket to shreds. But the wolf wanted more than just a jacket and he kept coming.

The vicious, guttural snarls of the wolf filled Vincenzo's ears and drowned out the heavy drumming inside his head. Hector was on his hind legs, clawing the air with his front legs, pulling on the leash, trying to reach his opponent. Saliva flew in every direction as the wolf frantically pulled against the constraint. If the rope snapped, Vincenzo's throat would be torn apart in a matter of seconds, and his death would occur instantly.

Escape was the only thought running through Vincenzo's mind; everything else was a blur. As the beast's jaws continued shredding his jacket, the cell phone in his pocket, along with the sugar packets, landed on the sandy shoreline.

Hector backed off when he heard the phone drop. When he did, the twist in the restraint holding him unraveled; the wolf gained an extra foot of freedom. The next time Hector jumped at Vincenzo, the man barely back-peddled far enough to avoid the jaws of death. Fearful for his life, Vincenzo turned and tried to run. But Hector was able to twist in midair and latched onto the heel of Vincenzo's left shoe, ripping it from the man's foot.

In that moment, Vincenzo escaped certain death. Leaving behind two fingertips, and one exquisite Italian leather shoe, as he ran for his life.

Chapter Thirty-Seven

A few hours later, Lou awakened; it was two and half hours earlier than usual and still hours before the night sky would begin to give way to the new dawn. His first thought was to check on Hector.

As he stepped onto the dock, Lou pointed his flashlight beam toward the doorway of the boathouse. Inside, Hector lifted his head. He knew from the scent in the air and the sound of the footsteps that the alpha male of his pack was approaching.

The image Lou saw in the boathouse was . . . interesting. The wolf was lying on a blanket, gnawing away at something held firmly in his grasp.

"Hey, Hector, what are you chewing on, boy?"

The huge wolf raised up on his back haunches and dropped what he had in his mouth; then stretched his two front legs forward and yawned.

Lou tilted his head to the side and paused. "What are you chewing on there, buddy? Looks like . . . a shoe to me. Well, what's *left* of one anyway. Where'd you get that?" Hector wagged his tail, in subservient recognition of his leader.

As Lou undid the harness he had placed around the wolf's shoulders the previous night, he realized it had seen better days. The seams were badly frayed. *Hmmm, I didn't realize the stitching was coming apart like this. One more good tug and Hector could have been roaming around at will last night.*

Then, as soon as Lou removed the harness, Hector rubbed up against his legs twice and walked over to the edge of the dock. There, he lowered his head and growled. Hector had picked up Vincenzo's lingering scent. When he kept growling and sniffing the area where the dock met the shoreline, Lou became curious.

"Whatcha got there, boy? What's got your attention? I figured you'd be off looking for your breakfast by now."

Earlier, when Lou's eyes had been on the boathouse, he hadn't noticed a jumble of shredded fabric by the water's edge he now saw. "Hector, get away from that, it's trash!" But the wolf didn't move until Lou gave him a light slap on the butt. "I said *go*. Find something for breakfast. *Scoot!*"

The wolf bounded off and quickly disappeared into the pines behind the lodge. Lou knelt down and scooped up what he thought was trash, most likely something that had fallen overboard from one of the boats and drifted ashore.

At first, he thought the object underneath the cloth was a stone. Then he felt its shape. "Whoa, somebody's going to be looking for this."

It was still a good hour before the sportsmen in camp would be coming down to the dock. So, Lou headed back over to his cottage, thinking he might have a quiet cup of coffee with

Kate before the twins were up. He'd get a better look at the object in his hand then.

EARLIER, Kate heard Lou leave and had gotten up to prepare a pot of coffee. When the man she loved walked into the kitchen, she greeted him with a smile. "I can imagine Hector was glad to see *you* this morning."

Lou let out a snort. "You might say that."

"That's an odd reply."

"Well, I was just thinking that I may have interrupted him from making a phone call."

"Say that again?"

Lou placed the cell phone he'd found in the middle of the kitchen table as he pulled a chair out. "Hector was growling at this."

Kate looked at the phone. "Whose phone is that?"

"Damned if I know. Somebody dropped it down at the dock."

"Well, that someone will certainly be looking for it."

"I know. I'll put a note on the message board about it."

She walked over to the table with coffee for Lou and a cup of tea for herself. "There's no need for that. Slide it over here and I'll tell you in a few seconds who owns it."

"I found it on the shoreline, it might be too wet to fire up."

"It looks like a satellite phone; those cases are pretty durable."

The screen lit up as soon as Kate pressed the button. "See, no problem. Okay let's see who this belongs to."

As Kate's thumbs raced across the screen, she kept shaking her head. "That's odd, nothing's coming up. But, this is an Android, so let's try this." Kate lifted the phone close to her mouth and commanded: *"Hey Google, call HOME."*

Still nothing happened.

"Now that's odd! Even if this was a new phone, you'd think the owner would have their *home* number in the contact list…but, apparently not everyone does that."

Lou was thinking. "Well, I guess I can ask folks when they come to the dock if they're missing a cell phone."

Kate shook her head as she opened the battery compartment. "No need; we'll find the owner from the SIM card." A second later, she said, "Oops, no SIM card. Okay! So, let's take a look under the phone's battery…and grab the IMEi card."

"The *what*?"

Kate ignored Lou's question as she concentrated on removing the battery.

"What did you just call that other card?"

"The IMEi."

"What the hell's that?"

"It's an acronym. It's shorthand for International Mobile Equipment Identity."

"You knew that?"

Kate nodded. "The meaning behind the acronym has become a trivia question of late."

"What'll that do?"

"It'll help us find out who the carrier is. The carrier will be able to tell us who's paying for the service. Hmmm, that's missing too. Okay, let's see who they called."

As soon as Kate replaced the battery, her thumbs raced across the phone, and in a heartbeat, she was looking at calls made from the phone.

"Well, they've only made a few calls, so, it is a new phone.

Hmmm, two of the calls were to a phone with a 506-area code. Now who would they have called in New Brunswick?"

Kate checked the time; it was approaching 6 a.m. "Well, I'm up, you're up, Angelo's up, and most of New Brunswick's up by now, so, let's call one of these 506-area code numbers and see who answers."

Kate pressed the call button and put the phone on speaker. They waited for the call to connect.

Hello, you've reached Brunswick Mutual Casualty Office. We're either on the line or away from our desk. Your call is important to us, so please leave your name, number and a brief message and we'll get back to you as soon as possible.

Kate looked at her husband, eyes wide. "Okay, let's see if there's any text messages on this phone."

"Why?"

"They called Brunswick Mutual! Let's see if whoever owns this sent them a text."

Lou ran his right hand across his forehead, through his hair and down the back of his neck. As he sat back in his chair, he thought: *My wife is a sleuth.*

Kate's eyes stayed glued to the phone's display window. "Nope, I don't see any text messages, but that doesn't mean they weren't erased." Kate put the phone down and looked across the table at her husband. "This just moved *way* beyond someone misplacing their phone."

"Whaddya mean?"

"This has all the earmarks of being a *burner* phone."

"And?"

"And, Lou, whoever had this phone, might be the one who sent that text to Brunswick Mutual cancelling your insurance. Just because I didn't see any text messages, doesn't mean whoever had this phone didn't *send* any."

Lou inhaled deeply. "Can you get any prints off it?"

"Yeah, yours and mine."

Lou stood up. "I'm going back over to the dock. Maybe there's something else laying around."

Crime scene analysis wasn't Lou's area of expertise, but he *did* excel at tracking and reading signs.

When Lou reached the docks, he stopped and canvased the area with his flashlight. The first thing he saw were circular dark brown stains on the first two planks. Kneeling down, he thought: *Could be dried blood.* His eyes shifted to the shoreline where he spotted several unopened sugar packets lying in the sand which he hadn't noticed earlier. As he stared at the small squares, he knew their presence near the dock was telling him something.

Then it came to him. *Shit! It was sugar! That's what the granules in those tank were…sugar doesn't dissolve in gasoline like it does in water.*

Lou scanned the shoreline carefully looking for anything else out of place, but found nothing. Standing up, he thought, *Well, let's go take a look inside the boathouse. Maybe I'll see something else.*

The harness Hector had worn lay on the floor. Lou picked it up and reexamined it. *Now I know the stitching on this harness wasn't this frayed when I put it on Hector last night. I would have noticed that.* As he ran the beam of his halogen flashlight over the wooden decking immediately outside the threshold leading into the boathouse, he saw what appeared to be gouges in the decking. *Are those claw marks?* He knelt down to get a closer look. The yellow color of the gouges contrasted against the rest of deck's weathered grayish color . . . they *were* freshly made. The longer he looked at the marks, the more he realized something had gone on last night.

Okay, he thought, *so, Hector was straining on the rope and digging in, trying to get at something.*

Next, Lou turned around in the boathouse and checked the eyebolt where he had fastened the rope. The longer he stared at it, the more he thought, *Hector, you almost pulled that damn bolt out of the wall, my friend. What were you after?*

As he picked up the blanket he had put down for Hector to lie on, he heard a clunk. The leather sole Hector had been chewing on lay at his feet. Lou reached down and picked up the remnants of the shoe. "Hector, I know you weren't carrying anything in your mouth when I brought you over here last night. So, how'd you get ahold of this?" Lou knew he never kept footwear in the boathouse.

Now he turned the mangled leather over a few times, examining it. *This is definitely not the type of sole they use on hiking shoes, at least not the ones I've seen. This looks more like the sole to a dress shoe. Hector, where'd you get this?*

Lou silently ran everything he was seeing through his mind, connecting as many dots as he could.

Well, Hector certainly would've surprised anyone who was foolish enough to came down to the dock last night. Even tied up, he'd get his licks in, if anyone came too close. Looking down at the sole in his hand, he noticed a shred of what appeared to be soft leather hanging on.

Somebody's walking around with one shoe. If those stains are blood, he has a little more damage, too. Hector must have grabbed hold of something they were wearing and torn it to shreds. I'll bet the bastard was figuring on putting sugar in those two tanks, again.

Just then, Lou heard the sound of voices. The night sky had begun to lighten; it was nearly dawn. As usual, the serious fishermen in camp were eager to get out on the water.

. . .

AFTER THE LAST boat left the dock, Lou walked back to his cottage. As always, the first thing he did upon entering his front porch was turn around and scan the horizon. Nothing looked different, or out of place.

"Lou, are all the boats out?"

"All but Luigi's and the kids'."

"Did you find anything else down at the dock?"

"Yup."

When Lou didn't say anything more, Kate came over to him. "What?"

"Enough to know how I'll recognize the owner of that phone."

"Really?"

"Yeah, all I need to do is keep my eyes peeled for someone missing a shoe, wearing a torn jacket and asking to borrow my phone."

Kate shook her head, "Lou this is serious. We need to find out who this belongs to."

"I know. I'm trying hard to keep my inner warrior at bay. I feel it stirring."

As Lou turned to leave, Kate asked, "Where are you going?"

"I'm going back down to the dock and look around some more. After that, I'm putting a couple of trail cameras down there.. One way or another, I'm gonna catch the smart ass who's been sneaking around and putting sugar in those gas tanks!"

Chapter Thirty-Eight

Vincenzo's right hand was throbbing. The flow of blood from the ends of his ring finger and pinky had slowed, but was still oozing out. The emergency first aid kit Luigi had in the medicine cabinet was barely adequate for cuts or scrapes, let alone amputated fingertips.

He shook with rage. Things like this weren't supposed to happen to him, not to the assassin known as "Popeye." He was supposed to be *invincible*, at least that's what people who knew him thought.

Suddenly, he grabbed his right wrist with his massive left hand and squeezed until he cut off the circulation. Now he held his bloody mangled hand up to the mirror and cursed. For the first time in his life, the assassin felt *pain*.

The wolf had literally torn the tips of his fingers off with his teeth. Vincenzo stared at his hand. *A friggin' wolf did this to me . . . a friggin **wolf**!*

He tried running his hand under cold water, hoping for relief. But all he accomplished was changing the color of the washbasin from white to crimson red from the blood. He closed his eyes, took a breath, and shook his head. *I gotta stop this friggin' bleeding.*

He didn't have a lot of options; he couldn't go for help, but he did have a switchblade and a cigarette lighter. He pushed the release on the knife and the blade snapped out. Then he held the lighter under it. When the steel blade turned blue from the heat, he dropped the lighter, took a breath and pressed the tip of his ring finger down onto the searing hot blade. In an instant pain shot up his hand, traveled the full length of his arm, across his shoulder, through his neck, into the thalamus section of his brain and on to the cortex. He had never felt such excruciating pain. The nerve endings in his finger were on fire. His brain was exploding from the shock. Instinctively, he pulled his hand back. The pain was unbelievable. Never in his life had he felt pain of this magnitude. He wanted to stop, but couldn't; the wound needed to be cauterized. He wanted to yell, but couldn't; he dared not let anyone hear him.

Now, he needed to steady the flame under the blade for his pinky. In a nanosecond, Popeye experienced the same sense of futility every one of his victims had felt before he killed them.

The smell of burning human flesh was nauseating. His mind was a blur from the mind-blowing waves of pain coming from his nerve endings that wouldn't cease.

Because the blade cooled down so quickly, he ended up reheating the metal several times, and actually rolling the end of each ragged and uneven fingertip in a circular motion to thoroughly seal the ends of his shortened digits.

It wasn't until the bleeding stopped, and risk of infection from bacteria was eliminated, that Vincenzo dropped the knife into the sink and collapsed into a chair. He first thought was of Hector: *Wolf, I'm gonna friggin' kill you!*

After the self-inflicted ordeal Vincenzo had just endured, he decided to skip breakfast. Because Luigi had daily maid service at the cottage, Vincenzo needed to clean up the bloody mess before the housekeeper came knocking on the door. With all the trauma he had been through, it wasn't until he got up from the chair that he realized he was missing a shoe.

As he kicked the lone shoe off his foot, he was out to kill. *Wolf, you're mine now, you bastard. You're friggin' mine, now!*

THE MORNING SKY was just beginning to turn gray when a lone female Tench worked her way from the depths of the first feeder pond to the aquatic vegetation along the shore. Her body was full of eggs, but another day would pass before she was ready to release. Until then, she would wait in the shallows, concealed in the vegetation.

She had been in the weeds a while when she felt a sharp searing pain in her upper back. Wounded, and uncertain of where her adversary was, she tried to retreat into the depths.

She had seen a shadow, and she had reacted, but only enough to throw off her attacker's aim.

The wound was more severe than she initially realized… she would not survive. The five-and-a-half-inch beak of the Great Blue Heron had ruptured her swim bladder and penetrated deep inside her stomach. Her muscles reflexed. She was struggling to keep the thousands of microscopic eggs she carried within her.

When the Heron struck a second time, she was on her side, her gills were rapidly opening and closing, she was gasping for breath. In one fluid motion she felt herself being lifted out of the water and flipped up into the air as if she were a feather. Disoriented, she fell into the heron's open mouth, head first, and then…she was gone.

A male Tench who had followed the female from the depths hung back, waiting for the Heron to spread its wings and leave. Once the bird took flight, the male returned to the safety of the deeper water.

LATER THAT SAME MORNING, seven ATVs and two backhoes caravanned from the village of Grey Elk to the feeder ponds.

The backhoes would create leach fields that would capture the future runoff from the Turnbridge fields before it could even reach the pools. After the fields were completed, the Abenaki would still need to address the algae already present.

The lab reports came back stating that algae existed in all three ponds. Algae, itself, isn't always a problem. However, when algae enters a phase of rapid growth and reproduction it produces toxins that affected organisms with gills: fish, freshwater mussels and the gill-breathing juvenile stage of frogs and other amphibians.

The report listed two different forms of algae in the ponds.

The bright lime green blanket covering the uppermost pond is referred to as green algae, not as harmful as blue-green algae which is far more difficult to deal with.

The recommended solution for the lime green algae was simple. Koby had assured them that form of algae would be eradicated by skimming, netting, and disposing of the sludge a distance from the shoreline. Once the surface of the pond was clear, she'd add beneficial bacteria to the water creating a natural balance, again, to enhance the overall quality of the water.

The two lower ponds had been found to contain Green Filamentous algae, otherwise known as String Algae. Unlike other algae, this form doesn't produce any toxins but does spread rapidly and quickly becomes unsightly. The recommendation from the lab had been to apply a non-copper algicide, which wouldn't harm the fish.

Once the tribal council had agreed to take action, Koby sent an email to the provincial authorities requesting permission to apply the recommended chemicals. Until approval was granted, the chemicals were on hold.

The Abenaki believed they were on their way to solving the algae problem, with minimal impact to the environment. Algae was the only problem they knew about . . . at the moment.

DURING THE TIME Jake had been on vacation, no snail mail had reached the resort. The first day Jake was back on the job, he returned home with a stack of mail that had collected. Among the letters was one addressed to Kate from the Boston postmaster.

She wasn't surprised there was no response from the United States Social Security Administration, yet, but she had expected a reply from the forensic lab at Mountie Headquarters. Before dialing Mountie headquarters, for a status update, she opened the letter from the Boston postmaster.

It stated that the owner of the P.O. Box which had appeared on Luigi's original reservation request was listed as a "John Holland." Holland had been the box owner since 1984. Before him, the prior owner was Frederick Jenne.

Next, Kate placed a call to Mountie headquarters in Fredericton which was answered on the second ring.

"Royal Canadian Police, how may I direct your call."

"Forensics."

"One moment."

After a brief wait, a male voice came on the line. "Forensics. Mahoney speaking."

"Hey, Tim, it's Kate O'Grady."

"Hey, how ya' doing, Kate? What's up?"

"I'm trying to get the status on a package I sent down a couple of weeks ago."

"Gimmie a minute and I'll check the log." It wasn't long before Tim came back on the line. "Kate, I'm not seeing anything with your name on it. Who sent it?"

"I did."

"Well, nothing's come in with your name on it."

"That's strange. Okay, I'll check with the carrier."

"All right. Sorry I couldn't help."

As Kate ended the call, she had a dire feeling. *I gave that package to Jake well over two weeks ago. I hope it hasn't been sitting in his plane all this time.*

Chapter Thirty-Nine

A round eleven that morning, Koby fired up the mahogany runabout she and Jake owned and left for Moose Cove. Today was one of the days she had committed to staffing the village clinic from noon until 5 p.m.

When she arrived at the cove, she secured the runabout to the cleats on the dock, backed the ATV out of the dockside shed and drove up to the village. As soon as she parked in front of the clinic, she noticed a young boy standing by the door.

"Hi, are you waiting to see me?"

"Yes."

"Have you been waiting long?"

"No."

Koby smiled and tousled the young boy's hair as she slid the key into the lock. "Good, come on in." Koby could tell her young patient was a little shy. As she closed the door she said, "Okay, take a seat and I'll be right with you."

It only took a minute before Koby had the lights on and her PC powered up. It wasn't long before she walked over to the doorway leading to the hall where the examination rooms were located. "Okay, you can come in."

When the young boy stood up, he reached down and grabbed hold of a 5-gallon pail.

"You can leave that out there," she said. "No one is going to bother it." When the young boy hesitated, Koby directed him. "Let's go, into room one!"

As soon as the young boy entered the examination room, Koby noticed he was scratching his arm. "Okay, so what's going on? Why are you here?"

"My arm's itchy."

"I can see that. Is it both arms, or just one?"

"Both, I guess, but this one the most."

"All right, let's take a look and see what's going on." After a brief look at both arms, she said, "Do you know what poison ivy looks like?"

"Yes."

"Have you been near any poison ivy lately?" As Koby stood up to reach a for a bottle of calamine lotion, he answered.

"I think so."

"Do you think so, or do you *know* so?"

The boy let out a sigh. "I guess I know so."

"Okay, well, we'll get you fixed up, but it's still going to itch for a while." Koby didn't actually care where the poison ivy was, she just wanted the boy to feel comfortable that he'd made the right decision coming to the clinic.

"So, where was this poison ivy?"

"At the pond."

"Which pond? There are three ponds."

"The first one."

"I was up there recently. There *is* a lot of poison ivy up there. Be more careful next time. Remember, 'leaves of three, let it be!'"

"I know, my father taught me that."

"That's a long hike for you. Did you go there for a reason?"

"To fish."

As Koby applied the soothing calamine lotion to both of the boy's arms, she said, "So, you like to fish?"

"I guess so."

"Did you catch anything?"

"Yes."

Hmmm, a man of few words, she thought. "Well, what did you catch?"

"I don't know."

"What do you mean you don't know?"

"Well, I usually catch trout. This time I caught something else."

"You're a fisherman, and you don't know what kind of fish you caught?"

The young man dropped his eyes. "No."

"How many fish did you catch?"

"Two."

"Well, *I* know a lot about fish. When we finish up here, we'll take a look at your fish. Maybe I can tell you what you caught. Would you like that?"

"Yes."

"Okay. Here, take this bottle of lotion with you. I want you to keep applying this to wherever it itches. Okay?"

"Okay."

"Now let's go have a look at the fish you caught." They both walked out to the waiting room and looked into the pail sitting on the floor. As soon as Koby saw the fish, she picked up her phone and called Lou.

THE TROPHY FISH that dwelled in the lake, defined the very essence of Havre de Poisson's unique reputation. They also represented a significant part of the diet consumed by the residents in the village of Grey Elk. Lou was aware of the threat the Tench represented to the waters of New Brunswick. Once he learned two Tench had been caught in the first, upper pond, he wasted no time calling an emergency council meeting.

Immediately after putting the word out, Lou fired up his runabout and headed down the lake to Moose Cove, and then up to the village to chair the meeting.

Word about the meeting traveled quickly throughout the village. In less than an hour the council leadership faced a standing room only crowd. After the traditional opening prayer, Lou stood up.

"My brothers and sisters, the algae problem we have in the upper ponds pales in comparison to what we've just learned. A very invasive and aggressive fish, one that is *not native* to the land of the Abenaki, was caught in the first upper pond. This alien species is extremely dangerous. If we allow it to flourish, it will completely overtake our waters and our source of food."

Lou waited for the murmuring to quiet down before he continued. "Many of you know Koby Callahan as the nurse who staffs the clinic here in the village. Koby is also a marine biologist who sits on the Provincial Wetlands Habitat Board. I'm going to turn this meeting over to her."

Koby came forward carrying the 5-gallon pail. She stood to the side of the head table so everyone sitting there, and those attending, could see her.

"When I arrived at the clinic today, a young boy was waiting for me. He had been fishing at the first pond. He caught two fish he'd never seen before. I asked him to show me the fish, and he did." At that point, Koby reached into the pail, grabbed a fish by its tail, and held it up for all to see.

"*This* is what he caught. Take a good look at it. This is called a 'European Tench.' The Latin name is *Tinca, tinca.* They are common throughout Europe and parts of Asia. They are *not* native to the Americas. The experts believe they most likely were introduced into the waters of western hemisphere as stowaways in the bilge water ships from across the Atlantic release into our harbors."

Again, Koby waited for the murmurs and grunts to subside. "The danger this Tench represents to any body of water in the western hemisphere is *devastating.* It outcompetes with every native fish species for space and resources. It uproots large masses of aquatic vegetation, which alters the habitat our own native species need and negatively impacts the water quality."

Someone jokingly asked in a stage whisper, "Is it good to eat?"

When the laughter settled down, Koby replied. "It's not a very tasty fish." She waited for the murmuring to quiet down again, before continuing.

"The eggs of our native fish, like the trout, suffer a ninety-eight percent mortality rate. Tench eggs have a mortality rate of only seventy percent. Additionally, the female Tench lays hundreds of thousands of eggs, whereas trout lay no more than a few thousand. And…because the Tench can also tolerate extreme changes in temperatures and water quality, they are truly survivors."

Koby paused partly for effect and partly to let that information sink in.

"The fish I have in my hand is a mature female. I've opened her up. She is full of eggs. The good news is, she wasn't ready to spawn. That said, if there is one female fish this size in the ponds, there are more, *and* there are males. I don't know how this fish found its way into your pond, but we now know it's here. This species of fish needs to be killed off before it is allowed to establish itself and destroy the entire fishery in the lake."

Among the murmuring, Kate heard someone say, "It's a big lake."

"Now, I just heard someone say: 'It's a big lake.' Now that's true. But, let me say this again, Once the Tench invade a body of water, if not eliminated immediately, they *will* cause the existing ecosystem to collapse. The first to go will be the bottom of the pyramid, the small snails and bivalves. Once they are lost, algae blooms that never occurred here before will become commonplace. Next, will be a decline in the population of smelt, and other small fry which the larger fish feed upon. Once the population of the food fish decline, the population of larger fish, like the trout, and the bass will collapse, leaving only the Tench"

Again, Koby paused to let what she had just said sink in.

"The length of time for this to happen will be measured in years, not in lifetimes. Once this begins to happen, the fishery in Lake 980, that you and your forefathers have known for generations, and depended on for food, will cease to exist."

It was apparent from the silence that filled the room, the Abenaki had fully received the message and now understood its grave warning. The lake, and their way of life, was in trouble.

Chapter Forty

Jake completed his mail run hours earlier than usual, for a change. As he flew up the lake, he passed over Moose Cove. Looking down, he saw the sun's rays glistening off the mahogany finish on both runabouts. *Hmmm, something's going on at the village for both of those boats to be at the cove,* he thought.

On days when the wind came from the East, like it was, Jake would usually lower the plane's flaps well before he approached the dock at Havre de Poisson, and come straight in. However, today he was early and as he approached the resort, he saw quite a few boats heading in toward the dock. So, instead, he pulled the flaps up and made a loop letting safety be his guide. He set down in the middle of the lake, directly opposite his cottage and taxied over to his private dock.

He wasn't the least bit surprised when his daughter, Gigi, didn't come running down the dock yelling, "Daddy!" as she usually did. With both runabouts tied up at Moose Cove, he realized Koby had taken Gigi elsewhere. Once he secured the de Havilland, and reached his cottage, he saw the note.

Jake,
Gigi is with me.
Kate

I knew something was up, he thought. When he reached Lou's front porch, he opened the screen door and called inside: "Kate, I've come to relieve you of my daughter."

"Come on in! Gigi's in the living room, glued to the TV, watching 'Helpsters' with the twins."

"What's up? I saw both runabouts down at Moose Cove."

"Koby called me shortly after noon today. Somebody caught a Tench in one of the feeder ponds. Lou has called an emergency council meeting."

"That doesn't sound good."

"No, it doesn't."

"Hey, I'll be right back; I need to ask Angelo if he wants me to bring in more eggs tomorrow." Kate pursed her lips.

"Ahh, you might wanna hold off on that."

"Why?"

"Angelo isn't having a very good day today."

"Why, what happened?"

"Well, apparently the door to the coop was left open yesterday. We've all been in the woods the better part of the day trying to round up the 'free range' chickens."

"There's a latch on that coop. Nobody goes near it but Angelo."

"I know, that's what has him so upset. He's blaming himself."

"I'm gonna go talk to him."

"Before you go, I have a question for you."

"Shoot."

"Do you remember the package I gave you that I was sending down to Fredericton before the shutdown?"

"Yeah, it was going to the Mounties, right?"

"Correct. I called Fredericton today and they haven't received it, yet."

"That's odd. I'll check on it tomorrow for you. The guy who flies that route has been out. It might have been sitting in Grand Falls. I flew a bag of mail down there yesterday."

"So, you think they have it now?"

"Well, if it was in the bag I took down, it's in Fredericton now."

Kate just smiled. *Boonies. I keep forgetting I'm in the boonies!*

"Do you mind watching Gigi a little longer, Kate? I wanna go see Angelo."

"Go ahead; she's no bother at all. "

"Thanks, I won't be long."

As soon as Jake walked into the lodge, he could hear Angelo muttering in the kitchen.

"Angelo, how you doing?" Angelo turned to his friend and Jake could saw his sour expression, He was upset.

"Jake, I'm losing it."

"Whaddya mean 'you're losing it?'"

"Everything's going wrong today! First, when I came in this morning, only half the lights worked. Every other bulb had to be screwed in tight. The door to the walk-in was open and the buzzer was blasting. The temperature was off. It was just the breaker, but still, what if I hadn't been here?

Everything could have been ruined! Then I find out half my birds are roaming around the woods. *Mamma Mia!*"

With that, Angelo slammed a meat cleaver down, imbedding the blade into a wooden chopping block.

"Hey, Angelo, go easy! Kate says things happen in threes. So, you're good to go for a while now."

"Let's hope so, eh?"

"Yeah. So, tell me, you need more eggs tomorrow?"

"I got no choice now. I can't count on my layers." Angelo paused before saying, *"Funculo!* Now I gotta make *pancakes* tomorrow."

"Angelo, I'll be back after dinner. We'll have a cigar; maybe we'll watch the movie *Skyfall* again."

Angelo let out a breath, "Maybe, or maybe we'll just drink some *grappa!*"

"I'm not touching that stuff; I gotta get up in the morning and fly a bird." Angelo waved his hand in a dismissive manner and Jake took his leave.

LATER THAT EVENING, when the front page of The Brunswick Daily Times rolled off the presses, the headline read: "Has the Fairytale Ended?"

The following article appeared on page one. At least it was below the fold:

Has the fairy dust that magically elevated Lou Gault's fishing lodge to enviable heights finally settled?

Gault's lodge, long considered a paradise in the minds of many outdoorsmen, apparently isn't what it used to be. The lofty image Havre de Poisson once held seems to be vanishing. At least some anglers who came to try their luck at Gault's esteemed lake are having second thoughts.

Unsolicited comments received by this editor seem to indicate that may be the case. One recent guest stated: "The whole experience just wasn't what I expected."

It was small amenities that made Gault's lodge a standout among the vast array of fishing holes. For better than a decade, Gault's lodge has been "the darling" of those with really deep pockets who love to fish. Now, it's the absence of those amenities that folks are apparently missing.

"For instance, boats won't start," the recent visitor said. "Not just once, but every day for three days? Now, c'mon! That's not what I'm paying for."

A week at Gault's lodge doesn't come cheap. The cost is actually approaching a semester's tuition at many colleges. It's been well known for many years, that trophy fish published in record books have come from Gault's revered Lake 980. But times are apparently changing as that no longer seems to be the case.

Lately, record-breaking game fish are being hauled in from waters in close proximity to Gault. As in all things, time marches on and it appears Gault's long run at being the premier, number one fishing camp destination, at least in this neck of the woods, may be coming to an end.

But let's not forget, folks, no matter how flat the pancake is, there's always two sides to it. Unfortunately, our repeated attempts to reach Gault for comment, before this issue went to press, were unsuccessful. Let's hope we can get his side of the story soon. Stay posted.

Chapter Forty-One

At the same time Jake was speaking to Angelo, Matteo Abruzzi was sitting in Santino Varni's office in Boston.

"So, Matteo, what's going on in Canada?"

"Popeye's still up there."

"And?"

"He hasn't called today, but Gault should be wondering what the hell is going on by now, so maybe he's trying to put out a few fires."

Santino waited for Matteo to elaborate, but when he didn't, Varni asked: "So, what *is* going on?"

"Gault's got . . . issues." Matteo smirked. "Popeye cancelled the bastard's insurance, then he busted a huge plate glass window which was no longer covered. Then, a couple of outboard motors bit the dust after not starting for a couple a'days in a row. And the lodge had a few problems, too. We're messing around with electrical breakers. Chickens are running all over the friggin' woods, and we dumped some kinda fish into his lake that'll destroy it. We got stuff happening."

Varni was silent while he mulled over all the news. Then he said, "That's not enough."

Matteo nodded. "Understood."

"When's Popeye coming back?"

"I don't know. Like I said, he hasn't called me today." When Matteo didn't say anything more, Santino motioned with his hand for him to continue.

"He has a burner. He'll call me. He calls every day. He's mechanical, like clockwork. He just didn't call today, that's all; no big deal."

Santino pressed. "Why?"

"Why, what?"

"You inferred you could set a watch by him. Why hasn't he called you today?"

"I don't know why he hasn't called!" Matteo was annoyed. "Look, it's not a big deal, okay? Sometimes things happened. He's in the friggin' woods. He'll call."

"I want Gault to ask me for my help when I'm up there next week."

"Wait, no! You can't go up there *next* week." But Santino waggled an index finger at Matteo who knew it was a signal to tread carefully. Matteo stared at the rug for a moment, then spoke his reason.

"Santino, the election's coming up, man. You need to do a little campaigning; pump a little flesh, mingle, kiss some babies, spread some vibes, let 'em know you're *one* of 'em."

Santino dismissed his consigliere's concerns. Then, he seemed to change the subject completely. "Matteo, I want you to take care of Monteverde."

"Who?"

"Monteverde. He needs to go away."

"Carmine?" Santino nodded. "Why?" Matteo asked in shock. "What the frig is the matter with *Carmine*?"

"He's a risk."

"He's *not* a risk, Santino. What the hell are you talking about?"

"He's planning to challenge me for the presidency."

"No way! Come on, Santino, Carmine's got a mouth, but he's not *stupid*."

"He wants this seat."

"He's *not* running against you. He doesn't have the *balls*."

"He's a sleaze. He stays in the shadows. He has a following. But somebody he thinks is on his side, isn't as loyal as he believes. No, he's too much of a risk. He needs to go away. Do it discreetly."

"Shit man, we *grew up* with Carmine!"

"I know that, but times change, my friend. Times change." When Matteo didn't say anything, Santino looked at him. "Is there a problem?"

Matteo took a deep breath. "No, it'll happen." Santino nodded. Then Matteo decided to change the subject, himself. "Is Nina going up with you?"

"I'm not going to the resort."

"I thought you just said you were going to Canada?"

"Not to the fishing camp. I'm flying up with Nardo Lombardi. He's found a lake he wants me to see."

"Are you moving to plan B?"

"We'll see."

"Don't be crazy man. You don't need to *build* a friggin' place up there."

"I don't intend to."

"Then what the hell is Lombardi doing?"

"All Lombardi is doing is buying a lake in Gault's neighborhood."

"So, you'll own a lake. Then what?"

"I'll promote the hell out of it."

"Promote *what*?"

"Fear. We're already driving Gault's reputation into the ground. If Gault believes he's going to have legitimate competition in his own backyard, he'll get financial jitters and be even *more* motivated to sell."

"*That's* Plan B?"

"That's all it is . . . Plan B."

"So, whaddya do with the lake once you buy Gault's place?"

"Gift it to the pension fund."

"*What* pension fund?"

"The union's pension fund, the one that's gonna buy it for me."

"*Shit* man, you can't do that."

"Really? Whose gonna know? Nobody but the three of us: You, me, and our treasurer, Rico. He'll cover it up."

"You talk about not taking risks, Santino, that's a *huge* risk. You said this was all about *eliminating* friggin' risks. Which, by the way, only *you* seem to see. Now you're adding messing with the pension fund to the pile?

In a dismissive tone, Santino replied, "But this one is necessary, Matteo; it eliminates the other risks."

THE FOLLOWING AFTERNOON, when Jake headed home after a full day delivering mail, he had a few extra copies of the Brunswick Daily Times sitting in the empty co-pilot's seat beside him. After securing the mail plane to the dock, he headed over to his cousin's cottage.

"Lou, are you home?"

Kate yelled from inside, "Jake, he's still over at the boat house."

"Okay, then that's where I'm heading. I'm gonna leave a copy of the Times on your porch. Take a look at the front page story."

"Okay."

Lou was just securing the door to the boathouse when Jake arrived and handed him a copy of the Times. "About time you're delivering the paper."

"Read the article on the front page."

Lou leaned back against the boathouse. His breathing became heavier the longer he read. At the end of the full article, he said, "This is bullshit! Where the hell does he come off spreading crap like this around?"

"Sounds like somebody dropped a dime on you, Cuz."

"Who? Who in hell would do that? Hell, I haven't had a comment card that wasn't all five stars in years!"

"Well, somebody wasn't happy."

"And they go to press without even *talking* to me? What the hell kind of journalists work at that paper?"

"Yeah, but, it kinda ends saying they tried to reach you."

"Yeah, well, they *didn't*. And 'trying' doesn't cut it in my book. *Trying* is nothing more than the noise you make before you actually *do* something!"

"So, give 'em a call, Lou. Tell 'em Tinker Bell is still alive and well. Hell, they gotta know every barrel has at least one bad apple in it; they'll understand that."

"That's exactly what I'm gonna do. In the meantime, do me a favor."

"What's that?"

"Leave all those papers with me. The lodge can go without the Brunswick Daily Times for one night."

WHEN KATE HEARD the screen door to the porch open and close, she stepped to the open doorway. As usual, Lou was scanning the horizon. It was the picture of him she watched every time she had a chance. The only thing different was that tonight, there were three copies of the Daily Times folded under his arm. When he turned around, Kate said, "Lou, have you read the article? It's awful! They said they tried to reach you. Why didn't you call them back?"

"I don't know. I saw they were calling. I just figured it was a slow news day and they were looking to sell me some advertising space."

"Well, I think you're right about it being a slow news day. But I wish you had called them back."

"Well . . . I didn't."

"If it were me, I'd call them back right now!"

"I need to settled down a bit more before I can do that."

"Lou, you have to call them. Their readers deserve the truth, not this malarky!"

"Right now, I can't decide if I wanna call them and give that editor a piece of my mind, or just let the damn thing blow over. Sometimes, if you just leave things alone, everyone forgets about it. Hell, it's just a dinky little paper that no one reads anyway."

"It is that, but it's also the kind of story that gets picked up by the wire service. You *need* to call them."

"I will. I'll call them in the morning."

"The twins are already over with Koby. I'm going to head over to the lodge to give Alessandra a hand with the tables."

"And I'm gonna get some of this crud off me," he said, indicating his muddy clothes, "then I'll be over."

A HALF HOUR LATER, as Lou stepped off his porch, he heard a noise which made him pause. *That's a plane*, he thought. *Either Luigi's coming in or someone's going home early.*

By the time Lou reached the dock, the plane had circled once, and the pilot had his flaps down. The Smyth Air pilot waved to Lou as he taxied over to the dock. Lou noticed no one was in the plane except the pilot.

"Charlie, you delivering packages, or picking up?"

"Picking up, Lou. I hope it doesn't have anything to do with that article in the Daily Times."

So much for it being a dinky little paper that no one reads, Lou thought. "Well, like the good book says, Charlie, ya' can't be all things to all people."

Whether that was in the bible or not, the pilot nodded, saying, "Ya' got that straight, Lou, ya can't win 'em all."

By this time, the pilot had turned the engine off. Yet Lou still hadn't heard anyone coming down the dock. However, when Vincenzo cleared his throat, he was literally standing right next to Lou.

The sound startled Lou and he almost jumped. When he turned around, he was eyeball to eyeball with Vincenzo. "Vincenzo! You're leaving?"

"Yeah, time to go."

"Did you eat?"

"No."

"Angelo can put something together for you; it won't take long."

"No, I gotta go. I . . . ah . . . I gotta go. I'll grab something later."

Lou picked up on the sudden sense of urgency, yet vagueness in Vincenzo's voice. "Well, it was nice having you here. I hope you'll come back up and visit us again, maybe do a little fishing next time." When Lou put his hand out, Vincenzo dropped the bag he was holding in his left hand and used that hand to shake with Lou.

Lou kept smiling but thought: *That was an odd shake, what the hell was that about?*

Then, as Vincenzo reached down for his bag, Lou said, "Hey, just get in; I'll hand your bag up. These flying contraptions are difficult enough to get into using both hands."

As Vincenzo stepped off the dock, his weight tipped the pontoon slightly downward; instinctively, he reached to grab the wing strut with this right hand to steady himself. Lou saw the makeshift bandage on Vincenzo's right hand, but said nothing.

So that's why he didn't shake with his right hand.

The damage to Vincenzo's two right hand fingers had weakened his grip and he struggled getting into the cockpit.

As Vincenzo crawled into the plane, Lou couldn't help but notice the shoes on Luigi's feet. The style and color were totally different from what he'd been wearing every other time Lou had seen him. *Humph, I wonder why he's not wearing his fancy shoes?*

"Take care!" Lou waved as the plane revved up and backed away from the dock. *I'm not sure about that guy,* Lou thought. *I wonder why he took off early? And, what the hell's up with the bandaged hand? If he got hurt up here, I need to know about it.* Lou's mind flashed back to the memory of Hector laying on the floor of the boathouse, chewing on a shoe the other morning and the brown spots he saw on the dock. As the plane taxied out to the middle of the lake, Lou had one last thought. *I'm not so sure any friend of Luigi's, is necessarily a friend of mine.*

Chapter Forty-Two

When Alessandra heard that Vincenzo had left, she saw the opportunity to get an early start on her Saturday change-over chores.

She had grown up in Italy, and from an early age, her parents raised her to be responsible and self-sufficient. Her mother's approach to life was: *Never put off until tomorrow what can be done today.* The lesson she'd held on to from her father was: *Don't expect others to do what you should be able to do yourself.*

It wasn't long after breakfast on Friday when she had the sheets and towels from Luigi's cottage in the washing machine. She had barely closed the lid before she heard a loud snap, and the agitator stopped.

Hmm, the motor is still running, she thought, *so, it isn't anything related to the generator.* But when she looked behind the machine, she saw the black belt lying on the platform.

"Well, if you had to go and break on me, it's best you did

it now, and not on a busy Saturday," she said aloud, to no one in particular.

After removing the wet linens and towels from the first machine, and placing them in the second one, she once again measured out the environmentally friendly plant-based detergent she used, closed the lid, and pressed the start button. To her surprise, the second machine lasted about the same amount of time as the first one did before she heard another snapping sound, and that machine's agitator came to a stop.

She knew immediately what the sound meant, but she looked behind the machine anyway. *This is odd*, she thought, *two belts breaking at the same time? That's most unusual. Well, let me see if I can move these things around to give myself enough room to get behind there and replace the belts.*

If the machines hadn't been filled with water, Alessandra would have easily jockeyed them around and given herself the extra room she needed to work. *Nope, I'm not moving these things without draining the water*, she thought, *and that's a waste of good water.*

She stepped back. "Either Lou or Jake will have to move these things for me. But I might as well take one of these belts with me; that way I'll come back with the right belt the first time."

As soon as Alessandra picked up the first broken belt, she looked at the breakpoint. After seeing the first one, she picked up the second belt. Both breaks were identical. *Most unusual*, she thought. Having spent many hours as a sous chef, slicing and dicing with various knives, she knew the difference between a tear, a break, and a cut. *This is a cut*, she thought. *Lou needs to know about this.*

She headed down to the boathouse where she knew he was working. "Lou?" she called.

"In here, Alessandra. What's up?"

As soon as Alessandra reached the doorway, she held out the belts. "Take a look at these and tell me what you think."

"Oh, they broke. No matter, we've got spares."

"No, Lou, take a *good* look at these." The tone in her voice made him stop. Lou took hold of the first belt, looked at the break, then looked at the second.

"Well?"

"Looks like a knife cut."

"Exactly. Who would do such a thing?"

"No idea, but there's been too many mishaps happening around here for this to be coincidental."

"Yesterday morning, half the lights in the lodge didn't work!"

"I know."

When Lou didn't say anything further, Alessandra said, "The machines are full of water; they're too heavy for me to push around. You'll have to angle them so I can get behind and put the new belts on."

"I'm almost finished here. I'll get to those machines next."

"Do you want me to leave the generator running?"

"Yeah, I'm just about finished here."

"All right, I'll be in the kitchen. Let me know when you've pulled the machines out."

Before Lou stepped out of the boathouse, he grabbed his toolbox. *If I have to pull those suckers out,* he thought, *I might as well finish the job and replace the belts myself.* He grabbed two spares and walked toward the shed.

• • •

ONCE HE JOCKEYED the machines forward, it didn't take long before both belts were attached and the machines were back in place. But when Lou pressed the start button, nothing happened. He pushed the button a second time. *Ha, Alessandra must have changed her mind about leaving the generator on.*

The washing machine generator was a small unit located just outside the shed in what Alessandra referred to as "a doghouse with a door." The generator had an electric start, but Jake had wired the line to a kill switch inside the shed.

When the generator didn't kick right in, Lou thought, *I guess she came back and turned the switch off.*

He walked around to the other side of the shed expecting to see the switch pointing down, but it wasn't. Lou stared at the switch for a moment, then flipped the toggle the opposite way. *Maybe Jake wired this one back-asswards.*

He walked back to the machines and pressed a start button. The unit didn't even make a clicking sound.

All right, let's go outside again and see if the generator ran out of gas and shut itself down. When Lou unscrewed the cap, the gas was nearly to the brim. "Well, you've got plenty of gas. Let's disconnect you from the line leading to the kill switch and see if you'll start on your own." He wasn't talking to anyone but himself.

When Lou couldn't get the generator to start, he brought the unit down to the boathouse to examine it. The first thing he did was check the fuel filter. It was clogged. Next, he took the gas cap off and peered in with a flashlight. Sitting on the bottom of the small tank was a grainy residue. "Son-of-a-bitch! This didn't happen on its own. Somebody is screwing around with me." Suspicions were growing in his mind by the minute.

First the boats, now the machines with this same residue . . . there's a rat hanging around here somewhere and I'm gonna find out who the hell it is!

WHEN HE FINALLY RETURNED TO his cottage, Kate said, "I thought you'd be back sooner."

"Kate, I really think someone's trying to sabotage us."

"Oh Lou, that's foolish talk."

"No, it's not. Think about all that's happened lately."

"What?"

"The outboard motors, the insurance, the broken window, the lights at the lodge, the walk-in freezer, the algae, the Tench. Now the washing machines, the generator . . ." he stopped and looked at her. "Even the news article. What guest talked to the paper?"

"Lou, the broken window, the Tench, the algae are all part of living this close to nature."

"Maybe. But nature sure as hell didn't clog the gas filters, unscrew the lightbulbs, or throw that breaker switch to the freezers. That's way too many things to be natural."

"Lou, don't go overthinking this."

"I'm not."

"No, you're getting paranoid. Machines break down, maybe the bulbs weren't screwed in tight enough to begin with. Breakers do trip; things break. Even though, I will admit, it does seem like a string of bad luck."

"Then there's that phone I found down by the boathouse."

Kate rolled her eyes. "How would you like your eggs this morning?"

"Scrambled. That's the way I'm feeling."

As Lou watched his wife crack a few eggs on the rim of the skillet, his thoughts kept circling. *I am not overthinking this, my gut tells me there's something going on. Maybe I'll take a walk over to Rocky Point and give this some serious thought. Maybe I'll take a closer look at that phone.*

Chapter Forty-Three

At the same time Lou was over at Rocky Point, Matteo was walking along the Boston docks that defined the working harbor. When he saw Carmine Monteverde nearby, he stopped dead in his tracks.

Carmine had worked at the docks since his early twenties. He had a solid work ethic and was well respected. Some thought he was "old school" while others referred to him as a "straight arrow." Matteo thought of him as a childhood friend.

There had been significant unrest among the union's rank-and-file after the most recent strike. The grievance had lasted longer than anyone expected. Many members thought the gains they'd won would never make up for what they'd lost during the strike.

Carmine had been vocal about his displeasure, and he had followers. He blamed local leadership for all the savings the rank-and-file lost during the strike by holding out too long;

Carmine was bound and determined that he'd never let it happen again.

Matteo spoke first. "Hey, Carmine, how you doing?"

"Hey, Matteo!" He was genuinely pleased to see the man and smiled broadly.

"You doing okay?" Matteo repeated.

"Yeah. Whaddya doing down here with all us working stiffs, huh? What's the matter, you a got nothing to do?"

Matteo smiled at the jest. "Nah, I just need to get out once in a while. Besides, I miss being down on the docks."

"Who you kidding? You telling me, you miss freezing your ass off in the winter, and sweating your ass off in the summer?"

Matteo slapped Carmine on the shoulder and laughed. "You're right, I don't! But you know what I miss? I miss shooting the shit with *you* guys after work, like we always did. I miss that."

"We still go to the same 'ole place. You should join us once in a while."

"Maybe I will."

"Yeah, the guys would like that," he said, looking at the man he'd grown up with in the neighborhood. "Mister Big-Shot, coming down and rubbing shoulders with us, buying us a beer! All kidding aside, the older guys are gonna enjoy seeing you again, Matteo."

THE NEXT DAY, Matteo showed up at the local watering hole that the dock workers frequented. When Matteo walked through the door, the fella standing next to Carmine elbowed him and motioned toward the door.

Carmine smiled. "Hey everybody, look who's here! Hey,

Matteo, how about buying a round?" Matteo smiled and nodded to the bartender who happily complied.

It wasn't Matteo's intention to mingle, or even spend a lot of time talking with Carmine. He had come into the bar for one reason and only one reason: to distract Carmine and keep everyone else inside the place. While Matteo played the "old buddy" card and spoke with Carmine, an accomplice of his searched the side streets for Carmine's car.

"Hey, Carmine, I heard a rumor that you're thinking of running against the big guy?" Matteo had to see if Carmine really had the balls to go up against Varni. It would make the job he had to do a lot easier having known Carmine for so long.

Carmine nodded. "It's time for a change, Matteo. He's been the head honcho long enough. They know him, now. They know how he thinks. We need someone new at the bargaining table."

"Santino is a good man."

"He didn't negotiate hard enough for us last time, he kept us out too long, and it cost each and every one of us." Matteo didn't disagree.

"So, Carmine," Matteo said, "you think if you ran the union things would be different next time?

"Damn right I do! I'll bring 'em to their knees, if they try to screw with me."

The stevedore standing next to Carmine butted in. "I'll drink to that! Carmine, you got *my* vote."

Over the past few years, even Matteo had benefitted from the influence Carmine had with the rank and file, especially when election time rolled around. He genuinely liked Carmine, but he was wedded to Santino.

In reality, Carmine was popular among the men, and the

only thing that stood between him and a chance at being the Voice of the Union . . . was pure evil.

A day later, a small article appeared in the back pages of the Boston papers:

Police and fire rescue responded to a car fire yesterday in the waterfront district shortly after 5 p.m. The lone occupant died at the scene. Area residents reported hearing an explosion shortly before the fire and called police. The identity of the deceased is pending further investigation and notification of family.

ON THURSDAY, when Santino Varni returned from lunch, he stopped at his administrative assistant's desk. "Nina, please bring our calendars into my office."

Nina didn't really have a physical calendar for herself, so she grabbed her cell phone and the *At-A-Glance* calendar she used for Santino, and followed him. When she entered his office, she saw he was heading toward his desk.

Pointing to a chair opposite his desk, Santino Varni said, "Please have a seat." As soon as Nina was seated, he cleared his throat. "Nina, we're going north again."

Nina nodded. "When will that be?"

"We're going to fly up on Tuesday."

"For how long?"

"Two days, maybe three. Ask Nardo Lombardi."

Nina paused. "You want me to ask *Nardo Lombardi*?"

"Yes."

"May I ask, why?"

"He's the one I'm going up there with."

Nina blushed; she had assumed when Santino said "our" calendars that he was referring to the two of them. But she recovered quickly. "I'll make flight arrangements for both of you. It will be easier going out of Hanscom field to Grand Falls. I'll book Smyth Air from there to the resort."

"We're not going to the resort."

Now Nina was confused. When Santino saw the look on her face, he said, "Nardo will be showing me some property northeast of Kedqwick. See if there's a small airport near there we can fly into, will you? We'll need a four-wheel drive vehicle, and a couple of rooms."

"Yes, sir."

"Did you bring your calendar?"

Nina nodded and held up her cell phone.

"I'd like you to accompany me to the Mayor's Ball."

"When is that?"

"This Saturday."

She opened the calendar on her phone, pursed her lips, and stared at the screen. That was the night she already had a longstanding commitment, one that would be impossible to change.

"Do you have an appropriate dress?"

Nina was distracted by the thought of her other commitment, but managed to say, "No. No, I don't . . . I'll . . . I'll get something appropriate to wear."

Santino smiled as he reached for his wallet and took out a credit card. "Here, use this. Take the rest of the day off and go shopping. Find something that will make you feel intoxicatingly alive at the Mayor's Ball."

Santino was a ruthless, murdering bully, but he was also a generous benefactor to those in his inner circle.

He confuses me, she thought. *Maybe he doesn't see me as anything more than an employee. But I'm going to find a dress that will make him open his eyes!*

• • •

MEANWHILE, Popeye had just returned to the Boston area on his own. At first, he had intended to tell Matteo that he was done, finished, through with it all. But once the pain meds kicked in, and he couldn't feel the constant throbbing in his fingers anymore . . . the only thing he thought about was revenge.

I'm going to kill that friggin' wolf!

Chapter Forty-Four

That afternoon, when Jake stopped at his cousin's cottage to drop off mail, one of the letters was addressed to *Lieutenant Kathryn O'Grady, RCMP.* The return address on the envelope was the United States Social Security Administration.

"Kate, you in there?"

"I am."

"You've got mail."

"I'm on the phone, Jake. Just leave it on the porch, I'll pick it up later."

"As you wish." His duty done, he headed over to his own cottage, glad to be home.

Lou had spent a good part of his day over at Rocky Point, a place of solitude for him. When he needed to clear his thoughts and reflect, it was the place where he always seemed to head; it was the place where his most revelatory discoveries came to him. There he set his subconscious free and allowed it to roam about making connections on its own.

The Point was where he first agreed to go undercover with Kate a decade earlier. Now, once again, he sat on the smooth boulders, alone with his thoughts, hoping to hear the wisdom of the warrior's spirit deep within himself.

Lou remained at Rocky Point for quite a while, trying to piece the puzzle together. It wasn't until he heard the boats returning to the dock that he left.

ONCE THE BOATS were all in, Lou readied them for their next outing. Then he closed the door to the boathouse and headed over to his cottage. As usual, the first thing Lou did when he entered his porch was turn around and scan the horizon.

It was late afternoon; the sun had moved lower in the sky and shadows were elongated. The light was more subtle, yet, if looking west, one still had to squint. The clouds were still white, but soon they would take on the brilliant hues of sunset. The slight breeze coming off the lake was warm. Unlike the day before, the wind barely disturbed the leaves on the branches of the ancient maple standing near the shoreline; there was a hint of smoke in the air.

Lou lingered longer than usual on the porch, his eyes taking in the beauty surrounding him. As far as his eyes could see, the land, the trees, the lake, the streams, even the sky, belonged to the Abenaki. This area of New Brunswick was the ancestral home of Grey Elk and his band of Abenaki. Legal title for the land might now be in Lou's name, but he knew he didn't own the land. No one could *own* the land, only be one with the land. Since the dawn of time, the Abenaki had been one with the land. It was theirs to hunt, to fish, to call their home, and to care for. Lou was merely this generation's custodian, the caregiver, the one who held responsibility for protecting the land and passing it along to the next generation.

Once Lou was satisfied that all was well, he turned and picked up the mail still sitting on a porch chair and walked into the cottage.

Kate was still on the phone, but she gave him a wave when he walked in, and signaled she'd only be a few more minutes. Lou placed the mail on the kitchen table and sat down on the couch next to the twins who were glued to the television while wearing headphones. He would reveal his thoughts to Kate later.

Lou lifted the left headphone earpiece off his daughter's ear. "What are we watching?"

Without taking her eyes off the television screen, Ayleen said, "Odd Squad."

"You like that show?"

Ayleen nodded.

"What's it about?"

"*Daddy*, I'm trying to concentrate!"

Lou smiled. Ayleen would grow up to be an exact clone of her mother. She was smart as a whip and even at this young age, strikingly beautiful, inside and out. Her brother, Tyrone, was no slouch either; it was obvious he would take after his father. His son loved the outdoors. The only thing he was unhappy about was his name. Tyrone didn't care for his given name and preferred his Abenaki name, "Little Otter." Ayleen responded to either her given name, or to "Spotted Fawn." She wasn't as fussy.

• • •

When Kate finally finished her call, she stood up. "Whew, I didn't expect us to go on as long as we did."

"What's up?"

"Nothing really, just the usual mid-year budget shuffling and shifting of funds from one pocket to the other."

"What time are you going over to the lodge?"

"Soon . . . Alessandra said a few of the cottages asked us to put a couple of tables together so they could all sit together."

"I heard some talk about that at the dock. Oh, the mail's on the table."

"Anything important?"

"I don't know; I didn't even bother to look at it."

"Well, I'm going to jump in the shower," she said. "I'll get to the mail after the twins are in bed."

"And I have something to share."

"What?"

"Not now . . . tonight."

Dinner went off without a hitch. The three cottages who wanted to sit together did so and seemed to enjoy it. Rearranging the tables afterwards, back to their regular formation, took a little time; Kate ended up returning to their cottage later than usual.

After the twins were read their bedtime story and put to bed, Kate sorted through the mail. She was pleased the Social Security Administration had finally responded to her request. But when she opened the envelope and read the single page letter, it wasn't what she expected to see.

The letter confirmed the social security number she had questioned did belong to an individual named "Luigi

Secondo," but to date, no earnings had been recorded against the number.

Now this is just plain wrong, Kate thought. *How can someone who can afford to come up here for the entire season not have any reportable taxable earnings?*

Then she remembered something: *Wait, I think I read somewhere that not everyone in the States pays into Social Security. I need to check on that.*

The letter from the Social Security Administration also contained Luigi's home address in Boston. Kate fired up her laptop. *Okay, let's see where you live.* When she keyed in the address, the website of the *Omni Parker House Hotel* came up.

Okay, so maybe he lives in a hotel, she thought. *He's obviously got enough money to do that if he wanted to. Let's find out if he does.* She punched the phone number for the hotel into her cell phone and waited. After three rings, an officious sounding young man came on the line.

"Omni Parker House, front desk; how may I assist you?"

Kate hesitated, trying to envision what this proper Bostonian must look like.

"*Hello!* This is the Omni Parker House. How may I assist you?" he repeated.

"Yes, would you please connect me with Luigi Secondo. I believe he is one of your residents."

Kate heard the clicking sound of a few keystrokes before the person on the other end came back on the phone. "I'm sorry, I'm not seeing anyone with that name. Do you have the room number?"

"I believe he's a permanent resident, not a guest."

"This is a hotel, ma'am. We have no permanent residents."

"Say that, again?"

"I said, we're a *hotel*, not a boarding house, ma'am. You may have us confused with Parker Square Shelter for Men."

Kate dismissed the young man's gnarly tone of voice and pushed back. "No, the address I was given is absolutely this address."

"I'm *sorry*, ma'am, there is *no* one by the name 'Luigi Secondo' at this address. Is there anything else I can do for you, ma'am?"

Yes, you can stop calling me 'ma'am,' she thought, but only said, "No, I'm fine. I'm sorry to have bothered you." Hanging up, Kate began thinking. *Am I trying to find a ghost? Why are there so many inconsistencies?*

Mentally, she began going through a checklist:

- The phone number he gave us doesn't belong to him.
- He doesn't come up anywhere on the Internet.
- The P.O. Box he gave us isn't his.
- His social security number matches, but there's no earnings against it.
- He doesn't live at the address we have on file for him, nor the US Government has for him.

Well, DNA and fingerprints don't lie, she thought. *I'll find out who Luigi Secondo is when the forensic lab gets back to me.*

Finally, she looked over at her husband who was half asleep on the couch. "Lou, hon, you said earlier you had something to share."

"It'll keep. Let's go to bed."

Chapter Forty-Five

Saturday mornings were always hectic at Havre de Poisson. Guests were packing up, float planes were flying in to pick up passengers, housekeeping was busy changing over linens in the cottages for incoming guests, and a few diehard anglers were still out on the lake hoping for one last shot at hauling in a trophy fish.

Jake didn't deliver mail on weekends, so he gave Lou a hand down at the dock, readying the boats for the next group of anglers scheduled to arrive.

"You got any plans for lunch, Jake."

"Koby didn't say anything. Why?"

"I wanna run a few things by you."

"We can do it now if you want?"

Lou looked around; they had the dock to themselves. "Somebody is messing with me."

"Yeah?"

"Yeah, too much is happening for it to all be coincidental."

"Like what, Cuz?"

"Well, you know about those two outboard motors."

"Yeah, how can I forget three days in a row?"

"Well, now I'm not even sure if it was a bird or a *rock* that hit that plate glass window in the kitchen. Then, when I called Brunswick Mutual, they said I had cancelled my policy."

"Did you?"

"Of *course not.* Why the hell would I go and do a damn fool thing like that?"

"I guess you wouldn't."

Lou reached into the boat house and grabbed the broken washing machine belts Alassandra had brought over. "Take a look at these. Yesterday, I had to replace the belts on both washing machines." Lou handed both belts to Jake. "Look at these. What's that break look like to you?"

Jake examined both breaks before handing the belts back to Lou. "I'd say a knife played a role in each one."

"Exactly. Earlier in the week, quite a few of Angelo's hens wandered out of the coop. Angelo's way too conscientious not to have secured the damn door on that coop. When have so many things gone wrong around here, so close together? Never! Then there's that damn article in the newspaper."

"You mean the one about Tinker Bell?" When Jake's attempt at humor fell flat, he asked, "Did you ever call them back?"

"Yeah, I did, for all the good *that* did. They said they gave me a couple of shots at making a statement, and it's my fault for not returning their calls."

"But the clincher for me was when I had to clean out the fuel filter on the generator that we keep behind the shed. *That* one was clogged with the same damn residue I've been finding in the two outboard motors, *sugar!*"

"You sure it's sugar?"

"Has to be. I found an empty packet on the ground nearby, I found a few empties down by the dock too.

"All this happened this past week?"

"Yeah. Not to mention the other morning when I had to screw in every other damn bulb in every other damn ceiling fixture in the lodge before breakfast. Add to that the breaker controlling the walk-in freezer tripped, for no reason, and the door was left open. Damn good thing Angelo insisted on having a buzzer connected to the thermostat. I'm saying nothing like all that has ever happened before. I'm saying somebody's behind all this."

Jake took a deep breath. "Breakers are designed to trip, but can't see Angelo leaving the door open. I'll admit, you add all this stuff up and it sounds fishy."

"I don't even wanna talk about fish. That's another problem. They pulled a couple of those damn Tench out of the first feeder pond. We'll have some *serious* trouble if those suckers ever get into the lake."

Lou paused as he let out a sigh and shook his head in frustration.

"At least we got the damn algae problem under control, but that was just another thing this week. The only thing that hasn't jumped up and smacked me in the face are the controlled burns. We haven't had a single issue with that. The fire marshal's office is monitoring that."

"Well, the algae and the Tench thing happened on their own, Lou. That's Mother Nature. But for all the rest, I get what you're saying. Something's not right."

"I told you about the cell phone I found the morning after Hector spent the night at the boathouse, didn't I."

"No, but I heard about it from Koby. Did you ever figure out who it belongs to?"

"No. Kate tried; she thinks it a burner phone."

"Really?"

"Yeah. Whoever had it, called two different 506 area code numbers; one was to Brunswick Mutual."

"And the other call?"

"I don't know. We called, but the line was busy and didn't go into voicemail. Then we got busy and didn't get another chance."

"You still got the phone?"

"Yeah. I put a note on the message board and asked around, but nobody's claimed it."

"Let's try calling the other 506 number again. It would be nice to know if the guy that dropped a dime on you used that phone to call the paper."

"Yeah, that's a good idea. I'll do it as soon as I finish up here. I'm also gonna take a run over to those ponds."

"You got time for that before the next crowd comes in?"

"It'll only take an hour to get down and back from Moose Cove…if I push it."

"I fly over those ponds at least two or three times a week, but I don't think I've been on the ground in over a dozen years."

"There's a few new fire lanes running directly there from the village now."

"Yeah, I know, I've seen 'em from the air every time I come in."

"You wanna come along for the ride?"

Jake thought a moment. "Sure, but let's fly down. It'll knock close to an hour off our travel time."

Lou nodded. "Okay. I got one more boat out, but I hear him coming in now."

"Good, I'll go let Koby know. Meet me over at the plane."

During the flight down to Moose Cove, Lou shared what he'd found the second time he went down to the boathouse the morning after Hector had been there overnight.

"Lou, the way you're describing the stitching on that harness and the claw marks in the dock, it sounds like something got Hector's attention. I'm surprised you didn't hear him"

"Jake, he's not going to bark; he's not a dog. He's just going to act."

"Yeah, you're right."

"It could've been an animal. Raccoons have gone out on the dock at night."

"Lou, an animal would have picked up Hector's scent… and as far as I know, none of 'em carry cell phone." Jake thought for a moment. "You said the cell phone was near the end of the dock, right?"

"Yeah, along with some trash and a few sugar packets."

"When was that?"

"Thursday morning."

"Did you have trouble with those boats Thursday morning?"

"Nope."

"Friday morning?"

"Nope."

"What's all this telling ya, Lou?"

"Like I said, somebody's been deliberately trying to sabotage me."

"I think you're right, Cuz."

"But, who?"

Jake turned his head and looked directly at Lou. "You want another clue?"

"If you've got one, yeah."

"Call that other number with the 506-area code on that cell phone and see what you get."

LATER, after Lou returned home, he dialed the second 506 number on the cell phone he'd found near the dock. Kate was standing by and Lou had the phone on speaker. When the ringing stopped, a recording kicked in.

Welcome to the Brunswick Daily Times. Press 1 to continue in English, press 2 for French.

Lou pursed his lips and inhaled deeply. "That seals it for me, Kate. Whoever had this phone was up to dirty tricks."

"I can't disagree with you on that, Lou."

"I'm gonna call a little get-together among ourselves. Maybe if we all talk this thing through, we can figure out who the culprit is."

"Lou we're not dealing with a 'culprit,' this person's a criminal."

Chapter Forty-Six

On that same Saturday, Nardo Lombardi and Santino Varni walked out to a private jet sitting on the tarmac at Hanscom Field, a regional airport just outside Boston which catered to smaller aircraft.

As the Gulfstream G550 taxied to the runway, Nardo turned to the only other passenger on board. "Santino, I'm curious, why are you traveling under a different name?"

Santino had no intention of disclosing his full reason. "There are those who try to track my movements, that's all. But, what's in a name? This is merely the name I go by whenever I visit Canada."

"So, do I call you 'Santino' or 'Luigi'?"

"Santino." Varni had his reasons for that as well.

Nardo nodded. "If we acquire this lake, whose name do we use?"

"I'm not sure yet."

The pilot's voice came over the public address system: *"Fasten your seatbelts and prepare for takeoff."*

Almost as soon as the pilot clicked off, thrust from the powerful twin engines began propelling the sleek aircraft down the runway at increasing speed. When the jet reached liftoff and began to rise, the pilot retracted the flaps in stages until they reached cruising altitude. Minutes later, the plane was heading toward New Brunswick at speeds over 500 mph and cruising at 37,000 feet.

Two hours later, a Delta commercial jet left Boston's Logan Airport also headed for Grand Falls, New Brunswick. The first-class passengers in row two were non-other than Matteo Abruzzi and Popeye.

JAKE HAD COMPLETED his preflight check and was sitting in the cockpit at the end of the dock waiting as Lou came around the corner from Jake's cottage.

The two cousins were the only ones with waterfront cottages, since rank has its privileges. Exterior dimensions on their homes were identical, and both were precisely orientated to capture the best possible view and breeze off the lake. Not more than fifty yards apart, the only difference between them were the interior floor plans. Lou's interior floor plan matched the cottage Kate still owned in Ireland. The inside of Jake's cottage somewhat replicated the seaside cottage Koby had rented in Nantucket after she'd left the Channel Islands.

JAKE'S DE HAVILLAND was no match for the Gulfstream G550's speed, but after being airborne for no more than five minutes, Jake was already circling Moose Cove and coming in for a water landing. Granted, they had far less territory to travel.

"You were right," Lou said. "This was a helluva lot quicker than the runabout, even at full throttle."

Jake smiled. "Yeah, well let's hope that ATV has enough gas in it to get us up to the village."

"I don't think we need to worry about that. Koby keeps it full. There's no way in hell she's gonna run out of gas and end up getting stuck in the woods."

The two cousins traveled six miles up to the village without incident.

"Wanna stop in and say 'hi' to Laughing Gull?" Jake asked.

"I'd like to but can't. Gotta get back. I've a got another full house coming in later today."

Laughing Gull is a first cousin to both Lou and Jake and the only close relative they have in the village. Her husband, Tall Tree, grew up with them and is their closest friend in the village. The four of them are close in age, as are all of their offspring. Like Jake, Laughing Gull stepped up and agreed to mentor the three Gault children in the ways of the Abenaki and what it means to *walk the red road*."

As Jake set down in Moose Cove he turned to Lou. "Have you been up to take a look at the new fire lanes?"

"Not all of them; I haven't had a chance to get away with everything that's been going on at the camp."

"I've flown over them a few times."

Once the mail plane was secured to the dock, the two men traveled up the road leading to the Village

Jake talked over the noise of the ATV. "There's a new turnoff that goes to the left up ahead. I've seen it a few times from the air. If we turn there, we'll start seeing where they've been burning, and we'll run into the new lanes."

"Well, I don't have time for much more than taking a quick look at the ponds today."

"Okay, then that's all we'll do."

They weren't more than a few miles from the village, when the lush green forest floor gave way to charred barren ground, left behind by the controlled burns.

"Lou, the deer will be in here thicker than flies with all the new growth that's gonna spring up. There should be some nice hunting up here next fall."

"That's for sure." Lou paused for a moment. "We need to start paying a little more attention to managing the forest."

"Might be time to do this a little closer to the village, too."

"You're right, but if the wind catches it and the burn gets out of hand, that could spell trouble. I think we'll just go in with brush saws and clean out the places that are overgrown close to the village."

"No sense in testing our luck, right?" Jake pointed to a spot. "This looks like the road that'll bring us over to the ponds."

"All we have to do is follow the power lines."

"The trees are a lot taller since I was last here."

Jake's comment pulled up a memory for Lou. "One time, this goes back awhile, I remember playing Butterfly Hide and Seek up here. I was tracking someone, I can't remember who the hell it was."

"It was me."

"Was it?"

"Yeah. Don't you remember the crazy she-bear with the two cubs? I never saw you run so fast in my life."

Lou laughed. "That damn bear chased me damn near all the way to the first pond. I thought she was coming in *after* me."

"Speaking of ponds, there's a break in the tree line coming up on the left."

"Then, we're close."

When Jake pulled the ATV over to the side of the fire lane, both men got off and headed toward the pond on foot.

"Ya got some trashy litter up here, Lou. Looks like somebody wanted to get rid of a few old plastic chest coolers."

"It's gotta be from the guys doing the burn. I'll have a talk with them."

"They need to haul 'em out. Plastic takes hundreds of years to decompose. Be sure you tell 'em that."

"I will. Watch out for the poison ivy, Jake, it's all over the place."

"I see it."

When they broke through the brush and finally reached the rocky shoreline, four turtles sunning themselves on a fallen tree, slipped into the water.

Lou frowned. *I wonder if the chemicals will kill the turtles? Probably not… they don't have gills, but time will tell.*

Jake stared out toward the center of the pond. "Grey Elk took us here all the time. This is where he taught us to fish at night with torches and the long spears."

Lou nodded. "The elders still come here to teach others. The canoes and spears are on the opposite side."

They both looked out across the pond in silence for a moment. Memories of the many times they'd fished here with Grey Elk filling their thoughts. Finally, Jake said, "Everyone must be happy there's a road coming up here now."

Lou sighed. "We were told the approach we're taking to remove the algae will only kill algae, our people are okay with that. But, to kill off the Tench, every living thing in these ponds must die. Some who came to the tribal meeting asked why? Others asked what ritual must we do before so many lives are taken."

Neither Lou or Jake had anything further to say, they were thinking: How does one ask the Creator to forgive when so many lives will be lost?"

After a few more minutes of silence, Jake spoke. "Koby says it will come back. Nature has a way of healing itself."

"Yeah. It'll take time, but it'll happen." Lou made one more complete scan of the shoreline. "You ready to go?"

"Yeah."

"Then let's go. I need to get back."

As they retraced their steps Jake pulled up short. "Lou, take a look at this."

"What?"

"Look."

When Lou joined his cousin, Jake kicked the plastic cooler closest to him and a swarm of flies rose from the decaying fish that were inside. Lou stared at the fish in the cooler. There were other dead fish laying on the ground nearby.

"Lou, who among our people would take fish and leave them to rot?"

"Take a closer look, Jake. Those fish aren't from our waters. Those are Tench."

Lou walked to another cooler laying on its side. "There's a dead fish in this one too. Jake, these Tench didn't find their own way here; they had help."

"From who?"

"Good question. I'd like to find out. Grab ahold of that first cooler, let's take it with us."

What Jake didn't notice when he picked up the cooler was the crudely etched name on the underside . . . *Turnbridge*.

Chapter Forty-Seven

Miles to the west, Nardo and Santino had just flown into Grand Falls. From there, they took a connecting flight to a small regional airport in Kedgwick, north of Havre de Poisson.

A few hours later, Matteo and Popeye flew into Grand Falls on the Delta commercial carrier. Once they cleared customs, they rented a four-wheel drive and headed toward Five Fingers and the Turnbridge enclave.

Lou had been anxious to return from Moose Cove and take his usual spot on the dock before the next round of sportsmen arrived.

A perennial guest, Josh Barnard, was arriving this week. It was Josh, an attorney, who had used a long-forgotten treaty document years earlier to block the Canadian Rail Lines, and a developer, from gaining control of land the treaty had given to the Abenaki long ago.

The bond between the Barnards and the Abenaki went back quite a while. It was Josh's grandfather who had initially counseled Lou's grandfather, Grey Elk, on an approach to legally protect his ancestral lands. Decades later, when Josh Barnard had crashed his float plane in a wilderness lake, known as Lake 991, it was Lou who came to his rescue. Even though Josh and Lou lived entirely different lives, they were similar in many ways. Both were masterful in their chosen vocations, and many of their shared values were intertwined.

When Josh emerged from the very last of the de Havilland float planes to arrive, and stepped onto the dock, Lou was all smiles.

"About time you got here! I was just about ready to call Search and Rescue."

Josh smiled. "We came up on the East side of Carleton Mountain."

"Did you run into bad weather?"

"No, actually the weather was fine. About halfway up, I told the pilot to swing over by Lake 991, for sentimental reasons."

"I thought you'd had enough of that lake after ditching your plane there and spending the night in a cold camp."

"Hey, I had a fire; I was fine. You oughta know by now that I come from hardy stock."

Lou gave his friend a good-natured slap on the back. "Come on, let's go get you settled in. Dinner is in an hour. Angelo will be glad to see you."

As they walked, Josh couldn't help but say, "I saw that fairy dust article in the Daily Times the other day. Did you and Tinker Bell have a little rift?"

Lou just smirked. *Tinker Bell...he sounds like Jake.*

"You knew I was gonna rag you about it."

"I figured as much."

"So things are really going okay?"

"Financially, they are. But...I seem to have a monkey on my back and I'm trying to find out who."

"Whaddya mean?"

"Somebody's trying to tarnish my reputation. Whoever it is has thrown a wrench or two into things these past few weeks."

"How so?"

"Well, you saw the article in the Times. Somebody dropped a dime on me."

"Lou, that's a *rag*. Nobody's going to pay much attention to that."

"Well, a number of other things have happened all of a sudden."

"Like what?"

Lou paused. "You know what, I'm holding a little family powwow tonight. Why don't you sit in. You can tell me what you think after I go over the story."

"Where?"

"My cottage; 7:30 p.m."

"I'll be there."

WHEN NARDO and Santino arrived at Kedgwick Airport, they chartered a float plane operated by Howard Air. Smaller than Smyth Air, Howard Air pretty much dominated the backcountry fly-in business that went in and out of Kedqwick.

As soon as the de Havilland DHC-3 Otter took off. Nardo leaned over to Santino. "The place I want to show you is on the far side of this mountain coming up." Santino merely nodded.

"The mountain is known as Carleton Mountain. There's not much on the other side of it. The land is mostly in the hands of logging companies."

"Does that mean anything?"

"Maybe . . . maybe not. They tend to sit on these land banks for decades. They don't go near them until it's worth their while to go in and haul out the timber. They're not in the habit of carving out small sections, but from time to time they do . . . if they need cash and the price is right."

Santino looked down at the vast sea of green stretching as far as the horizon in every direction. "So, what's the price?"

"Like told you, there's not a lot of real estate activity up here. A couple of wood lots hit the market a few years ago at a low price. We'll use that as our starting point."

"What the hell's a 'wood lot'?"

"It's an expression. This far off the grid, people don't have many options beyond wood to heat their homes. It takes about a seven-acre lot to keep a single household in firewood year after year."

"I don't see any roads down there. How are people going to get to where we're going?"

"The same way we are, from the air."

"No, I'm talking about construction vehicles. Is there a road to this place?"

"Look down and you'll see Highway 180."

When Santino leaned over and looked down, he saw the road. He also saw a large lake, just west of Carleton Mountain.

"What's that body of water down there?" Nardo took a

quick look, then pulled out a map of the area. After studying it a few moments, he answered.

"That's Lake 980, the one the resort you're interested in buying sits on."

"It looks different from up here. What's the lake you said we're going to?"

"Lake 991. It's just on the other side of Carleton Mountain."

IT WAS late afternoon when Matteo and Popeye reached the hamlet known as Five Fingers. As they approached the local watering hole where they initially met Oswald Turnbridge, they noticed the parking lot was full.

"You gonna pull in; see if he's there?" Popeye asked, as Matteo let up on the gas pedal.

"Might as well."

After Matteo shifted the SUV into park and pressed the off button, he noticed Popeye rubbing the bandages on his right hand. "Is that still bothering you?"

"Yeah, friggin' thing itches like hell. It's nonstop."

"What'd the doc say? You had a doc look at it, right?"

"Yeah."

"So, what'd *he* say?"

"There wasn't a friggin' thing he could do. He wanted to know how it happened. I told him I was slicing friggin' garlic."

"You told him *what*?"

"I . . . never friggin' mind what I told him."

Matteo just shook his head. "Come on let's go inside."

• • •

EVEN THOUGH IT was late afternoon and light was fading, when Matteo and Popeye entered the building, it took a couple of minutes before their eyes became accustomed to the dimly lit barroom.

Like the previous time they were there, most of the bar stools were taken by locals who'd stopped in to guzzle down a few beers before happy hour ended.

Mattero scanned the bar and the tables. "He's not here."

"So, let's give him some time. Shit, we got time."

"Yeah, okay. Whaddya want?" Matteo asked and signaled the bartender.

"Gimmie a Pink Lady"

"Cut the shit. I ain't ordering you *that* here."

Popeye smiled. "What's the matter, you afraid of a bar fight?"

"Whaddya want?" Matteo growled again.

"A shot and a beer, maybe that'll take the friggin' edge off."

Every time the door opened, they expected to see Oswald. When Matteo finished his third draft, he pushed back his chair. "He's not coming. Let's get the hell outta here."

"Where to?"

"That hellhole of a place he lives in."

QUITE A FEW MILES to the northeast, the floatplane Santino and Nardo had taken from Kedqwick, sat idling in the middle of Lake 991.

"So, Santino, whaddya think? Is this lake big enough for you?

Santino looked out the window. "How long is it?"

"It's shaped more round like a circle than long. The map says about two miles across in any direction."

Santino leaned forward and tapped the pilot on the shoulder. "Hey, drive around, go close to the shore." The pilot nodded and pushed the throttle forward just enough to begin gliding across the surface. There were a few coves, which they didn't enter, but most of the shoreline was open.

"Nardo, what kinda fish are we talking about here?"

Nardo took a breath; he wasn't fully prepared for that question. "The data I have on this lake is dated." When Nardo hesitated, Santino gestured for him to continue.

"It's a remote lake. It's on private land; not very accessible, so we can't expect the information to be 100 percent." Santino merely shrugged his shoulders.

Nardo pulled out a sheet of paper. "The depth in the center is well over 150 feet. The shoreline is rocky. There's table rocks under the surface in some areas. It's spring fed, and there's a few tributaries that flow into it. There's no vehicular access to it. So, I'd guess the fish population is the same as it was the last time they gill-netted here."

Santino was looking out at the shoreline. When Nardo stopped talking, he turned and repeated his question. "So, what fish are in here?"

"The last time they gill-netted was twenty years ago. Back then they found lake and rainbow trout, whitefish, small mouth bass, some pickerel, yellow perch, blue gills, and smelt." The answer made Santino raise his eyebrows, obviously pleased.

"How much should I offer?"

"That depends on how much land you want."

"I want everything in from that highway. And I want at least two miles on the other sides. How much is that?"

"I'll have to work up the numbers tonight, Santino."

"Okay, do that. We'll make them an offer tomorrow."

"Tomorrow's Sunday. We won't reach anybody 'til Monday."

Santino smiled. "Okay, Monday. Now, let's go up again and take a look at where we'll build the lodge."

Nardo leaned forward and tapped the pilot on the shoulder. The plane turned away from the shoreline, taxied out to the middle, lifted off the water and circled back.

IMMEDIATELY TO THE WEST, the foreman in charge of all the crews executing the controlled burns called everyone together.

"Okay, listen up! The boss man says we're all done with the burning. Everybody's worked hard, we're all tired, so, let's call it a day. Tomorrow's Sunday, everybody's got the day off. I want every one of you back Monday morning, understood? Every single one of you, and I mean *everybody*. Be here bright and early, no excuses and no exceptions! I wanna pack up and clear the hell outta here before 10 a.m."

"You want the tanker trucks filled with water before we leave tonight?"

The foreman thought for a minute. "Fill one about halfway, dump whatever's in the others. I don't wanna waste gasoline lugging water we don't need over the highways."

"You got it boss."

Chapter Forty-Eight

It was after dark when Matteo pulled off the highway and drove down the dirt lane leading into the valley known as Turnbridge Hollow.

The Turnbridges rarely had visitors. Once the dogs started barking, the men folk came out to get a look-see at what had riled them. It wasn't long before the Turnbridge men saw the headlights off in the distance. Moonshine was how they made the little cash they had. To their way of thinking, headlights coming down their road after dark meant only one thing - trouble.

Well before their headlights reached the cluster of broken-down, weathered shacks they called home, the men had taken off for the hills and the oil lamps inside the shacks were snuffed out. When Matteo reached the barn, he stopped and rolled down the driver's side window. "Oswald! Oswald, it's me, Matteo! I need to talk with you. I have more work for you."

The womenfolk were the only ones within earshot of Matteo. They'd been left behind to mind the slew of bare-foot, ragtag kids hanging onto the porches. Many of them had never seen headlights before.

When Oswald didn't appear, Matteo pushed on the horn. Finally, a woman's voice called out: "He ain't here."

"I need to speak to him. Where is he?"

"He's gone."

"I'm a friend. I have work for him."

A couple of men hadn't retreated too far into the woods and were listening. When they heard Oswald's name mentioned a couple of times, one of them nodded; the other went to fetch Oswald. The man who stayed behind, cupped his hands and yelled, "He'll be a-coming."

Matteo turn the ignition key off, doused the headlights, and stepped out of the SUV. Close to fifteen minutes passed before Matteo heard a voice call out.

"What you want?"

"Oswald, is that you?"

"It's me . . ."

"Where are you?"

Oswald tapped Matteo on the shoulder. "Behind you."

Matteo nearly jumped out of this skin, when Oswald touched him.

Holy shit, how the frig did he sneak up behind me like that? When Matteo turned around, he saw not only Oswald, but four other figures, each armed with a shotgun of some type.

"Oswald I'd like to talk with you about something."

"Go ahead and talk."

Matteo hesitated. "I thought we might talk alone."

Oswald waved his hand and the men who were with him melted into the darkness. "You can talk now."

"Oswald, I'd like to play another trick on the Abenaki. You interested?"

"What kind of trick? I ain't doing no more fishing, if that's what you're asking 'bout."

"No, what I have in mind has nothing to do with fish."

"What then?"

"How would you like to really scare the *bejeebers* outta the Abenaki?"

"How?"

"How'd you like to really make 'em pay for sending Arthur Turnbridge to jail. Would you like that?"

"You gonna pay me for it?"

"Absolutely. Are you interested?"

"I suppose so. But like I said, I ain't doing no fishing."

"Trust me, this has nothing to do with fishing."

"What is it then?"

"How'd you like to teach those Abenaki what it's like to play with *fire*?"

Even in the dark Matteo was able to see the smile on Oswald's face.

Matteo spent more than a few minutes talking to Oswald. Finally, Matteo took out his wallet; there was an exchange of money before he got back into the SUV.

"You all set?" Popeye asked.

"Yeah. He's gonna create a real nice diversion for us."

"All right let's go find someplace to eat. Tomorrow's another day."

When the SUV reached the top of the hill, Matteo turned left onto the highway. "We'll stay in Nictau tonight. That'll put us close to that logging road."

• • •

LATER THAT NIGHT, the year-round adult residents, along with Josh Barnard, assembled at Lou and Kate's cottage. After a few pleasantries, addressed mainly to Josh, Lou called the assembly to order.

"All right, we've had a number of things happen around here recently, none of which I believe were accidental or a quirk of fate."

Angelo was the first to speak up. "Lou, we had a string of bad luck. Things happen, that's all."

"Angelo, last week I might have agreed wholeheartedly with you, but not now."

Josh spoke up. "Lou, didn't you say you found a phone?"

"Yes, I found a cell phone at the edge of the dock near the shoreline. So far, no one's claimed it."

Now Kate spoke. "It has all the markings of a burner, Josh. It's been stripped and it hasn't been in use for long."

Lou turned to Josh. "I believe whoever had that phone is the one who canceled our policy with Brunswick Mutual and gave a scathing review to the Brunswick Daily News."

"Did you have a lot of unhappy guests last week, Lou?"

"No, we didn't. Two cottages had to deal with outboard motor issues, but even their comment cards were positive." There were a few murmurs as everyone nodded in agreement.

Lou turned to his wife. "Kate, you had something you wanted to share."

Kate waited for everyone to settle down before she began. "In all probability everything that's been happening is the act of one or two individuals. If we know what's behind this, we'll have a better chance of figuring out who it is. Does anyone have any ideas on motives?" There was dead silence until Josh spoke up.

"This isn't a motive, but my guess is, whoever's behind this wasn't your typical guest; may be they were a loner, maybe they weren't into fishing as much as everybody else. Those are just a couple of thoughts to consider."

Lou nodded. "Okay, so who stood out; who seemed like they didn't fit in last week?" The name "Vincenzo" was almost said in unison.

Kate cleared her throat "Vincenzo was pretty easy to pick out. But, sometimes it's not always the most obvious person."

"Right," Jake said, "but I think we can rule out the guys who had the outboard motor issues." Kate nodded in agreement.

"Kate, where's that burner phone?"

"It's on the desk, Lou."

"Wasn't there an 800 number on the phone's *recently called* list?"

"There was."

Lou walked over and grabbed the phone, powered it up, scrolled down the short list of outgoing calls until he came to an 800 number, and pressed it, then he put the phone on speaker.

"Good evening, this is Smyth Air."

Lou just stared at the phone. When he said nothing further, the person on the other end terminated the call.

Kate put her hand out. "Lou, let me see that phone a second." Lou no sooner handed the phone to his wife, than her thumbs were clicking away on the screen. "That call was made Wednesday night, just after 11 p.m. What's that tell us?"

Jake smiled. "Sounds to me like somebody was making plans to get the hell out of Dodge."

"Possible, but not necessarily," Koby said. "They could have been confirming their Saturday pickup."

"Nope, I'm with Jake," Lou said. "Everyone who flies in here with Smyth Air has a return reservation with a specified time they're getting picked up the following Saturday; there's no need to confirm." What he didn't say, but immediately thought was, *the only one who left early was Vincenzo.*

Kate looked at the faces around the room; some appeared to be deep in thought, but no one looked like they had anything further to say. "Okay, so, we believe the individual was a loner," she continued. "We've pretty much determined the perp dropped his phone and there's a possibility he left early. I'm saying 'he,' because we didn't have any female guests last week. So, who left early?"

Lou took in a deep breath and let it out before speaking. "Only one person left early; everyone else stayed the full week."

Jake stifled a yawn. "Okay, that does it for me. I'm ruling out Colonel Mustard and going with Vincenzo, in the boathouse, with the phone."

Josh ignored Jake's comment. "You know this is all circumstantial evidence. I haven't heard one thing that a prosecutor would jump on."

Kate chimed in. "Josh is right, this is all supposition. Alessandra, I know you've stripped the linens from Luigi's cottage, but have the housekeepers gone in there yet?"

"Not yet."

"Good, have them hold off."

Lou looked at the cheat sheet he was working from. "All right, so here's something else for us to ponder. The name of the local paper is no secret. Hell, we leave enough copies of the Brunswick Daily News lying around in the lodge. But here's a question: How could someone figure out who we use for insurance?"

When no one spoke up, Josh asked, "Who *do* you use?"

"Brunswick Mutual."

"Do they advertise on your website or on any of your marketing material?"

"No."

Josh continued with a follow-up question. "Okay, could it have come up in conversation somehow?"

"That's not anything I talk about with anybody. But, back to Vincenzo, here's what makes me question if we're talking about one person, or two. He stayed in camp the whole time he was here. Yet Jake and I found evidence over at the feeder ponds which absolutely tells me the Tench didn't end up in our waters all by its lonesome."

Josh nodded. "Okay, so, maybe there's more than one person involved, or maybe the Tench thing is totally separate."

Lou took a deep breath. "That's what I'm beginning to think, Josh."

Alessandra looked at Lou. "How would whoever's doing this know about the Tench?"

Koby spoke up quickly. "The infiltration of the Tench has been in all the papers lately, it's public information. What's interesting to me though is how they found out who insures us."

"Me too," said Kate.

"Maybe they overheard one of us talking about insurance," Koby offered, as she innocently shared her thoughts.

Kate looked around. "Did any of us talk about Brunswick Mutual in front of any guests last week at any time?"

"Angelo and I did," Lou said. "But that was *after* the window was shattered. The text on the phone was sent to Brunswick a few days *earlier*."

Angelo had been quietly thinking, but now he spoke up. "A few weeks ago, Luigi and I discussed the resort during one of our outdoor walks and insurance came up. But he and I talk about *everything* under the sun, and, besides, we all *know* Luigi. He'd never to anything to hurt us."

Lou held up his hand. "I agree, we all know Luigi. But ask yourself, where did Vincenzo stay? He stayed in *Luigi's* cottage. That doesn't implicate Luigi, but none of us know a damn thing about Vincenzo, or what kind of a relationship he has with Luigi."

Angelo shrugged his shoulders and kept his thoughts to himself. *Lou's right, we don't know anything about Vincenzo at all.*

Alessandra sat up straight before she spoke. "I don't know if this means anything, but I'm going to share it. I found it strange that every time I reset the table Vincenzo sat at I had to refill the sugar bowl. Like I said, I don't know if that means anything."

Lou took in a breath and let it out. "I'm positive it was sugar that fouled up those two outboards and the generator. All the signs point to that. Actually, all the signs I'm seeing are pointing at Vincenzo.

"But," said Josh, "if he never left camp, he couldn't have been the one who put the Tench in the pond."

"No, you're right."

Jake stretched and rolled his head around his shoulders. "Maybe he wasn't working alone."

When no one said anything else, Lou stood up, signaling the meeting was over. "Okay, this firms up what I've been thinking. It's getting late and tomorrow's an early day for all of us. Let's keep thinking and sharing."

What he didn't share was, *I'm going to have a talk with Luigi about this friend of his.*

Chapter Forty-Nine

Whenever a sportsman requested a fishing guide, Lou had contracts with a handful of Abenaki from the village of Grey Elk. It was rare that Lou, himself, went out as a guide, unless it was with Josh Barnard.

Josh never *requested* a guide, but ever since the two men spent a night in the woods bordering Lake 991 when Josh's plane went down, they'd had a special bond.

On Sunday morning, when Josh walked down to the dock, the only boats still tied to the dock, were Luigi's, which nearly never went out, and the one assigned to his cottage. After setting his fishing gear down, Josh walked inside the boathouse to find Lou.

"Got time to do a little fishing today, Lou?"

Not even bothering to turn his head, Lou answered, "I've been waiting on you."

"Good, I'll put my gear in my boat."

"No, we'll use the runabout. Just bring your tackle box. I've got the rods all rigged up that we're gonna use."

"Whatever you say. You're the boss."

ONCE THE 26-FOOT mahogany Classic backed out of the boathouse, Lou leaned toward his friend and shouted over the rumbling noise of the powerful engine: "We're going down to Osprey Cove. The fishing's good there this time of year."

"Works for me."

Once they reached the center of the lake, Lou pushed the throttle full forward. In a matter of seconds, the sleek bow rose out of the water and the boat came up on plane. Osprey Cove is about a mile beyond Moose Cove and is the smaller of the two coves. Unlike Moose Cove, Osprey is devoid of barrier islands. The winds that rule the lake also define the surface conditions in Osprey Cove.

Lou kept the throttle full forward the entire trip and maintained a straight course down the center of the lake. As he entered the cove, he backed down on the throttle and veered to the left, avoiding a pair of mergansers floating on the surface.

Once they were inside the cove, Lou stood up, keeping one knee on the seat. "Josh, we'll head over to where the stream comes in; there's a huge drop off about thirty feet offshore. We'll get into some decent size fish there."

As they approached the area Lou had in mind, he turned to Josh. "Get the anchor line ready. But make sure you check the connection before you toss it over; that's the only hook onboard."

As soon as Lou cut the engine, Josh released the anchor over the side and counted the length of rope as it played out.

"We're in about ninety feet of water here, Lou."

"That's about right."

"How far down are we gonna go?"

"You go down about sixty feet, I'll go a little lower."

"You hooking 'em under the dorsal?"

"Yeah, these smelt are pretty lively."

Josh had barely set his fishing rod in the rod holder when the tip arched over and touched the water. The sound of the line peeling off the reel caught his attention. After setting the hook, he turned to Lou. "Looks like you were right about sixty feet."

"Let 'em take as much line as he wants. Ya gotta really play these big one's when you're using light tackle. That line will break, if you try hauling 'em in."

Josh could feel the strength of the fish tugging on the line. He could tell by the resistance that he'd hooked a fairly large fish. Just then the tension on the line went slack. Josh wasn't sure if he still had the fish on the line until it jumped a full foot out of the water, forty feet from the boat.

"Whoa, that's a nice fish, Josh! There's some good-sized rainbows in this cove."

Josh began reeling in the line. "I think this 'bow's coming up again. Yeah, he's coming toward the boat. I can see him coming up. Lou, get the net."

"Ya might wanna play him some more; that fish is still pretty green."

Just as the fish came to the surface, it turned around and sounded. The rod was bent over; its tip touching the surface of the water. Josh's fingers moved to adjust the drag. Then the rod tip straightened up and the line went slack. "Shit. I should have let up on the drag sooner."

"Josh, there's plenty more of 'em in here."

"I hope so."

As Josh tied another hook on the line, he made small talk with Lou. "There was a float plane sitting in the middle of Lake 991 the other day when I was coming up."

"Really?"

"Yeah. Ya know, I can't even remember the last time I was up this way. I think it was two years ago."

Lou smiled. Josh enjoyed a fairly large practice now. Clients lined up and waited for him. He was nowhere near as hungry as he once was. He now used far more discretion on the type of client he agreed to take on.

"Air smells like something's burnt, Lou."

"We've been doing controlled burns in this end of the valley. Before that, we had a lot of timber taken out and added a slew of new fire lanes."

"Did you haul out much?"

"Enough to cover costs and then some. It was a safety initiative, more than anything. Next year we'll put in a few new fire lanes closer to the village. That'll knock my insurance rates down even more."

For the next few hours, they stayed in Osprey Cove jawing about a number of things, in between catching and releasing some trophy-sized fish from the depths.

SHORTLY AFTER LOU and Josh left the dock that morning, Kate was on her way to Luigi's cottage. The bathroom held the greatest potential of finding clues and that's where she headed. After collecting a few strands of hair from the drain and lifting fingerprints from a glass tumbler, she let Alessandra know that housekeeping was free to tidy up the cottage.

As she walked back to her own place, her thoughts were active. *This time, I'll let forensics know I'm sending something down. I can't believe I haven't received any results from the other packet yet.*

AT JUST ABOUT the same time Josh was pulling up the anchor, Oswald Turnbridge walked onto the lands of the Abenaki with his cousin, Nathan.

"Oswald, you doing this thing for that same fella?"

"Yeah."

"He gonna give you money, like he done last time?"

"I already got the money."

"You gonna give me some of it?"

"I said I was."

"I ain't been on Abenaki land but one time 'fore this, but it looks familiar. We goin' where we left them fish?"

"I ain't sure. I gotta look around some."

"Why?"

"Cause I gotta git something first."

The two Turnbridge cousins traveled only a short distance before Oswald said, "I figured those would be here."

"What's that?"

"Trucks."

"We gonna steal us a truck?"

"No, don't be stupid."

"I *told* you, Oswald, don't you be calling me that."

"Quiet."

"Why, ain't nobody here but us?"

"Shush, we don't know that. There might be a guard."

"Well, I don't see nobody."

"That don't mean nothing. You just hush."

"Why I gotta hush? Ain't nobody but us here!"

"Cause, somebody might be sleeping inside one of them trucks. Ever think of that? Come on, let's go take a look."

The two young Turnbridge boys moved cautiously down the line of trucks, neither one trusting the other's ability to determine if anyone was inside a cab sleeping. When they reached the last water tanker truck, Oswald's cousin turned to him.

"What'd I tell you, huh? Ain't nobody here, 'cept us."

"You got what I told you to bring?"

"Yeah."

"Well, give it here. I gotta use it now."

As Oswald's cousin pulled a length of clear plastic tubing out of his pocket, Oswald began unscrewing the gas cap on one of the trucks.

"Whatcha gonna do? You gonna siphon some gas?"

"Yeah. Take that container out of my backpack and lay it down right in front of me."

"I ain't never seen it done afore. I knows my paw done it though. He told me he did it."

Oswald ignored his cousin as he knelt down. He put one end of the tubing inside the gas tank and drew on the other end with suction from his mouth. He intended to spit the tubing out just as the gasoline began to flow. When that didn't happen, he spat out the gas that had reached his tongue and, inadvertently, the gas coming out of the tube soaked his pant leg before he placed the line in the container he'd brought.

When Oswald felt he had siphoned a sufficient amount of gas out of the tank, he pulled the tubing out of the container he was filling and lifted it high enough up in the air to stop the flow.

"Okay, let's go. I got what I come here for."

"Where we going?"

"We're gonna go toward that Abenaki village. But we gotta be careful. I don't want no Abenaki seeing us."

When Oswald stood up, he let go of his end of the siphon, but didn't remove it from the tank. Unbeknownst to him, as soon as he dropped the tube, gravity kicked in and once again, gas began flowing out of the tank, this time onto the ground.

THE UNDERGROWTH in the forest surrounding the village hadn't been cleared in over a decade. When the Turnbridges were about the length of a football field from the village, Oswald stopped and turned to his cousin. "Okay you step back a few feet. I'm gonna pour a line with this gasoline. Once I put a flame to it, you run like you're being chased back home. You got that?"

"Is that when you gonna give me some money for helping you?"

"Yeah, when we get back."

"Don't you forget."

Oswald ignored his cousin and began pouring the gas in a straight line on the ground. When he was satisfied he'd doused a long enough line, he lit a match and threw it on the gas. Unlike some accelerants, when gasoline is poured out, fumes fan out at ground level. When the gasoline ignited, it exploded into a massive fireball igniting the dry underbrush, including the trousers of both Turnbridges.

Shocked, the men immediately tried extinguishing the flames that engulfed the lower half of their bodies by rolling on the ground. Before the flames were out, they both suffered severe second-degree and third-degree burns.

"Oswald, you gotta help me! I'm in awful pain!"

"Shut up! We gotta get ourselves outta here, 'fore them Abenaki come. Come on, we gotta run!"

"I can't, it hurts!"

"Quit your bellyaching. I'm hurt too, but we gotta git! Now follow me across that field, you hear me?"

Chapter Fifty

The section of forest nearest the village that hadn't been cleared of undergrowth in years ignited quickly; in no time, sparks were flying, and towering flames were reaching the upper branches of trees.

A saving grace, if there was to be any, was the wind. It was coming from the east at barely 4 mph, just enough to direct the fire and embers floating upward away from the village without fanning the flames.

It was the frantic barking of the dogs that first alerted the people in the village something was wrong. Tall Tree raced to the council lodge and sounded the fire alarm. Within minutes, the men in the village were running toward the lodge. Tall Tree made two phone calls: the first to 911 and the second to Lou.

Lou was just pulling into the boathouse when his cell phone rang.

"Lou the forest is on fire!" Lou recognized Tall Tree's

voice. But he had difficulty hearing him clearly with all the background noise.

"*What* did you say?"

"The forest is on fire!"

Lou's first thought was that the fire must have been burning underground and somehow reemerged.

"Did you call 911?"

"Yes!"

"I'll call the company we hired for the burns. Their equipment should still be there. I'm on my way. We drilled for emergencies like this, Tall Tree. Which way is the wind blowing?"

"Away from the village."

"Good! You know what to do. I need to refuel before I can make it back down to the cove."

"The smoke is heavy."

Lou stepped out of the boathouse, phone still at his ear. "I can see the smoke from here. Take charge. Everyone knows the drill. Wet everything down, especially the roofs."

"We will."

As soon as Lou called the company that had orchestrated the controlled burn, they mobilized their crews and had them moving.

Lou made one more call before heading out.

"Jake the woods near the village are on fire. I'm heading there now. Cover for me at the dock."

"No problem."

"One other thing."

"What's that."

"Keep this close to the vest. We'll handle it."

"Got it."

. . .

Oswald Turnbridge and his cousin were both terribly injured in the explosion.

Oswald pushed his body and made it across the dirt road separating Turnbridge land from the ancestral lands of the Abenaki. The burns his cousin sustained were far more severe than his own. Once his cousin reached the grassy area bordering the dirt road, he collapsed. The massive thermal injuries he had sustained forced his body into burn shock. He wasn't able to continue on and collapsed.

In addition to the Abenaki and crews who orchestrated the controlled burns, firefighters from surrounding areas all responded to the 911 call.

Once the wildfire had been brought under control, crews were assigned to monitor the area throughout the night. Lou invited everyone who had battled the flames to the village's council lodge for food and water.

The new fire lanes, and that the minimal wind never changed direction, played a key role in saving the village. Many believed the battle would have ended sooner, had the only water truck with any water in its tank reached the fire before it ran out of gas.

After expressing his appreciation to all who had responded and fought the fire, Lou excused himself and huddled with the fire chief from Five Fingers.

"Lou, I can't speak for the fire marshal, but this fire is definitely suspicious."

"Say more."

"There isn't a snowball's chance in hell that fire was the result of an underground flare up. There's no doubt in my mind this was arson."

"What makes you say that?"

"It's too far from where they did the burning. Lou, there's no question that fire will travel underground, but not that far. Secondly, you go look at that initial burn line. It's long and straight, that wasn't a flare-up or spontaneous combustion. There's something else, too. I'll give you whatever odds you want that the fire marshal's gonna find residue of an accelerant."

"You think so?"

"Not a doubt in my mind! Go look at the burn marks on the trunks where it all started. Flames would never have gone that high without an accelerant."

Lou took a breath as he processed what he'd just heard. Finally, he said, "Well, at least we got through it without anyone getting hurt."

"I wish that were true."

"Someone got hurt?"

"Yeah."

"Who?"

"That I don't know. The Mounties found someone lying in the grass. I heard he was in tough shape."

"Was it a fire fighter?"

"No, everybody's accounted for."

"Did they take him over to the clinic?"

"Hell, no; they airlifted him over to the trauma burn unit in Grand Falls."

"I heard a chopper but I was still coming up from Moose Cove. I thought it was more equipment coming in. Guess it wasn't."

. . .

THE FOLLOWING MORNING, when Jake flew out, the package Kate was sending down to the forensic lab in Fredericton was on the seat next to him. Jake had left earlier than usual to ensure he'd arrive in Grand Falls before the plane to Fredericton left.

Lou was up at his usual early hour and at the dock well before his guests began arriving. It wasn't long after the boats were all on the water, when Lou returned to his cottage.

When the screen door opened, Kate called out, "Lou are they all out?"

"Yup."

"Gigi is in here watching "Odd Squad" with the twins. Can you watch them? Koby and I are going for our run."

Lou had been married long enough to understand his wife wasn't actually asking a question. "Yeah, sure," he called back. "Are you doing three or five miles today?"

Jake's wife, Koby, emerged from the living room. "We're not sure yet, Lou. We'll figure that out on the run."

"Okay, have at it."

"Oh, Lou, before I forget. I received an email this morning from the Provincial Wetlands Habitat Review Board. They've approved our request to clear the ponds of all aquatic life."

Lou nodded. To him, it was bittersweet news. The thought of killing all the marine life in the ponds weighed heavily on him and all the Abenaki. He headed over to the kitchen counter for a cup of coffee.

Before Kate left, she snuggled up to her husband, reached up to tousle his hair and whispered softly into his ear, "Thanks for watching the kids, hon. I'll make it up to you tonight. I promise."

Lou smiled. *How the hell did I ever get this lucky?*

• • •

WHEN KATE and Koby set out, they chose a familiar trail. It meandered east, and would parallel the lake until it reached the beaver pond. At the pond, the road forked and you had a choice; you either went left a mile toward Grey Elk's Village before looping back, or right, toward the old logging road and back to the lodge. They had a choice to make.

Both women had long strides and ran with the grace and endurance of true long-distance runners. As usual, whenever they ran the forest trails, Hector was their escort. The wolf loped along at an easy pace, constantly shifting from side to side, falling behind, and taking the lead.

When Hector decided to adopt his humans, years ago, he became the protector of his pack. Yet he was always a free spirit, and it wasn't unusual for him to break away during a run, only to return home much later. Sometimes he returned with an animal he had caught still in his mouth; other times, it was evident he'd enjoyed a meal somewhere out in the forest.

As they approached the fork in the road and the decision point, Koby was in the lead. "Which way Kate?"

"Go right. I need to get back."

As they passed the old wooden gate at the end of the logging road, Hector stopped. Usually, if he caught a scent, and was hungry, he was off in a flash, this time he just sat back on his haunches, sniffing the air. The wolf had caught a lingering scent in the air, his ears twitched as he listened for movement.

HOURS EARLIER THAT SAME MORNING, an SUV had pulled off the highway onto the old logging road.

"How far up are you gonna drive Matteo?"

"I'm gonna go right up to the gate."

"Then what?"

"We'll just scout around. We're coming back tonight."

"You know I can't go walking around in there, right?"

Matteo nodded.

"And the way you're dressed, *you're* gonna stick out, too."

"I know that." When the SUV stopped at the gate, the sky was just giving way to the early signs of dawn. As soon as Matteo pulled the key out of the ignition, he turned to Popeye. "Ready?"

Popeye merely nodded.

"Then let's go."

As they stepped out of the vehicle, the cool moist morning air and the earthy scent of the forest hit their senses. Popeye breathed it in deeply. *What the frig am I doing back here?*

When they reached the outskirts of the resort, both men stopped. Matteo saw movement, and whispered, "Whaddya think's going on?"

"They're just heading down to the dock. They'll be gone most of the day."

"Do they lock their cabins?"

"Nah, what for?"

Waving his hand Matteo said, "Let's go." He approached the cottage nearest him. When he reached the door, he knocked. After waiting a half minute, he turned to Popeye and whispered, "No one's here."

"So?"

"So, let's go ruffle some feathers."

"What the frig for?"

"Maybe that paper you called would be interested in doing a follow-up story on a little B & E that's going on here."

Popeye smiled. "You take this one. I'll go next door."

"Five minutes and we're back at the gate."

"I hear ya." With that, Popeye slipped into the shadows and snuck over to the next cottage.

Chapter Fifty-One

Miles to the northwest in Edmonston, New Brunswick, Nardo Lombardi and Santino sat across from an attorney representing Adler Forest Products, a division of Michigan Consolidated Industries.

"Mr. Lombardi, I must tell you up front, Adler Forest Products is not in the habit of selling off even wood lots, let alone sizable acreage like you're looking for in the land banks it holds."

"I understand," Nardo acknowledged. "That being said, everything does have a price. My client is willing to make what I'm sure management at Adler Forest Products will find to be a *very* attractive offer for the small parcel we're interested in."

After clearing his throat, the attorney said, "I suppose it is my duty to review such matters as this. What exactly is the offer, Mr. Lombardi?"

"My client is prepared to offer $3.2 million dollars for a clear title."

When Adler's attorney sat back and did the math in his head, he double checked.

"What was the amount again?"

"Three point two million."

That's an outrageous price for undeveloped land, he thought. *They must know something I don't.*

"May I ask what you intend to do with this property? I'm certain Adler would require that information."

Nardo Lombardi gestured toward Santino. "My client is a wealthy environmentalist and sportsman. It is his desire to create a retreat for like-minded people of means, who wish to experience a wilderness adventure."

"I see."

"We're prepared to sign a purchase and sales agreement today, if that's possible."

"You do realize that I do not have sole authority to say, 'yay' or 'nay' on a matter such as this."

"Of course."

"Will you be looking for Adler to hold some of the paper?"

"No. This will be a cash deal."

The attorney's eyes widened upon hearing that. "Really. Are we talking Canadian dollars?"

"No, U.S. dollars!"

"I see. Well, gentlemen, I will absolutely forward this on to the proper individuals."

For the first time, Santino spoke up. "When will we hear back from you?"

"Matters like this are difficult to gauge. It could be rather quickly, or it could take longer."

Santino replied, "Mark it 'urgent.' we'd like a quick reply."

The attorney smiled his best fake smile. "I'll certainly do that, sir."

When Nardo handed the attorney his business card, everyone stood up, signaling the meeting was over.

As SOON AS they left the building, Nardo turned to Santino. "I'm not walking away feeling like we're going to strike a deal with Adler. I'll do some more research when we get back. There's lots of lakes up here; maybe not as close, but we'll find something."

"Nardo, we've found something. It's perfect."

"Santino, I doubt they're going to agree to sell at *any* price."

"I wasn't aware Adler owned the property. I have *leverage* with Adler."

Nardo tilted his head. "What kind of leverage?"

Santino ignored the question as he dialed his phone.

"Rico, it's Santino."

"Hey, Santino!" Nardo couldn't hear the other person's voice on the phone.

"Rico, how many shares of Adler Forest and Michigan Consolidated Industries does the union own?"

"Let me check." After a brief pause, Rico came back on the line. "We got a hundred thousand shares of Adler, and we got one point two million shares of Michigan. Michigan just did a stock dividend. You wanna dump some?"

"What's the total number of outstanding shares for Michigan?"

"Looks like a little under three point five."

"So, we own about a *third* of the company?"

"Just about. We got a seat on their board, too, but we don't use it."

"What would happen if we dumped all their shares in our portfolio?"

"Hell, it'd bottom out. Trust me we *don't* wanna to that."

"How much debt are those two into us for?"

"Ah, let me see; I gotta go to a different book. Hold the line."

When Rico came back on, again, he said, "Adler's into us for six hundred K, Michigan's into us for half a mil."

"What'd happen if we called in all that debt?"

"They'd likely go into receivership. We don't wanna do that, they don't have the liquidity."

"Who's the treasurer at Michigan?"

"Let me see, that's in another file, too. Gimme a sec."

"I need his direct line."

When Rico came back, again, he said, "Aaron Seeka"

"You got a number for him?"

"Yeah; you got something to write it down with?"

"No."

"Then I'll text it to you."

"And text me all the numbers you told me."

"I will. Hey, where the hell *are* you; the connection is lousy."

"I'm traveling."

"Must be nice. Enjoy."

"One last thing."

"What?"

"How much liquidity do *we* have right now?"

"I'm sitting on just under 4 mil. I gotta find some place to put it."

"Leave it in cash."

"You sure?"

"Yeah, for now."

As Santino put his phone away, he looked at Nardo, "I need to make one more call. Then we'll go to lunch."

THAT EVENING, just before dinner, two guests walked over to Lou, while he was standing near the entrance to the kitchen.

"Hi fellas. How'd things go today?"

"Everything was fine out on the water. It's what we discovered when we were back on shore that's got us peeved."

"Whaddya mean?"

"I'm missing a laptop. It was there when we went out this morning. I know because I emailed my wife just before we went out on the water."

The other fella added, "And it sure as hell looks like someone rifled through the dresser drawers and our luggage."

Lou was upset at the news, but he tried remaining calm. "I'm not doubting a single thing you're telling me, but in all the years we've been operating, this is the first time I'm hearing *anything* like this."

"Well, times change Lou. We'd appreciate it if you'd put a padlock on our cottage."

"I'll do that immediately. I'll also ask Kate to sit with you and get your statements. We have insurance, so we'll file a claim for that. Whatever the insurance doesn't cover, I will."

"Much appreciated. Lou."

"I'm sorry, fellas. I don't know what else to say; like I said, we've never had an issue like this before."

As Lou was about to head into the kitchen, Kate came over to him. "Lou, the two men sitting at table six want to talk to you."

"What about?"

"They didn't say."

"Thanks. I'll go right over."

Table six sat four people, so Lou just pulled up an extra chair and sat down. "What's up, fellas. Kate said you wanted to see me."

"Lou, someone was in our cottage after we went out this morning."

Lou clenched his teeth; he couldn't believe what he was hearing. Thoughts began roaming in his mind and when he didn't immediately say anything, one of the other man sitting at the table said, "Lou? Did you hear what he just said?"

"I did. I was just processing it. The fellas in the cottage next to you just told me the same thing. In all the years I've been running this place, we've *never* had a problem like this. Was anything missing?"

"Well, Fred here, is missing a laptop; I'm missing a Kindle reader, and I found my electric razor on my pillow."

The first man said, "I think we'd like to have a lock on our door."

"I'll do it. I'll also cover your losses. After the boats are out tomorrow morning, I'm going to have someone patrol the area during the day. I'd like you fellas to sit with Kate before you go back to your cottage tonight. She'll take a statement from each you. That way, the Mounties will have a complete report on it. Anything my insurance doesn't cover; I'll make good on."

"Thanks, Lou. We appreciate that."

When Lou got up from the table, he overheard a stage

whisper: "Nothing like closing the barn door after the horses are out."

Lou walked into the kitchen. "Angelo, are you in here?"

"I'm back here, Lou. What's up?"

"I'm not exactly sure."

Angelo tilted his head in an inquisitive manner, and stopped what he was doing. As Lou walked toward him, he could see the troubled expression on his friend's face.

"A couple of cottages are missing things."

"Like what?"

"Personal stuff."

Angelo understood the gravity of the situation. A place like Lou's lived or died by its reputation, just like his cooking. Angelo asked, "I thought everyone went out today. All the lunches were gone."

"I'm trying to figure that out. All the boats went out early, and no one came back in until close to 3 p.m. No one from the village was in camp today, either."

"Which cottages?"

"Naturally, the two furthest out."

"Up where the path comes in from the gate?"

"Yeah."

LATER THAT EVENING, Lou couldn't dismiss the word "arson" from his thoughts. Then the conversation at dinner about the thefts filled his head. *Someone is deliberately messing with me,* he thought. *Why?* The more he thought about it, the more he felt the warrior spirit within him begin to stir.

· · ·

WHEN SANTINO CALLED AARON SEEKA, treasurer of Michigan Consolidated Industries, the conversation was direct on Santino's part, but cordial.

"Aaron, it's Santino Varni."

"Ah, Mr. Varni, it's so nice to hear from you," Seeka lied. He had reached out to Santino Varni numerous times and never received the courtesy of a reply.

"Aaron, I need a favor."

Intrigued, Seeka responded, saying, "How can I help?"

"One of your attorneys has received a request to sell off a small section of land. I would consider it a . . . personal *favor*, if you would support this."

Seeka knew he was walking a fine line when he said, "I don't know that I can help, Mr. Varni. Well over a year ago, the board voted to aggressively acquire land. I doubt they'd agree to sell anything. But they might be open to doing a lease."

"A lease is no good." Varni's voice was gruff.

Seeka paused and chose his words carefully. "Then, I'm not sure I'll be able to help you with this, even as much as I would *like* to, Mr. Varni." Aaron Seeka had survived in life by always keeping his options open.

"That's most unfortunate. I was hoping this would be an opportunity for you to . . . *return* a favor."

Aaron Seeka paused a moment. "What favor is that, Mr. Varni?"

"Well, it has come to my attention that the administrator of the Union Pension Fund is considering putting out an immediate call on the outstanding debt the fund is holding. Naturally, I told him to absolutely avoid touching anything involving Michigan, or Adler."

Aaron Seeka was astute enough to draw the inference; he

knew the *exact* amount of the debt Santino Varni was referring to. The assets Michigan Consolidated held were primarily land and equipment. The balance sheet had minimal liquidity. Aaron Seeka's primary responsibility, the one that kept him awake at night, was keeping a cash-poor operation financially afloat. If the debt Varni's union held on Adler, or its parent company Michigan Consolidated were *called*, both entities would be forced into receivership. Seeka thought feverishly of all the potential chess moves that might work if that happened. There was only one that would.

"Actually, Mr. Varni, the more I think about it, the more appealing such an offer actually might be to the board. As a matter of fact, I'm *positive* I could make this happen."

"Thank you, Aaron." Varni's voice was calm, and as soft as butter on a hot day.

"Oh, there's no need to thank me, Mr. Varni. I sincerely appreciate the opportunity to . . . to return the favor."

LATER THAT MORNING, an investigating officer with the Royal Canadian Mounted Police entered Grand Falls General Hospital and approached the receptionist.

"May I help you, officer?"

"Which floor is the Burn Unit on?"

She handed the officer a visitor's day pass. "The trauma unit is on level six."

"Thank you."

Oswald Turnbridge's cousin had second, and third degree burns over sixty percent of his body. Even with medication, the pain he was experiencing was beyond intense. He was heavily sedated, barely awake, and singularly focused on the trauma he was going through.

Turnbridge had no identification on him when the EMTs brought him in. The name on his hospital chart merely stated: John Doe, Burn Victim, Room 12.

The Mountie approached the nurse's station and inquired which room the John Doe burn victim that had been brought in was in. "I need to speak with him."

The nurse sitting behind the desk didn't even look up. "He's in twelve. He's heavily sedated, and you'll have to follow full burn protocol."

"What does that mean?"

She continued typing on her keyboard but still answered him. "You'll need to put on full personal protective gear meaning gown, cap, mask, gloves, booties over your shoes, the works. It's all hanging on the door outside his room. He's very susceptible to infection at this stage, from you, or anything you might bring in, even on your clothes."

"Is he awake?"

"Let me buzz his nurse." She pressed a button. "Marge, is your patient awake? There's a Mountie out here who wants to talk with him."

"He's not responding to me. If the Mountie wants to come in and try for a few minutes, he can. But I'd tell him to come back later."

As soon as the call ended, the nurse at the desk looked up. "You can go in after you gown up, but you'd be better off waiting a while."

"Are we talking hours?"

"Officer, his injuries are extensive. This young man's not going anywhere. I'd hold off for a couple of days. We've got him heavily drugged."

"Any chance you could hold off on his pain meds so I could speak with him soon?"

This time, the nurse looked straight up at the Mountie. "Sir," she said stiffly. "If the person in that room was someone you actually *cared* about, would *you* want the nurse to hold off on their pain meds?"

The Mountie sucked in a breath, held it, then released it slowly. "I guess I deserved that. I'll be back."

AT THAT EXACT MOMENT, elsewhere, Popeye was having another lengthy conversation with the editor of the Brunswick Daily Times.

Chapter Fifty-Two

The following day, Jake had a light schedule. Once he returned home and secured his plane to the dock in front of his cottage, he walked over to Lou's cottage.

"Kate, are you in there?"

"I am."

"I have an envelope for you from Fredericton." Kate wasted no time coming out to the porch.

"I think this maybe the one you've been waiting for."

"If the return address says, 'RCMP' it certainly is!"

Jake smiled. "They kept putting it on the wrong plane all week, but I searched it out. Here's the rest of your mail and the paper."

"Thanks Jake." Kate ripped open the envelope to read the forensic report.

Three of the six fingerprints she'd collected came back belonging to Antonina Cataldo. The other three prints weren't clear enough to make a positive identification and were still under review. The DNA testing on the hair samples were all a positive match with Antonina Cataldo.

Kate read the report a second time. *How did I miss picking up Luigi's prints or anything with his DNA? Well, it's too late now.*

In actuality, it would have been highly unlikely for Kate to find even a trace of Luigi Secondo's presence since he didn't exist, and Santino Varni was far too clever.

Over a decade earlier, a district attorney had put a contemporary of Santino Varni away on the basis of DNA evidence and fingerprints. Since then, Santino had been fastidious about not leaving any trace of his presence behind. He even went so far as to capture shaving cream off his razor when he shaved. He wiped the razor blade on toilet paper and flushed it; nothing ever went down any drain. He brushed his teeth over the toilet. Nail clippings went into the toilet as did the hair in his comb. His toothbrush sat in a glass filled with hydrogen peroxide his dirty clothes went into a special plastic bag that went into the washer along with his clothes. Whenever he touched any surface where prints could be lifted, he moved his fingers in such a manner that he avoided leaving a clear print. Showers at Havre de Poisson were outdoors, and communal, therefore, they posed no risk. The fact that his bed linens were changed daily also lessened any risk of him leaving DNA behind. So, he felt safe.

THE NEXT ARTICLE about Havre de Poisson that appeared on the front page of the Brunswick Daily Times, below the fold, wasn't noticed by either Jake or Kate that day. If they had, copies would not have been left on the table in the lodge. The content of the story was as follows:

A while back, this paper ran a feature story questioning whether the so-called "fairy dust," which has long been the suspected magic behind Lou Gault's success, might have finally run its course and vanished?

Since publishing that article, additional unsolicited comments have been received by this paper from unnamed sources. The woes plaguing this once highly esteemed venue seem to be continuing.

Recently, a rash of thievery has been reported in what was once considered "paradise" among the crowd of well-heeled sporting enthusiasts who trek there annually, eager to drop a bundle of cash.

Surprisingly, not one, but two crime reports were recently filed by none other than the proprietor's wife. Gault's wife, Kathleen O'Grady-Gault, holds the rank of Lieutenant in the Royal Canadian Mounted Police force, so it's safe to assume her reports reflect an accurate account.

Earlier, a guest stated to this paper: "The experience just isn't quite up to what it once was."

Sadly, it appears that, like the poem Casey at the Bat, the grandeur that once held Gault's lodge above all the rest, is no more, for - mighty Casey has struck out.

Later that night, when Lou read the article; he felt like the earth had moved under his feet. The day had already been a downer for him and the people who lived in the village of Grey Elk.

At midday, they had stood in silent prayer, watching as the chemicals that would eradicate the Tench, and every other living creature in the three upper ponds, entered the now algae free water.

• • •

THAT EVENING, Lou and Jake walked over to Rocky Point to have a cigar and talk.

"Cuz, I can't figure out who's got it in for you. But somebody sure as hell does. This is crazy."

"Yeah, it's like somebody's trying to send me a message."

"Like what?"

"I don't know. It almost feels like someone wants me to fold the tent."

Jake took a long draw on his cigar and let it out slowly, blowing smoke rings in the air. "Ya know, that might be an interesting way to look at what's going on."

"I thought about that."

"And?"

As Lou let out a puff of smoke, he said, "I dismissed it."

"Why?"

"Because it makes no sense to me. Besides, I have no intention of going out of business."

"Didn't you tell me that someone wanted to buy you out?"

Lou tapped his cigar on a rock. "Yeah. That was Luigi. But that's all over and done with."

"You sure? I thought you said he came on pretty strong."

Lou took a draw on his cigar. "He did, but then the next time he came up, he apologized."

"What'd he say?"

"That he didn't know what had come over him."

"And?"

"And that was that. He said if I ever needed any financial help to let him know."

"Did he say he wasn't interested in buying the place anymore?"

"Not in so many words, but, yeah, that's what he was saying."

"That's interesting."

"What?"

"The way he left it."

"Say more."

"Well, think about it. From that point on . . . up to right now . . . if we were tracking something in the forest, what would all the signs we've seen be telling you?"

"What the hell are you talking about?"

"You said you can't figure out what's going on, right?"

Lou nodded and tapped the tip of his cigar on the rock next to him. When Lou didn't say anything, Jake pushed.

"So?"

"So, what?"

"So, let's put our heads together, and look at everything that's been going on and piece it together, like we're tracking something."

"You know what?"

"What?"

"I don't know how the hell they continue to let you to fly a plane. You're plain batshit crazy, man. You need to lay off that damn Grey Poupon."

"No, I'm serious, Cuz."

"Jake, you don't have a serious bone in your body."

Jake dismissed Lou's comment. "Why did the elders give you the name Raven Claw? Because you saw signs no one else could."

"Jake, I'm not tracking a lost hunter."

"It doesn't matter. Lou, the gift you have is a transferable skill. What are the signs telling you?"

"I haven't looked at it that way."

"Me, neither, until now." Jake swatted the bug flying around his head. "Whaddya say we go inside and talk about this? I think we've pissed off enough mosquitoes with all this second-hand cigar smoke they're inhaling, they've called in reinforcements.

"Good idea, otherwise, the warrior spirit within me is going to explode."

ABOUT NOONTIME THE FOLLOWING DAY, when Josh Barnard set his fishing rod in the holder, he fired up his cell phone and called his office.

"Claudine, this is Josh. I'm just checking in. Anything going on that I need to be aware of?"

"You've been on my mind all morning."

"Claudine, no, no, no! You're a married woman, now! I know that because I was best man at your wedding." Josh smiled, knowing the neck and cheeks of the young, fair-skinned French-Canadian admin he shared with two other attorneys would be turning various shades of crimson by now.

"Josh Barnard, you stop that! You know that wasn't what I meant."

"Good, because I really encourage people I work with to practice monogamy. Divorce is so costly, and not an area I practice."

There was a deep sigh on the other end. "Why can't you be polite like my other solicitors?"

"You have people soliciting you?"

"Josh, you are definitely trying my patience this morning, *and* you are teetering on the edge of sexual harassment."

"Well, if you need an attorney, I know a few."

"Can we move on? I do have other things to be doing."

"Yes. Is there anything I need to be aware of?"

"A request came in from Adler Forest Products. They're selling off a parcel of land and they want you to research the title. There's a possibility they'll need you to handle the whole transaction."

"That all?"

"Everything else can wait. You're back on Monday, right?"

"Not sure. The plane I co-own with your husband is available Monday, so I thought I might get some flight hours in."

"Adler said they wanted you to move quickly. I didn't mention that you're out this week. Should I get back to them?"

Josh paused before saying, "No. I should be able to get the title search done from here. Transfer what you have over to my account."

"I will."

"Okay, Ciao."

"Au revoir."

ALTHOUGH THE GAULT twins didn't live in the village of Grey Elk, Kate had agreed they would grow up understanding the ways of the Abenaki and what it meant to "walk the red road." The traditions of the band had always passed from generation to generation through mentoring. Like their father, the twins would be assigned their own mentor at an early age. To be a mentor was an honor; they were the ones who taught the next generation the ways of the Abenaki, the ways of the forest, and the life values necessary to lead an honorable life.

Kate had been more than a little apprehensive when she learned Jake, the jokester in the family, had stepped forward to mentor the twins. But her concerns were put aside when she saw the serious side of Jake.

An integral part of every mentor's role was teaching their mentees the game of "Butterfly Hide and Seek." The game originated with the Pequots centuries ago. Grey Elk's predecessors had copied it after realizing its value. Over time, the game became part of the mentoring process. As times changed, traditions changed. Becoming masterful at the game was now looked upon as a rite of passage for both young men and young women in Grey Elk's band as they approached adulthood.

The game was somewhat similar to the child's game of hide and seek, only far more involved and it lasted for days. Mastery was achieved through one's tracking skills, self-discipline, and both physical and mental endurance. The ability to blend into one's surroundings, remain quiet, and not be seen by others, was the very essence of the game. It was believed to be good luck for the one hiding if they remained still long enough that a butterfly landed on them.

From all accounts, even at their young age, the twins were already showing signs of becoming adept at the game, and in the ways of the forest.

Jake encouraged his two mentees to practice the game whenever they had free time. The only conditions he placed upon the twins were; an adult needed to *know* they were playing the game, the game could not go beyond three hours' time and they had to stay within a mile of the lodge.

At first, Kate wasn't at all pleased with even this much free rein. But she acquiesced when Lou lobbied her for the one-mile radius. Once they were older than their almost seven years, the radius would expand, and the game would last for days.

The game had one more component: It was played in pairs with one person being the seeker, and the other, the quarry or "adversary" who would hide. The one who hid had a head start. Once an hour passed, the seeker had two hours to find their quarry.

Little Otter would have preferred more time and a larger radius. His twin sister, Ayleen, was fine with the format. On this day, when they chose up to decide who would play which role, Ayleen won and chose the adversary role, her brother would be the seeker.

When Little Otter agreed to the roles, Ayleen put both hands on her brother's shoulders. "Look at me! I want a *whole* hour this time; no early head start, that's cheating!"

"I'll leave from Alessandra's house. She'll tell me when it's time to go."

"It's not fair if you bring Hector."

"I'll tell him to stay behind. Just go!"

Satisfied her brother would be truthful, Ayleen changed into her moccasins and took off. At first, she headed toward the lodge, then she zigzagged and headed back toward the old logging road.

It took her about a half hour before she settled on a location to hide that she felt comfortable with. It was on a knoll, near the gate at the logging road. The area wasn't overgrown, but there was plenty of cover to hide in. She had deliberately avoided leaving traces of her passing by jumping from fallen tree to fallen tree. When she had a fairly good view of the logging road, she stopped and hunkered down to wait.

As she nestled in, completely camouflaged among the

flora, she thought: *He won't find me this time, unless he cheats, and Hector is with him.*

Over an hour passed after Ayleen settled into her hiding place. She had been passing time listening to the sounds of the forest, when she heard the distant sound of a vehicle.

It wasn't unusual for delivery trucks to travel up this road, but the sound of the approaching vehicle didn't quite match that of a truck. It sounded more like a car.

Chapter Fifty-Three

After reading the most recent article in the Brunswick Daily Times, Matteo decided to throw a little more angst Lou's way. When their heavy SUV pulled off highway 385 onto the logging road, Popeye looked at Matteo. "You got a plan, or are we going free-style?"

"We're gonna hit the same two cottages again."

"That's it?"

"You got a problem with that?"

Popeye shrugged his shoulders, "Hey, this is your show."

"When we come back tonight, we'll light a few fires."

When the SUV stopped in the turnaround just before the gate, Ayleen, still hidden, expected the driver to get out and open the gate. Instead, two people exited the vehicle, walked around the gate and walked up the road, toward the resort.

That's odd, she thought. As she was about to sit up, so she could continue to observe the men, movement across the road caught her attention. Little Otter had found the path she'd taken. *Well,* she thought, *at least Hector isn't with him.*

. . .

WHEN MATTEO REACHED the first of the two cottages that had been targeted earlier, he saw the padlock on the front door and waved for Popeye to come over.

"They put a friggin' lock on the door."

"Mine, too. Shows they ain't stupid, huh?"

"They just live in the friggin' boonies. How stupid is that! You see another cottage you want?"

"No, everything else is out in the open, man. They're gonna see us. They know my face; remember, I'm 'Vincenzo' to them."

Matteo let out a sigh, "Okay, let's go. We'll come back tonight and roast a few marshmallows over an open fire."

Popeye smirked at the sarcasm. "Yeah, let's go."

WHEN LITTLE OTTER reached the point where his sister began jumping from fallen tree to fallen tree, he began searching in a wider circle.

I know you came this way, sister; I will find you. I always do, he thought.

As Little Otter knelt down to inspect a disturbance in the forest floor, he heard a voice. When he heard it a second time, he stood up, and instinctively blended his silhouette with the trunk of a tree. His sister's trail had led him within thirty yards of the old wooden gate. When he heard the voice a third time, his eyes glanced toward the gate and he saw the SUV. Then he watched two men walk around the gate and stand by the vehicle talking.

They must be lost, he thought. *I'll help them.*

Neither man expected to see a young boy dressed in

deerskin emerge from the forest, much less ask: "Are you lost?"

When Popeye turned around, Little Otter immediately recognized his face. "Hey, you stayed with us!"

Matteo acted quickly, and Little Otter found himself in a neck hold, his right arm twisted halfway up his back. He yelped in pain.

"Who's *this?*"

Popeye let out a breath. "One of Gault's brats."

"Well, he's not going anywhere."

"Whaddya wanna do with him?"

Little Otter began to squirm and scratch, as he attempted to wrest himself from the man's grasp. When that happened, Matteo applied a sleeper hold. In a matter of minutes, the youngster hung like a rag doll in his arms.

Again, Popeye asked, "Whaddya gonna do with him?"

"I'm not sure. Maybe he'll be a bargaining chip."

"Maybe."

"Get the door."

As Popeye opened the rear door, he heard a low menacing growl; it was close by. A smile came over Popeye's face. "Matteo, you got the kid. I got a little unfinished business I gutta take care of."

Matteo glanced over as Hector emerged from the brush. "Make it snappy." Matteo threw the limp body of Little Otter into the back seat, shut the door and slid into the driver's seat.

In one fluid movement, Popeye stepped away from the car. Then, like a seasoned prizefighter, he began shifting his weight from leg to leg, sizing up his opponent. In an instant, the garrote was out of his pocket, the wire creating a deadly arch that linked his massive arms.

Hector remained still, hunched at the shoulders, ready to pounce. His teeth were bared, his yellow eyes locked on his quarry. His nose flared as the scent he remembered so well filled his senses.

Popeye reached his arms out, the garrotee raised, as he taunted his adversary. "Come on . . . Come to poppa!" The wolf sidestepped slowly, carefully circling his prey; his yellow eyes fixed on the man, studying him.

When Ayleen saw her brother go limp, then thrown into the back of the vehicle, she did the only thing she could do. Emerging from her hiding place as quietly as possible, she raced toward home.

Both combatants were aware that the dual taking shape at the gate would be to the death. Hector circled Popeye cautiously, looking for the right angle to attack this strange adversary. He saw the thin wire in the man's hands, but had no understanding of what it could do.

Popeye studied the wolf's movements, ever vigilant, waiting for the charge he knew would come. He gripped the garrote, the mere feel of the handles gave him a sense of the victory that would be his.

Four times, Hector measured his opponent's readiness and gauged his opponent's reaction using false attacks. Wiser, now, on how the man would react, the wolf held back.

Each time the wolf had feigned a charge, Popeye had raised his massive arms, hoping to encircle the wolf's neck with the deadly wire. The muscles in his massive forearms bulged; his hands had fused with the wooden grips.

Finally, Hector tired of teasing his opponent and lunged, purposefully coming in low. The force of his impact pushed

Popeye off-balance and back a step. When his arms came down, it was only on air. He hadn't been able to entrap the wolf, yet. But what Popeye didn't know was how quickly the wolf was learning how to fight this adversary. Now the wolf knew more about how his quarry would react.

Unlike the wolf, Popeye had never looked into the face of those he had killed. Facing an adversary, one actually capable of fighting back, was a different dance step for the assassin.

Each time Hector circled, looking for an opening, Popeye turned with him, maintaining eye contact. The wolf had tested his prey enough; now he was ready. It was only a matter of time before Hector would charge.

"Come to poppa! Come on boy! Come to poppa!" As Popeye taunted the wolf, saliva gathered at the corners of his own mouth. The assassin was ready, he had never known defeat.

Popeye had studied the wolf's movements. He'd noticed that the wolf circled him three times before each fake charge. The wolf was approaching his third pass. Popeye separated his wrists as wide as possible, a preliminary move to snare the wolf. The assassin smiled, thinking, *Come to poppa, come so I can watch the life go out of your eyes.*

Popeye readied himself. The wolf was approaching the end of his third circle. This time, when Hector stopped. Popeye knew the time had come. *We'll end this now. Come to poppa!*

On cue, the wolf lunged forward and the garrote came down around his neck. Popeye smiled as he crossed his arms at the wrist. He pulled back, tightening the loop. *Poppa's got you, you son-of-a bitch!*

The wire enraged Hector even further. The wolf was actually taller than Popeye when he stood on his hind legs.

Slowly, Hector's strength and fury began pushing Popeye backward, reducing the assassin's ability to maintain pressure on the garrote.

The muscles in the neck of a wolf are far different from a human's. As Hector twisted his head, his jaws found Popeye's right wrist. When his teeth came down on Popeye's wrist they not only punctured Popeye's skin, they damaged a few tendons. The pain wasn't immediate, but there was a slight loss of strength in that arm.

When Popeye's grip on the garrote lessened, the wolf pushed off Popeye's chest with his front paws, freeing himself from the snare, then continued circling his prey.

Popeye readied himself for another attack, but instead, the wolf made a fake charge, then halfway around the next circle, charged again. Popeye wasn't expecting it, but his arms went up instinctively, hoping to encircle the wolf's neck again.

The wolf's speed surprised Popeye and his arms came down over the wolf's shoulders. He was unable to cross his arms and lock the beast into a death hold.

Tipping the scales at some 140 pounds, a full grown male grey wolf is a formidable adversary. Hector was all of that and determined. Popeye found himself repeatedly stepping back to remain upright. Never before had the assassin been in a situation where he had to fend off his chosen victim.

The wolf sensed it had the momentum, and kept pushing, snarling; his jaws constantly snapping. Popeye struggled to contain his adversary. Then suddenly, he realized he was on defense, not offense. Desperately, he tried crossing his fists at the wrist to regain an upper hand over the wolf. But Hector gave his adversary no quarter and constantly lunged at Popeye's neck.

When Popeye felt the wolf's breath and saliva on his neck,

a wave of panic set in. All that separated him from the wolf was the thin wire of the garrote. In an unprecedented move, Popeye lowered his hands in an attempt to push the beast away. When that happened, Hector twisted his head and tore into Popeye's right forearm, mangling more tendons and damaging more muscle.

Popeye lost his grip on the garrote from his already weakened right hand. The wolf lunged forward again. With one end of the garrote now flailing in the air, there was no longer a constraint. The soft flesh of the assassin's neck was completely exposed. The wolf's open jaws came together with a force close to 1500 psi.

Popeye's head snapped back; his eyes widened; his left hand completely let go of the garrote. Seeming to reach for his throat, Popeye's hands and arms went slack. Once the assassin's carotid arteries and windpipe were ripped from his neck, the battle was over.

As Popeye began to collapse, Hector gave a final push with his front paws and jumped aside.

Matteo only had a partial view of the battle from the side view mirror. He watched Popeye backing up, but when he fell, Matteo lost sight of him. Grabbing hold of the rearview mirror, he tried angling it differently, hoping to see Popeye. Seconds went by, suddenly Matteo recoiled in horror as Hector's front paws pounded against the driver's side door. Matteo froze as he stared at the snarling beast.

All Hector knew was that a pack member he cared about was inside the vehicle . . . and he wanted *in*.

When the wolf dropped down from the driver's side window and disappeared, Matteo checked both sideview mirrors and the rearview mirror for any sign of Popeye.

Suddenly the wolf was on top of the hood, looking

straight through the windshield at Matteo, growling even louder than before. Blood and saliva dripped from the wolf's mouth, his paws smearing it into the windshield. The wolf began clawing at the window, destroying the wiper arm on the driver's side. There was no mistake; he wanted *inside* the car!

Matteo's thoughts were racing. *What the frig is this! Where the hell is Popeye?* Matteo blew the horn twice and yelled, "Popeye!" There was no Popeye, Popeye was dead.

All the while, the wolf continued pounding and clawing at the windshield. His paws blurring the glass even further with a combination of saliva, blood, and dirt.

Matteo rolled down the passenger side window slightly. "Popeye, get in the friggin' car!" When no one answered, Matteo leaned on the horn and again yelled: "Popeye get in the *friggin'* car!"

The wolf was now frantically pounding on the windshield, desperately trying to get inside. Then Matteo saw the glass actually bow inward from the wolf's last pounce, something deep inside him snapped. For the first time in his life, he knew fear.

Looking in the rearview mirror one last time, he whispered, "Popeye, there's no friggin' way I can reach you, man." Shifting into reverse, he backed into a three-point-turn. The thought of running over the wolf came to his mind, but Hector was far too agile for that to ever happen.

As he drove away, he looked in the rearview mirror one last time and saw Popeye's body lying in the dirt. Flight and self-preservation had completely overtaken Matteo.

For the moment, he'd forgotten there was an unconscious child in the back seat.

Chapter Fifty-Four

At the resort, Kate had just stepped out onto their porch and taken the wicker chair next to her husband. Lou would have preferred the more durable traditional Adirondack chairs. Kate thought the wicker was more comfortable, so, that's what they had.

So far, the day had passed without incident. Earlier it had been cloudy, but now the sun's rays danced across the surface of the lake like a thousand sparkling jewels.

"Well, it turned out to be a grand day after all," she said.

When Lou didn't respond, she turned her head ever so slightly and glanced at the man who made her life complete. He was deep in thought, his eyes straight ahead. Physically he was next to her, but his mind was elsewhere.

"Is it the boats, or the sun glistening off the water, that's got ahold of your thoughts?" When he still didn't respond, Kate reached over and touched his forearm. "I'll give you *a copper* for your thoughts."

Kate's touch, more than her words, broke his train of thought.

"I'm sorry. I didn't hear what you said."

"Well, it's no wonder. So, what got ahold of your thoughts?"

"I was just thinking about a conversation Jake and I had recently." When Lou left it at that, Kate waited a beat before saying anything.

"And would you happen to be in a mind to share that?"

Lou smiled at the lilting tone of his wife's Irish brogue. "It's nothing, I was just reflecting on how many times Luigi's name came up the other night, when Jake and I were trying to connect a few dots."

Before Kate could comment, Ayleen came bursting through the screen door. "Mom! Dad! Come quick! Someone's taken Little Otter!"

Both parents looked at their daughter for a split second before Lou said, "What!? Say that again!"

Aylene was half out of breath after running all the way from the gate. "Two men took him…we were playing hide and seek…he was looking for me; all he did was walk over to them…they grabbed him and threw him in their car…I saw it! Hurry!"

"Where?" Kate yelled.

"At the gate!"

As Lou jumped up he checked that the sheath holding his hunting knife was on his belt. "Kate, meet me there." As he ran out the door, she headed toward the gun cabinet.

Kate was a natural with a pistol; she had represented Ireland twice on the Olympic pistol team.

By the time Lou reached the gate, the SUV was long gone. The first thing he saw was a body lying on the ground, it was too large to be his son. He circled over to it. The ground was littered with Hector's paw prints.

He could tell from the clothing that it was a man's body. The face was no longer recognizable. As Lou assessed the overall build and saw the massive forearms he knew it was Vincenzo.

It was clear there had been more activity near the gate. A couple of yards away there were fresh tire marks and fresh footprints. Two appeared to be those of grown men, wearing shoes. His eyes scanned the area for telltale imprints of his son's moccasins. The ground told him there had been a scuffle. Finally, he saw his son's smaller footprint coming in from the edge of the forest. They entered the area where there had been a scuffle, then disappeared.

The longer Lou stared at the signs, the more enraged he became. The warrior spirit within him finally erupted with a fury. Lou knew Kate wouldn't be far behind. He tried to calm the warrior within as he continued studying the area. Clues left behind were telling him the story.

"Lou!"

"Over here, Kate. Where's Ayleen?"

"She's coming, she's just winded. I wasn't sure what we'd find. I told her to stay well beyond the gate until she heard the sound of the whippoorwill."

"Call 911."

As tough as Kate was, her heart was sinking as she punched in the number. Lou cupped his hands around his mouth, "Tyrone! Can you hear me?" There was no response. He called out a second time.

"Ty…Tyrone…can you hear me?"

"Daddy!"

Lou's head swiveled around like an owl's when he heard the reply.

It was his daughter's voice. "Ayleen, is this where your brother was?"

"Yes!" She pointed to her left. "I was right over there."

"I need to study the signs more, honey, so stay back, okay?"

Kate watched the scene between father and daughter and thought to herself: *Well, so much for the sound of the whippoorwill.*

WHEN MATTEO REACHED HIGHWAY 385, at the end of the logging road, he came to a full stop. His visibility was impaired, the windshield was a total mess from the bloody drool and paw prints left by Hector. The wiper was destroyed on the driver's side, and the only thing spraying windshield fluid did was exacerbate the problem.

In his effort to distance himself from the maniacal beast that had pounded on his windshield, Matteo had raced up the dirt logging road and hit just about every bump and washout there was. The jostling was enough to wake Little Otter from his stupor. At first, he didn't realize what was happening, then the boy's mind cleared.

The horror of what had happened at the gate still filled Matteo's mind. When he got out of the SUV to try and clean the windshield, he never even gave a thought to the back seat. His thoughts were on Popeye, the crazed wolf, cleaning off the windshield and getting the hell away. For the moment, the kid in the back seat was the furthest thing from his mind.

Little Otter hunkered down as he watched from the rear seat. When Matteo took out his handkerchief and tried to clean off the windshield, Little Otter tried to quietly open the driver's side rear door. The boy's timing was off. Matteo was focused on the windshield, but the movement inside the vehicle attracted his attention.

"Hey, kid, freeze!"

Little Otter immediately slid across the seat to the far side and grabbed the opposite door handle. Matteo dropped the hankie and moved just as fast to the side of the car. As Little Otter tried to open right rear door, Matteo pulled open the left rear door, reached in and grabbed Little Otter by the leg. Matteo snarled. "You ain't going nowhere kid."

Although frightened, Little Otter still had his wits about him and reacted quickly. He began kicking with both legs as his arms pushed the rear right passenger door open. Matteo thought he had a firm grip on Little Otter's deerskin leggings, but all he had was the decorative fringe. As Matteo reached in with his other hand, Little Otter released the snap on his waist and the loop holding the legging to his belt came loose. In a heartbeat the youngster was out the door, leaving Matteo holding an empty deerskin legging.

Matteo excelled in track and field during high school and had kept in shape. When Little Otter took off, Matteo lit out after him.

"You ain't getting' away from me kid!"

Little Otter took off like a jack rabbit and his legs were pumping, but Matteo was quick and had long strides.

The boy heard the footsteps behind him. When he turned his head and saw how close his captor was, he literally dove head first into the thorny underbrush on the side of the road, scrambled beneath the brambles and ran for all he was worth once he was free of the thicket.

Had Little Otter stayed on the road, he wouldn't have

escaped Matteo. As it was, he had almost come close enough to reach out to grab the youngster. As he stared at the thorny underbrush where Little Otter had left the road, he shook his head. "Frig you kid!" With that, he returned to the SUV, threw the soiled handkerchief he'd left on the hood to the ground, got in and turned onto the highway.

BACK AT THE GATE, Lou had taken off his shirt and placed it over the disfigured face of the body lying in the dirt. Kate was nearby scanning the area, looking for anything unusual. Hector sat calmly off to the side, beside Ayleen, his tongue hanging out as if nothing had happened.

Even though Kate was now on the phone talking to the 911 dispatcher, her eyes continued to survey the area. When she finally concentrated on the figure lying in the dirt, she too recognized the massive forearms. As soon as Kate was satisfied the dispatcher had the correct information, she hung up.

"Lou is that who I think it is?

Lou nodded. "Yeah, it appears he was planning to visit us again. Ty must have accidentally come upon him."

Kate continued to stare at the scene, her left hand subconsciously covering her mouth; her son's whereabouts and safety consumed her thoughts.

Lou's own mind was racing. *What was Vincenzo doing here? He didn't come here to take my son. So, why was he here? Who is he, really? What's the connection between him and Luigi?*

Without taking his eyes off the scene, Lou yelled over to Kate. "Have you figured out what Luigi does for a living yet?"

"No, not yet."

"Well, add Vincenzo to your list."

MEANWHILE, over in Grand Falls, the Mountie assigned to interview the unknown burn-victim, returned to the hospital and was given full access to the patient whose identity was still a mystery.

In all the time the young Turnbridge lad had been in the hospital, no next of kin or friend had made any inquiry or reported a missing person to the police. The name on the chart still read: John Doe, Burn Victim, room 12.

The Mountie was a seasoned veteran and guessed the patient lying in the bed was no older than his middle teens. Now sitting at the bedside, he saw the victim stir. After clearing his throat, the Mountie asked, "Are you awake?"

The young man opened his eyes and turned his head slightly.

"Can you tell me your name?"

There was a lengthy pause. Between the stupor of pain medicines, the trauma, and the strange surroundings, the young man's brain was misfiring more than usual. Finally, he whispered, "Nathan."

"Okay. Nathan, I'd like to ask you a few questions. Are you okay with that?"

Turnbridge turned his head and looked directly at the officer but said nothing. The Mountie waited, but when there was no further response, he continued his questioning.

"Nathan, what brought you to the land of the Abenaki the day of the fire?"

It took a while for Nathan to process the question, but finally he understood. "We was there," the young Turnbridge whispered.

"I know you were 'there,' Nathan. The question is '*Why* were you there?'" When there was no response, the Mountie asked, "Nathan, did you go there to help fight the fire?"

Turnbridge winced in pain, then shook his head.

"Okay, so you weren't there to fight the fire. Why were you there, Nathan?"

The young Turnbridge inhaled deeply, closed his eyes, then slowly exhaled. "Oswald took me."

"Okay you were with Oswald. Does Oswald have a last name?"

Turnbridge nodded slowly, painfully.

"Can you tell me Oswald's last name?"

When there was no response the officer said, "Can you tell me your last name?"

"Turnbridge."

"Okay, so you're Nathan Turnbridge. Is Oswald's last name Turnbridge also?"

Nathan was beginning to fade in and out.

"Nathan…Who is Oswald? What's Oswald's last name?"

It was a lengthy process, but the youth finally gave Oswald up. Not only did he confess to helping set the fire, but that they had dumped buckets of fish into the waters of the Abenaki earlier.

When the nurse gave Nathan another round of meds, he faded out and was unable to respond to further questions. The Mountie had enough information and quietly left the hospital.

It took a while to track down the whereabouts of Oswald Turnbridge. The last known address for him was the foster home he had lived in years earlier. When two patrol cars arrived at the Turnbridge compound, true to form, there wasn't a soul in sight.

The menfolk had taken off for the hills, thinking it was another raid on their stills. The womenfolk huddled behind closed doors with the children hoping they wouldn't be bothered.

The Mountie in the first cruiser picked up the microphone mounted on the dashboard inside his cruiser and pressed the button on the side. It sounded like a bullhorn when his words came blasting out.

"Oswald Turnbridge, come on out. We want to speak with you."

Whether Oswald heard the Mountie, or not, was irrelevant. He had also suffered second-and third-degree burns over most of the lower half of his body. While his injuries were nowhere near as severe as his cousin's initially, without proper treatment, his wounds had become infected. Currently, he was inside on a filthy bed sweating and suffering horribly.

Finally, the officer heard a woman's voice call out: "He's hurt bad."

Oswald Turnbridge was in the third stage of sepsis and toxic shock. By the time the ambulance arrived, and he was airlifted to the burn unit at Grand Falls Hospital, there was little anyone could do for him.

The damage to his organs was irreversible. He wasn't yet 20 years old.

Chapter Fifty-Five

When the 911 call regarding a child abduction in the vicinity of Highway 385, went out, an RCMP cruiser pulled over.

"Car 34 to base."

"Base."

"Do you have anything further on the abduction?"

"Roger. The caller said it occurred on a logging road near mile marker 221."

"Roger that. In route."

Within minutes, the cruiser was at the logging road and had turned in. The actual distance from the highway to the gate was a little under three miles. About a mile in, the road straightened out. When the cruiser reached that point, the officer saw a young boy walking in the middle of the road up ahead.

· · ·

WHEN LITTLE OTTER heard a vehicle coming up behind him, he immediately thought: *He's coming back for me!* In an instant he was off the road and blending in among the trees and underbrush. When the Mountie flashed his strobe lights and gave the siren a single blast, Little Otter let out a sigh of relief. From an early age his mother had schooled both of her children that the police are always your friend. Shortly, he reappeared on the road, waving his arms.

As the Mountie proceeded forward, he picked up the mic for his radio.

"Car 34 to base"

"Base."

"Possible sighting of abductee."

"Roger that."

KATE HAD ALSO CALLED for a crime scene investigation, as well as the medical examiner and gave their location. She, Lou, and Ayleen were still at the gate when the first cruiser – Car 34 - arrived.

Tyrone jumped out of the front passenger door yelling and waving his arms. "Dad, Dad, you're not going to believe what happened!"

Lou held up both hands, fully aware of the gruesome sight nearby. "Son, stay right where you are! We'll come to you." Kate took Ayleen by the hand and all three quickly, but carefully, walked around the perimeter of the crime scene.

Reaching his son, Lou knelt down and placed both hands on his son's shoulders, and looked him squarely in the eyes. "Are you okay?"

"I'm fine, Dad; they got me in a sleeper hold, that's all."

Kate looked at her stoic son who was acting as nonchalant

as if nothing had happened. *Oh my God,* she thought, *he's just like his father.*

Lou noticed Little Otter was missing one of his deerskin leggings and the scrapes all over his leg. "How'd you get away, son?"

"I just jumped out of the car when he stopped at the highway."

Lou smiled and tousled his son's hair. *I'm sure there's more to it son. He didn't pull over to let you off at a bus stop! But, I'll wait, one day you'll tell the full story around a campfire.*

By this time the officer had exited his cruiser and was standing beside Lou. "Sir, I'm going to have to ask you to step aside. I need to check this lad out and get a statement from him." Instead of moving, Lou continued talking to the boy.

"Tyrone, are you *sure* you're okay?"

"I am, Dad, honest."

"Sir, I need you to step aside, *now!*"

Lou looked up at the officer. "Back off. I'm talking to my *son.* You're on *Abenaki* land. Your jurisdiction here is limited *at best.*" Even crouched down, Lou left no doubt who he believed was in authority at the moment.

"*Sir,* I am a member of the Royal Canadian Mounted Police. I'm asking you *politely* to step aside."

Lou stood up and looked the Mountie straight in the eye. The young Mountie took a step back; instinctively, his hand moved toward his pepper spray.

"Don't do anything stupid," Lou said.

Kate was about to step in thinking she might need to

defuse the situation before it escalated just as a second cruiser arrived.

Instead, she said, "Lou, let's allow this officer to do his job."

With that, Lou turned around and tousled his son's hair a second time. "Tell him everything you know, son."

Kate walked over to the second cruiser, identified herself, and gave the officer a brief description of what she knew. Then pointing to the body lying on the ground, she told him what she expected him to do.

Next, she walked over to where Tyrone and the first officer were talking. "Excuse me, officer. I need to check my son's fingernails."

"Not now, ma'am. You'll be able to do that as soon as I'm finished."

Kate realized she hadn't made herself known. "I apologize officer; I failed to introduce myself. I'm Lieutenant Kate O'Grady, RCMP. I'm not trying to pull rank here, but I do need to check to see if there's anything under my son's fingernails that we might be able to use to identify his abductor."

It took a couple of seconds for the officer to process Kate's words. Then the officer relaxed and gave her some space. Kate shrugged her shoulders and smiled. "It's standard procedure with abductees. Could you get the evidence packet out of your cruiser? It should be in the trunk. It's in a brown bag."

When the officer returned with the packet she smiled again. "By the way, just so you know, my husband is an auxiliary Mountie. He served with your Sargeant Major in Afghanistan. They're both ex-commandoes. Had you done something foolish, it probably wouldn't have turned out very well for you."

"I was just trying to do my job, Lieutenant."

"I know that. And he wasn't wearing a name tag."

When Lou looked over and saw the second officer bending down to examine the dead body, he pulled his daughter aside. "Ayleen, take Hector and go into the woods, and stay there. Use this handkerchief to wipe the blood off him as best you can. Whatever you do, don't let him come back here, okay?"

"Okay, Daddy."

"And *this* time, stay there until you hear the sound of the whippoorwill. Promise?"

"I promise."

Once Ayleen had hold of the fur on Hector's neck and they were out of sight, Lou walked over to the second officer. "I've got a good idea who this fella is," he said.

"That'll help because his face is pretty mangled. Any idea what got at him?"

"Could have been a bear," Lou lied.

The officer pointed to paw prints in the dirt. "Those don't look much like bear tracks to me; more like a wolf or large coyote. Either case, game warden's gonna have to find that one and kill it."

"Problem is . . . finding out which one did it."

"Probably some old loner who can't hunt for himself."

Earlier, Lou had seen the garrote lying on the ground. He had an idea what had happened and decided that pointing it out to the officer would only complicate matters. When the officer wasn't looking, Lou discreetly picked it up, and tossed it into the brush.

"Well, we'll certainly be on the lookout for an old loner,"

Lou said, walking back. As the officer got up off his knees, he pointed to the material covering what was left of Vincenzo's face.

"That your shirt?"

"Yeah,"

"Well, you can take it. I'll place a tarp over him. No telling how long I'll be here before the medical examiner arrives. They're the only ones authorized to move the body."

"If you think you're gonna be here awhile, I can send over some coffee."

"Nah, I got a thermos, but thanks."

WHEN THE FIRST officer to arrive finished talking with Tyrone, he walked over to Kate. "Lieutenant, someone will be contacting you about counseling for your son. In the meantime, you should keep a close eye on him."

"I'm aware of that office, but thanks for mentioning it."

"Not a problem, ma'am." He touched the brim of his hat and nodded, then walked back to his cruiser to begin making out his report.

ONCE KATE, Lou, and their son were a distance from the gate area, Lou stopped, and made the sound of the whippoorwill. Then he stared back at the gate.

"What are you thinking, Lou?" Kate asked.

"We've become too lax about watching our backdoor."

Kate nodded in agreement. Her thoughts shifted back in time momentarily. *Two good men gave their lives defending that backdoor,* she remembered. *It seems so long ago, now.*

"Kate."

Lou's voice brought her back to the present.

"Yes?"

"I'm going to put a few trail cameras up around the gate area."

"I thought being concerned about our back door was all behind us." She dropped her shoulders in resignation. *But I guess taking steps to stay safe will never be behind us.*

It wasn't long before their daughter and Hector emerged from the forest. The moment Ayleen joined them, Lou knelt down and embraced both his children. Lou let out a deep sigh. "The spirits within us are no longer at peace. You are old enough now, it is time I teach you how to build a sweat lodge."

Kate looked at the people who defined her world. *I can never lose them,* she thought, *or I would be lost myself.* Then she looked at the evidence bag in her hand. *But first, this is going down to Fredricton with Jake tomorrow. I want to know everything there is to know about what the forensic lab finds under Tyrone's fingernails. And it better not get lost in the mail like the last package I sent did.*

Chapter Fifty-Six

After Santino made the call to Aaron Seeka's office while standing on the sidewalk outside the office of the attorney representing Adler. He was confident title to the lake known as 991, and its surrounding property, would soon change hands.

While Varni had traveled to Canada using Luigi Secondo's passport, he hadn't allowed his *alter* persona to emerge this time. He constantly struggled to repress the gentler persona of Luigi Secondo. At night, the mental confrontations between the two personalities kept him emotionally and physically drained. Varni had violated the one thing that had always separated the two personas: When he entered Canada, the physical world of his alter persona, Santino weakened the tenuous truce that barely existed between the two identities. Not once did Santino allow Luigi to come out, not even once. He simply couldn't chance it, not now.

The next morning, Santino Varni and Nardo Lombardi were up early and arrived at Kedgwick Airport shortly after 8 a.m. When Varni arranged for a flight over to Grand Falls, he specifically requested a float plane.

"Sir, a float plane won't be necessary, you're flying from one airfield to another," the agent explained.

"I plan to make a brief stop at Havre de Poisson," Santino replied.

"Oh, well, in that case, you *will* need a float plane. I'll arrange it."

A PLANE FLYING into Havre de Poisson from the north side of the lake was common on a Saturday, but not on a weekday. When Lou heard the sound of the approaching prop, he thought, *I wasn't expecting anyone to come in from Kedgwick this morning, maybe Angelo ordered something special.*

All but two boats had already gone out for the day. Lou knew one boat wouldn't be going out until later. The other boat rarely went out; it was Luigi's. Because there were always a few odds and ends that required attention, Lou had lingered in the boathouse longer than usual. Today's task was stripping the frayed line off a couple of reels and replacing it with new line. But the unexpected plane now arriving caused him drop the task.

As the plane banked into the wind, Lou walked down to the far end of the dock and waited. When the plane taxied in, Lou snagged the front pontoon, secured it to a cleat with a half hitch and moved to the rear tie down. As he turned around, a familiar face was staring at him.

"Hey, Luigi! I wasn't expecting you. Angelo didn't say anything about you coming up."

"I had business in the area, that's all. Are you okay? Is everything okay?"

Lou hesitated. The abrupt tone Luigi was using, even his voice, was unlike the benevolent Luigi that he knew. Finally, Lou responded. "Of course, everything's fine. Why wouldn't it be?"

"I read you were having a few mishaps up here."

"Where? Here?"

"I believe there was an article that mentioned something about fairy dust."

Lou laughed. "Don't tell me you get that dinky little rag sent to you in Massachusetts?" He was surprised Luigi had brought that up.

Santino deflected Lou's question. "Actually, I thought somebody was playing an April Fool's joke on you, Lou," Santino lied. "Then I realized it wasn't April." Quickly changing subjects, Santino said, "I was in the vicinity. I thought I'd stop."

"You were in the *vicinity*?"

"Well, Quebec City," Santino lied again.

"You certainly must like this place to give up a direct flight back to Boston."

"You look tired, Lou. But that's what comes from shouldering the full load of owning a business, doesn't it?"

Lou ignored the comment, still thinking about the change in Luigi's voice and his mannerisms. Then he cleared his throat, and asked, "Angelo's going to be happy to see you."

"I can't stay, business calls."

"Not even for lunch?"

"No."

Another curt comment, Lou thought, but he also saw the opportunity to ask a question. "I've been meaning to ask you,

Luigi, what business *are* you in? In all the years you've been coming up here, we've never actually *talked* about that."

"High finance, Lou, high finance," Santino lied again. "A roll of the dice here, a roll of the dice there. Eventually it all pays the rent."

Lou noticed movement inside the plane and realized Luigi wasn't traveling alone. "Is that Nina with you?"

"No. No, that's . . . that's just, that's just another player, another player in the game. Another player in the world I live in. Well, Lou, I just wanted to stop in and say hello. Remember, I'm here for you financially. You have any financial problems, you let me know, and I'll be there for you."

"Hey, before you go. I do have a question."

"Fire away!"

"How well do you know Vincenzo, the fellow you let take your cottage?"

Santino hesitated; he hadn't anticipated the question. Once again, he lied. "Not at all, actually. Never met the man. He's a friend of a friend of a friend of my sister. She thought a week up here might help him clear his head. Was there a problem? I hope he didn't do anything wrong?"

Lou hesitated again; his senses told him he was talking to someone other than Luigi. "No, we're cool."

"Okay, and remember what I said, if you need *anything*, you let me know. I consider you to be family, and I take care of family."

Lou ignored the comment. "So, where are you heading next?"

"Grand Falls, and then on to Boston."

"I can't believe you went this far out of your way to stop by, Luigi. Angelo will be sorry he missed you."

As the plane lifted off, Santino Varni looked down at the receding resort. *Gault, your days are numbered. One way or another, you're going to lose everything.*

THE ONE BOAT that could have gone out early that morning but didn't, was assigned to the cottage Josh Barnard had taken. Uncharacteristically, Josh was inside laboring over the title work he needed to research to create a clear transfer for the Adler, Michigan transaction to go through.

The database he usually found to be technically dependable and succinct was somehow lacking. Entire quadrants of land involved in the title search were inexplicitly missing from the database.

"Aargh! What is it with this?" Josh sighed as he expressed his frustration. "Three quarters of the land in this deal isn't even showing up on this database." He tried two additional access points, but still failed.

"Okay, the rulers of the Internet are telling me to kick this one to the curb, for now." With that, Josh grabbed his lucky rod and reel and headed down to the dock.

THAT SAME MORNING, in a different cottage, Kate sat in front of her own laptop, staring at the burner phone Lou had found by the dock. The one thing she hadn't checked were the *in*coming calls to the phone. She only found two. Both came from the same number. Kate was curious and initiated a return call.

"Longshoremen's Union, Mr. Varni's Office." The voice sounded somewhat familiar. Kate hadn't expected that and now hesitated.

When Kate didn't speak up, the person who answered the phone repeated: "Mr. Varni's Office, may I help you?"

Kate stayed on the line until she heard a click. Then she moved the phone away from her ear. *You may have already helped me, you just may already have.*

Chapter Fifty-Seven

When Lou returned to his cottage, the first thing he did was go to the bathroom and look in the mirror. When he came out, he walked over to his wife. "Kate, do I look tired to you?"

She tilted her head back and stared at her husband. "No, no more than usual. Why?"

"Luigi just said I looked tired."

"Is that who flew in?"

"Yeah, said he stopped in to say 'hello."

"He didn't stay?"

"No, he's on his way back to Boston; he was in the *vicinity* doing business and just stopped by."

"Where was he?"

"Quebec City."

"Did he say what kind of business?" The comings and goings of Luigi Secondo, along with what the man did for a living, was a mystery Kate long wanted to solve.

"Not really."

"Did you even ask?"

"I did."

"And?"

"He gave me some cockamamie answer, something about being in *high finance* and *rolling the dice*." Just then there was knock on Lou's door.

"Lou, you in there?"

"Yeah. Come on in, Josh."

"When I didn't see you at the dock, I figured you'd be here." As soon as he entered the cottage and saw Kate, he added, "Morning, Kate!"

Kate smiled and nodded her head. "Morning, Josh."

Turning to Lou, Josh continued. "Are you ready for this? It looks like you're going to have new neighbors."

"Who?"

"Someone's buying Lake 991, and the land around it."

"Do you know who it is?"

"I'm only doing the title work, but I'll find out, if you wanna know."

"I do, but don't go breaking your neck over it. I've got enough to do without worrying over who's gonna be pitching a tent on the far side of Carleton Mountain."

"Josh don't listen to him," Kate said. "I definitely want to know."

THE PUZZLE LOU and Kate found themselves dealing with was beginning to take shape, albeit there were a few critical missing pieces . . . actually, more than a few.

Kate had been receiving copies of reports related to the wildfire investigation. The Fire Marshal had confirmed that an accelerant had been used. Nathan Turnbridge had confessed to being present when his cousin ignited the accelerant that caused the wildfire to rapidly spread.

Nathan Turnbridge had also confessed to being a participant in the plot to introduce the invasive Tench into Abenaki waters. The motivation behind both acts committed by the Turnbridge cousins was still a mystery to law enforcement and Lou and Kate.

Physical evidence, along with eyewitness statements from his children, confirmed that someone besides Vincenzo had been involved in the abduction of their son.

Lou and Jake had determined the operational mishaps and property damage that had occurred at Havre de Poisson were, in all probability, the work of one man, Vincenzo. The now deceased Vincenzo.

Still open were questions on who entered the two cottages furthest from the lodge and stole private property. They had nothing yet to go on.

Circumstantial evidence suggested that whoever had the cell phone Lou found at the dock was the same person who called Brunswick Mutual and the Brunswick Daily Times. But the motive behind both calls was purely speculative.

Kate had recently established a connection between the burner phone and the Longshoreman's Union. But what that connection actually meant still remained unclear.

Back in Boston on the following day, Matteo walked into Santino Varni's office unannounced and sat down in front of Varni's desk. He said nothing but clearly was upset. Varni looked up in surprise.

"What?"

"Popeye's dead."

Santino paused. "Where's the body?"

"I don't know."

"What the hell do you *mean* you 'don't know?'"

"I had to leave him! I went back later, but he was gone."

"If he was *dead,* he didn't get up and walk away. What happened?"

"I left him on that dirt road into the resort. A huge friggin' dog . . . it looked like a wolf , I don't know. . . killed him."

"Where were *you*?"

"At Gault's place."

"*Where* at Gault's place?"

"We'd gone up the logging road. There were too many people walking around the place, so we decided to leave. We were almost back at the car when Gault's kid popped out of the friggin' woods and recognized Popeye."

"Why didn't you just take the kid?"

"We did, but then all hell broke loose." When Matteo didn't say anything further, Santino motioned with his hands to continue.

"Honest, this friggin' crazed dog came out of the woods snarling at us. I wanted to put the kid in the car and get the hell out of there, but Popeye decided to take the damn thing on."

"Yeah, okay, Gault has a pet wolf running around up there."

"Yeah, so…Popeye's all mouth, saying he was gonna kill the thing. Well, guess what, it didn't work out that way. Then the friggin' thing starts jumping up at me, trying to get in the friggin' car. His mouth was all blood. He killed Popeye. There wasn't a friggin' thing I could do about it. So, I got the hell out of there."

"Where's Gault's kid?"

"I don't know."

"What the hell do you *mean* you don't know!!?"

"I don't know! One minute the kid is in the back seat, knocked out, the next thing I know . . . I'm chasing the little bastard, he jumps into the woods and he's *gone*."

Varni pushed the button on his desk phone.

"Yes Mr. Varni?"

"Nina, come in here."

When Nina came in, she immediately knew something was terribly wrong. Matteo sat slumped in the chair across from Santino, both hands holding his head.

"Nina, I want you to drop whatever you're doing. I need you to expunge any and all references to Popeye ever having any connection with the union. Employee files, pension funds, tax records, you name it. I don't want a *single* record connecting him to the union anywhere. Do you *understand* what I'm saying?"

"Yes. Popeye never existed."

"Correct. Put *everything* else aside. *This* is your top priority."

"I understand."

THAT EVENING, Lou walked over to Angelo's to have a cigar with the chef and his cousin Jake. It was a good thing, too, because Angelo wanted to talk with Lou about what Alessandra had told him earlier in the day. He couldn't believe it.

"Lou, Alessandra said Luigi stopped by."

"He did, Angelo. He was heading back home."

Angelo took a long pull on his cigar and let the smoke out

slowly. "I'm surprised he didn't come up to the lodge to see me." His disappointment was clear.

"He didn't seem like himself, today, Angelo. He wanted to get home. You might not even have recognized him as your old friend."

"Well, if he wasn't feeling well, then I can understand him not coming up to see me."

Lou lit his cigar. "No, that's not exactly what I mean. It was strange, kind of like I was talking to a completely different person. It didn't even sound like him; even his mannerisms were different." Lou paused to let out a puff of smoke. "It was odd."

Angelo nodded his head. "I've actually noticed that same thing on a few occasions, myself. It's as if something comes over him."

"Yeah, I asked him straight out what business he was in, and I thought I was going to find out. Instead, he gave me a silly answer."

"He *has* to be in some kind of business. He seemed quite knowledgeable when we were talking about insurance."

Jake leaned forward to tap his cigar on the ashtray. "I, for one, am very impressed. I find the mystery surrounding that man intriguing," he said jokingly.

Lou dismissed Jake's comment and looped back to what Angelo had said. "Angelo, *when* did you and Luigi talk about insurance?"

"It was a few weeks ago."

"Did you mention who we use?"

"Probably."

"Interesting."

"We talked about it for a while. He was firing question after question at me about the resort."

"What kind of questions?"

"Operational questions. How do we do *this* and how do we do *that*. I was beginning to wonder if he was planning to go off and try running a place like this himself."

"Hmmm. Okay, I'm gonna change subjects. Remember that lake Josh Barnard crashed into some years back?" Both Jake and Angelo nodded. "Well, Josh told me earlier today that someone's buying it."

Jake tilted his head back and blew a thin stream of smoke skyward. "Must be another lumber company. Who else would be interested in it."

"I agree," Lou said.

"Although, on second thought, Angelo, this could be something for *you* to keep an eye on."

"Why is that, Jake?"

"Well, if it turns out to be another fishing lodge, you might be in line for a big fat employee sign-on bonus."

Lou stood up when his cousin "poked his bear" as the expression goes. "All right, I gotta get up early. I'm leaving before this conversation spirals down any further."

"Wait, Lou. I'll walk back with you. G'night, Angelo." Jake snuffed out his smoke and walked out with his cousin.

THE FOLLOWING MORNING, when Josh came down to the boathouse, he asked Lou a question: "Does the name 'Santino Varni' mean anything to you?"

Lou thought a moment. "Not off hand. Why?"

"Well, that's the name of your new neighbor."

"Really? Well, that's a new name for me."

. . .

When Lou returned to his cottage, he paused just long enough to scan the horizon before stepping inside. Kate was already on the phone, so, he made a mental note to mention later who was buying land on the far side of Carleton Mountain.

Not long afterward, Kate was off the phone and called over to him in the next room. "Lou, the Mounties officially identified the body at the gate as that of Vincenzo Pierro."

"Well, we knew that was gonna happen."

"Yeah, but we didn't know he has, well, he *had* a pretty long rap sheet."

"By-the-way, did I mention I found a garrote near his body when we were over at the gate."

"No."

"Yeah. I wonder if he tried to use it on Hector?"

"Lou, that's an assassin's weapon." Kate silently tried to envision why in the world an assassin would have come to Havre de Poisson. Then she got up and walked over to where Lou was sitting in the kitchen. "Here's an interesting thing, the file said he was a longshoreman. And here's another coincidence: There were two calls made to that burner phone you found by someone at the Boston Longshoreman's Union."

"So, you did a little more digging, huh?"

"A little. I just called one of the number's on the phone and a person answered saying: Longshoreman's Union, Santino Varni's office."

Lou stopped dead still. "*Who's* office?"

Not sure that she was pronouncing it correctly, Kate looked at her notes. "Someone by the name of 'Varni.' Santino Varni, why?"

"That's the name of the person Josh said is buying Lake 991."

Kate took in the information. "Ya' know what else is weird?" She took a breath. "The voice who answered sounded familiar. I'm sure I've heard it before."

"How so?

"It was a Boston accent. I could have sworn it was Nina Cataldo."

"Who?"

"Luigi's fiancée. What else did Josh say?"

"Nothing much other than he's having trouble clearing the title for the sale."

"Oh, I meant to tell you, a mental health case worker called today, looking to set up time with Tyrone."

"For what?"

"It's just part of the child abduction follow-up protocol. The shrinks the RCMP use don't make house calls, so we're doing a zoom call. I'll only be allowed to be present for part of the call because they want him to have the freedom to say what he wants without feeling pressure from a parent. We'll do it in his room, that'll give him some privacy."

"What about Ayleen? She saw the whole thing. Doesn't she need some professional TLC, too?"

"She's also scheduled. I just didn't mention it. Sorry."

"Good. Let's take advantage of every opportunity to help these kids put this whole thing behind them. We don't need them having nightmares."

Chapter Fifty-Eight

The suspicious explosion that took Carmine Monteverde's life created a firestorm within the Longshoreman's Union. Carmine had been a popular figure among the rank-and-file members. Quite a few had already begun publicly supporting his bid for senior leadership.

What was not lost on the media was the growing backlash surrounding the questionable cause behind the death of a serious contender for the presidency of the union; nor was it lost on those who sat in oversight positions.

The Massachusetts State Department of Labor Relations and the National Labor Relations Board both initiated investigations. Whistleblowers brought into question various issues including whether union officials at the helm were consistently upholding their fiduciary responsibility to safeguard union assets.

In past years, the degree of influence the union had on state and independent auditors had been excessive. As a result, the annual audits on the union's financial records, and pension fund, had been little more than a wink and a nod, a sham in many aspects. Now, the more astute local politicians facing re-election saw an opportunity to gain free publicity and began calling for an investigation and more oversight. Soon, teams of handpicked auditors, each and every one, an ethical public servant, descended upon union headquarters.

In a matter of days, auditors were asking to see supporting documentation and justification behind every expenditure, including travel and business meetings for the two prior years and the current year.

Alex Biondi, a special auditor assigned to audit the pension fund, requested the corresponding entry for a sizable check recently sent to an attorney representing Adler Forest Products.

When word of Biondi's request reached Rico Gardella, the union treasurer and pension fund manager, he got up from his chair and took a walk over to the small office Biondi was using.

"Hey Alex, listen, my schedule's kinda crazy this week. But I try to get together with every auditor at least once. It's close to lunch time now, so whaddya say you and I head out and beat the crowd?"

Alex smiled and picked up a brown paper bag. "Thanks, but I'm all set."

"Ahh, come on...you can save that for tomorrow; I'm buying. Besides, there's a *real* nice place, and I *mean* nice, you're gonna love it, within walking distance. And, we may not have another time to get together like this, again."

"I appreciate the offer, but I'll pass. Wife's got me on a strict diet."

Rico sensed the auditor's resistance and backed off.

Gesturing with both hands in the air, palms facing the auditor, Rico said, "Okay, okay, I'm just trying to be helpful."

Biondi ignored Rico's attempt at playing the *good cop* card. "By the way, Rico, your balance sheet's off by about six million dollars right now. If you *really* wanna help, I need to see the corresponding entry for a check that was made out to Adler."

"Yeah, I, uh…I already got a guy running that one down for ya."

"That's great. Thanks."

When Rico returned to his office, he made out an entry increasing the debt holdings with Adler in an amount equal to the check that was made out and gave it to a staff member. "Put this on that friggin' auditor's desk as soon as he leaves today."

When Josh Barnard's admin called a third time to let him know the attorney representing Adler Forest Property had called yet again, requesting the status on the title search, Josh Barnard put a call into Smyth Air. After he packed, he walked over to the boathouse, thinking he might find Lou.

"Lou, are you in there?" When no one answered, he took a walk over to the lodge. Lou was in the kitchen, steadying an extension ladder, with both hands, while a fella from Noonan Glass took the measurements of the broken plate glass window.

"Lou, I gotta say goodbye."

"You're leaving?"

"Yeah, I gotta. I need to finish the title survey on this Lake 991 deal, or I'm going to lose a good client. I thought I'd be able to get it done from here, but I can't."

"Well, I'll comp you the time you're not using. Come back up when you can."

"No, that's not fair to you, Lou. This is all on me."

Lou shrugged his shoulders. "Hey, my monkey, my circus. Besides, I like having you up here, Josh. So, that's what's happening."

Just then the sound of a float plane could be heard coming up from the west end of the valley.

"That sounds like my ride, Lou. I'll be back in touch."

WITH LOU'S URGING, Kate increased her efforts to learn more about Luigi Secondo and what he did for a living. So far, she'd only been able to ascertain a few things:

1. He's Sicilian
2. He's bilingual
3. He has a direct connection with Nina Cataldo, who is employed by the Boston Longshoreman's Union
4. He has absolutely no online presence

Another list of suppositions about the man was just a tad longer:

1. He obviously has money
2. He's single
3. He's supposedly engaged
4. His calendar seems flexible
5. He has some connection to Vincenzo Pierro
6. He presumably lives in, or around, Boston
7. He comes to the resort to relax, not fish

As she sat back in her chair she mused over her lists. *Maybe I'll learn something if I do a little drill down on Vincenzo.*

Like Luigi, Vincenzo Pierro didn't have a presence on social media. He did, however, have a lengthy criminal record. Pierro's last known address was Revere, a suburb across the bay from Boston, with a *checkered* history. Noteworthy among the information in his file was a reputed connection to a small crime syndicate believed to be controlled by a man named Santino Varni.

'Varni', she thought. *That's the name of the person Josh said was buying Lake 991. That's also the name I heard when I called the number on the burner phone. I think I'll try something.*

Within a minute, Kate searched: *Officers - Boston Longshoremen's Union.* Three names came up:

Santino Varni – President

Matteo Abruzzo – Executive Vice President

Enrico Gardella – Secretary / Treasurer

Well, look at that . . . how interesting that the name Santino Varni all of a sudden keeps showing up, she thought, *but the name Luigi Secondo doesn't show up anywhere. I think I'll take a real shot in the dark.*

Kate grabbed the burner phone and clicked on incoming calls to look at the listings, again. Both calls came from the same number. It didn't matter which one she selected, so she chose the first one and pressed the call button. The phone rang twice before someone picked up.

"Mr. Varni's office how may I help you?"

The voice was the same familiar voice she had heard before. Kate was ready this time. "Nina?"

"Who is this?"

"Nina Cataldo?"

"Yes. Who *is* this?"

"Nina, it's Kate, Kate Gault, from Havre de Poisson." The silence was deafening. "Nina, I'm sorry to disturb you. I'm trying to reach Luigi. Could you give me a number where I can reach him?"

A flustered Nina Cataldo recovered quickly. "I'm sorry, Kate, I have another call coming in; let me put you on hold. If I lose you, I'll call you right back." Nina quickly made note of the number appearing on her caller ID. Of course, she had no intention of calling back once she disconnected. When the line went dead, she blocked the number.

Kate put the burner on speaker and waited. When several minutes passed, she hung up. Then it dawned on her: *Wait a minute. Angelo said Luigi calls him to let him know he's coming up here.*

When Kate walked into the kitchen she found Angelo busy at the stove. "Angelo, do you have your phone with you?"

"Of course."

"May I see it?"

"It's on the shelf."

In a nonchalant voice, Kate said, "Angelo, who calls you on this phone?"

"Suppliers, and Jake does, if he's picking something up for me."

"Is this the phone Luigi calls you on?"

"That's the only phone I have."

"Do you ever use this phone to call him?"

"No . . . he's a busy man . . . he calls me."

Kate pulled up the list of incoming calls. With the exception of one number that showed up periodically with a Boston area code, all the calls were from phones in the New Brunswick area.

"Do you mind if I use your phone to call Luigi?"

Angelo shook his head. "Go ahead."

Kate selected the Boston number and pressed "call." The phone rang once then went directly to a message that voicemail had not been set up and the call ended. Kate made a note of the number that had called Angelo's phone and returned to her cottage.

As she walked from the kitchen, back to her cottage, she decided to try a totally different angle. Perhaps doing a little research on Vincenzo's crossings into Canada would yield something of value.

Canadian Customs had Vincenzo Pierro entering Canada three times, always through Grand Falls. The first time he arrived via private jet. The second and third time he flew in on a commercial flight. Kate requested, and received, a list of the passengers who also came in on the Delta flights Vincenzo had taken from Boston to Grand Falls. On one flight, the name "Matteo Abruzzi" appeared as a fellow passenger. When she noticed that Abruzzi sat in the seat adjacent to Vincenzo on the Delta flight, she made a note. *Now that's just coincidental enough to peak my interest.*

The next thing she did was call the car rental companies servicing Grand Falls International Airport. Not one had any record of a Vincenzo Pierro renting a vehicle. However, Matteo Abruzzi had rented a black SUV twice when he'd recently arrived in Canada.

It may only be circumstantial, Mr. Abruzzi, but right now I consider you to be a person of interest in whatever mischief Vincenzo was up to including kidnapping my son. Let's see if I can find a mug shot of you.

When Kate googled the name "Matteo Abruzzi," several

pictures came up. But what caught her attention most was an image in the section below, titled: *"People also searched for."*

Kate stared at one photo. It was grainy and wasn't taken head on. It had all the markings of a paparazzi photo taken with a long-distance lens. The name under the photo said, "Santino Varni." But the facial features were definitely similar to Luigi Secondo's.

Chapter Fifty-Nine

The solar shades in Santino's office were drawn from floor to ceiling. Still, the glare from the early morning sun caused Matteo to squint as he sat across from Varni now in a foul mood.

Matteo was beginning to feel pressure from all sides. He no longer had Carmine Monteverde as his mouthpiece with the rank-and-file union members. His trusted ally, Popeye, the one who did his dirty work, was gone. The auditors were now coming to him with questions he didn't want to answer, and the police investigation into the death of Carmine was ongoing, something Matteo wished would go away.

From day one, Nina Cataldo had always been at her desk long before Santino arrived at the office. Every morning when he stepped off the elevator and approached Nina's desk, she would ask if he'd like a coffee. Some days he said, "yes," and some days he declined.

This particular morning, when Santino arrived, Nina was on the phone rearranging meetings and Santino walked briskly past her, into his office and closed his door. Matteo had walked past her desk earlier, while she was on the phone, and gone into Santino's office. *Something's up,* she thought.

Instead of knocking on Santino's door and interrupting the two men, Nina decided to press the intercom and ask if they'd like coffee. As she waited for an opportunity to speak, she innocently listened to their conversation.

"Santino, Rico says the auditors are asking about the money you took from the pension fund." Santino smirked and shrugged his shoulders.

"Santino!"

"What?"

"Come on man, we gotta *do* something! Our names are on that friggin' check!"

"So, maybe this auditor needs to go away."

"Come on, we can't do that. They'd be all over us."

"So, we pay it back."

"Yeah, right. How's that gonna friggin' happen? Shit, even together we don't have that kinda cash."

"We will; we just need to take a little trip."

"Yeah, where? You gotta friggin' gold mine someplace?"

Santino smiled, thinking about the stream near Lou's saw mill and nodded. "I just might have one."

Matteo lowered his head, placed both hands against his cheeks, and growled. "Aargh! Santino, if we had any sense, we'd just walk away and wait for all this to blow over."

"Relax. Rico's gonna take the heat on this."

"Why? So you and I can walk? Santino, there's no friggin' *way* that's gonna happen. He'll *talk* before that happens."

"He won't have a choice."

"What's *that* supposed to mean?"

Santino ran his index finger slowly across the front of his neck.

"No! We're not *doing* that!" Matteo protested. "That's *not* on the table! That's never going to be on the table."

"He knows too much, Matteo. Think about it. He's a risk."

"Come on, Santino, that's *crazy* talk, he's *not* a risk."

"He's a risk if I *say* he's a damn risk!" Santino banged his fist on his desk. "As long as he's alive, he's a damn *risk*, dead men don't talk." Matteo closed his eyes and sat back in his chair.

After a moment, Santino let out a breath and whispered, "It needs to be done." Hearing those words, Matteo knew it was a *fait accompli,* there was no point in arguing, Santino had made his decision.

When Nina overheard Santino's last comment, she instinctively held her breath and covered her mouth.

"Leave a note. Make it look like he was dipping in, and we had no knowledge."

Matteo took a breath and cleared his throat, as if he was going to protest again; then he nodded in submission. Rico had grown up with both of them; he was an old friend, they went to school together, he came from the very streets they all grew up on.

"All right, I just gave you something to do. Tell Nina I need to see her."

As Matteo stood up, he cleared his throat again. Neither man heard the slight metallic click on the intercom as Nina released the button and clicked off.

Two floors below, Alex Biondi, an auditor sent in by the National Labor Relations Board, stared at the journal voucher that had been left on his desk. As he paged through the archaic, handwritten records, he wondered, *When the hell are they gonna invest in an automated system?*

Earlier, when he'd originally seen the original journal voucher, the entry recording the payment to Adler Forest Products and crediting cash, a flag went up for him. *Where's the second half of this JV entry? They should have made a compound entry; hell that's basic accounting 101 stuff.*

The next thing he did was compare the dollar amounts on the two entries; they matched. The first voucher was numbered 149, the second was 149A. The numbering scheme wasn't all that uncommon, for an adjusting or corresponding entry. The dates on the two JV's were the same, but the handwriting and ink color were different, both of which Biondi picked up on.

Biondi continued to stare at the two entries, shaking his head. *It's really odd they didn't use a single compound entry. Well, as long as they have the supporting documentation and it's in the general ledger, I guess, it doesn't matter.*

But when Biondi opened the general ledger and looked for the entry under the asset labeled *Investments in Debt Securities*, the only thing he found was a yellow sticky note with 'See miscellaneous JV 149A' on it.

Another flag went up for Biondi and he went back to the book of journal vouchers. JV 150 was missing. If a JV is subsequently determined to be incorrect, Generally Accepted Accounting Principles (GAAP) dictated that the original entry should remain as is, and an adjusting entry made.

Interesting, he thought, *JV 149A wasn't in the book and JV 150 was taken out.*

Biondi decided to go back to the general ledger, thinking he might find evidence of where JV 150 might have been posted, perhaps, under an asset. The only thing that caught his attention on any asset account was an illegible line on the Loan to Officers page. What appeared to have been a previous entry, had been erased.

Alex Biondi was "old school," and there wasn't much that got by him. He didn't look like a bean-counter, but he was. He was known for both his thoroughness, and his integrity. He was no stranger to challenging audits or uncovering deceptive practices. He had been with the SEC when they audited the ENRON meltdown. He was with the FTC when the mortgage fiascos surfaced, and that industry nearly collapsed.

No, Biondi was nobody's fool. He knew what a rat smelled like. But for the time being, he considered the issue to be lousy bookkeeping practices.

The next thing he did was call Adler Forest Products to request a copy of the debt agreement they had with the union. But after the first two rings, the call went into a recording:

Welcome to Adler Forest Products. Please listen closely, as our menu has changed: For Sales, press one. For all other departments, press two. If you know your party's extension, you may dial it at any time.

Alex pressed two and ended up leaving a message requesting a call back. After that, he called the bank the Union had drawn the check on, and requested a copy of both sides. Alex Biondi was nobody's fool.

WHILE BIONDI WAS MAKING progress in Boston, just the opposite was true for Josh Barnard. He hadn't been able to move the ball forward one iota on the title search.

None of the court records in Northumberland County, nor any recorder's office or any assessor's office, had any records corresponding with the coordinates on the purchase and sale document Adler had drawn up. Josh was stymied. Finally, in frustration, he decided to start over, but this time, taking a different approach.

ELSEWHERE, Nina Cataldo walked into Santino's office and he motioned for her to take one of the chairs facing his desk. Then, without even waiting for her to sit down, he started giving instructions.

"Matteo and I will be traveling north. I need you to make the arrangements."

"Just the two of you?"

"Yes."

Nina nodded that she understood and made a note on the pad she had in front of her. "When will you be traveling?"

"We'll head up tomorrow."

"Will you be staying at the cottage?"

"Yes."

Nina remained seated, notepad and pen in hand, waiting for more information. But abruptly, Santino said, "Okay, that's all I have for you."

"If you can tell me the length of your stay, I'll book your return flight and rearrange your appointments appropriately."

Santino inhaled deeply and held his breath before exhaling. "I'll get back to you."

Nina nodded, stood up and returned to her desk. The recent conversation she'd inadvertently overheard, along with the abrupt conversation she'd just experienced, troubled her. It left her even more confused about where she stood with Varni. For the first time, she began to question her own deep feelings about him.

Santino and Matteo grew up with Enrico Gardella, she thought. *If Rico's a risk because he knows too much . . . what am I?*

When Nina left his office, Varni picked up his cell phone and made a call. The phone rang twice before someone picked up.

"Passiatore Jewelry."

"Let me speak with Frederico."

"May I say who's calling?"

"Santino."

Within a minute, Frederico came to the phone. "This is Frederico."

"Frederico, how many gold nuggets can you move?"

Frederico knew immediately who he was talking to. "As many as you give me."

"What's the turnaround?"

"A few days, probably no more than three, maybe four."

"What would sooner cost me?"

"How soon?"

"On delivery."

Frederico's free hand reached up and pulled on his pencil thin mustache. He knew he'd have to front the money himself. He also knew if he tried to move too much product at once, the price would plummet.

Finally, he answered. "I'm gonna take a guess at twenty percent, maybe a little more."

"Line it up," Varni said. "I'll be in touch."

Chapter Sixty

When Josh Barnard entered the vault his firm had containing every inactive client folder and legal case they had ever been involved with, he wasn't exactly sure what he was looking for, or even where to start.

It was Felix T. Barnard, Josh's grandfather, who had inspired him to pursue a career in law. When Josh was a law student, the elder solicitor had taken his grandson under his wing numerous times. He had repeatedly coached him on the importance of researching the law for obscure precedents, how to look for oddities and grey areas that could be used to argue in a client's favor. Josh had learned from a master.

As he stood next to a worktable, facing row upon row of storage boxes, Josh thought about his grandfather. *Your work has helped me in the past. So, I'm going to start with you.*

His grandfather hadn't done a lot of real estate work. His practice had focused more on commercial law, primarily in Fredericton and New Brunswick's southern counties.

Although his grandfather had practiced law for over fifty years, all that remained of his career were seven dusty storage boxes in a basement vault.

Now as Josh thumbed through the tabs on the folders, he pulled anything involving real estate, or pertaining to Northumberland County.

One folder he selected had served him well several years earlier. He'd used the contents in that folder to build an iron clad case proving that the Abenaki had exclusive rights to their land. He set that folder aside and continued perusing through the rest of the folders. When he saw one marked *supplemental*, he put that one aside.

After whittling it down to six folders, he returned the boxes to the shelves and headed up the stairs to his office, the folders he had selected, in hand. *I need to be able to complete the rest of this title transaction, otherwise, I'm not making a dime on this one.*

RICO GARDELLA LIVED ALONE. He was a survivor. His life had always been a challenge, first on the streets, then on the docks. Between excessive drinking, habitual brawling, and the passage of time, the abuse on his body had taken a toll. He wasn't even forty, yet looked older. He already depended on a variety of meds to function, and his liver was shot.

Matteo had traveled enough times with Rico, on union business, to know his friend was a creature of habit. Rico did things mechanically, by the numbers; you could set the hands on your watch by him. It was the only approach to life that worked for Rico.

Rico was never fully awake when he poured his morning coffee and took his pills. Even if the overhead light in the kitchen had been on, the cyanide pill nestled inside his pill box looked exactly like the medicine it had replaced.

When he failed to show up at work that morning, someone called his sister. She went over to check on him like she did every time she got a call the morning after he had "tied one on."

But this time, it was different. This time she dialed 911. This time the EMTs came. This time, the police found a typewritten letter. The letter stated that he, and he alone, had repeatedly diverted money from the pension fund for his own personal use. The letter alluded to a gambling problem. At the end, the letter said he was sorry for what he had done and asked for Santino's and Matteo's forgiveness.

ABOUT THE TIME the EMTs were arriving at Rico Gardella's house, Matteo was on his way to the airport. He was aware that Santino would again be traveling under a different name. Nina had told him to expect to see a change come over Santino once they arrived in Canada especially once they reached the resort. In spite of the warning, he wasn't prepared for what he actually saw when they deplaned in Grand Falls.

Holy shit, Matteo thought. *Nina wasn't kidding!* The Santino he knew walked differently, his posture was different, his facial features were different, even his voice was different.

BEFORE THEY DEPARTED BOSTON, Santino handed Matteo a list. "Take this and listen to me: no matter *what* happens, no matter what I *say or do* while we are there, *this* is what we need to accomplish before we leave Gault's place."

First on the list: "Search the stream bed for gold nuggets."

When the Smyth Air flight carrying Santino, now traveling as Luigi, and Matteo arrived at Havre de Poisson, Lou was waiting at the dock.

"Lou, it's good to see you, my friend," Luigi said, as he stepped out of the plane.

"Welcome back, Luigi. Angelo told me you were coming up today."

"Thanks, Lou. I brought a friend up this trip."

Lou had noticed movement inside the plane and expected it was Nina. But it was Matteo who emerged from the plane.

"Lou, this is Matteo," Luigi said. "Matteo, this is Lou Gualt, the fella I've been telling you about."

Lou stuck out his hand. "Welcome, Matteo. We're a little rustic here, but if there's anything you need, just let me know." Like always, Lou was getting an instant "read" on Matteo, from the man's handshake.

"Thanks, I'll do that."

"You've come up at a good time, Matteo. The fishing's been pretty good lately. Do you do a lot of fishing?"

"No, I just came up to get away."

"Well, there's a boat here for you, and I'll fix you up with all the gear you'll need if you change your mind. I can hook you up with a guide, too, if you'd like."

"I think I'm good."

When the pilot began handing the luggage out, Luigi said, "Matteo, grab your bags; we'll drop 'em off at the cottage then I'll take you over to see Angelo."

"Hold on a second," Lou said. "Matteo, there's one thing I need to make sure you're aware of."

"What's that?"

"We have a wolf that roams the area. He may appear

domesticated, but he's not. That being said, he won't bother you if you don't bother him. Just give him a wide berth." Matteo nodded, as a disturbing flashback entered his thoughts.

It was mid-week, and as the two new arrivals turned and headed toward the cottages, Lou called after them. "Let me know if you need anything."

Without looking back, the man Lou knew as "Luigi," waved his hand in the air. "We will."

As soon as they were away from the dock, Matteo quietly asked, "Where's the streambed with all the gold?"

"Over to the left. See the sawmill?"

"Yeah, it's kinda in the open."

"Nobody goes near it; they'll all be out fishing."

BEFORE ALEX BIONDI could move forward with his audit, he needed to know what the offset account was on the balance sheet for the 3.2-million-dollar check Adler Forest Products had cashed.

The bank had sent him a copy of the front and back of the check. It was endorsed with a stamp. When he zoomed in on the image, the stamp read, Aaron Seeka, Michigan Consolidated Industries.

Hmmm, it's probably a promissory note, he thought. *Adler hasn't returned my call. So, let's just give Mr. Seeka a call and see if we can get a copy of the note.*

When the phone rang more than three times, Biondi was certain he'd end up leaving a voice message. Instead, right after the third ring, Aaron, himself, picked up the phone.

"Aaron Seeka."

"Mr. Seeka. My name is Alex Biondi. I'm conducting an

audit on The Boston Longshoremen's Union Pension Fund. Do you have a minute?"

"I do."

"Adler Forest Products is one of your subsidiaries, is it not?"

"Yes, it is."

"I'd like a copy of the recent promissory note Adler just took out with the pension fund." The line went quiet for a few seconds.

"Adler didn't pick up any additional debt on that transaction."

"I'm talking about a 3.2-million-dollar transaction, Mr. Seeka, I'm guessing that was note."

"No, that was a cash deal. Adler sold off a section of land."

"Oh," Biondi was surprised. "Could you email me a copy of the purchase and sales agreement?"

"Sure. I'll make a call and have someone get it right over to you. Do you have a fax?

"Just send it as an email attachment."

When Alex hung up, he began calculating in his head: *Hmmm, land holdings, I didn't even see that listed as a separate asset on the balance sheet. Their balance sheet is off by over six million. The transaction with Adler is only going to account for half of it. Something's still off.*

Chapter Sixty-One

Life at the resort was no longer the same after Little Otter's kidnapping. Jake and Lou had reduced concerns somewhat by linking the trail cameras around the resort, and its perimeter, to everyone's cell phones. Jake also altered the sensitivity settings so the alarms wouldn't go off unless it was something larger than a small deer.

The first morning Matteo and Luigi were in camp, Matteo woke at his usual time, even as a child he'd been an early riser. Luigi was still asleep. Since Matteo thrived on coffee, he decided to head over to the lodge.

The morning air was brisk, but tolerable, and Matteo wandered out to the deck wrapping around two sides of the lodge to enjoy the view as he sipped his first cup of coffee. Glancing across the open field, his eyes settled on the brook by the sawmill.

What the frig, he thought, *nobody's gonna see me.* With that, he casually walked across the open field until he reached the brook. There was a low picket fence set some ten feet before the stream, which Matteo easily stepped over.

The sun hadn't fully risen and the light wasn't that bright yet, but the water was crystal clear. He saw a stone that appeared to be orangey-yellow in the stream bed. He looked around, didn't see anyone, rolled up his trousers and stepped out of his shoes. Once he was in the water, his eyes scanned the stream bed as he tried to locate the stone that had attracted his attention. Just as he thought he saw it, he heard someone clear their throat.

"The stream is off limits to guests."

Matteo turned but didn't recognize the person standing a few feet from the picket fence. When Matteo didn't move, the man said, "That's a spawning stream. No one's allowed in there, that's why there's a fence. I need to ask you to come back over on *this* side."

Matteo obliged, and stepped back over the fence, shoes in hand. "Have we met?"

"Not before now."

"Mind telling me who you are?"

"Name's Jake. I live here."

"Oh, well I guess I didn't realize I was trespassing."

"What were you doing in there?"

"I saw some, uh…I saw some fish. I thought I might be able to catch one with my hands."

Jake laughed. "Which cottage are you staying in?"

"I don't know. I came up with Santino."

"Who?"

Matteo was about to say, "Santino," again but caught himself. "*Luigi,* I'm staying with Luigi."

"Oh, yeah, I heard Luigi brought a friend up. Well, welcome! Just stay in the common areas, okay?"

"Yeah, sure thing."

As Matteo headed back to Luigi's cottage, Jake watched him for a moment, then walked over to the boathouse. "Lou, you in there?"

"Yeah."

Jake looked around to make sure no one was within earshot. "Lou, I just chased Luigi's friend out of the stream bed."

"Really?"

"Yeah. He said he was trying to catch fish with his hands. I don't believe that's what he was doing, but who knows. You might wanna keep an eye of him."

"I will."

WHEN ALEX BIONDI opened the file attached to an email, containing the purchase and sale agreement from Adler Forest Products, he wasn't happy. Between the sloppy accounting, the missing JVs, and the Adler property passing directly to Santino Varni, versus to the pension fund, he wanted answers. When he walked over to Rico Gardella's office . . . it was empty.

Biondi returned to his work area and began examining records for the past *five* years. It wasn't long before he found numerous checks made out to Santino Varni. The notations were always the same: *Loan to officer*. The problem was, the loans were never recorded as a receivable in the books, nor could he find any documentation supporting the loans, or any indication any payments had been made against the loans.

When Biondi added up all the checks made out to Varni

over the years, and combined them with the 3.2-million-dollar check paid to Adler, the books finally balanced.

In the past, whenever he'd gone to Rico Gardella with a question, Biondi came back with a vague answer. He sensed Gardella was a puppet for Varni and the man probably did whatever he was told to do. When he learned of Gardella's sudden death, he smelled a rat.

Biondi requested a copy of every check issued to Santino Varni over the past five years. Then he put a call into his manager, letting him know he was altering his audit approach from routine to a full scale, due diligence, investigative audit. Biondi was a man on a mission.

LATER THAT SAME DAY, Luigi and Matteo came down to the dock looking for Lou. "Hey Lou, you around?" Luigi called out.

"I'm in the boathouse."

"Lou, we've decided to do a little shore fishing."

"All right! Give me just a minute and I'll fix you up with some gear," Lou called back. "The stream that flows into the lake is a good spot. It's not too far and the fish wait offshore for whatever comes floating down. Don't go upstream, you won't find anything up there this time of year, and that's a spawning ground anyway. A little further over is Rocky Point; that's also a decent place to fish from shore."

As the two men headed off, Lou had only one thought. *That's different. But at least Luigi is doing something besides hanging around jawing with Angelo.*

When an hour had passed, Lou decided to take a walk to see how Luigi and his friend were doing. As he approached the stream where it entered the lake, he didn't see anyone. *They must've gone over to Rocky Point,* he thought.

When he reached Rocky Point, he didn't see anyone there either. *Well, they must have given up, and gone back to their cottage.*

As he retraced his steps, he noticed the two fishing rods leaning against a tree, near the stream. When he looked at the rod tips, he could tell instantly they hadn't been used, the unique way of securing the hook to the tip that Grey Elk, his grandfather, taught him was still intact.

When he looked at the ground, he saw where they, or someone, had obviously decided to take a walk up along the stream bed.

After what Jake said this morning, I think I better go check this out.

Lou worked his way through the heavy scrub that grew on both sides of the stream near the mouth. About thirty yards further up, the brush had been cleared away from the stream. Once Lou passed beyond the scrub, he saw Luigi bent over, standing in the middle of the water.

"Hey Luigi, this area's restricted. The smelt spawn in this stream," he called out. Luigi straightened up, but didn't say anything. When he didn't move, Lou yelled louder, "Come on, get out of there! You're messing up the spawning grounds.

It wasn't until Luigi turned around that Lou noticed his front pockets were wet and seemed to be bulging a little.

"Luigi, come on, you can't be in here, it's off limits to guests." Lou no sooner said those words when he heard a metallic click. He turned around and saw Matteo coming toward him with a stiletto.

"Whoa! Whatcha planning on doing here, fella?"

Lou could tell from the way Matteo was holding the knife, the look in his eyes, and how he was moving that he was no stranger to close work. Lou's right hand went to his belt and quickly unsheathed his own blade. Then he braced for the attack he knew was coming.

When Matteo came at him, the six-inch blade of the stiletto came in low. At the last second, Matteo slipped on the wet grass, giving Lou just enough time to dodge sideways. His own blade drew blood as it slashed Matteo's bicep.

Matteo touched his wound. It wasn't deep, but Lou had sent a message. Matteo was more cautious now. Lou heard Luigi move.

"Stay where you are Luigi!" Lou yelled. Matteo took advantage of the distraction and lunged toward Lou. Again, Lou shifted just enough and Matteo's blade failed to make contact.

Lou had been in numerous close quarter, hand-to-hand knife fights in Afghanistan. But this duel was different. He wasn't up against a poorly trained young Afghan rebel, pumped up on adrenalin, or something else; this opponent was a savvy street fighter.

Twice, the two combatants made a complete circle as they gauged the other. Their eyes gave away nothing; each ready to fend off their opponent if attacked. Lou studied every move his opponent made. What could he learn beyond being up against a right-handed street fighter who knew how to hold a blade?

Without warning, Matteo switched the knife to his left hand and boldly came at Lou, thrusting his blade as if it were a sword. Lou back peddled, caught his heel on an exposed root, and fell. Matteo smiled at his sudden advantage.

Lou's eyes never left Matteo. He was ready when Matteo

attacked again. Now knowing his opponent was ambidextrous, Lou took a chance, rolled right and sprang to his feet like a cat. Matteo tried to twist, but he tripped and landed on the ground, the arm holding the knife momentarily pinned under his chest. Lou's knife drew blood a second time but, again, it wasn't a disabling wound. The warrior spirit within Lou was now in full control of his thoughts, and actions.

Once again, the two combatants circled, each watching the other, each waiting for the chance to end this dual in their own favor. Matteo knew the one tactic that had always served him well was to constantly drive his adversary backward. He'd seen Lou trip once, maybe he could cause him to fall again. He began tightening his circle around Lou's position. Each time that happened, Lou moved back a step.

By now, they had moved away from the stream and had moved to within a few feet of the thick underbrush. Lou's eyes were focused, glued on Matteo. At first, Lou dismissed a subtle movement he noticed in the corner of his eye. Then he thought: *I need to be aware of where Luigi is.*

He was about to turn his head when he heard something. It was faint, and the noise from the stream disguised it. Either Matteo hadn't heard it or didn't recognize it. But now Lou had a plan. He began forcing Matteo more to the left so his hand holding the stiletto was closest to the underbrush.

Suddenly, Lou yelled, "RELEASE!"

In the bat of an eye, Hector's jaws wrapped around Matteo's wrist, and chomped down hard. The wolf's entire upper body was shaking back and forth, its prey in his teeth. Matteo was stunned. The knife, still in his hand, was useless.

Without warning, Luigi came up behind Lou with a rock the size of a softball in hand.

Lou was about to slam the butt of his blade against Matteo's temple when the rock smashed into his back, sending him sprawling. When Hector saw the second adversary attach his pack mate he released his grip on Matteo's wrist and leaped forward, knocking Luigi on his ass.

Lou was in pain, but still more than able to defend himself.

Hector had badly damaged Matteo's wrist. Visions of the wolf clawing at the windshield completely filled Matteo's mind and he took flight.

Lou turned around just before Hector was about to tear Luigi's neck apart and yelled, "HEEL!"

The huge beast let out a growl, but obeyed.

Luigi sat in the water, wide eyed, staring at the snarling beast hovering less than a foot from him.

Lou turned toward Luigi and yelled, "On your knees!"

Luigi rolled over and knelt down on one knee, acting like he wasn't sure what to do. From the moment Santino Varni had set foot on Canadian soil two days earlier, he had resisted morphing into his alter persona. His *core* and *alter* personalities had continued to struggle for dominance over the other. The back-and-forth mental jousting between the two had created a virtual grid lock, neither persona had the upper hand. Every time Santino Varni's core persona attempted to aid Matteo, Luigi Secondo's persona mentally stepped in and thwarted the attempt. Both persona's inside Varni's skull were determined to undermine the other, the conflict and confusion inside Varni's head was both real and disabling.

Lou was oblivious to the conflict going on inside Varni's head, or as he knew the man, Luigi's head. However, he did sense, as long as Hector was there, the man was no immediate threat and he took out his cell phone. "Kate!"

She immediately heard the urgency in Lou's voice. "What's the matter Lou?"

"Kate, I'm over at the stream, just below the sawmill. Bring over two pair of handcuffs, or two plastic zip ties, I don't care which…just hurry!"

"You need what?"

"Two handcuffs or two zip ties. Just do it! *Now!*" She didn't argue with his tone of voice and immediately hung up. Then Lou turned to Luigi. "All right, get off your knees and empty your pockets!"

Luigi didn't move. "There's nothing in my pockets."

"The *hell* there isn't."

With that Lou reached forward with his knife and sliced open the front left pocket on Luigi's pants. When several gold nuggets fell out, Lou pursed his lips. After what Lou had just been through, he wasn't taking any prisoners.

"Empty your other pocket!"

"Luigi was still on one knee. When he tried taking a swing at Lou's groin, Lou countered, using his knee and deliver an uppercut with his knee to Luigi's jaw. Luigi fell backward, into the stream, blood trickling from his mouth.

Within minutes, Kate came running with plastic zip ties and two handcuffs. When she saw Luigi in the water and her husband soaking wet, she began to open her mouth, Lou cut her off. "Put a set of cuffs on Luigi, I need to go take care of the other one."

Kate stepped into the stream and quickly secured Luigi's hands behind his back. "What happened?"

"His friend came at me with a knife. Give 911 a call."

Pointing at Luigi, Lou said, "Our pal was stuffing his pockets with nuggets from the stream."

Kate had her phone in hand, slowly shaking her head. "I can't believe I'm calling 911, *again*."

"Me, neither. Give me one of those zip ties and keep an eye on this guy. I'm going after his friend."

"Lou, be careful, please."

As Lou stepped out of the stream, he called back: "I need to get something from the sawmill first."

Lou returned carrying a canvas bag. When he began collecting the gold nuggets and tossing them into the bag, Kate stopped him. "Whoa, stop! Lou that's *evidence* you're tampering with."

"Damn right it is. Evidence that nobody is ever gonna know about! Like I said years ago, if word ever got out about this, there'd be folks climbing and crawling all over the ancestral lands of the Abenaki. Kate, that just *ain't* happening, not on my watch, anyway!"

Chapter Sixty-Two

Lou pushed his way through the thick brush at the exact spot Matteo had passed. Even if Matteo hadn't left a trail that a blind person could follow, he never would have eluded a tracker like Lou.

With "Luigi" now cuffed and under the watchful eyes of the alpha female in Hector's pack, the wolf turned and followed Lou into the woods.

Matteo hadn't traveled very far. His latest encounter with the wolf had left him even more traumatized than the first. Varni's *consiglieri* may have lost his nerve, but he hadn't lost his switchblade.

Lou moved carefully. The trail was easy to follow, but he knew the one he hunted could be hiding anywhere. The last thing he needed was to stumble into an ambush.

When Lou heard a low growl coming from Hector, he knew his quarry was close.

"Show yourself and this will all end peacefully," he called out.

When Matteo didn't answer, Lou was in no mood for games. He patted Hector on the shoulder, and could feel the tension rippling through the animal. After counting to three, he whispered, "Release!"

Hector took off like he'd been shot out of a cannon! It was a matter of mere seconds when Lou heard Matteo cry out, "Okay, okay, I give up! Just get this thing away from me!"

Twenty paces ahead, Lou found Matteo, sitting in the crotch of a small tree, frantically trying to stay above the snapping jaws below him. The imagery was almost funny, and had Lou not been so damned pissed off, he might have laughed.

After sheathing his knife, Lou reached into his pocket and pulled out the zip tie. "All right, climb down."

"No, you call him off first!"

With Kate's arrest powers as a Mountie, she took both individuals into custody. Later that afternoon, she received a two-page fax from Mountie headquarters. The transmission contained mug shots that identified both men, along with their prior records.

The individual charged with the attempted murder of Lou was identified as Matteo Abruzzi. He was listed as a known associate of a crime syndicate based in Boston. Abruzzi's record included arrests for assault and battery, grand theft, and extortion charges. Aside from serving two years' probation on a B&E when he was in his early twenties; his record showed no other convictions.

The individual charged with accessory to attempted murder had been identified as Santino Varni, a known high-ranking member of a crime syndicate based in Boston. Varni also had a long list of charges, including accessory to murder, but interestingly, he had never been convicted of a crime.

When Kate read the text beneath the photo of the man she knew only as "Luigi Secondo," she called to Lou in the next room.

"Lou, come see this."

Once Lou finished reading the text under Luigi's photo, he said, "Well, I'll be damned. I'll bet he's been coming up here and hiding out in plain sight all along."

"Didn't Josh say Lake 991 was being bought by someone named 'Santino Varni?'"

"He did."

"This other one, the one who tried to stab you, is no saint either." Just then there was a knock on the front door.

"Special Delivery! Letter for Lieutenant Kate O'Grady." It was Jake's voice.

"Hey, Cuz, come on in . . . you gotta see this."

As Jake entered the cottage, he handed Kate a letter. "This came in today, right before I left." Then, he looked at his cousin. "Whatcha got, Lou?"

Lou handed him the two-page fax. "Take a look."

Jake quickly scanned the fax, then read it again, more slowly. "Well, I'll be damned! You two certainly had a fun day. Has Angelo seen this?"

"No. All he knows is that Luigi's friend tried to *field dress* me with a knife, and that the Mounties hauled both of them away in cuffs. He's pretty upset."

"Luigi had us all duped, didn't he?"

"Yeah, but Angelo more than anybody else. He's gonna feel like a real patsy."

"So, how'd you disarm the other guy?"

"I had a little help from Hector."

"That bad boy sure earns his keep around here!"

"Lou," said Kate, after reading the letter. "Take a look at this."

"What is it?"

"It's the DNA results on the samples I took from under Tyrone's fingernails."

As soon as Lou read the letter, he handed it over to Jake. "Son-of-a-bitch! The guy that tried to stab me is the bastard who kidnapped Tryone!"

Kate shook her head. "Interesting, isn't it? And what gall to come back here, just as bold as can be. He was right under our noses, not scared of anything!"

"We all tend to see what we choose to see, Kate, and believe what we choose to believe. He must have thought nobody could touch him."

"Amazing how we all followed Luigi around like the children of Hamelin followed the Pied Piper."

"What Piper?"

Kate smiled, "It's nothing Lou. Just a fairy tale . . . it isn't real."

"Well, he didn't beguile *every*one. Hector wasn't taken in."

Kate shook her head, "Can you imagine what might have happened if we didn't have Hector?"

"Nope, and I don't wanna even go there," Lou said. "But I'll tell you one thing, I'm gonna start paying a helluva lot more attention to who's coming up here, and what's in their background."

He turned to Jake. "We've become too complacent. We let our guard down, maybe even gotten a little soft. This is the second time trouble came up that logging road, and people died. We need to eliminate that risk."

"I'm with ya', Cuz."

"Good."

Then, Jake reached into his pouch and looked at Kate. "Hey, not to change the subject, but here's another letter for you."

Kate ripped open the envelope after she read the return address: *Captain John B. Nesbitt, Caribbean Yacht Charters, Ltd.*

After reading the contents, she held the letter out. "Lou, look at this! After what we've just been through, this six-day cruise we're taking in the Caribbean on a private yacht, can't come fast enough."

They would learn to regret her words, very soon.

Epilogue

Alex Biondi, auditor for the National Labor Relations board, stayed focused and built a credible case of embezzlement against Santino Varni. After Varni was indicted by a secret grand jury, Biondi's name was inadvertently released to the press. Once Biondi began receiving death threats, he retired; he and his family subsequently entered the witness protection program. Their exact whereabouts are unknown to this day.

Santino Varni, a.k.a. **Luigi Secondo**, notoriously aversed to any risks, was ultimately brought down by a risk he, ironically, chose to take - *willingly*. U.S. prosecutors successfully negotiated Varni's extradition back to the States. Upon his return, he was immediately taken into custody by Federal Marshals. Varni was tried for embezzlement of pension funds, tax evasion, and violations of the Federal RICO laws, and was found guilty of all charges. In separate trials, Varni was also convicted on numerous counts of murder, accessory to murder, intent to murder, assault and battery, bribery, and grand theft. He is currently serving six concurrent life sentences in the U.S. penal system, each without the possibility of parole. Canada has waived the right to extradite Varni and try him for accessory to attempted murder.

Matteo Abruzzi was allowed extradition to the United States by the Canadian government in order to testify in the trial of Santino Varni. The agreement included an understanding that once the trial concluded, Abruzzi would be returned to Canada to face kidnapping charges along with assault with a deadly weapon. Abruzzi agreed to testify against Varni in exchange for a plea deal. Abruzzi's testimony against his former boss was overwhelming. Seeking retribution, Varni put out a contract on his lifelong friend. Abruzzi died from stab wounds in a holding cell while awaiting extradition back to Canada. The unprovoked attack remains under investigation.

Josh Barnard finally made partner in the law firm his grandfather co-founded and where his father had been a partner. His appointment was several days before he finally went through the folder marked 'Miscellaneous' which he had pulled from his grandfather's files. Among the papers in the folder was a single sheet with a note stapled to it. The note read: "File in Grey Elk's folder." The single sheet he subsequently found in that folder was a rare court addendum correcting a decision made in 1921. The 1921 court decision had misstated the eastern boundary lines drawn up in the treaty of 1796 between the Abenaki and the British Crown. The eastern boundary of the lands, over which the Abenaki held sovereign ownership, extended beyond Carleton Mountain to a point just east of Lake 991. The document invalidated the pending sale and purchase agreement between Adler and Varni. Barnard subsequently filed to transfer the additional property to Lou Gault through probate.

Solicitor Barnard, always the opportunist, is currently bringing a claim against his former client and its parent company, seeking reparations on behalf of the Abenaki for over a century of illegal Havresting of timber on Abenaki lands. Settlement is estimated to be approaching a quarter billion U.S. dollars.

Jake Gault and **Koby Callahan** continue to enjoy their married lifestyle along with their individual careers. Koby now chairs the Wetland Habitat Board. Jake has turned down a management position with Canada Post Corporation, as it would require relocating from Havre de Poisson. Their little daughter, Gigi, is growing up fast and has aspirations to follow in her mother's footsteps.

Chef Angelo has recovered from the shock of learning he had been duped by Luigi Secondo aka Santino Varni. He and **Alessandra** continue enjoying their life at Havre de Poisson and being the "adopted" grandparents to the three Gault children.

The owner/editor of the jaded **Brunswick Daily Times**, still the quirky personality, entered bankruptcy proceedings shortly after summer. The paper is no longer being published.

Havre de Poisson and the ancestral lands of the **Abenaki** continue to thrive under the capable stewardship of **Lou Gault.** His wife, **Kate's** role with the Canadian Mounties has returned to normal. However, as mother of rambunctious and fast-growing twins, life will never be "normal." Shortly after the incident at the gate, Kate completely redesigned the resort's registration system; all first-time visitors now undergo a background check. Neither twin is demonstrating signs of anxiety or Post-Traumatic Stress Disorder (PTSD) as a result of the attempted kidnapping.

The Boston Longshoremen's Union held a regularly scheduled election shortly after the arrest of Santino Varni, A new slate of officers is now in place.

Antonina Cataldo was repeatedly questioned by prosecutors, but never charged with any crimes. The incoming union leadership felt it best for all parties to sever ties with her. She was given a generous separation package and quietly released. Her lengthy association with Santino Varni proved to be a career obstacle, but she eventually accepted employment as the hostess in a touristy restaurant in Boston's north end. Upon occasion, she corresponds with Varni, but to date, there is no one else in her life.

Neither **Oswald** nor **Nathan Turnbridge** ultimately survived the horrific burns each received during their botched attempt at arson. Their bodies were laid to rest in the Turnbridge family cemetery in a private ceremony.

Hector, the wolf, as of this writing, continues to watch over all members of *his* adopted pack, and continues to roam the resort at will.

Angelo's Recipes

Chef Angelo invites you to try three of the recipes he
prepared in this edition of
The Lou Gault Thriller Series!

Mangia, Mangia!

Sautéed Mushroom Bruschetta

Sautéed Mushroom Bruschetta Ingredients:
- 1 ½ lbs. Champignon mushrooms (if not available use a blend of oyster and portabella)
- ½ onion, chopped
- 1 ½ oz. unsalted butter
- ¼ cup extra virgin olive oil
- ½ cup Marsala wine
- 1 cup heavy cream
- Grated Pecorino Romano cheese, to taste
- Fresh thyme, finely chopped
- Salt and pepper to taste
- 1 fresh baguette or rustic country style bread

Instructions:

1. Preheat a 12″ sauté pan over medium heat. Once hot add 1 oz. of butter and let melt. Meanwhile, slice the mushrooms and cut into quarters. Cook mushrooms for 5 minutes, until soft, but haven't released their moisture. At this point add the finely diced onion, the rest of the butter and season with salt and pepper.

2. Continue to cook for 4 to 5 minutes over medium heat to caramelize the onions.

3. Once the liquid from the mushrooms has almost evaporated, remove the pan from the heat and add the Marsala wine.

4. Return pan to the heat and reduce wine by a 3rd, then add the cream. Bring mixture to a boil and simmer until the cream thickens. Taste and adjust salt to taste and keep the sauce warm until serving.

5. Slice bread into quarter inch slices and drizzle each with EVO. Sprinkle a pinch of salt and pepper on each and toast in the oven or on a grille until slightly crisp.

6. Cover each slice of bread with grated cheese, then sprinkle with leaves of thyme followed by the mushroom sauce. Serve immediately.

Frittata coi Piselli Omelet, Veneto Style

Frittata coi Piselli Omelet, Veneto Style

Ingredients:
- 4 Tbsp unsalted butter
- 1 onion, finely chopped
- 1 red bell pepper, finely chopped
- ½ cup diced ham
- 1 small bulb fennel, shredded
- 2 cups shelled green peas, fresh or frozen
- 6 eggs
- ½ cup boiling water or stock
- 2 – 3 sprigs parsley, finely chopped
- Salt and pepper, pecorino cheese to taste

Instructions:
1. Melt half the butter and sauté the onion until caramelized. Then add the ham, bell pepper, fennel, and peas for a few minutes
2. Sprinkle with salt and pepper, add a little boiling water or stock, and simmer until the fennel is tender.
3. Beat the eggs lightly with a pinch of salt and stir in the parsley and grated cheese
4. Drain the vegetable mixture and add it to the beaten eggs.
5. Melt the remaining butter in a large frying pan. Pour in the egg mixture and fry until the underside is set and golden brown.
6. Turn the omelet out onto a large plate and slip it back into the pan to brown the other side.
7. Serve flat, not folded over, as you would a French omelet.

Coniglio alla Molisana

Coniglio alla Molisana
Skewered Rabbit with Sausages

Ingredients:
- 3 ½ lbs. boned rabbit (boned chicken thighs can be substituted)
- 1 sprig parsley, finely chopped
- 1 sprig rosemary, finely chopped
- 12 slices of thinly sliced prosciutto
- 12 sage leaves
- 6 Italian sausages, hot or mild
- ½ cup olive oil
- Salt and pepper to taste

Instructions:

1. Wipe the rabbit (or chicken thighs) with a damp cloth. Cut rabbit into 12 even-sized pieces. Flatten the meat lightly, using a mallet and season with salt, pepper, the finely chopped parsley and rosemary.

2. Place a slice of prosciutto on each slice of rabbit and roll up tightly.

3. Using 6 skewers, thread a roll of rabbit, 1 sage leaf, 1 sausage, another roll of rabbit and another sage leaf on each skewer.

4. Brush the skewers with oil and grille over charcoal, if possible. Or, broil on a rack placed as close as possible to the source of heat, cooking until the rabbit has an internal temperature of 160F. Alternatively, the skewers can be baked in a slow oven (350F) for about 1 hour, or until the internal temperature of the sausage reaches 160F.

5. Turn the skewers occasionally, each time brushing with oil

Other Books by Dave McKeon

THE LOU GAULT THRILLER SERIES
BY DAVE MCKEON

Relentless Pursuit
War Chief
Howl of the Banshee
Sabotage

Coming Soon:

Curse of the Caribbean

Sneak Peak into Curse of the Caribbean

Book Five of the Lou Gault Thriller Series

"Not everything is as it seems, and
not everything that seems is."

Jose Saramago

ONE

By the time he was nineteen, Antonio Sanchez had made his bones by killing people. The devil owned his wretched soul. The only allegiance he had in life was to himself.

The cartels favored Sanchez's work, even though his services were pricey. They preferred him for three reasons: He didn't care who the mark was, he would track them down, and he never failed.

But his latest kill was unique, even for him. He had bribed his way into prison to kill a man who had foolishly crossed the cartels.

When Sanchez passed through the prison gates, he wasn't searched. A bribe took care of that. As always, he used an alias, even though the guards suspected who he was. The guards even knew why he had come, what would happen, and especially the role they would play. Cartel money talked.

The kill happened within hours.

Sanchez was the last prisoner the guards escorted to

lunch. When he entered the cafeteria, he scanned the line ahead of him. Only one man stood out - the mark.

His anxious demeanor gave him away; he knew he wasn't safe. With eyes darting from left to right, he kept shifting his weight onto the balls of his feet. He held the metal lunch tray up around his chest like a shield. No, he wasn't safe.

Sanchez bribed his way forward in line, dispensing cigarette after cigarette until he was directly behind his victim.

The assassin wasted little time.

At first, the mark thought the odd sensation in his side was simply a muscle twitch. By the time his hand reached back to massage the area, the stiletto had penetrated deep and had done it's work. The thin blade sliced his right kidney in half and severed the renal artery.

There was no recovery from such a wound, yet, the assassin twisted the blade in a wide arc, scrambling the mark's interior even further. When he finally withdrew the blade, the mark dropped to his knees. An eerie hush came over the room. Time stood still . . . until the metal tray crashed to the floor.

In seconds, the line parted and Sanchez was exposed, standing next to the dying man who was on his knees, gasping for breath.

The first guard approached the assassin and held out his hand. Sanchez understood and handed over his knife. As he was led away, he heard whispers of *"El Carnicero."*

Sanchez smiled; he liked being called: "The Butcher."

He knew he'd be placed in solitary once the contract was filled. Sanchez also knew the cartels' money would free him. They owned everybody.

Less than a day passed before the door to Sanchez's cell opened. Harsh light from the hallway flooded the dark windowless "hole" where he had waited. After ensuring the corridor was empty, the guard looked at Sanchez momentarily then raised a finger to his lips and beckoned the assassin forward, mouthing the words, "Follow me."

The guard knew who Sanchez was, just not by name. Not even the cartels knew his birth name. There had been much talk among the guards. Yet, no one questioned what had gone down was the work of the ruthless one, *'El Carnicero,'* himself.

As the guard listened to the assassin's footsteps echoing off the walls behind him, he repeatedly made the sign of the cross. Whenever they came to an intersection of hallways, the guard stopped and checked the coast was clear. Once they reached the service gate at the outer wall, the guard turned to the assassin:

"Carlos will meet you," he whispered.

"Where?"

"In the *piazza.*"

Sanchez watched the guard punch in the code for the gate before he whispered again.

"Hold out your hand."

When Sanchez felt the familiar knife handle in his palm, he smiled. *"Gracias!"*

The guard nodded. *"De nada."*

Sanchez left prison during the early morning hours, a time when shadows of the night teased the eyes and darkness still ruled.

The killer had never been to the nearby village before. But it didn't matter; the road from the prison led to the piazza and all piazzas were alike. At one end there would be a church, with a bell tower At the opposite end, it would be open. The sides of the town square would have archways for the merchants. There would be a fountain in the middle of everything. All roofs would be terracotta; all walls would be bleached a chalky white from the sun.

Sanchez knew it was the cartels who had freed him, and he was thankful for that. But he was also a cautious man, and caution had been his savior more than once. He had no fear, yet he would remain in the shadows until whoever "Carlos" was, would show himself.

For the moment, Sanchez rested, back pressed against a wall he had chosen while he would wait, listen, and stay alert for even the faintest sounds. The air was heavy, his senses were sharp, even the trickle of sweat working its way through the stubble on his cheek captured his attention. His eyes shifted from left to right.

The piazza was quiet, but soon, the eastern sky would turn indigo, only to be pushed aside by the reds, pinks, and oranges of the dawn. Pigeons would reappear with the dawn as sounds of the marketplace would begin filling the square. But, for now, the only sound was water, dripping from the fountain . . . tier by tier to land in its pool.

As the light edged out the darkness, Sanchez realized the wall he had chosen faced east. He would need to move before the shadows disappeared.

A noise broke the silence. It was subtle, but he tensed when he heard it.

Was that the wind? When he heard it a second time, he recognized it as wings fluttering at the far end of the piazza. A smile came to his face. *Something, or someone, has disturbed the pigeons nesting near the church.* He remained still, listening. A quarter minute passed, then half a minute.

The pigeons have quieted down. Whatever it was, is gone, he thought. More minutes passed as he strained to hear even the slightest sound. He reflected again on the birds.

What caused them to stir? It could have been the one who opens the church to ring the bells who disturbed them. Sanchez took a breath. *But the birds would know him. Maybe it was someone else, maybe it was Carlos.* He let out a sigh and leaned back against the wall as he remained in the shadows, listening for footsteps.

A moment later, his senses told him someone else was in the piazza . . . but where? His mind raced. *Who is this Carlos? Is he a killer, like me? Has my usefulness to the cartels finally run its course? Why is this Carlos being sent to meet me?* His eyes darted back and forth, still searching for the slightest movement. He saw nothing. Then, he heard it. Someone very close to him cleared their throat.

He froze.

Sanchez readied his switchblade and whispered, "The church is not open yet. Have you come to pray?"

"No. I am Carlos."

Sanchez relaxed a little upon hearing the name. "It is strange, I did not hear you approach."

"I was here when you arrived."

Sanchez turned toward the voice, not sure what to think. *If he was sent to kill me, I would already be dead.*

His mind cleared enough to ask: "Why did the cartels want us to meet?"

"Come, we will eat, *then* we will talk."

Book Five:

Curse of the Caribbean

Coming Soon.

Acknowledgments

A special thank you to my early readers: Alan Adler, Barry Colvin, Carl Johnson, Tom Mullin, and Kathy Zimmer. Your willingness to carve out time to review my early drafts, and offer your unabashed critique, opens my eyes to what I am unable to see.

Again, a shout out to Paula Howard, my editor and publisher, who continues to put up with me. Thank you Paula, for all you do. You are a joy to partner with.

Lastly, a tip of the hat to Bob Hurley, the talented graphic artist who turns my ideas into exciting covers.

About the Author

Dave McKeon is an award-winning author of short stories and creator of the Amazon best-selling Mystery/Action/Adventure series, *The Lou Gault Thrillers.*

His stories reflect his own diverse background, life experiences, and his unquenchable love affair with the outdoors.

A native New Englander, he has hunted, fished, hiked, camped, skied, and traveled in the eastern United States and throughout New Brunswick and Quebec, Canada, his entire life.

A Vietnam-era veteran, Dave has formerly held both a Top-Secret Clearance and the Department of Energy's "Q" Clearance. His stores are influenced by his experiences working with the NSA, the EPA, and the Department of the Navy.

To Learn more about Dave McKeon
Visit www.avillagewriter.com